INSIDE HOLLYWOOD

By

Jodie Rhodes

PROLOGUE

"Will you please stop telling me you're just his answering service!"

"But I am just his answering service," the girl said, her voice trembling.

Erin took a deep breath and tried to control herself. "Now look," she continued, dropping her voice to the warm contralto that had successfully charmed a number of people into doing things they didn't want to. "I, of all people, understand Keith Ramsey's need for privacy. As the most exciting and sought-after actor in the industry today, I know he's constantly besieged by people who want to grab a piece of his glory. But I am not one of those people and I assure you that Keith will be not merely upset but infuriated if he learns that you have refused to put me in touch with him."

"Erin Connolly?" the girl from the service repeated uncertainly. "Are you a personal friend? I don't see your name on this list he gave me."

So he had left a number where he could be reached! Erin slumped back in her chair and breathed a sigh of relief. You never knew about that independent bastard. He'd been known to disappear for months at a time with no one knowing his whereabouts.

"My dear," Erin said softly, "I am a little more than a personal friend. He has been waiting for word on a major script that I've been negotiating to get. Well, I've got it for him now, and I need to talk to him immediately!"

"Oh!" The girl sounded slightly awed. "In that case, I'll certainly pass your message on to him right away. Could you give me your number?"

"There's no need for that," Erin said quickly. "Just tell me how to contact him, and I'll call him myself."

"I can't do that," the girl said firmly. "Mr. Ramsey specifically instructed me to do nothing but pass on messages."

"I think you're making a major mistake, young lady," Erin said threateningly. "Mr. Ramsey could lose the most important role of his career due to your obstruction. Would you give me your name and the name of your supervisor?"

"My ... my name is Susan Laskey, and my supervisor is Mrs. Morganstem, but you won't be able to reach her until tomorrow." The girl started to cry. "I'm sorry, Miss Connolly, but I have to do what I'm told."

Jesus Christ, Erin muttered to herself. Have I sunk so low I'm now down to intimidating innocent kids from an answering service?

"It's all right, Susan," she said. "You're doing the right thing. Just make sure that Keith calls me as soon as possible. I'll give you two numbers."

"Thank you very much, Miss Connolly," the girl sniffled as she wrote down Erin's business and home phone.

The minute Erin hung up the receiver, her intercom button flashed red She punched it down and picked up the phone. "Yes, Nancy, what is it now?" she asked.

"Sheldon Avery is on line two. He's been waiting almost five minutes, and he's really steamed."

"Oh God." Erin groaned. "That's all I need right now. All right, I'll take him."

"Hi, Shel. Really sorry to keep you waiting, but the damn phones have been screwed up all afternoon. Would you believe that I placed a call to Marty Jessup at CBS in New York and ended up talking with a housewife in Crestline, Ohio? I mean, honestly . . ."

"Just cut out the shit, will you?" Sheldon said furiously. "I want to know now if Keith Ramsey has signed a contract for the part."

"Shel, luv, what in the world has got you so upset?"

"You know damn well what! I've been stalling my agent for two weeks now because I was nuts enough to believe you when you said you could deliver Ramsey. You got any idea what it's like to stall Irving?"

Erin laughed. "Darling, I most certainly do. It's like trying; to stall a bulldozer that's headed straight at you with its throttle open wide."

"It's not funny, Erin. Irving told me today that Columbia's dropping the option on my book unless they get a definite commitment in the next forty-eight hours. That's a million dollars we're talking about, darling," he added viciously. "So it's put-up or shut-up time for you."

"I don't much care for your tone of voice," Erin said evenly. Now I do understand the kind of pressures you've been under, so I think I can excuse that last remark. But I would appreciate it if you'd remember that you're not talking to some cheap, one-shot producer or money-hungry agent. You're talking to Erin Connolly who, among other things, won both the Oscar and the Cannes Film Festival award for Street Scene "

"That Oscar was four years ago," Sheldon snapped. "What have you won lately?"

For one terrifying second Erin went completely blind as the white rage generated by Sheldon's remarks blazed inside her. A few seconds later the room came back into focus and she looked up gratefully at the late afternoon sun streaming through the sheer curtains and reflecting off the brilliant paintings hung on her walls.

"Hello? Hello? For Christ's sake, is anyone there?"

"Sorry, Shel," Erin said calmly. "Must be those damn phone lines acting up again. Anyway, to get back to what we were talking about, I'd like you to answer one question for me. And; I want you to think about it very carefully before you answer."

She paused for a beat and when she did speak again there was an almost solemn tone to her voice.

"Do you really believe wholeheartedly and without reservations, as I do, that Keith Ramsey is the only actor alive today who can be totally trusted to portray the most important character you've ever created without compromising the artistic integrity you wrote your guts out to give him?"

"Well yes, of course I do," Sheldon said, momentarily distracted by the thought of his artistic integrity being compromised. "But . . ."

"No buts." Erin said firmly. "That's the answer I was looking for, and you gave it to me. Now, can Columbia guarantee you Keith Ramsey?"

"You know damn well they can't. There isn't a studio in town who can, because nobody knows how to reach him." Sheldon's suspicions flared up again. "And I think that includes you."

"Really?" she replied coolly. "Then it must have been my overactive imagination that spent a full sixty minutes earlier today talking to that very same Keith Ramsey. He absolutely loved your script, by the way."

There was a stunned silence on the other end of the line. When Sheldon finally managed to speak, he was so excited his voice cracked.

"He did? I mean, he really said that?"

"Among other things. Like it was one of the few scripts he'd ever read that was worthy of the book that inspired it. He told me something else I think you might be interested in hearing. 'Erin,' he said in that marvelous, deep resonant voice of his. 'When I finished this, I knew I was holding an Academy Award picture in my hands.'"

"My God. Oh my God, I can't tell you what that means to me," Sheldon babbled. "I am so thrilled. Did you know Keith Ramsey has always been an idol of mine? My whole life I've dreamed of having him play one of my characters."

"Of course."

"Well, this is such wonderful news I hardly know what to say. Listen, Erin, please accept my apologies for the way I talked earlier. I was just so uptight with this deadline hanging over my head that I didn't know what I was saying."

He gave a small, embarrassed laugh. "I know this probably sounds a little crazy, but do you think there's any chance you could set up a luncheon or something where I could meet him in person now that he's signed the contract?" Sheldon paused. "He did sign the contract, didn't he?"

"'Luv, can you imagine that he wouldn't after the way he fell in love with the script?"

"Erin, that's not an answer." There was a sudden ominous note in Sheldon's voice. "Now, either he did or he didn't. Which is it?"

"Honestly, Shel, sometimes I wonder why 1 put up with you." Erin sighed. "I give you everything you've ever asked for and in return I get hit with your paranoid fears. "No!" she said sharply as he started to protest. "You listen to me! Now I told you I just finished talking with Keith. The operative words are talking. As your own wonderful agent along with all those super powerful studios reported to you," she said sarcastically, "no one could get Ramsey for your picture because no one could reach him. Well, I reached Keith Ramsey and sent him your script. And he called me to say he wanted to do it. But he's two thousand miles away in one of his hideouts. So we're just going to have to wait till he gets back for the actual signing."

"I can't wait, Erin."

"Then you want to lose the whole thing?"

"Look," Sheldon said desperately. "You know I don't want to lose him, and I'd never ask him to come back here just to sign a contract. But I have to have that contract. Now you know where he is, so why can't you fly up to wherever that is and have him sign it there?"

"You really ask a lot, Shel."

"I'll pay you for it," Sheldon said frantically. "The plane tickets, your time, whatever you want to charge. I don't have any other choice. Do you understand that? Forty-eight hours. That's all I've got."

"I understand," Erin said slowly. "Okay, Shel, I'll get back to you."

There was a hesitant tap at the door. "Excuse me, Erin." Nancy peeked in. "I just wanted to check and see if there was anything else you wanted me to do before I left for the night."

Erin gazed at her blankly for a moment then blinked. "Is it five already?"

"Five-thirty, actually."

Erin looked at her watch, a faintly startled expression on her face "The day seems to have gotten away from me," she said vaguely. "I'm sorry to have kept you overtime."

"Oh for heaven's sake, you didn't keep me overtime!" Nancy burst out impulsively. "Why, I remember when we worked straight through till ten o'clock every night and… " She stopped abruptly.

"It's all right," Erin said gently as she watched Nancy flush crimson. "I remember too. But don't worry," she announced with sudden grim determination. "We're going to get those days back!"

"You betcha," Nancy grinned. "We'll show 'em all! Right?"

"Right," Erin smiled. The smile faded as she thought of the forty-eight-hour deadline facing her. Sheldon Avery's script was her last, her only chance to make a comeback. But she was going to lose it unless she got Keith Ramsey. And at the moment she couldn't think of a single way to do that.

"Are you okay?" Nancy asked anxiously.

"Of course I'm okay," she said, forcing the smile back on her face. "Now run along, Nancy, and enjoy your evening."

"You're sure?"

"I'm sure. Now scat!" she said firmly.

"Well, all right then." Nancy started for the door, stopped abruptly, and whirled around.

"Oh wow, I almost forgot! David called and asked me to remind you that he was picking you up for dinner at seven." She grinned and gave a cheerful wave as she headed back for the door.

"Have a nice evening," she called over her shoulder. "You deserve it."

****

The traffic was unusually heavy as Erin headed west on Wilshire Boulevard toward the elegant high-rise apartment building that dominated the skyline of the expensive Westwood Village area.

She whipped her white Porsche around the big Cadillacs and Lincoln Continentals that moved with maddening slowness in front of her, switching from one lane to another, accelerating rapidly as she came up to each intersection, trying to beat the light.

Pulling up to the iron gates that guarded the entrance to the underground garage of her apartment building and inserting her plastic card into the electronic lock, she cursed as she looked at her watch. Despite all her frenetic maneuverings to get home quickly, it was already six-twenty. Erin had been counting on at least an hour to relax and pull herself together before David arrived. Now she'd barely have thirty minutes by the time she got up to her apartment. That was hardly enough time to bathe and dress, leaving no time for the relaxation she so desperately needed. And if David was in one of his sullen, depressed moods, which was about the only mood he'd been in for the past month, she thought irritably, then she was going to have to deal with that along with everything else that had gone wrong on this rotten, miserable day.

Well, the hell with it. There's no law that says I have to meet his damn seven o'clock timetable. He made the date, not me. So I'll do what 1 need for me, and he can wait till I'm ready!

Erin stepped off the elevator on the lobby floor to check her mailbox. It was stuffed with envelopes: bills from Saks, Bonwit Teller's, Gucci's, Giorgio's, Jorgensens, and Vendome Liquors. There was also a small white envelope, unstamped, from the manager of her building reminding her that the rent on her apartment was now five days overdue.

"Welcome home," she announced with a grim smile. "It sure is good to get all these loving letters from family and friends."

She shoved the envelopes into her bag and walked back across the lobby to the elevator, stepping inside as it opened with at faint hissing sound, and pressed the button for the penthouse apartment.

The six-foot grandfather clock bonged one slow, solemn note as she walked into her apartment. Erin had discovered it an antique shop in a small Connecticut town four years ago and had paid for refinishing and shipping it to California at ten times its original cost.

"I know." she muttered to it, shivering as a cold blast from the air conditioner hit her. "It's already six-thirty." Goddamnit. Why couldn't she remember to turn the damn thing off when she left in the morning? That's going to be another hundred-dollar electric bill, she thought unhappily

Walking quickly into the living room, she clicked off the switch, then pulled back the drapes and opened the sliding glass doors to the balcony that looked out on the distant Santa Monica mountains.

Taking a deep breath, Erin stepped out on the balcony and looked up at the brilliant stars dotting the sky, their presence revealed by the Santa Ana winds that had swept down from the mountains, blowing the ugly smog out to sea, then went back into her bedroom, stripping off her clothes and

filling the tub as she stepped in until nothing was supporting her except her feet braced against the faucets, the back of her head now barely above water level and her hair soaked with the rich pink bubbles.

Faintly, she heard chimes. They stopped for a moment and then sounded again.

"Jesus Christ!" she exclaimed, sitting up abruptly. It was the doorbell. It was David! She scrambled out of the tub, grabbing a robe and wrapping it around her as she ran to the door, her bare feet leaving damp imprints on the thick pile carpet.

"Sorry not be ready. It was one of those horrible days. Let me fix you a drink."

`"Why don't I fix my own and let you get dressed?"

"You're a dear." She blew him a kiss and pattered down the hall to her bedroom, standing in front of the closet that took up one whole wall, trying to decide what to wear. She finally settled on the red velvet pantsuit that had set her back five hundred dollars. But it was worth every penny, she thought happily as she admired her image in the mirror.

The pants, which she wore without any underwear, clearly outlined her small waist, flat tummy, slim hips, and firm, tight ass. The short velvet jacket was cut to reveal the low-necked white silk blouse with its crisp ruffled front. The contrast of the sheer white blouse against the rich red velvet jacket set off to perfection her small triangular face with its flawless ivory complexion, brilliant jade green eyes and lustrous short cap of dark hair.

Not bad for a thirty-year-old broad," she announced thoughtfully to the mirror. Then she laughed. "Hell, it's damn good for a twenty-year old broad."

"Well, I'm ready," Erin announced brightly as she appeared in the entrance way of the living room. "Now that didn't take too long, did it?" Then her eyes widened in shock as she saw the oversized double old-fashioned glass in David's hand which was filled to the brim with a dark amber liquid.

"My God, David, is that all Scotch in there?"

"You don't mind, do you?" He raised the glass and gulped down a third of its contents.

"No, of course not," she said uncertainly. "It's just that I . . . well, I've never seen you drink like that."

He gave her a twisted grin. "I'm celebrating," he announced. "An anniversary."

"'Anniversary?" She looked at him blankly. "What anniversary?"

He took another large swallow. "I guess it was foolish of me to think you'd remember. You see, it was exactly a year ago tonight that I left my wife and family for you."

Erin's eyes narrowed in anger. "Is this going to be one of those blame-Erin-for-everything-that's gone-wrong evenings? Because if it is, I'm going to cancel it right now before it starts."

"Oh no, my love, you're not going to cancel this evening," he said softly. "This is very definitely a non cancellable evening."

He stood up and walked over to her, his hand cupping her chin and tilting it up to him as he kissed her lightly on the lips. "You're looking unusually beautiful and desirable tonight," he murmured in the deep, warm voice that had turned her on so totally when she first met him.

Unexpectedly, tears stung her eyes as she looked at the husky, broad-shouldered man with the dark, intense eyes and remembered how things had been then. They'd been so much in love, so ecstatically, wondrously in love that the whole world had glowed. And he'd been everything to her. Friend, lover, the father she'd always longed for. Why had it gone wrong? Why had she lost it?

"I still love you, David," she said tremulously.

"Do you?" He looked at her intently. "But you're not in love with me anymore, are you?"

"I don't know." She gave a helpless shrug. "If only . .”

"If only you still wanted to go to bed with me," he interjected harshly. "That happens to be one hell of an if, doesn't it?"

I can't help it," she said unhappily. "It's not something I can force."

"But you're not the kind of woman who can go too long without a man," he said broodingly. His eyes clouded. "Soon, very soon, you'll find someone who turns you on," he murmured half to himself. "And that's the one thing I cannot stand to see."

"David, you promised it wasn't going to be one of those evenings. I told you, I just can't take it tonight."

"That's right. You did, didn't you?" He smiled suddenly, an engaging smile that lit up his face. "Well, as a man who keeps his promises, I now declare a moratorium on the subject. It shall never be mentioned again."

He offered her his arm. "Shall we leave for dinner, my lady?"

"Oh Christ, I almost forgot!" she groaned. "David, I've got to call my answering service and tell them where I'll be this evening. Where are we having dinner?"

He frowned. "You're not planning to meet anyone later tonight, are you?"

"Don't be silly. Of course I'm not." She patted his cheek. "It's just a business thing."

"What kind of a business thing?" he asked suspiciously.

"It's a long story." She smiled. "No, that's not true. It's a very short story. About forty-six hours short, now. I'll tell you about it at dinner. Which is going to be? "

He hesitated. "I made reservations at Melisse" he said finally.

Erin lifted her eyebrow, wondering just what was going on in that complex head of David's. The elegant Santa Monica restaurant had been "their place" for every special occasion in their lives. It was where they'd first admitted they were in love with each other. It was the place where David told her he was getting a divorce and wanted to marry her. It was where they first talked about having a child. Her eyes closed in sudden pain at the last memory.

"I hope you don't mind," David said quickly. "I was just hungry for their food, that's all."

"No, I don't mind." She forced a smile. "Now that I think about it, I'm a little hungry for their food myself."

He looked relieved. "Good. You go ahead and call your answering service, then, while I finish my drink."

****

The maitre d' broke into a delighted smile as Erin and David walked into the restaurant, and rushed toward them. "Miss Connolly, Mr. Bernstein, what a pleasure to see you again. It has been so long!" He looked at them reproachfully. "Why do you stay away for such a time? It is not right for friends to behave so."

"You're absolutely right, Henry," David agreed solemnly. "But you see Miss Connolly's business has been most demanding lately. And how could I come here without her?"

"Ah." Henry nodded. "In that case, you are forgiven." Then he shook a reproving finger at Erin. "But you must not let business deprive you of the joys of life. Work less and enjoy more," he commanded her as he led them briskly to their booth where a waiter stood at attention. "The lobster Fra Diavolo is superb tonight."

"Henry never changes, does he?" Erin laughed as David gave their drink orders and the waiter scurried away to fill them. "He's been making that same speech for as long as I can remember."

"Henry is one of the few things in life that remains constant." David said somberly.

"Hey," she warned. "You promised no gloom tonight,"

The waiter appeared at that moment with their drinks. "Would you like to see a menu now, sir?"

"No. We want to relax for a few minutes first." David picked up his double Scotch on the rocks and leaned toward Erin as though he were about to propose a toast. Then his eyes, which had been fixed on her, suddenly grew distant. He brought the glass to his lips and drank deeply, staring into space.

Erin shifted uncomfortably as the brief pause in their conversation grew into a lengthy silence. "How are things in politics these days?" she asked with determined brightness.

"So so," David replied briefly. "How are things in the silver-screen business?"

"Worse than so so." she said with a grimace. "Christ, I don't know what I'm going to do if I lose this picture!"

She began telling him in detail about the conversation with Sheldon Avery, then trailed off as she saw the amused glint in his eyes.

"And just what the hell do you find so funny about all this?"

"Your attitude." He smiled. "To hear you tell it, you're the innocent victim of a cruel and malicious fate. While the truth is it's your own sweet, charming, lying, cheating, conniving, manipulating self that put you in this box."

"Why, you supercilious son of a bitch!" she spat, white with rage. "Who the hell do you think you are to talk to me that way?"

"The person who knows you better than anyone else in the world," he said, the faint smile still on his face.

"Don't flatter yourself," she said contemptuously. "After all, you're just one in a long line of men who felt the same way."

David's fists clenched involuntarily as rage blazed out of his eyes. With a visible effort, he regained his composure.

"Well, that tender loving moment in your apartment didn't last long, did it?"

"None of them do." Erin was furious. "Because you spoil them all. We should have ended this whole relationship two months ago like I wanted to. It's become destructive for both of us, and I have enough problems without having you drag me down too."

"Poor Erin. You do suffer terribly, don't you?" he mocked.

"There was a time you cared about my problems. Now all you care about is your own sick self!"

"That's certainly sick," he agreed coldly. "After all, what could be more important than the meteoric rise and fall of Hollywood's most important producer? Especially when her fall is almost as meteoric as her rise."

"You have two choices. We can order, or you can take me home now. And frankly I don't much care which you choose as long as I don't have to talk to you. Because I am really, finally, finished with you. I just hate to hurt Henry's feelings."

"By all means let us spare Henry's feelings." David signaled the waiter. "Henry wanted us to have the lobster Fra Diavolo. Shall we go along with that, for Henry?"

"Just order it and let's get this travesty over with," she snapped.

"The lobster Fra Diavolo for two," David told the waiter. "And a bottle of Pouilly Fuisse. He glanced at Erin. "Unless the lady wants another drink?"

"No, just the wine." She looked up at the waiter. "And could you bring it now?"

"Of course, madame." He bowed politely before leaving.

"Miss Connolly?" Henry appeared suddenly in front of them, a frown on his face. "There's a telephone call for you. Do you wish to take it?"

Erin's face lit up. "Indeed I do, Henry!" She looked triumphantly at David. "I told you I'd get through to Ramsey," she gloated as Henry brought the phone to the table.

"Hello, this is Erin Connolly," she announced with a vibrant warmth.

"It's Susan Laskey," the worried young voice answered. "I'm terribly sorry to disturb you at dinner, but you did say how important it was to call you. The thing is . . . well, I haven't been able to reach Mr. Ramsey. His housekeeper at their lodge told me he's backpacking in the mountains and isn't expected for at least another day."

"For Christ's sake, don't they have forest rangers or something that can reach him in an emergency?"

"I ... I really don't know anything about that. Is it really an emergency?"

"His whole career is hanging in the balance and you ask me if it's an emergency?" Erin took a deep breath and lowered her voice. "Susan, maybe I didn't explain it fully. If Keith doesn't get back to me in the next twenty-four hours, he's going to lose it all. The script, the picture, the Academy Award. Now do you understand?"

"I didn't realize all that, Miss Connolly. Let me try to reach him again."

"Mr. Ramsey and I would both appreciate that, Susan. Just make sure you succeed this time." She hung up the phone with a crash.

"Bravo!" David smiled sardonically. "A virtuoso performance."

"Oh just shut up." If this kid from the answering service did reach Ramsey, would he call her, she wondered?

Yes, she decided, he would. Not because her dramatic messages would arouse his curiosity. He was too smart and savvy to fall for that. No, the reason he'd call her would be to give her hell for scaring that little Susan Laskey half to death. Which was just fine with her. All she needed was that vital personal contact with him.

Once she got that, somehow she'd figure out a way to persuade him to read the script, even if she did have to end up doing what Sheldon had begged her and fly up to that godforsaken wilderness where Ramsey was camped out. But the timing is so goddamn fuckin' tight, she thought desperately. What if he doesn't come back to his crappy rustic lodge before the forty-eight-hour deadline is up? Well he's going to, she told herself. I am willing him to come back, and it's going to happen.

"Pardon me, madame."

Erin looked up, startled, as the waiter stood patiently beside her, holding the steaming plate of lobster Fra Diavolo. "Sorry," she murmured automatically, leaning back to allow him to set it down in front of her. Her eyes focused on David, who was staring at her with a peculiarly intent expression.

"Are you all right?" she asked apprehensively.

"Couldn't be better." He continued to stare at her with the strange glitter in his eyes. "And how are you?"

"Tired." She eyed him carefully. "I'm really very tired, David. I'd appreciate your taking me home as soon as we finish dinner."

"That's too bad," he frowned. "I'd planned for us to go to the Polo Lounge."

"The Polo Lounge?" she said incredulously. "David, what is it with you this evening? Considering how things are between us now, this nostalgia thing with dinner here tonight was a bit much. But going to the Polo Lounge is really too much.

That's absolutely wallowing in sentimentality. No," she said emphatically. "We're not going to the Polo Lounge. You can take me home, or I'll call a cab."

"Don't get upset," he said softly. "I'll take you home. But I have to make a phone call first."   He stood up abruptly and walked away, leaving Erin to gaze after him bewildered.

****

An elderly man carrying a miniature poodle under his arm was coming out of Erin's building as she and David walked up to the entrance. He smiled and held the door open for them, bidding them a pleasant good evening as he set the dog down and headed off down the block.

"Some swell maximum-security building," Erin grumbled as they crossed the lobby to the elevator. "Might as well send out engraved invitations to every burglar in West L.A. and be done with it."

"Um," David murmured noncommittally.

Erin shrugged irritably and gave up all attempts at polite conversation as they rode in silence to her floor. The headache which had started in the restaurant was now pounding steadily at her temples, and her hand rubbed nervously at the charm bracelet on her wrist.

One of the hall lights had burned out, and Erin stumbled as she stepped out of the elevator, cursing under her breath as she fumbled in her purse for the key to her apartment.

"It's all right, I've got it," David said as he opened the door.

She glared at him in outrage as he reached inside and switched on the light in the foyer. "Goddamnit, David, what are you doing with a key to my place?"

"Don't get so excited. It's an extra one I just discovered after I gave you back the others."

"Just discovered? Don't give me that shit! I know damn well you've kept it all this time. What the fuck were you planning to do with it? Catch me with someone else? Well, maybe that's what you deserve. But it's not going to happen that way. So give it back to me right now," she demanded.

"I was planning to," he smiled. "We'll have a nightcap, and I'll turn over all the keys of your kingdom to you."

"No nightcap," she said grimly. "Just the key."

"Well, then, just the key." He looked down at her, his body blocking the doorway. "But I do have to bring you your gift."

"Oh Christ, David, no more gifts!" she exclaimed. "You're always bringing me gifts, like you think they're going to solve all our problems. Just give me the key."

"No, this time you're wrong. You want this," he insisted. "It will only take me a minute to bring it up from the car."

"David, please. Just leave me in peace tonight. I am totally wiped, and I need to be alone. Can't you understand that?"

"Of course I understand that," he said gravely, "That's why you need this."

"All right," she said resignedly. "Bring me the gift. But do me a favor, okay? Bring it into the bedroom where I am going immediately to collapse. You can leave it there along with the key."

Erin padded down the hallway to her bedroom without waiting for David's response, kicking off her shoes and unbuttoning the white silk blouse.

"What a waste," she muttered as she walked into the bedroom and stared into the mirror. "Five hundred dollars worth of clothes for a two-bit evening." Angrily, she ripped off her pants and jacket, threw off the blouse, then crawled into bed, pulling the covers up to her chin and closing her eyes.

She didn't hear the soft opening and closing of the door when David returned, and the thick-pile carpet muffled the sound of his footsteps as he walked down the hall and into the bedroom. The first intimation she had of his presence was when the bed moved under his weight as he sat down at the foot of it.

Her eyes opened lazily and she turned her head to the pillow next to her, David's favorite place for putting the beautiful expensive presents he loved to get her. But there was nothing there. Puzzled, she turned away and looked down the length of the bed, then gave a short, choked gasp as she saw the gun in David's hand. He held it loosely, its long black barrel pointed at her.

"What kind of filthy, sick joke is this?" she demanded hoarsely.

"It's not a joke, Erin."

"Stop it, David! Stop it this minute!" She sat up in the bed, clutching the covers to her. "This cheap melodramatic trick is beneath you. Now take that ugly thing out of here right now!"

His fingers played with the gun, turning it over so that it lay flat in his palm for a moment. He gazed at it idly, then brought it upright again, the snout directed at Erin.

"I am warning you, David, I will not put up with this! You take that thing out of here or I'm calling the police."

"Are you afraid?" He smiled at her, amused. "That would certainly be something to see. I thought Erin Connolly was never afraid of anything."

"I am not afraid," she said evenly. "I am disgusted. Now, do you take it away or do I call the police? You may not care about yourself or me anymore, but I don't think you'll want your kids reading about something like this."

"Oh, they'll understand," he said quietly. "They know what it's been like for me lately." He looked at her quizzically. "I thought you realized that. Didn't you know I was calling them when I left you for a moment in the restaurant?"

And then for the first time Erin was afraid. It was impossible, of course. This whole scene was impossible. David couldn't do a thing like that, she told herself. She swallowed hard as she looked at the man who'd given her so much love. The man she'd loved at one time almost as much as she needed him. No, this couldn't be real. It was just another Hollywood scenario. He would beg her forgiveness when it was over, and she'd make him pay long and hard before she gave it to him. But eventually she'd forgive him. Despite everything, they were still too close to stay away from each other for very long.

"I'm calling your bluff," she announced with narrowed eyes. "Right now!" As she reached for the phone, the shockingly loud report of the gun echoed throughout the room, making her ears ring.

David leaned forward on the bed, his arms outstretched as though he were reaching for her, and Erin dropped the phone as she flung aside the covers and held out her hands toward him. But she was too far away and he slid off the bed to the floor, dragging the bedspread with him. She scrambled frantically over the rumpled bed to where he had fallen.

"David? David, what did you do?" she whispered.

His eyes were open, looking at her, and tears of relief streamed down her cheeks. "Oh, David, you fool, you goddamn fool," she cried. "How could you do a stupid thing like this?"

He refused to answer her, and rage mixed with her tears of relief. She grabbed his shoulders, shaking him savagely. "Tell me," she commanded. "Tell me how you could try such a thing!"

His head fell against her breast. It was terribly, terribly heavy. And then she knew he wasn't going to answer her. Ever.

ONE

Two days after Erin Connolly arrived in Los Angeles and moved into the small apartment just off Sunset Blvd, she met Ron Fletcher. It had been another long, hot, and frustrating day for her. She had spent the morning poring over Variety and The Hollywood Reporter, and the afternoon answering every ad in the help wanted columns that promised even a possible entry to the movie industry.

It had been a disillusioning experience. Employers who billed themselves as Hollywood producers turned out to be greasy little men looking for topless dancers. Employment agencies that guaranteed jobs at major studios demanded previous experience in jobs that had connections to the film world and every place she went, she found offices jammed with pretty young girls who glared with undisguised hostility at each new applicant who walked in the door.

It was almost six when she finally returned to her apartment, not sure whether her head or her legs ached the most. Collapsing on the couch, she kicked off her shoes and massaged her feet, then paused for a moment to look out the window. The pool sparkled in the last rays of the afternoon sun, a clear, clean inviting blue. It was exactly the therapy she needed, Erin decided. She got up and ran down the hall to the bathroom, stripping off her clothes as she went and leaving them in a careless pile behind her. A minute later, wearing an extremely brief bikini and carrying a brightly colored beach towel, she was out the door and down the steps.

The pool area was deserted as she dropped the towel on a chaise and dove into the water. It was cool and deliciously refreshing, and she forgot all about the aggravations of the day as she floated dreamily on her back for a moment before turning over and heading for the deep end, stretching out her muscles in a long, powerful crawl.

Ron Fletcher opened the sliding-glass patio door of his first floor apartment and walked over to the pool, testing the water temperature by tentatively dipping one foot over the side. Satisfied, he sat down on the edge and then slid in, wading slowly toward the center. Erin, completely unaware of him, had just completed a racing turn at the deep end and was now stroking vigorously back, arms pumping and head low in the water, when she rammed Ron dead center. He gave a queer gurgling gasp and sank toward the bottom.

Horrified, she dived down and grabbed him under his arms, bringing him to the surface. Paddling frantically, she carried him to the safety of the steps at the shallow end, where she flipped him over and started pounding on his back.

"Stop! You're killing me!" he moaned as he struggled to sit up.

"I thought I had," she panted. "Are you all right?"

"Maybe. I'm not sure." Cautiously, he put his hand over his heart, which was thumping at an alarming rate.

"Put your head down between your legs," Erin ordered.

He obeyed obediently and began to relax as Erin rubbed his back and neck.

"Better now?" she asked anxiously.

The ominous thumping began to subside. "Yeah." He finally managed to take an easy breath. He lifted his head and then his heart began thumping again, for he got his first good look at Erin.

"On the other hand, I could have a relapse any minute. I think you owe it to me to make sure that doesn't happen. So how about checking out my condition over dinner?"

"Well." Erin frowned and started to shake her head, but when Ron dramatically clapped his hand over his heart and began to choke and wheeze she couldn't help breaking into laughter.

"Okay! Just remember, though, that I'm the only one who will be doing any checking out."

He took her to a small Chinese restaurant on Pico Boulevard and during their meal Erin discovered that Ron was not only a short, fat middle-aged man who was recently divorced and very lonely, but the head of publicity at Film-Star Studios. Almost trembling with excitement, she asked if he expected to have any openings for a beginner like herself. "Of course I know I'm totally inexperienced but I would take any job just to get a start. I'd mop the floor and empty the trash, I'd....

"Wait right there," he grinned. "We can't have you taking jobs away from our janitors. Let me see if I can find something for you."

TWO

It took two weeks, before Ron was finally able to manufacture a job for her in his department. But that Friday evening when she opened the door after his knock, she knew that it had all been worth it.

"Congratulations, Miss Connolly!" he beamed, handing her a bouquet of red roses. "Starting this coming Monday morning at eight-thirty sharp, you will be an official employee of Film-Star Studios."

"You did it?" she cried excitedly. "You really did it?"

"1 did it," he smiled.

"Oh tell me!" She grabbed his hands and pulled him into the apartment. "Tell me all about it."

"You'll be working with Andi Steiner, a very smart, very sharp little gal who handles the publicity releases on our major stars. Now Andi just happens to have her sights set on bigger things, and she's cultivated some pretty good contacts. So if you should turn out to be the most helpful assistant she's ever had, I'd be very surprised if you didn't get promoted right into her job. How does that prospect grab you?" he chuckled.

"I love you, Ron Fletcher!" At that moment, she really meant it.

****

Erin's heart skipped a beat as the studio guard scanned the list of names on the clipboard in front of him and frowned uncertainly.

"What was the name again, miss?"

"Connolly" she said tremulously. "Erin Connolly. I'm supposed to report to Mr. Fletcher in the publicity department."

"Oh, here it is!" He looked up and smiled at her. "Your first day, isn't it? Well, good luck."

"Thank you. Thank you very much." Erin gave him a radiant smile in return, and as she walked into the lobby of the arrogantly phallic glass and steel tower on the Film-Star lot, she knew she'd found the world she'd been looking for. The very air seemed charged with excitement, intrigue, and the heady scent of power. She paused for a moment, throwing back her head to drink it in before heading for the elevator.

"Welcome aboard," Andi Steiner said pleasantly, offering her hand. "Ron says you're a crackerjack at detail, and God knows we need someone like that. Our files are in a total mess. She waved her hand toward the back of the office. "Just look at that!"

Erin stared in horror at the mountainous pile of newspapers and magazines sitting in front of open file cabinets that bulged with yellowed clippings spilling out of their folders.

"It's not as bad as it looks." She grinned. "It's worse."

"Well, it does seem like it could use a little reorganization," Erin said shakily. "So maybe we should update files on our important stars first, and store the other files that are filling up those cabinets some other place until we have a chance to reevaluate them."

"That's good thinking, Erin. Very good thinking." Andi stared thoughtfully at her new assistant. "But how would you know who's important and who isn't?"

"I wouldn't, of course. I'd have to ask you."

"Right." Andi smiled coldly. "Yu will always check with me first before you ever do anything, because I am the one who makes the decisions. Just remember that, and we'll get along fine."

"Oh I will," Erin assured her. "And I want you to know how happy I am to have this opportunity to work for you. Mr. Fletcher said I'd learn more from you in two weeks than I would in a year from most people."

Andi snorted. "He did, did he? Well, that's the first bright observation the old fart's made in the past ten years."

She started to laugh as she saw the startled look on Erin's face. "Shocked you. did I? You thought because he's the head of this department and got you this job that he was a big wheel?" Andi shook her head pityingly. "Kid, have you got a lot to learn! Tell you what. Stow your purse and stuff in this desk, then trot your little fanny down to personnel to fill out the eight million forms they give all new employees. When you get back, we'll get you started on clipping stories out of this pile of junk, and then I'll take you out to lunch and fill you in on who's really important in this place."

By the time Erin finally completed the voluminous documents handed to her by the personnel director's assistant, she felt that Andi hadn't exaggerated by too much. Her fingers were stiff from writing the answers to endless questions about her background when she returned to the publicity department some forty minutes later.

She found a note on her desk from Andi. "Clip out every article on actors and actresses with a red check mark against their names on attached list," it stated tersely. A pair of scissors lay across the note, acting as a paperweight. Andi was noticeably absent from the office.

With a resigned sigh, Erin began dragging the pile of newspapers and magazines over to her desk. An hour after she began the tedious task, Ron Fletcher marched into the office, followed by two men talking rapidly and waving their hands.

Erin looked up and smiled eagerly as he came up to her desk. He strode by without even saying hello. Cheeks burning with humiliation, she bent over the papers again, turning the pages without even seeing what was on them.

Two hours later she sighed, leaned back in her desk chair, and absently rubbed the painful crick in her neck. When she brought her hand back down to turn the next page, she saw with horror that it was stained black with the ink from the newsprint. Which meant that in rubbing her neck she had put a big, black, ugly stain on her blouse. Oh God, how could she go out to lunch with Andi Steiner looking like that?

Panicked, she fled to the ladies room, where she took off the blouse and examined it frantically. There was a definite smudge on the collar, but it wasn't too bad, she decided. She wet a paper towel with a squirt of liquid soap from the glass container over the sink and scrubbed vigorously. The smudge went away, and Erin smiled with relief as she hurried back to the office.

Another twenty minutes passed as Erin sat at her desk, lifting her head every few minutes to stare expectantly at the door. But there was still no sight of Andi. Her stomach growled, and she frowned as she looked at her watch. It was almost one-thirty. She got up and walked over to the girl who was sitting at the receptionist's desk, busily polishing her nails.

"Excuse me," Erin said hesitantly, "but would you happen to know when Andi Steiner is expected back in the office?"

"Well, she usually gets back from lunch around one-thirty or two, unless she's had some special presentation to go to." The girl absently waved her hand in the air to dry the polish. "Today she just went out with some friends from the art department after their meeting this morning, so she should be back any minute now."

"She's already gone out to lunch?" Erin exclaimed.

"Well yeah, sure." The girl looked at her curiously. "Something wrong? I mean, like were you supposed to see her before?"

"No," Erin said in a small voice. "There's nothing wrong."

She returned to her desk, having learned her first important lesson about Hollywood. Promises meant nothing.

Two weeks later, Andi Steiner invited Erin to lunch again, and this time it actually happened.

Erin had been kneeling in front of the file cabinets, stuffing old folders into storage boxes and replacing them with crisp, new, updated folders that she had painstakingly organized and cross-indexed when Andi tapped her on the shoulder.

"Hey, kid, I think you're due for a break. Another day buried in those files and you're going to forget your own name. Grab your purse and let's get out of here."

Andi took her to a small, pleasant restaurant with dark paneled walls and red leather booths. "Well, cheers," she announced as she lifted her martini glass.

"Cheers," Erin echoed with a smile as she picked up her glass of white wine. She took a sip and looked around the room with obvious pleasure. "This is really nice, Andi!"

"You deserve it, kid. You've been doing a hell of a good job for me, and I wanted to show you I appreciate it." Andi cocked her head, her bright inquisitive eyes peering out from the fringe of bangs that framed her small but attractive pixie face. "I'll bet this is the first lunch you've had since you started working here that hasn't come out of a brown paper bag."

Erin laughed. "You win."

"How old are you?"

"How old?" Erin looked at her uncertainly. "Why, uh, I'm twenty."

"Twenty. Jesus!" Andi stared into her martini. "I was thirty last week. Most depressing experience of my entire life."

"But thirty isn't old," Erin protested.

"Oh yeah? Maybe where you come from, Idaho or Iowa or whatever hick place, it isn't. But out here it's not only old, it's ancient." Andi moodily stirred the olive in her drink. "And if I don't get a break pretty soon, it's gonna be too late for me. Just too fuckin' late."

"Why?"

"All the rules have changed, kid. It's not like when I started here five years ago. Then publicity was a great job, a step up on the ladder. We had contract players, we produced fifty-two films a year. It was a production-line approach, and I was right in the middle of that production line and steadily moving forward every day. You don't have the faintest idea what I'm talking about, do you, kid?" she said with a crooked grin. She finished her martini in one large gulp.

"No," Erin admitted in bewilderment. "I really don't."

"Well, I'll try to explain," Andi signaled the waiter to bring another martini.

Erin listened intently as Andi recounted what had been happening in Hollywood over the past few years and gave a gasp of horror as Andi told her that Film-Star was currently in debt to the tune of more than 70 million dollars.

"Take it easy, it's okay," Andi assured her. Then she gave a dry laugh. "Well, of course it isn't okay. What I mean is, it's nothing for you to worry about. Film-Star isn't in any danger of going out of business. Abe Lieberman is too smart to ever let that happen. Smart? Hell, he's a goddamn genius. Our studio is going to come out of this just fine."

She took a swallow of her martini and frowned. "But it's going to be a whole new ball game from now on. There's going to be a big emphasis on television, on syndication; and we're going to have a lot of independent producers coming in here with their own packages for feature films.

"So you see," she concluded gloomily, "with that kind of a setup, there's just no way to advance your career through the publicity department."

Erin could see all too clearly, and she silently cursed herself for her incredible naivete in believing Ron Fletcher when he'd bragged about his importance. Well obviously there was only one solution. She had to get out of publicity and into another department, one with real power, as quickly as possible. But how? If Andi Steiner, who was a sharp, savvy woman with five years of experience and contacts at Film-Star, hadn't been able to manage it, what chance was there for someone as new and green as herself?

THREE

It was a sobered Erin who returned to the office to organize the files which just a few short hours earlier she had viewed with patient boredom, and now regarded with a passionate hatred.

Andi Steiner did manage it, though. A month later—a month that had opened Erin's eyes to the hopelessness of her position as Andi handed all her dreary work over to Erin, work that would never lead to a promotion, as she went out on long leisurely lunches, many of them interviews for jobs with a future, leaving Erin with a job that had no future at all.

Then one day Andi burst into the office and grabbed her around the waist.

"Erin, baby, come with me!" she shouted ecstatically. "We are going out to celebrate!"

"I made it, kid," she announced, waving around her martini with such vigor that the icy cold gin slopped over the side of the frosted glass. "I finally made it! You are looking at the new production assistant to Leland Devereaux!"

"That's great," Erin said enthusiastically. "But who's Leland Devereaux?"

"Oh God, kid!" Andi groaned. "Haven't you learned anything since you've been here? Leland Devereaux just happens to be the most exciting, most gifted director Broadway has seen in the last decade. And Abe Lieberman got him! He's coming out here in three weeks to create and direct a special new series of quality programs for television. Major plays and dramas, documentaries, all top-drawer stuff. It's going to make Film-Star the most important, prestigious studio in this town, and it's going to give me a solid gold ticket to success!"

Andi sat back in the booth, a dreamy smile on her face as she envisioned the rosy future ahead of her.

'But what exactly will you be doing?" Erin asked curiously.

"Nothing much at first," she admitted with a little shrug. "A production assistant is really just a glorified gofer. But, you see, that isn't the point."

Andi leaned forward, her face intent. "The point is getting in on the ground floor of this kind of a project. Because if you're smart, all the opportunities are there. And believe me, kid, I'm going to take advantage of every one of them."

"That you didn't have to tell me. You'll be running the show in no time at all." A pensive look crossed Erin's face. "I hope you'll remember me when you're famous."

"Of course I will," Andi said generously. "Which reminds me. The second reason I took you out to lunch today was to tell you that you're going to be in charge of our little area in the publicity department for the next ten days."

Since Erin had actually been in charge of everything for weeks now, doing all of Andi's work without her title, this was hardly exciting news.

"And if you do a good enough job while I'm gone, I'll recommend you for the position on a permanent basis," she smiled.

Erin was feeling more depressed by the moment. "But where are you going?"

"On vacation, my child." Andi lifted her glass and took a deep, pleasurable drink. "This little gal is taking off for Puerto Vallarta on the first flight out of here tomorrow, to have a ball while she can. Because once Devereaux arrives, there won't be any vacations at all. There won't even be any evenings off, if what I hear about him is true. He works his people twenty-four hours a day. So I'm going to get my batteries recharged in the next ten days, and come back ready to take on anything they throw at me."

"Puerto Vallarta," Erin said wonderingly. "Isn't that where Elizabeth Taylor and Richard Burton used to…"

"Right. And it works its wonders equally as well on us lesser mortals. It is the place to go for R and R. That stands for romance and recreation.

"Anyway," she continued, seriously, "I'm trusting you to handle things while I'm gone. And the most important task I'm assigning you is to keep your eyes and ears open about what's going on. Not that I really expect anything important to happen. But I'm giving you my vacation itinerary just in case, so if something comes up that's a problem, or something you think I should know about, you can get in touch with me immediately. Understood?"

"Understood."

"Good." Andi relaxed and picked up the menu, then peered over it. "By the way, I meant what I said about recommending you for my job."

"I really appreciate that," Erin said dismally.

Leland Devereaux arrived in Hollywood two weeks early, due to unexpected complications in his romance with the beautiful young actress-wife of a famous Italian producer. The producer, a highly excitable man, had arrived at Devereaux's hotel suite in the middle of the night, screaming and brandishing a revolver. "If you're not out of Rome before daybreak, you're a dead man!"

Devereaux prided himself on being a man of considerable physical courage; however, the present moment did not seem like the most propitious time to demonstrate it. He had packed hurriedly as the producer stood in the doorway tracking his every movement with the gun, and fled into a waiting cab and off to Rome's Fiumicino airport.

During the long flight from Rome to Los Angeles, Devereaux repeatedly told himself that he had taken the only action possible; that it had been an act of wisdom, not cowardice. Nevertheless, the experience rankled and he was anxious to put it behind him and forget about it. And the best way to accomplish that was by immediately plunging into work.

Having made that decision, he began to feel better. After all, he mused, as he stroked his silky Vandyke beard, the work was all that really counted. The brilliant creative work that only Leland Devereaux could bring to a world so desperately in need of it.

That realization so cheered him, he playfully pinched the luscious, pear-shaped buttocks of the stewardess who leaned over him to ask solicitously if he wanted another drink, and made a date with her for his first night in Los Angeles.

Executives at Film-Star were thrown into a state of total panic when Leland Devereaux charged into their offices two weeks ahead of schedule, full of ferocious energy and demanding that production start immediately on his first project, a screen adaptation of a highly acclaimed Broadway play. Frantic studio personnel shifted work schedules, grabbing people wherever they could find them to put together a staff for him. And the most frantic among them was Joel Gerson, the bright young man who had just been promoted to the coveted position of administrative assistant to the executive producer in charge of the new television series.

"Where is she?" he demanded frantically of the girl sitting at the receptionist's desk in front of the publicity department.

"Where's who?"

"Steiner! Andi Steiner! For God's sake, who else would I be asking about?"

"I...I don't know." the girl stammered, cowering back in her chair as he glared at her. "But if you want Andi Steiner, she's on vacation."

"Vacation? Oh Christ, I don't believe this," Joel moaned. He took a deep breath. "Okay then, we just have to get her back here. So where is she on vacation?"

"I don't know that either. I'm just the relief receptionist."

'Then who does know?" he roared.

"Her assistant." With a trembling hand, the girl waved behind her toward the desk where Erin was bent over, engrossed in cutting out articles from a pile of fan magazines.

"Thanks," Joel said curtly as he strode over to Erin.

"Hey!"

Erin continued clipping away. "Hey. Hey you!" he shouted.

Erin dropped the scissors and glanced up in alarm at the frantic man looming over her. "You Andi Steiner's assistant?"

She swallowed. "Yes."

"You know how to get in touch with her?"

"Uh, yes."

"Good. Then do it. Immediately! Get her back on the first plane from wherever she is and tell her we expect her back here tomorrow morning at eight o'clock sharp if she wants to keep her job as Devereaux's production assistant. You got that?" he yelled.

"I got it," she said faintly.

"Glad to hear that. Then I won't have to repeat it." He turned on his heel and marched out of the office.

Erin pulled open her top desk drawer, took out the envelope containing Andi's itinerary, picked up the phone and stared thoughtfully at the piece of paper in front of her which listed the name, address, and telephone number of the hotel in Andi's sharp, angular handwriting.

Then she hung up the receiver and quietly stuffed Andi's itinerary under the pile of old magazines in her wastebasket.

FOUR

Erin set her alarm for six-thirty the next morning and she was instantly awake and fully alert the second it went off. She bathed and dressed quickly, ate a hurried breakfast, and arrived at the Film-Star lot a few minutes before seven-thirty.

The studio guard blinked at her in surprise. "You sure are early today, Miss Connolly. Got some big project going on in publicity?"

"In a way, Harry," Erin smiled. "At least it's big to me."

"Well, good luck on it," he said cheerfully as he checked off her name on his clipboard. "I'll keep my fingers crossed for you."

And darned if I won't, he thought to himself as Erin blew him a kiss before hurrying past him into the lobby. She deserved the luck, because she was just as nice as she was pretty. Always greeted him with a smile, and usually took time to stop and chat with him a bit. Not like some of those stuck-up snobs who couldn't even take the time to get his name right. He found himself hoping that her project, whatever it was, would succeed, and he had a feeling it probably would. Over the years, Harry had developed a sense about the people who passed through his gates and that sense told him Erin was one of the winners.

Erin was considerably less confident than Harry as she took the express elevator to the executive suites located on the twentieth floor, nervously fingering the strap on her purse as she rehearsed her speech.

Knowing that Devereaux had ordered production to start on his first venture promptly at eight o'clock, she had no doubts that Joel Gerson would be in his office at this early hour. But she had serious doubts about his response to her proposal.

Her mouth was dry, and she had problems swallowing as she stepped off the elevator and walked into his office.

"What do you mean, you couldn't reach her?" Joel screamed in outrage. "It's your job to reach her!"

"I've been trying, Mr. Gerson," Erin announced quietly. "I've called her hotel every hour on the hour since you came into my office yesterday. I even called from my home until midnight last night."

"Are you looking for an award or something? What the hell do I care if you called until midnight? All I want is to have Andi Steiner here. Now!"

Gerson poured water into a glass from the handsome silver carafe sitting on his desk, shook two pills out of a small vial and gulped them down, then broke into a sudden coughing fit as one of the pills lodged in his throat.

Erin leaned over and refilled the water glass, handing it to him hastily.

"Thanks," he said weakly as he swallowed and the choking spasm ceased. "For something, anyway," he added balefully.

"I'm really terribly sorry about this, Mr. Gerson," Erin said earnestly. "But I'm sure I'll be able to contact Andi today. Unless, of course," she frowned, "Andi decided to accept that invitation from her friends in the area to spend the week with them. Unfortunately, she didn't leave me their name and phone number. Not that I think that would be a problem," Erin said quickly. "You know how dependable Andi is. I'm sure that whatever she's doing, she'll be checking in with her hotel. And I'll keep calling, naturally."

"Well, isn't that just swell," Joel said bitterly. "I can't tell you how much you've reassured me. Good old dependable Andi Steiner, who didn't even leave the name and number of friends she might or might not visit, is going to call at some unknown time. And that is supposed to take care of my problem?"

He leaned over and smashed his fist on the desk so hard that the silver carafe leaped up and toppled over. "Well, it doesn't take care of my problem," he exclaimed furiously. "My problem is today! Today!! Do you understand?"

"Yes. Yes, I certainly do," Erin said apprehensively. "So that's why I decided to ask you if I could help out by taking her place until she gets back," she concluded in a shaky voice.

"You?" He stared at her incredulously. "You take Andi Steiner's place on the Devereaux production set?"

"I could do it, Mr. Gerson," Erin assured him feverishly. "I know I could. Andi and I have worked very closely together. She's even recommending me for her job in publicity. That's how much trust she has in me. And she's told me everything about this new job."

"You've got to be kidding," he said flatly. "You're a green kid who can't even manage to get hold of her boss in an emergency. How could I ever believe you could handle something like this, even for a few days?"

"I can't guarantee someone else's performance, Mr. Gerson," Erin said evenly. "But I assure you I can guarantee my own."

"Well." Joel sat back in his chair, a speculative look in his eye. "That's very interesting. Very interesting indeed. I wonder why it didn't occur to me earlier."

Erin felt perspiration forming under her arms as he continued to stare at her, a thoughtful smile playing around his mouth. Then without warning he abruptly brought his chair forward with a crash, and she jumped in fright.

"All right, little girl, we'll give you your chance. I'll call Faraday and tell him I've okayed your filling in for Andi Steiner for the next few days."

He stood up, placed his hands flat on the desk, and leaned over her, his eyes drilling into hers. "But just remember one thing—if I hear one complaint about you, if you so much as foul up a coffee order, you're through! Not just with the Devereaux production, but with Film-Star Studios. Understood?"

"There won't be any complaints, I promise. And I want to thank you for this, Mr. Gerson. I just want to thank you so much."

"Stop thanking me and get the hell out of here and go to work!"

"Yes sir!" Erin leaped up from the chair and fled the office.

There were no complaints, of course. At least not from any of the production crew on the set, who found Erin an absolute treasure. She was quick, bright, efficient, unfailingly cheerful, and engagingly eager to do anything and everything they asked of her. There was one extremely bitter complaint, though, from an initially stunned, then outraged, and finally heartbroken Andi Steiner who returned a week later to find that her trusted assistant had completely, totally, and irrevocably stolen her one big opportunity.

"I'm telling you she never called me!" Andi cried in anguish to Joel Gerson. "You know me, Joel." Her eyes pleaded with him. "You know I'd never go anyplace where the studio couldn't get in touch with me any hour of the day or night."

"But I didn't know how to get in touch with you," he observed mildly.

"That's true." She reflected miserably that none of this would have happened if she hadn't deliberately withheld her vacation plans from him for fear that he might ask her to cancel them.

"I should have told you, and I apologize for not doing so. But I never dreamed there'd be any problems. I trusted that little bitch. I trusted her completely . . ." Andi broke off with a choked sob, then dug into her purse for a cigarette to help calm her. Her hand was trembling so much, she couldn't work the lighter.

Joel graciously leaned over and lit the cigarette for her. "Now just try to relax, Andi," he said soothingly. "You're not helping yourself at all by getting this excited."

"You do believe me, though, don't you?" she asked feverishly. "You do know I'm telling the truth?"

"Yes, Andi, I believe you," he smiled.

"Then why haven't you gotten her off that set?" she demanded hysterically. "She was only allowed to be there until I got back. Well I'm back now! I'm back, Joel! And it's my job!!"

"Unfortunately, they're into almost a full week's production by this time and the crew is used to Erin now. They really don't want a change."

"Joel, don't tell me that! You know as well as I that you can change a production assistant any time you want. Pull her out and put me back there!"

"I'm sorry, Andi," he said regretfully. "But I'm afraid I really can't do that. Devereaux himself has gotten used to her and you can imagine how upset he'd get with any change in personnel."

"You cruddy fake!" Andi stormed. "What you're really saying is that you're sleeping with the bitch. I took you into my bed for a whole year, a year when you were nothing! I catered to your weird, kinky needs. I did everything for you! Well, if you think I'm going to keep quiet about this, you're crazy. I'm going to tell the whole world!"

"And the world will find it just as boring as I did," Joel said icily. "I took pity on you, which was obviously a mistake. You are a rather sad example of a woman trying to trade on a body that has seen better days. You are also, apparently, severely emotionally disturbed. I will try to be kind when I inform personnel why we must terminate you.

"By the way." he added as she started to cry hopelessly. "I have never been to bed with Erin Connolly. She made it on her own."

FIVE

Andi made one brief stop before exiting Film-Star Studios forever.

"Hey, wait a minute!" the security guard protested as Andi pushed her way past him. "You can't go in there. It's a closed set."

"I've got an important message for one of the crew members," she announced grimly.

"Well, gee, I don't know," he began uncertainly. But Andi hadn't waited for his permission. She was already through the door and marching toward the front of the set before he'd finished speaking. He frowned, then started after her.

Erin was crouched by the side of the script girl, rapidly feeding her revised pages of the teleplay which she'd just run off on the Xerox machine, when she felt the sudden sharp pain of fingernails digging into her arm. She looked up in surprise, and then stared in disbelieving horror as Andi Steiner glared down and yanked so hard at her blouse that it was literally ripped off her shoulder.

"Bitch!" Andi hissed. "Filthy, lying, cheating bitch! I've got a message for you. I'm going to get you one of these days." She stood up and waved the torn scrap of Erin's blouse around the room. "And I've got a message for everyone here, too. Watch your back when you're around this bitch if you don't want to end up with a knife in it!"

The panting security guard came up and grabbed Andi around the waist as everyone in the studio looked on in stunned fascination

"It's all right. I'll go quietly." She allowed the guard to lead her away, then turned around just before they reached the door. "But remember what I told you." she screamed at the astonished faces. "You let a killer in here, and you'd better watch out."

"I . . . I'm so sorry," Erin stammered, crimson with embarrassment. "I can't imagine what she's talking about, but I apologize to all of you for having been the cause of this terrible interruption. "Please forgive me," she added in a voice that sounded on the verge of tears.

"Hey, it's okay." Kevin Anderson, a burly stuntman who had become Erin's devoted slave from the moment she appeared on the set and took it upon herself to massage his back and neck between takes with a special lotion she'd bought, came over and roughly caressed her head. "Don't you know that you're nobody in Hollywood until you've made your first enemy?"

Both the cast and the crew broke into appreciative laughter, which was quickly stilled when Leland Devereaux smashed his gold-handled walking stick, a Devereaux trademark, across the arm of his director's chair.

"Perhaps we should ask Miss Connolly to make more enemies," he intoned glacially, "since this is the first genuine emotion I've seen on the set all day. Now shall we get back to work and see if we can produce some?"

Chastened, the crew scurried back to their cameras and the actors took their places as Devereaux snarled. "Action!" But their pace had been put off by Andi's appearance, and it was a bad take. They had to sweat through ten more takes before Devereaux was satisfied, and by that time everyone had completely forgotten about the incident, including Erin. There would come a time, however, when Erin would remember it all too clearly, but by then it would be much too late to do anything about it.

During the next ten months Erin worked harder than she ever had in her life and loved every second of it, unhampered by a single unpleasant incident. She was at the studio every morning before eight and often stayed as late as eleven at night, even on days when the Devereaux unit wasn't shooting.

Although she found television interesting and often exciting, only the creation of movies truly fascinated her and fired her imagination. So whenever she wasn't needed on a Devereaux project, she would appear on the set of whatever film company was currently shooting and shyly offer her services.

People soon grew used to the slim, long-legged girl with the glowing green eyes who was always available to bring them coffee and sandwiches and run errands for them and Erin was allowed to roam freely throughout the studio.

She watched, listened, asked questions and poked into every area of filmmaking; absorbing knowledge like a sponge. She saw how a film's soundtrack was recorded, mixed, and edited; became familiar with set design, costume design, and special effects; perceived the importance of a music score in creating atmosphere; discovered how a skilled cinematographer could command audience attention for a movie just through his control of light and shadow and learned the vital function of the cutting room where, finally, all the confusing bits and pieces were shaped into a cohesive whole.

She also realized that the people who designed, photographed, cut, and scored a picture were tools. Absolutely necessary, but tools nonetheless. Power belonged to actors, directors and producers. There was no way she could become an actor. She simply didn't have the ability to be anyone but Erin Connolly. Nor could she imagine herself as a director. But a producer, now that was something she could become. She'd loved books all her life and instinctively sensed which ones could be made into Oscar winning pictures. But when Erin confided her ambition to the friends she'd made at the studio, they stared blankly at her for a moment, then burst into laughter.

"Honey, I think maybe you need to be told the facts of life," Mavis Coulter said with a kindly smile as she saw the crushed look on Erin's face. "We weren't making fun of you. It's just that we know your dream is totally impossible."

"Why? Why is it impossible?" Erin demanded.

"Because you don't have connections. Because you don't have money. Because no one would ever take you seriously."

Erin never mentioned her aspirations about becoming a producer to her friends again, and they assumed she'd given up the idea. She'd done nothing of the kind, of course, but she'd wisely decided that if the idea of her becoming a producer made people laugh, she could only do herself harm by talking about it. She would just bide her time until the right opportunity came along, and when it did she would take swift decisive advantage of it.

But as the weeks went by and turned into months, she became increasingly discouraged. Because it didn't seem as though there would ever be any right opportunities. Not that her career was without progress. Lois Parton, the plump, rather homely, but thoroughly professional and totally dedicated script girl for the Devereaux production unit, had astounded everyone first by getting married and then by becoming pregnant. Leland Devereaux offered Erin the position when Lois left on maternity leave. It was considered by everyone except Erin to be an incredible honor, and she was deluged with congratulations.

Just a week later two different directors for independent production companies, whom Erin had worked for while they were filming on the studio lot, asked her if she'd be interested in joining them as an assistant editor.

"Jesus, you've really got the world by the tail!" Cheryl Green exclaimed with more than a touch of envy. "I mean, you've been at Film-Star less than a year and here you are with three incredible job offers. I worked five years before I got even one offer like that." She shook her head wonderingly as she stared at Erin. "It's unbelievable! What are you going to do?"

"I don't know." Erin forced a smile and tried to sound enthusiastic. "It's . . . well, it's all so exciting I'm just not sure what the right choice is."

But television really isn't your thing, is it?" She flushed as Erin stared at her curiously. "What I mean is that I thought you were more into the film side. Major motion pictures, that kind of thing."

"You want the job as script girl for Devereaux, don't you?" Erin said softly.

Cheryl looked down at her hands, which were clutching a coffee mug with desperate intensity. "Yes," she admitted in a barely audible whisper. "The studio productions I'm working on now are dogs. I'd give anything to get on the Devereaux set."

She lifted her head and gazed at Erin. "Would you recommend me for the job if you decide to turn it down?" she said pleadingly.

"Of course I would, Cheryl," Erin told her as she stood up and absently patted her on the shoulder. "But right now I think I'd better go and get a bite to eat before Devereaux starts shooting again. Anyway, whatever I decide I promise to let you know about it first."

"You're a really nice human being," Cheryl said gratefully. "And whatever you decide, I want you to know how much I appreciate your help and understanding."

"Well, isn't that what friendship is all about?" Erin smiled as she walked out of the office.

But her smile faded abruptly as she made her way to the Film-Star commissary. In a few short days she would have to make a decision about the positions offered her, and the unhappy truth was that she didn't want any of them. They were all dead-end jobs that would lock her into obscurity. But there was no way she could turn down all of them without seriously jeopardizing her future in the business.

Erin was still frowning unhappily as she entered the commissary and glanced around the room for an empty table. Then her eyes widened in amazement as she saw the figure sitting at a small table in the back.

"Jimmy? Jimmy Norton, is it really you?" she shouted with delight as she raced over to him.

"My God! Erin!" He stood up and stared at her. "What in the world are you doing here?"

"I was just about to ask you the same question," she said happily as she pulled out a chair and sat down. Then she started to laugh. "We always seem to be meeting this way, don't we? Remember that day in the student union?"

"Yes. Yes, I certainly do." He lowered himself slowly back into his chair, then reached out and took hold of her hand. "Just wanted to make sure you're real."

"Oh, I'm real all right," she assured him.

"And more beautiful than ever," he smiled. "You look absolutely terrific, Erin."

"You look pretty terrific yourself." Her eyes approvingly noted the casually elegant cashmere jacket, the custom-tailored shirt, the thin gold Rolex watch, and the perfectly manicured nails on the hand that rested lightly on top of hers.

"You sure have changed from that kid in jeans and a T-shirt I knew in college," she grinned. "It's a wonder I even recognized you."

"Well, the color's still the same," he said dryly. "That probably helped."

"Hey, what's with the hostility? This is me, Erin. Remember?"

He looked into the brilliant green eyes and saw that nothing had changed since those college days where he was ostracized as the only black until Erin walked over to him one day in the student union and started talking to him and he realized the fact he was black meant nothing to her, that she didn't even think of him as black.

He nodded in acknowledgement, then continued briskly, eager to change the subject, "But let's forget about the past and catch up on the present. What's been happening with you, and what are you doing here?"

"You first," Erin insisted. "Because you owe me an explanation. I wrote you the minute I knew I was coming out here and the post office returned the letter. You didn't even leave a forwarding address for me. That was mean, Jimmy," she pouted. "You promised to introduce me to Hollywood."

"Well, I've turned into a pretty mean dude. Especially when someone doesn't answer my letters for a whole year."

"Okay, truce time," she laughed. "Now tell me about you!"

"Oh, not all that much to tell," he said offhandedly. "Came out of USC's film school and went to International Pictures. I'm a writer and director now."

"A writer and a director?" Erin's eyes glowed. "Jimmy, that's marvelous. That is absolutely marvelous!" Then an expression of doubt clouded her face. "But how come I haven't run into you before if you've been working here at Film-Star?"

"Because I don't work for Film-Star. I'm under contract to International. They just loaned me out for a special project."

"Loaned you out?" Erin repeated puzzledly. "I never heard of a studio doing that."

"That's because you haven't heard about me. I'm a special project all on my own," he added with a wry smile.

"What?"

"Never mind," he said quickly. "It's just a management thing."

"Hey, James Lee! Great to see you here." A short, stocky man with iron-gray hair, who was dressed in a somber but impeccably tailored black suit, white shirt, and regimental tie, stopped at the table and offered his hand.

"We're really delighted to have this chance to work with you, James Lee. Please call me anytime if you have any questions or problems." He gave Erin a quick, quizzical glance before walking away.

Erin gazed in awe as he continued his brisk passage across the commissary, pausing briefly to chat with a few people at the tables near the window. "That was Lee Golden!" she said breathlessly. "He's second-in-command to Abe Lieberman and just about the most powerful person in the whole studio!"

"I know," he replied tonelessly.

"You weren't kidding, were you?" Erin said admiringly. "You are really someone special." She looked at him inquiringly. "But why did he call you James Lee?"

"Because that's my name now, I changed it to James Lee Norton. Jimmy sounded too much like a kid."

"It's exactly the right name," Erin announced with a thoughtful nod. "Jimmy is who you were. James Lee is who you are now. A very successful man." She flashed him a quick gamine grin. "So when are you going to introduce me to Hollywood, Mr. Success?"

"After you tell me what's been happening to you. No," he interrupted as she started to protest. "I won't do a thing for you until you bring me up to date on everything that's been going on in your life since we last saw each other."

"Well, if you insist," she sighed. "But it hasn't been all that exciting, I've got to warn you."

"I'm warned," he smiled, "So go."

She gave him a brief description of her deadly dull work at Film-Star, then leaned forward, staring at him intently.

"Jimmy . . ." She checked herself immediately. "James Lee, I know I have the talent and ability to become a producer. And I want it more than anything in the world. Can you help me?"

"Erin, you're really asking the impossible," he said sadly, shaking his head. "Your friend Cheryl Green was right when she told you why it can't be. You've got no contacts, no money."

"Suppose I could find the contacts and the money? Would that make it happen?"

He started to shrug, then froze as an incredible idea occurred to him. Was it possible? He looked across the table at the vibrantly beautiful woman who still made his pulse race, despite the hopelessness of any relationship between them. Yes, goddamnit, it was possible.

"I think I might be able to help you after all," he said cautiously. "If you'll do exactly as I say."

Erin's green eyes blazed with hope. "Just tell me what you want and I'll do it," she promised excitedly.

"There's a party I'm invited to the end of this week. A very exclusive party at the home of Martin Weinguard. I'll take you with me."

"You mean Martin Weinguard the studio head of International Pictures," Erin said wonderingly.

"The one and only." He smiled.

"And you'll personally introduce me to Martin Weinguard?"

"Oh, well, you'll meet him too. But the really important person I'll be introducing you to is Anthony Wellington."

"Anthony Wellington?" She gave him a baffled look. 'I never heard of him. Is he a new director or a producer?"

"No, he isn't even an important studio executive."

"I don't understand," she said uncertainly.

"I know you don't." He gave her a wolfish smile. "But just listen very closely as I tell you about Anthony Wellington, and then you'll understand perfectly.

SIX

Hollywood executives were baffled by the tall slender man with the prematurely balding head, stooped shoulders, and apologetic smile who arrived in their midst and shyly offered them financial backing for their upcoming productions.

For one thing, nobody had ever heard of him. He had no credentials in the entertainment industry on either coast. Even more disturbing was the way he approached them. It was totally unheard of for a potential investor to suddenly appear in a producer's office and open his checkbook. Things just weren't done that way. The standard procedure was to send out word that a certain party might be interested in making a deal; then emissaries from both sides got together and cautiously explored the possibilities; finally a meeting was arranged where the principals, armed with their attorneys, would come together face to face.

Anthony Wellington had ignored all these time-honored customs, and it made them very nervous. Either he was conning them, or the whole thing was a put-on. Suspicious and distrustful, they backed away from him, leaving him hurt, bewildered, unhappy, and very lonely. Then he met Marcia Weinguard.

It happened at a party thrown by Martin Weinguard to celebrate the nomination of two of his pictures for the Academy Awards. George Banner was an independent producer who was enjoying the unusual privilege of being courted by every major studio in Hollywood after his low-budget picture on California surfers had broken box-office records around the country. He was also one of the few people who really understood Anthony Wellington. Out of genuine liking, as well as pity for the gentle diffident man, he invited him along as his guest. Anthony was so overwhelmingly grateful for the invitation that Banner immediately began to regret his impulsive kindness.

"Now look, Anthony," he warned. "Don't get any wrong ideas. I'm not taking you there for the purpose of meeting anyone who's looking for a financial backer. In fact, I don't want you to even bring up the subject. This is strictly for entertainment. Just relax and enjoy yourself."

"George, I wouldn't dream of talking about money at a party," Anthony said, deeply shocked. "How could you possibly have thought such a thing?"

Banner, who knew that money was always a major topic of conversation at every Hollywood party, shook his head at his friend's hopeless naivete. "Well, it's been known to happen," he remarked dryly. "But don't you get involved in anything but a good time."

"You can count on that," Anthony smiled.

And at first Anthony Wellington not only had a good time, he had the time of his life. Beaming with wide-eyed delight, he shook hands with some of the most glamorous stars in Hollywood, almost beside himself with excitement. Then George Banner, after thirty minutes of shepherding his charge around the room, gently deposited him at a table and left him with a tray of delicacies from the buffet as he went off to take care of business. And Anthony Wellington stopped having a good time.

Initially he looked up and smiled eagerly at each person who passed by his table, and when he saw someone to whom he'd been introduced earlier he would leap to his feet and offer them a place to sit down. But it was like they'd all suddenly turned deaf and blind, gliding by him unseeing and unhearing, only to break into animated cries of pleasure at a voice that called to them from a table just beyond his.

Gradually his smiles faded and then disappeared altogether as he forlornly watched the party where, as usual, he was fated to be only a spectator, never a participant. He was on the verge of gathering together enough courage to leave his isolated corner and join the noisy, laughing crowd around the bar when the band filed into the room. They took their places on the stage and launched into a wild driving beat that brought everyone charging onto the small dance floor, where they exploded into joyous contortions.

Anthony blinked in confusion as multi-colored lights flashed on over the dance floor and the candle on his table flickered briefly before going out. It took several seconds before his eyes were able to focus again. Then he saw the woman sitting at the table next to him. She, too, was alone with a tray of food from the buffet sitting in front of her. But unlike himself, she was stuffing it into her mouth with ferocious energy.

"You must have found something better than I did," he smiled as he leaned toward her.

"What?" Marcia Weinguard looked up from her plate and stared at him blankly.

"Your selection from the buffet," he said, nodding toward her plate. "I was wondering what it is."

She cupped a hand around her ear. "You'll have to speak up. I can't hear a word in this racket."

"I said, I wanted to know what you're eating," he shouted. "Because you're evidently enjoying it very much."

Marcia, who was easily forty pounds overweight, pulled back and glared at him indignantly. "What the hell kind of crack is that? You trying to be smart or something?"

"I beg your pardon?"

The band's drummer executed a frantic paradiddle with his sticks as the guitarist, hips gyrating like Elvis Presley's, grabbed the microphone and let out a high, keening wail as he apparently experienced a major orgasm. A brief silence followed as the band's members fell back and lit up, the sweetish odor of marijuana mingling with the more conventional cigarette smoke in the room.

"Marcia, I've been looking everywhere for you!" An incredibly handsome young man in his early twenties came rushing up to her table. The ceiling lights reflected off the lustrous cap of dark curly hair and illuminated the sparkling blue eyes that glowed out of the tanned face. "Now you promised me a dance." he smiled engagingly. "So I'm claiming this next one."

"I never promised you anything, Rodney," Marcia said bluntly.

"Well, I guess that's true." With an effort, Rodney managed to keep the smile on his face, his perfectly capped teeth gleaming whitely at her "Maybe I just promised myself, because I was looking forward to it so much."

"Oh get off it, Rodney," Marcia said impatiently. "You've done your duty. Now go away and leave me alone."

"Marcia, what are you talking about?" He bent over and kissed her hand. "I want to be with you. Don't you understand that?"

"I understand very well," Marcia replied in a low, ominous tone. "But what you don't understand is that I don't want to be with you."

"1 hear you," he answered nervously. "But your father ..."

"It's all right, Rodney," she said wearily. "I'll tell him you came over and did just what he asked you to."

"Well, if you're sure ..."

"I'm sure. So do me a favor and split!"

As Rodney turned and walked away, Anthony was horrified to see two big fat teardrops spill out of Marcia's eyes and roll down her cheeks. Whipping out a large white handkerchief, he pressed it on her and murmured, "I'm so sorry that young man upset you. Is there anything I can do?"

"No," she said with a muffled sob. "But thanks." She mopped her checks and handed his handkerchief back, then bent over her plate again.

"Forgive my rudeness in not introducing myself. I'm Anthony Wellington," he offered shyly.

"Marcia Weinguard," she mumbled as she shoveled a forkful of food into her mouth.

"Marcia Weinguard!" he exclaimed. "Are you by any chance related to Martin Weinguard?"

"Daughter." She began eating faster.

"Why, how exciting!" he beamed. "This is a real honor for me, meeting you."

She put down her fork. "Forget it," she announced curtly. "You'll just be wasting your time trying to play up to me, because nobody gets a penny out of Marcia Weinguard!"

He gazed at her in astonishment. "You think I'm interested in your money?"

Her eyes traveled over him coldly. "Well, it's pretty obvious that you're no actor, so you're not cozying up to me to get a part in a picture. That leaves money."

"Money," he repeated. Then as the incredible irony of the situation hit him, he started to laugh. And the more he thought about it, the funnier it became to him. His laughter grew into a roar, causing people at nearby tables to turn and stare.

"Hey! Hey, what's the matter with you?" Marcia asked nervously.

"Oh, my dear girl, if you only knew," he sputtered as another wave of laughter overcame him. He finally managed to bring himself under control, wiping his eyes with the handkerchief that was still damp from Marcia's tears. "You see, I've spent the last five months trying desperately to give away money. And now you think I want to take money. It's just too incredible!"

"What in the world are you talking about?

"Well, I guess I do owe you an explanation," he said, embarrassed. He became aware of the fact that his loud laughter had attracted attention to them from every table surrounding them.

Hunching his shoulders and lowering his voice, he leaned close to her. "Actually, what happened was . . ."

Marcia listened in growing wonderment. At first suspicious, she quickly realized that Anthony was telling the absolute truth.

"It's the craziest thing I've ever heard. What are you going to do now?"

The leader of the band blew into his microphone and absently scratched his crotch as he announced, "And now a mellow number for the folk."

"I'm going to ask you to dance," Anthony smiled as the slow, easy sounds of a Bossa Nova wafted through the room.

"This is really nice," Marcia breathed softly into Anthony's rather stork like neck as they glided around the room.

"Yes, it certainly is." Anthony contentedly hummed off-key as they continued to circle. "Perhaps we could do it again. Would you by any chance be free for dinner tomorrow evening?"

"Dinner?" Marcia was so startled she tripped over his foot. "You're asking me to dinner?"

"Why, yes." He looked at her a little uncertainly. "Is that all right?'"

"Oh, Anthony, of course it is!" Her face lit up like a child's on Christmas morning. "I accept with pleasure."

Marcia Weinguard was so overwhelmed by the discovery that a man who had as much money as her daddy was seriously interested in her, she fell in love with him immediately. Anthony was so overwhelmed by the discovery that the daughter of Hollywood's most powerful studio head was seriously interested in him, he talked himself into believing he could fall in love with her. Martin Weinguard simply fell on his knees and thanked God that his homely, overweight daughter, whom he loved more than anybody or anything in the entire world, had finally found a man.

Marcia and Anthony were married three month later, on the occasion of her thirty-second birthday. "This way you'll never have an excuse for forgetting our anniversary date." she'd chuckled.

It was the most spectacular wedding Hollywood had seen in two decades. Over a thousand people attended the reception at Martin Weinguard's palatial Beverly Hills mansion, and the guest list read like a who's who of the royalty of the entertainment industry. Anthony wandered around in a euphoric daze as the idols he'd worshiped from afar all these years came up to shake his hand and warmly offer him congratulations. At last he was a participant in the marvelous world he'd dreamed about and longed so much to become a part of.

But Anthony's euphoria quickly faded when he learned that his new bride had no intention of holding parties where the elite of Hollywood would gather to discuss the future of the film business. She had no interest in the film business at all —past, present, or future. There were, in fact, only three things that interested Marcia Weinguard: eating, watching television, and sex.

Of the three, Anthony was most depressed by the sex. A shy, fastidious man, he was also a hopeless romantic who envisioned the act of love as a tender, exploratory adventure leading to heights of breathless pleasure that could only be expressed in terms of silent joy as the loving couple looked deeply into each other's eyes. That was not Marcia's way.

"Let's fuck, honey," she would exclaim happily as she threw herself upon him, her lips still greasy from the fried chicken she'd just gorged herself on. "Let's do it all, from top to bottom!"

Anthony dutifully did it all, but his heart wasn't really in it. And as time went by he became increasingly disheartened, not only by the way his marriage had turned out but by the way his entire life had turned out. For he was no closer to the magical world of show business now than he had been when he'd first met Marcia. Martin Weinguard had been kind but firm when he'd hopefully offered his services to International Pictures.

"Face it, Anthony, you weren't meant to be a producer. You know nothing about pictures, and I'm afraid you'll never be able to learn. You see, you just don't have a feel for the business."

Martin had paused for a moment, then smiled. "But if you want the job of handling financial deals for our corporation, well, I could arrange that. Because money is something you really have a feel for."

"Thanks, Mr. Weinguard. I appreciate that, but it isn't exactly what I had in mind."

"Not Mr. Weinguard!" he chided him. "It's Martin to you, my boy. Got it?" he asked as he affectionately thumped Anthony on the back.

Yes sir," Anthony said dispiritedly.

In an effort to keep his mind off the depressing specter of his failed dreams, Anthony began dabbling in real estate again and in the next few years his net worth increased from eighty to over one hundred million dollars. Two attorneys and three accountants worked full-time on his growing empire. And they were probably the happiest attorneys and accountants in Los Angeles, for Anthony was not only incredibly successful but astoundingly generous, offering them a share in his enterprises on top of the very healthy retainers he paid them. The only thing that troubled them was his peculiar reaction to success.

"I swear, he gets unhappier with every buck we make," Herman Weiss whispered to his partner. "It's not only unnatural, it's scary. Do you think we should talk to him?"

"No!" his partner announced decisively. "Let's not rock the boat. The more miserable he is, the more money he makes. It could be a disaster for all of us if he got happy."

"Yeah, you got a point," Herman admitted. "So we just leave him alone, right? And tell the others to do the same?"

"Right!"

Anthony was unaware of the decision made by his staff. All he knew was that they were considerate enough to handle more and more of the business on their own without bothering him, something that Irving Schwartz back in New York had never been willing to do. But occasionally something stirred inside him and told him he should call a meeting. He was always vaguely nonplussed to find these impromptu sessions sent his staff into a frenzy of activity with much scurrying around and exchanging of papers. But the end results were always the same. More money, more profits.

"Don't underestimate that man!" Herman Weiss hissed after one of those unexpected meetings. "The lawyers for Howard Hughes never saw much of him, either, but they were smart enough to realize he knew everything that was going on. I say we play straight with this guy!"

Everybody nervously agreed, and Anthony's empire continued to grow.

But his empire was the last thing on Anthony's mind as he peered into the mirror over the dressing table in his private bathroom on the second floor of the Bel Air estate he'd built for Marcia, and tried for the third time without success to knot his white tie properly. Because all he could think about was the fact that he was forty years old on this day, and he'd accomplished nothing. Not one of his dreams had come true.

"Here, let me do that for you." Marcia cried out as she burst into the bathroom. "You know you'll never get it right yourself."

"Probably not," he admitted. Docilely, he leaned over so she could reach the bow. "And how was your day, dear?" he inquired politely.

"Just like every day before one of Daddy's big parties," she muttered crossly. "Wearing myself out running all over town looking for a new dress, then putting up with all that tiresome fuss of fittings. And I had to wait a whole hour before Elaine was free to do my hair. I don't know why I bother. I never end up looking any better, anyway."

"Now that's not true, dear. You look lovely when you get dressed up, and you know your father always notices."

"Oh I suppose so," she said grudgingly. "But it makes a nervous wreck out of me, and I miss all my favorite television programs. I'm just so much happier staying home."

Her fingers paused in the act of tying his bow. "Hey, how about a quickie, honey?" she said hopefully as she gazed up at him.

"No!" he cried, cringing involuntarily. "I mean, we don't have time," he added hastily. "Your father was very specific about screening the new picture precisely at seven, and he'll expect us to be there to help him greet all the guests first."

Marcia looked momentarily dejected, then brightened. "Well, maybe it's better to save it for later when we can relax, and I don't have to worry about rushing to get dressed. It's more fun rushing to get undressed," she giggled. "Right, sweetie pie?"

"Right," he echoed dismally.

"I want you to promise me something, though. I don't want you going off and leaving me alone tonight. I know what you're like when Daddy screens a new picture. You get all excited and start trailing around after the stars and the director, pestering them with questions. And then you forget all about me. It's a terrible feeling," she said with sudden passion. "So please don't do that tonight. Promise?"

"I promise."

That night, for the first time in his life, Anthony Wellington broke a promise. Because the minute he laid eyes on Erin Connolly, he was transported into an ecstasy of feeling he hadn't experienced since that long ago evening in the Orpheum Theater in Stroudsburg, Pennsylvania, when he looked up from his bag of hot buttered popcorn and saw Ingrid Bergman.

SEVEN

"Now I'm not promising anything for sure," Erin warned an excited Cheryl Green as she sipped from her wine glass at the same restaurant that Andi Steiner had taken her to a year before. "But if things work out like I hope," she grinned, "then I'm looking at the new script girl for Leland Devereaux."

"Oh, Erin, that would be so wonderful! Do you think there's any real chance at all of my getting it?"

" Well, I've set up a preliminary interview for you with Peter."

"Peter Faraday?" Cheryl squealed in excitement. "Devereaux's assistant director?"

"That's the man. But listen to me very carefully," she cautioned. "Devereaux doesn't know anything about this. So when you appear on the set this afternoon, as far as he's concerned you're just filling in for me while I'm out sick with the flu. This will give you two days to become familiar with my job."

Erin was genuinely fond of Cheryl and wished her well in her interview with Peter Faraday as she dropped her off at the Film-Star lot after lunch and headed for Beverly Hills. She would be sure to give Peter a strong recommendation for the hard working script girl.

But now she needed to get ready for Project Anthony Wellington.

Then, as though fate had decreed that it was all meant to be, everything went right. The first shop Erin went into had the perfect dress. It was an exquisite white lace, cut low off the shoulders and gently undulating around the body.

"You look like a sexy angel," the salesgirl said admiringly as she saw Erin step out of the dressing room and pirouette in front of the mirror.

"Exactly what I want to look like." Erin smiled. "Now do you have shoes to match? And someone to adjust the waist and hemline?"

"Yes, of course.'" The salesgirl scurried off, and a few minutes later both the shoes and a seamstress appeared.

"The dress must be ready by tomorrow afternoon," Erin told her.

"It will be," the small, elderly seamstress promised as she bent over and inspected the fit. "Ah, so lucky," she sighed through the pins in her mouth. "To have such a dress, and look like you. You're a very fortunate young lady."

"Thank you. I'm hoping to be."

"You will. You will. Take my word for it." The woman gently patted Erin as she pinned up the hem. "You've got the look of success about you."

****

"You look too good to be true," an awed James Lee Norton said reverently as Erin opened the door of her apartment and invited him in.

"I am too good to be true," she grinned wickedly. "That's the basis of my charm. You want a drink before we go?"

"No. I want a hundred million dollars so I can have you instead of Anthony Wellington," he said huskily. Then he gave a quick, nervous laugh as he saw the startled look on her face. "Just a little joke," he assured her.

"Well, it would be nice if it weren't a joke," she murmured, kissing him on the cheek. "I think we'd make great partners."

"Partners!" he cried in mock anguish. "I wasn't talking about being partners." Erin gave a relieved laugh as the familiar mischievous twinkle appeared in his eyes, replacing the intent hungry look that had been fixed on her.

"Maybe someday we'll have a discussion about whatever you were talking about," she said lightly. "But right now I think we'd better concentrate on our current project. Any last minute tips on strategy?"

James Lee frowned thoughtfully. "Your biggest job is going to be separating Wellington from his wife. She sticks to him like glue, and he's too much of a gentleman to deliberately walk away from her. But unless you get him alone, you're never going to have a chance."

"Can't you distract her?" Erin asked as she picked up her purse, and they walked out the door.

"Nobody distracts Marcia Weinguard," he said wryly.

"But you can try, can't you?" she insisted as they got into his sporty white Porsche and drove off.

"Sure, babe." He down-shifted abruptly, tires squealing and motor roaring as he rounded the corner and then whipped out into the traffic of Sunset Boulevard, heading north for Martin Weinguard's home. "I'll do my best, but I can't promise anything. You'll understand better when you meet this broad," he told her with a crooked grin as they screeched to a halt at a red light. "In the meantime, start thinking."

Erin and James Lee rode in silence for the next ten miles, absorbed in their own thoughts. But no one would ever have been able to guess what was going on in their minds when they finally pulled up to the impressive gates outside Martin Wcinguard's house and stepped out of the car. Their faces were as blandly gracious as those of all the other guests who arrived with secret thoughts hidden behind a smiling facade.

"James Lee!" Beaming, Martin Weinguard took a step forward and grabbed his hand, pumping it vigorously. "So glad you could come!" Then his smile faltered as he saw Erin. "And this is . . ."

"A business associate of mine at Film-Star," James Lee replied smoothly. "Miss Connolly, Mr. Weinguard."

Martin's face cleared. Having a black man in his home was one thing. Having a black man with a white girl as his date was something else altogether. It was unthinkable! But if she was just a business associate, well, that was different. As a matter of fact, he decided on reflection, James Lee had shown quite good judgment in bringing this girl. It would have been quite awkward for everyone if he'd shown up with one of those jungle bunnies he probably went around with.

"A pleasure to have you here, my dear," Martin said pleasantly. "And what is it you do at Film-Star?"

"I work with Leland Devereaux."

Martin's eyebrows shot up. "Well, that must be very exciting for you." He took a closer look at the lovely young creature standing in front of him. "I take it, then, you're directly involved in this exciting new television series that all of us in the industry are watching with such enthusiasm?" he asked with a speculative gleam in his eye.

Erin, aware of his sudden interest in her, played a hunch. "I have been very fortunate in that respect," she said demurely. "Mr. Devereaux has been kind enough to both guide and teach me, and as a result I've enjoyed the marvelous privilege of working personally on every project."

Martin had a difficult time restraining himself from jumping up and down and shouting with joy. That James Lee is some wonderful, smart nigger, he thought ecstatically. Every major studio in town had made surreptitious approaches to Leland Devereaux when they found out what was going on over at Film-Star, all to no avail.

But James Lee had bypassed the obvious, zeroing in on Devereaux's new romantic interest instead. It was a stroke of genius, because the famous Broadway director was notorious for his slavish devotion to whomever was the current love of his life. Neither the love nor the devotion ever lasted very long, but while they did, he would do almost anything for the object of his passion. So all that was necessary was to cultivate this little girl with tender loving care, and she would deliver Devereaux to him. At that moment, Martin loved James Lee like a brother.

"I'm sure you're being much too modest. Miss Connolly," he announced softly as he took hold of both her hands and gazed intently into her eyes. "Leland Devereaux would never devote time to anyone who didn't show exceptional talent and promise. I would bet money that you are headed for some very big things, given the right opportunity. And I never bet money unless I know I'm going to win," he added with a chuckle.

"You're very kind," Erin murmured.

"Nonsense! All I am is right." He laughed then. "If you can forgive what sounds like an old man's vanity, I'd like to prove it by talking with you later. International Pictures is always looking for special people, and I think you might be exactly what we need for a major new project we're just starting."

"Daddy, the line of people is getting very long," Marcia whispered. She shifted her weight and tried flexing her toes in the shoes that were beginning to pinch painfully.

"What?" he said, startled.

"The line, Daddy!" she repeated irritably.

"Oh. Oh yes, of course." Martin coughed and released Erin's hands. "Miss Connolly, let me present my lovely daughter Marcia and her husband Anthony Wellington."

"A pleasure, I'm sure."

Anthony said nothing. His mouth was too dry to utter a word as Erin looked up at him, her luminous green eyes gently caressing his face. He vaguely felt the iron grip of his wife as she hooked her arm through his.

"Anthony, I want you to take care of this young lady," Martin announced briskly. "Get her a drink and get her comfortable. And make sure she has a good seat for the screening."

"I'd be delighted," Anthony said hoarsely, finding his voice with difficulty. He tried to offer Erin his arm, and there was a slightly awkward moment as Marcia continued to cling to it.

"Marcia!" Martin hissed.

Reluctantly she let go and then watched unhappily as Erin and Anthony walked off together. "Why did you do that, Daddy?" she whimpered.

"Because that little girl is going to do something very nice for me." He winked at her, a smug smile on his face. Martin would quickly find out how terribly wrong he was.

One week after the party at Martin Weinguard's home, all of Hollywood was buzzing about Anthony and Erin's torrid love affair, which was being carried on right in front of their delightedly scandalized eyes with a blatant lack of discretion.

"A toast to Hollywood's newest celebrity," James Lee chuckled, getting to his feet as Erin came out of the kitchen of her apartment and handed him a drink. "Long may she reign."

"'Oh, she's planning to do that, all right," Erin said with a smile. "But not as a gossip item."

"Which, I imagine, leads us to why you invited me over tonight." James Lee sat back down on the couch and raised an inquisitive eyebrow as Erin curled up opposite him. "Am I supposed to guess, or are you just going to come out with it?"

"I've got it, James Lee!" she exclaimed, her eyes sparkling. "I've got the script for my first picture. But I need your advice on where to go from here."

He blinked in disbelief. "What do you mean, you've got a script? You don't even have a production company."

"Oh, don't worry about that." She waved an impatient hand at him. "Anthony has already agreed to set up one."

"Christ, Erin, you don't waste time, do you? How in the hell did you accomplish that in one week?"

"It wasn't all that difficult." She gave a tiny shrug. "All I have to do is marry him. Anyway," she continued eagerly, "let me tell you about this script."

"Marry him!" he shouted. "What the fuck are you talking about, Erin? We never planned on your marrying him!"

"I know," she admitted. "But that's because we didn't really understand what Anthony was like when we started this. He's awfully old-fashioned, James Lee, and the thought of having an affair would horrify him."

She leaned forward, clasping her hands together. "Believe me, this is the only way I can make it work," she told him earnestly. "Besides, it won't be all that bad. He's actually a very nice man."

"Jesus!" James Lee stared into his drink for a long moment. "You realize how much trouble you're buying yourself with this? I mean, it would be one thing if you had a little fling with him, got the money to produce your picture, and then returned him to his wife. But if you break up Marcia Weinguard's marriage, her father will never rest until he destroys you."

He took a long swallow of his drink and shook his head. "You have any idea of the power that man wields in this town? There's not a studio that'll let you in its doors to shoot this picture. There's not a single major star or director who'll sign with you."

"Those things occurred to me," she said with a wry smile. "Why else do you think I asked you to come over tonight? Obviously, I need some advice."

"Advice?" he repeated incredulously. "Erin, I thought you were listening to me. The only advice I can give you is not to marry Anthony Wellington, which you apparently refuse to accept. So that's it, babe. You're playing with a totally stacked deck, and you don't have one winning card."

"That's not quite true. I have Merry-Go-Round."

James Lee almost choked on an ice cube. "You've got to be kidding." He stared at her, unbelieving. "I mean, are you talking about the book that's been number one on the bestseller list for the past six weeks?"

"Of course," she grinned. "What else would I be talking about?"

"But Film-Star has the option on that! They locked it up cold before the book was even published. There's no way you could touch it!"

"Past tense. The option has expired, and they only paid a lousy $2500 for it because no one had ever heard of the author and since the book hadn't been published yet, they had no idea it would become such a fantastic bestseller. Film-Star promised to get back to the agent with a major new 5 figure offer by the end of this week but that leaves 48 hours before they make that offer in which no one owns the film rights.

"And since you work at Film-Star, you had no problem getting a copy of the screenplay, right?"

"Right."

"But there's not an agent in this town who'll take a call from you, Erin, so how could you possibly even get a chance to offer on it, much less win it?"

"I paid a visit to the author."

EIGHT

Who?" Alan Corry said puzzledly as he picked up the phone in the den of his rented beach house.

"Erin Connolly, with Film-Star Studios. I'm terribly sorry to bother you at home, Mr. Corry, but something very important has come up about the picture and we can't reach your agent. Is there any chance at all that I might come out to your place late this afternoon so we can go over it?"

"Good Lord, there's no problem about renewing the option, is there?" Alan cried in alarm. "I thought everything was set. We're supposed to meet with you people tomorrow."

"Well, I wouldn't want to call it a problem," Erin said slowly. "But I do think we should get together as soon as possible."

"Oh my God! I told Harvey he was pushing too hard."

A long silence followed, intermittently punctuated by Alan's rapid breathing. "Look, Miss Connolly," he finally said in a nervous rush. "I'm a writer, not a businessman. Harvey, my agent, always handles that part. I- I really don't know what to tell you."

"Mr. Corry, please believe me when I say there's nothing to be upset about. You have written an absolutely marvelous book, a book any studio would be proud to have. And speaking for myself, I would like to say I think it's the finest work any writer has produced in the last decade."

"Really?" Alan said shakily. "You really feel that way?"

"Without question! Now if we can just get together to iron out these problems, it will be smooth sailing from that point on."

"Well, if it's that important . . ."

"It is," she announced firmly.

"All right, then." He gave her directions to his beach house, realizing belatedly as he hung up the phone that she'd never told him what exactly the problems were. Was it possible they were so bad she couldn't bring herself to mention them over the phone, he wondered anxiously. Surely they weren't going to refuse to renew the option, because if that was the case there'd be no reason for her to come out to see him. So what was left? The price they were willing to pay for the option renewal, that was one. Harvey had pushed for a major five figures. The start date on production of the picture, that was another. Harvey had inserted a clause in the contract that photography had to start within three months, so that he'd receive his full money on the deal. Screen credits were the third. Harvey had insisted that the studio let him write the screenplay.

"Screen credits," he muttered. He began picking up books from the floor of the den and stacking them neatly in piles, blowing dust off the desk and polishing its surface with the sleeve of his shirt as he passed by.

"They hate my script, and they want to bring in a new writer," he told his computer. On the other hand, it could just as well be the production date. Maybe the studio is jammed with other pictures in production, and they're not going to start mine for another whole goddamn year.

Both thoughts were so depressing that Alan Corry gave up his halfhearted cleaning attempts and went into the small kitchen where he took out a large glass, a bottle of vodka, a can of tomato juice, a tray of ice cubes, and a lime. After a moment of reflection, he returned the tomato juice and lime to the refrigerator and just poured the vodka straight over the ice cubes.

Alan Corry had a number of problems of his own. Merry-Go-Round was his first book, and he'd been stunned when it hit the bestseller list. In a feverish glow of excitement he had given his ex-wife a cash settlement, bought a three-thousand-dollar wardrobe, moved out of the dingy one-room apartment in New York that was located on the fringes of Harlem, and moved to California where he rented a beach house and settled back to enjoy the good life while he wrote the screenplay for the picture. It hadn't turned out to be such a good life. The bills kept pouring in, but the money didn't.

"I'm a bestselling novelist," he'd screamed at Harvey, his agent. "So how can I be poor?"

"Because you never listen to me," Harvey had sighed. "I told you it would take time. You can be a hardcover bestseller and barely make any more than your advance. The money is in paperback, rights sales and film rights."

"So when are you going to get those for me?" he'd demanded.

"Soon, kid, soon. Trust me."

Well I trusted you, Harvey, and you can see how far that's gotten me! Alan shouted furiously as he got up and headed back to the kitchen for a refill, tripping over a stack of books on the way. As he bent down somewhat unsteadily to straighten them, the doorbell rang.

Oh Christ, that can't be her, he thought in panic. It's too early. I'm not ready. He peered at his watch, squinting to bring it into focus. Five o'clock. How could it possibly be five o'clock already?

The doorbell rang again, an impatient edge to it now, and Alan swallowed hard as he trudged down the hall to answer it.

"Mr. Corry, I can't tell you what a pleasure it is for me to meet the author of Merry-Go-Round in person," Erin announced sincerely as she held out a slim, tanned hand.

"You're Miss Connolly?" he blurted. Alan had been prepared for a crisply efficient, no-nonsense woman in her late thirties or early forties with horn-rimmed glasses and a matronly figure encased in a sensible tweed suit. This girl standing in front of him couldn't be more than twenty-two or twenty-three, and she was one of the most excitingly beautiful creatures he'd ever seen in his life.

"I hope you'll call me Erin," she smiled.

"Erin," he repeated in a daze. "A beautiful name. It's just right for you."

"Thank you, you're very kind." Erin gently extricated her hand from his grasp and took a firmer hold on the large envelope under her arm. "Do you think I might come inside?"

"Good Lord, of course. Of course!" He flung the door open wide. "Come in and make yourself comfortable wherever you'd like. I work in the den, but maybe you'd rather sit in the living room where you can see the ocean?"

"Wherever you're the most comfortable is where I'd be the most comfortable," Erin murmured softly.

"Well, what a nice thing to say." Alan led her down the hall, looked around at the dusty, cluttered living room, and thought about the equally dusty, cluttered den. "I'm afraid writers aren't very good housekeepers," he said with a nervous laugh.

"They're not supposed to be. Cleaning ladies are good housekeepers, but they rarely make great novelists. And I'm here to talk to a great novelist."

A sudden rush of heat engulfed him as he gazed into the luminous green eyes fixed on him. "That does put a different perspective on the situation, doesn't it?" he said huskily.

"The right perspective, I would say." Erin absently stroked his arm. "And one I'm very eager to explore."

"Yes. Explore." Alan felt suddenly dizzy. "How about a drink?" he stammered. "Would you like a drink?"

"That would be lovely."

"Good. Good. I'll go get it now." Alan went off toward the kitchen, then stopped abruptly. "All I have is vodka. Is that okay with you?"

"Vodka is all I ever drink," Erin assured him. She walked over to the couch and curled up on it. "Now isn't it a marvelous omen that we share the same tastes?"

"Very marvelous. Even absolutely marvelous."

But Alan's euphoria turned into puzzlement and finally suspicion as he sat opposite Erin on the couch and listened to her.

"I don't get this," he growled. "I thought you were here to talk about my contract with Film-Star, but that's not what you're talking about at all."

"What I'm talking about is you," she said quietly. "And isn't that what's really important?"

"Yeah, to whom? You're asking me to kill a deal with a major studio like Film-Star to go with some totally unknown outfit, and you expect me to believe that's in my best interests? Boy, you must think I'm some dumb idiot!"

"Not dumb, Mr. Corry. Hopelessly stupid is more like it. Apparently you've never heard of International Pictures?"

He blinked in surprise. "International Pictures? You never told me International Pictures was involved in this."

"That's because it never occurred to me it was necessary. I thought everyone knew Anthony Wellington was the son-in-law of Martin Weinguard, the studio head of International."

"Anthony Wellington?" he repeated uncertainly.

"Really, Mr. Corry," she snapped. "Didn't you even read this contract?" Her finger stabbed at the letterhead on the piece of paper he was holding. "Anthony Wellington, a principal partner in Con-Well Productions."

"But what exactly does that mean?" he asked with a hesitant frown.

"I'm afraid it means I've wasted my time this afternoon." Erin removed the contract from his hand, collected her purse, and stood up. "It's a personal disappointment to me, because I believed so much in your book. However, you are certainly not the only bestselling novelist in this country. 1 can think of several, notably that world-famous author whose current book is edging you right out of first place on The New York Times bestseller list, who would be more than delighted to sign with us for half a million dollars. Anthony was right when he told me to contact him first."

Erin sighed. "Well, live and learn. In the meantime, thank you for the drink, and good day, Mr. Corry." She turned on her heel and marched briskly out of the living room.

"Half a million dollars?" Alan exclaimed in a strangled voice. His agent had only gotten $2500 for the first option. "Where does it say half a million dollars?" He stared at his empty hands where moments before the contract had rested. "Hey, Erin! Miss Connolly! Wait!!" He raced after her.

"What is it now, Mr. Corry?" Erin said impatiently. "It's late, and I must get back to my partner so we can make other plans. We have a production date to meet for our first release."

"I think we should talk more," he said breathlessly. "I didn't understand everything clearly at first. You know how writers are. We get all involved in what we're doing in our own little world and just don't relate properly to the business world outside. You do understand, don't you?"

****

Erin turned the car radio up to full volume as an old Beatles hit came pouring out of the speakers, moving her body in rhythm to the demanding beat and pausing occasionally to caress the envelope lying beside her, which contained the signed contract from Alan Corry.

"It's going to be all mine," she shouted exultantly to the skyline of Los Angeles which began to appear in silhouette against the mountain ranges as dusk fell and lights winked on in the tall office buildings. "This whole place is going to belong to me!"

But it didn't work out the way she'd thought it would. Erin had been confident that once she owned the screen rights to Merry-Go-Round, all the doors of Hollywood would open wide to welcome her. In fact, they remained locked tight. An enraged Film-Star Studios, in concert with an equally enraged Harvey Goldberg, Alan Corry's agent, filed class-action suits against both the fledgling production company and Erin personally, charging them with virtually every crime under the sun except murder and Hollywood avoided Erin Connolly like the plague. Even secretaries hung up on her when she called. Trade papers had a field day with the lawsuits, reveling in the sensational background of the case; and the smart money in town predicted that Merry-Go-Round would shortly return to Film-Star.

It was a prediction that caused Erin increasing anxiety. "Anthony, are you sure this contract your attorneys drew up is fully binding?" she asked for the fifth time one evening as she paced nervously around her apartment.

"Honey, you just have to stop worrying yourself to death like this," Anthony said with concern as he walked over and put his arms around her. "The contract is as legal as any contract can be, and these are some of the best attorneys in the country."

"Then why does everybody say I'm going to lose?" she wailed.

"Well now, they're not law experts, are they?" he smiled. "They're just very opinionated people. And that's not the same at all. So come on and relax, honey. It's all going to work out."

"I wonder," she said dismally.

"There is one thing that's occurred to me." Anthony gave a gentle cough. 'To help the situation, I mean."

Erin whirled around. "What, Anthony? Please tell me, because I feel like I'm at the end of my rope."

"The half of a million dollars Alan Corry is claiming. I think maybe we should pay it to him."

"Are you crazy?" she exclaimed in shock. "I told you he misunderstood. That money was just a projected figure, based on his profit shares in the movie. Nobody pays an author that much just for the option rights to his book. Even Film-Star isn't contesting that!"

"I understand," he said with an apologetic smile. "But the young man does seem to believe he was getting that sum. And if we pay it to him, don't you think the controversy would go away? It would certainly make his agent happy. Ten percent of that is considerably more than Film-Star is willing to pay. "Besides, we can afford it, you know. So why don't we do it, and take care of all these problems in the process?"

For one of the few times in her life, Erin was struck speechless. That amount had seemed an impossible sum to her, but Anthony was right. He could afford it. Which meant she could afford it. Until that moment, Erin hadn't fully comprehended just how much money Anthony really had. God, what a fool she'd been worrying about costs. Anthony could buy a small country if he wanted to.

"My love, my marvelous love, why don't I listen to you more often?" Erin murmured as she wrapped her arms around him and nuzzled into his neck. "You are so brilliant, and you know how to take care of everything. Will you always take care of me?"

"As long as I live," Anthony promised fervently as her warm lips caressed him and her deliciously wicked tongue found its way into his mouth. "Oh, Erin," he groaned as she began stroking his body. "Oh, Erin, what are you doing to me?"

"Loving you, Anthony," she whispered. "Just loving you."

"Please love me more," he whispered back, and then dissolved into mindless ecstasy as she did exactly that.

****

Anthony's assessment of the situation regarding Merry-Go-Round was completely accurate, for the lawsuits were dropped immediately after Alan Corry received a check for $500,000. Without the support of the now delighted author and his equally delighted agent, Film-Star had no case. But Erin, who thought her troubles were now over, quickly learned how wrong she was as James Lee's grim prophecy came true. When Martin Weinguard put a red-eyed, weeping Marcia on the plane for Reno a month after that fateful party, he promised her that Anthony and Erin would pay for what they'd done. He kept his promise. There wasn't a studio in town who would let her use its production facilities for shooting the picture. There wasn't an actor or actress who would sign with her. There wasn't a director who would talk to her. She couldn't even get a technical crew. And time was running out.

Against the advice of Anthony's lawyers, she had given Alan Corry a three-month option instead of the usual twelve-month contract. "Film-Star has already stalled him for a year on the picture," she had argued. "We have to offer him this in order to get him."

It had never occurred to her that she'd even need three months to exercise the option. Wildly eager to start filming her first picture and supremely confident that ownership of a bestselling novel combined with Anthony's money would open all doors, she had planned to start production immediately. Much too late she realized that Hollywood was a feudal society and it took more than money to buy it. Nor did it help to have Anthony apologetically remind her that he'd warned her of just this very thing, since he'd been similarly unsuccessful in buying his way into Hollywood.

Erin clenched her fists and rocked back and forth in an agony of despair. Two weeks, that was all she had left. Then the option would expire unless she'd started production by that time. "It just can't happen this way," she told herself fiercely. "It can't!" She leaned forward and picked up the phone.

"Yeah, babe, I've heard," James Lee said sympathetically. "But don't say I didn't warn you."

"Oh, James Lee, don't tell me that!" she begged, close to tears. "Tell me how to get out of this trap! Tell me how to save my picture. Please. I trust you. You're my only true friend."

"Jesus, Erin. Jesus, what are you asking?"

"I want your mind," she told him feverishly. "You've got the best goddamn mind I've ever known. You have to have some ideas!"

"Wow, you really ask a lot."

"Is it too much?" Her voice suddenly became soft and confidential, "Is it too much to ask for what we've been to each other all these years?"

He started to laugh. "Erin, I think you'd con the gravedigger on the day of your funeral."

"Does that mean you'll help me?"

"I guess it means I'll try." He hung up the phone and shook his head. Then, sighing, he picked up the phone again and called New York.

NINE

"Tom Jeffries?" Erin looked up from the menu she had been absentmindedly perusing and regarded James Lee with a puzzled expression. "I never heard of him. What pictures has he directed?"

"He's a commercial director. Television commercials."

"What?' she cried in horror. "You want me to hire some hack who's spent his whole life with diapers and detergents to direct my picture? I'll give up the picture before I ever allow that to happen!"

"Well, that's your only other choice," he observed dryly. "But before you make the worst decision of your life, 1 suggest you listen to me for a moment."

"Listen to what? How I'll have the whitest whites and brightest colors of any movie ever produced?"

The preposterous statement, uttered in tones of anguished outrage, was too much for James Lee and he broke into helpless laughter.

"I don't see what's so funny," Erin said sullenly.

"I know you don't," he agreed, wiping his streaming eyes; with the napkin. "Maybe someday you will. In the meantime, be a smart girl and listen to me like I told you earlier."

"Okay, but it better be good. This wasn't what I had in mind when you called today and said you had the answer to my problems."

However, as Erin listened to James Lee, she realized he had indeed come up with the answer to her problems. Tom Jeffries was more than a talented, ambitious young man who aspired to the world of films: he was a craftsman who commanded such respect from his peers that they would literally follow him anywhere he went.

Which meant he not only had his own services to offer, but those of camera crew, photographers, musicians, sound mixers and, most importantly, studio facilities and a first-rate lab to develop the film. He was also based in New York, with no ties to the Hollywood power structure.

"You're a genius, James Lee," Erin said gratefully. "I don't know how to thank you. But are you sure he knows how to direct a film?"

"I'm sure," he smiled. "I know it's hard for you to believe, but that's because you don't know anything about shooting television commercials. It takes an enormous amount of skill and professional know-how. Tom Jeffries will do a first-class job for you."

"Well." She leaned back against the booth and gave him a relieved grin. "It looks like I'm back in business. I've got everything I need now except the actors, and I'll bet we can get them from the New York theatre."

"Not quite," he said slowly. "I'm afraid there's one very major thing you're lacking, and frankly I can't figure out any way to help you with it."

"I don't understand," she said with a puzzled frown. "What are you talking about?"

"Distribution."

"Oh my God!" The implications of what he'd just said sank in. "Those fucking studios control distribution, don't they? They'll never let my picture into the theaters. And what good is producing a picture if no one will ever see it?"

The realization that Hollywood, despite all her efforts and James Lee's help, still held the trump card was so bitter she had to blink back tears. Then anger and a grim determination replaced her momentary feelings of hopeless despair. All her life she'd had to fight to get what she wanted and she wasn't about to quit now. Because Erin Connolly wasn't a quitter. She was a winner!

"I won't let them kill my picture," she told James Lee fiercely. "I'll beat them at their own game, and one day they'll all come crawling to me! There are independent distribution companies, aren't there? I'll go to them. I'll pay them to take the movie, if I have to."

"And you'll be wasting your money. Oh sure, you could buy some of the small outfits, but you know what that would give you? An exclusive showing at a drive-in theater in Steubenville, Ohio. No, babe, that isn't the way."

"Then what is the way?" she asked desperately.

"Make them want your product. There are only two major independent distribution companies. Forget about the rest. So what you have to do is create such demand for your picture, they'll be hungry enough for it to ignore the pressures from the big studios. But don't ask me how to accomplish that. You're saddled with an unknown director and no stars."

"I have a bestselling novel, though. I do have that, don't I?" she demanded.

"Right, babe. That's what you've got. Now try and figure out a way to capitalize on it."

It took Erin a week to figure out how to do it, but the idea she came up with was pure dynamite. It wasn't a new idea. In fact, it was one of the oldest ideas in Hollywood. But under these circumstances, it was a stroke of genius.

Merry-Go-Round had the usual standard ingredients for a successful novel. There was sex and violence, salacious inside looks at the world of high fashion, a sinister suggestion of Mafia influence, and a glittering overlay of show-biz personalities. However, what catapulted it to the top of the bestseller list was none of these things. It was the love story between two characters who had captured the eagerly romantic hearts of America in a fashion that hadn't been achieved since Margaret Mitchell created Rhett Butler and Scarlett O'Hara in Gone With The Wind.

Erin instigated a nationwide talent search for the actor and actress who would play these sizzling roles. Ten million dollars of Anthony's money went into the promotion of that search. Hopefuls from Bangor, Maine, to San Jose California, applied for the parts. National magazines carried stories from their readers on their visions of the two characters. Television talk-show hosts interviewed possible candidates and asked their audiences for ratings on a scale of one to ten. The promotion built up to a feverish pitch a month after it had been launched, and then the word was leaked that the stars had been found.

By this time the country was in a state of tense excitement, because the identity of the stars was shrouded in mystery. None of the contestants who had appeared in public were being considered. A terse news release went out from Con-Well Productions. "We have just discovered the perfect two individuals who personify the incredible brilliance and sexual magnetism of the characters in Merry-Go-Round. You will meet them shortly."

Reporters jammed the small offices of Con-Well Productions in New York after that release. C'mon, Miss Connolly," a reporter from the Daily News pleaded. "Just give us a hint. When are you going to unveil them?"

"Soon."

"But when? You can't hold back much longer."

Erin knew that. The only thing she wasn't sure of was how to unveil them. The expensive public relations firm Tom Jeffries had introduced her to was hot on going with a public unveiling on a big television special. Erin wasn't convinced that was the best way to go. Then, watching CBS one night in her exclusive suite at the Plaza, she knew immediately what the best way to go was. A feature story on CBS's "60 Minutes." A hard news story on her personal achievement.

The Nielsen ratings went into double numbers when "60 Minutes" introduced the new stars of Merry-Go-Round, and the usually unflappable Leslie Stahl found herself taken aback by the sheer sexual power of the two people Erin had found. But Erin didn't leave it there. During the entire six month filming of the picture, America was treated to the explosive inside story of what was happening on the set. The male star was accused of fathering the child of the girl who tried to win him in the picture. The incredibly sexy female lead was threatening to leave the set if her co-star, who was now reputed to be her lover didn't return to her. It was the story of Merry-Go-Round happening in real life, and the whole world thrilled to it. It was also the story of Hollywood at its best, and Erin reveled in every second of it.

****

Nine months after Erin Connolly had appeared at Martin Weinguard's exclusive screening party in his palatial Beverly Hills mansion, Erin Connolly Wellington held her own screening party in the equally palatial Beverly Hills mansion that Anthony had bought for her. It wasn't as exclusive a party as Martin had held, and there was a distinct difference in the guest list.

Martin Weinguard had successfully commanded the presence of major stars, important studio heads, big name directors and producers. Erin hadn't wasted her time inviting people who would turn her down. Besides, who needs them she told herself exultantly. Merry-Go-Round is breaking box-office records all over the country in its first week."

But Erin was anxious to make sure her picture continued to break those box-office records, so she'd opened her home to every important film critic and syndicated columnist in Hollywood. These were the people who could ensure her continuing success, and she was determined to make them welcome. The party had been publicized for weeks, promising not only the appearance of those dynamic young stars who had drawn audiences into the theaters by the thousands but the most opulent entertainment Hollywood had seen since Cecil B. De Mille had thrown one of his extravaganzas.

It was a wildly gala festival, and the crowds poured in. But as Erin stood by the door and counted the well-known faces who rushed up to kiss her on the cheek, she grew increasingly upset. Where was Randy Allen, Hollywood's most celebrated columnist?

"Hi, Mrs. Wellington," a breathless little voice announced. "I'm Lynn Powers, Randy Allen's assistant. He's terribly sorry he couldn't make it tonight."

No one would ever have been able to guess the cold fury that raged inside Erin as she graciously greeted the dumpy little Jewish girl who was so nervous she stumbled over her words as she tried to explain why Randy Allen hadn't been able to make it to the party. But as Erin, with a determined smile, continued to talk with Lynn Powers she realized that the terrified girl was considerably more than a dumb secretary. She was bright, perceptive, and astoundingly knowledgeable about Hollywood personalities. And then Erin flashed a very genuine smile as the idea came to her.

Of course Erin had no idea, as she set about to change Lynn Power's life forever, that she was about to create the deadliest enemy she would ever encounter.

TEN

Lynn Powers officially came into existence on April 10, 2010, her creation inspired by a picture of a pretty young Hollywood starlet in an old issue of Screen Romances who bore the same name. Actually, however, she'd been around for some time before that. But during that time she'd been known as Shirley Silverstein, and that was a period of her life Lynn Powers wanted to forget about totally.

Because being Shirley Silverstein meant being fat, homely and unpopular. It meant being poor. It meant a constantly aching back from bending over sewing machines, hand-me-down clothes, and the pervasive odor of boiling cabbage. Above all, it meant the continuous nagging criticism of her mother. Then one day she picked up a movie magazine left in the tailor shop by one of the customers, and then she knew absolutely and without a doubt what she did want. To go to Hollywood and make her mark in that fabulous, magic world. And she worked with single-minded devotion toward that goal.

The counselor at the Los Angeles employment agency Lynn had signed with tore out her hair in frustrated rage as the stubborn star-struck girl turned down one job after another.

"This kid's a potential gold mine," she wailed to her co-workers. "Types ninety words a minute, takes shorthand at one hundred eighty. And she can spell and punctuate, too. I got ten companies who'd hire her this very instant! Then 1 could switch her around to another job every three or four months and make a fortune in commissions. But the little pisher refuses to even consider a position unless it's connected with the movie industry. What did I do to deserve this?

"My advice is to get her what she wants," the woman at the next desk told her unsympathetically. "Otherwise, you're gonna lose her."

"Yeah. Yeah, I know," the counselor sighed unhappily. "You're talking about that new listing that just came in."

The new listing was for a secretarial position with Randy Allen, the acid-tongued syndicated Hollywood columnist. The job paid peanuts, and the commission earned by the employment agency would barely cover the cost of a dinner for two at a good Los Angeles restaurant. The counselor had debated with herself for several days about letting Lynn Powers know about the opening, because it was such a waste of her talent and skills. But now she reluctantly conceded the wisdom of her co-worker's remark and dialed Lynn's telephone number.

Lynn was not particularly excited when she walked into the employment agency early the next morning. She was used to getting calls from the counselor telling her that just the right job had come up, only to find out when she arrived at her office that it wasn't right at all. But this time she was in for a surprise.

"Randy Allen!" Lynn cried, her eyes as wide as saucers. "You mean Randy Allen, the famous columnist?"

"Yeah, that's the one I mean," she said glumly. "But I'm telling you, it's a lousy job. Just typing all day long, and the pay is really rotten."

"Oh how wonderful!" Lynn exclaimed joyfully. "I don't know how to thank you."

"Listen, kid, keep in touch with me," she begged. "I can get you twice this salary any time you want, with fringe benefits you wouldn't believe."

But Lynn hadn't heard a thing that had been said after the magic words Randy Allen had been spoken. "Oh hell," the counselor sighed as she watched the ecstatic girl race out the door for her interview.

Randy Allen hired Lynn thirty minutes after she walked into his office, which was the exact length of time it took her to take down his rapid-fire dictation and turn it into five crisply perfect typewritten pages. And for the next three months, he started every day with a prayer of thanks to the kind gods who had given him this jewel. Lynn was everything and more than she'd promised to be. No task was too big or too small for her. Her energy was inexhaustible and her cheerfulness constant. She had a real feel for the business too, bringing him little gems of gossip for his column and offering them to him shyly, along with the fresh, home-baked pastries she brought with her every morning to serve him with his coffee.

But in the fourth month, Randy started feeling a little uneasy. Maybe Lynn was just a bit too good to be true. She handled a lot of his phone work now and was on a first name basis with most of his contacts. Was it possible she had ambitions of her own? At first he was embarrassed by such thoughts. After all, she was such a hopeless-looking klutz. Maybe his friends were right when they told him he had a tendency toward paranoia. He discussed the possibility at length with his psychiatrist, who just looked at him and said "Hmm?" Which was no help at all. But then the fucker never had been any help, he thought angrily.

Randy was still trying to decide what to do about Lynn when Erin Connolly Wellington sent out her invitations for the extravaganza press party celebrating her first picture. He might have covered it himself if the incredibly beautiful young boy who'd become an overnight sensation in his first starring role (thanks in large part to Randy Allen's promotion of him) hadn't called in desperation and begged his mentor to come and see him because he was going out of his mind trying to decide whether he was really gay or not.

Randy had a deep, personal interest in such discussions, so he sent Lynn out to Erin's party. He couldn't believe he would be missing anything important anyway. Erin Connolly was just a little cunt from nowhere who'd snagged that strange man previously married to Martin Weinguard's daughter. She wouldn't be around too long.

Lynn was so excited about the assignment, she couldn't eat or sleep or think about anything else. But when the day of the big party arrived, her feverish joy turned into teeth-chattering terror. Suppose they refused to let her in the door? After all, they'd invited the famous Randy Allen, not some dumpy little Jewish secretary from Brooklyn. And even if they did let her in, wouldn't they be furious to learn that Randy had snubbed them in this way?

"Nobody will talk to me," she moaned to the mirror. "I'll end up against the back wall with the catering service."

Lynn had a sudden terrible vision of herself huddled in a corner as a tall, imperious woman strode up to her and icily demanded to know where the tray of hot hors d'oeuvres was. "I'd probably go out to the kitchen and get them," she said sadly to her mirror image. "And then tomorrow Randy will fire me."

It didn't happen that way at all, although Lynn experienced a brief, heart-stopping moment of panic when she introduced herself to Erin.

"Randy Allen's assistant?" Erin had said, staring at her through cold, narrowed eyes. "And just exactly what is it you do?"

Frantic to establish her right to be at the party, she'd babbled on about researching the material for Randy's columns and even co-authoring some of them; praying that what she was saying would never get back to Randy. He'd fire her quicker for that than for ending up serving hors d'oeuvres.

Several times Erin broke into her desperate recital with sharp, pointed questions. None of them caused Lynn any problems, because she really did know what she was talking about. In fact, although she was innocently unaware of it, she actually did perform the important functions she thought she was inventing for Erin's benefit. But at the moment, all she knew was an incredible sense of relief as the woman in front of her suddenly favored her with a warm smile.

"Well, my dear, we're certainly all sorry to hear about dear Randy's health problems, but it appears he's done us a real favor by sending you in his place. Colitis, was it?"

"Colitis?" Lynn repeated confusedly, still involved in relating the inside story of a famous television star who'd suddenly quit his hit series. "Gee, I don't remember any rumors like that about Paul Denton. It wouldn't go with his he-man image at all. Torn ligaments, caused by his doing his own stunts, is what I heard. Of course that's a lie. He made the whole thing up to get out of his contract, so he can sign next month with Peckinpah for that new picture. And to tell you the truth," she confided, "I think he's making a mistake. That picture is going to bomb!"

She flushed in embarrassment as Erin burst into laughter. "Well, maybe I'm mistaken," she mumbled. "You can't call them right all the time."

"That's not why I'm laughing," Erin assured her, still chuckling. "The colitis I was referring to belongs to your dear employer Randy Allen. Or at least that's what you told me. I mean, isn't that the reason he couldn't make it tonight?"

"Oh my God! How could I possibly have forgotten?" She swallowed hard and then bravely met Erin's eyes. "Especially since he's suffering from it so much. You must think I'm really terrible."

"No, I don't think that at all," Erin replied thoughtfully. "Why don't we get together for lunch next week and talk about it?"

"About Randy's colitis?"

"No. About why you forgot it."

ELEVEN

"Wow, Mrs. Wellington! I mean, Erin," she corrected herself hastily as Erin gave her a friendly warning look. "I never dreamed you had anything like this in mind when you asked me to lunch. I . . . gosh, I just don't know what to say!"

"Why not say yes?" Erin suggested pleasantly.

"You really think I could do it?"

"Of course. You're a bright, sharp, ambitious girl, and you've developed a lot of very valuable contacts during the time you've worked for Randy Allen. All you need is a little financial backing to get started, and Anthony and I would be delighted to provide it."

"Wow!" Lynn reached absently into the basket of rolls on the table. She flushed as she saw it was empty.

"Gee, I'm sorry. I have this terrible habit of eating when I get nervous. I don't even realize I'm doing it."

"I think that's something you might consider changing," Erin said gently.

"Yeah, I know," Lynn mumbled, hanging her head. "Not that I haven't tried before, because I have. I really have," she told Erin earnestly as she looked up at her. "But giving up eating just seems to be the hardest thing in the world for me."

"Maybe you'll find it easier this time." Erin smiled. "After all everything else in your life is about to change."

"That's true, isn't it?" she said wonderingly. "I still can't believe it, though. Fat, dumb Shirley Silverstein from Brooklyn becoming a famous Hollywood columnist. Boy, will that kill my mother!" she declared joyfully. "I can hardly wait to tell her!"

"Well, we've got a little work to do before you tell her." Erin laughed.

Under the warm, encouraging guidance of Erin Connolly Wellington, Lynn managed to diet off thirty pounds, learned how and where to shop for clothes, found the courage to have her nose done, changed her limp, mousy hair into a gleaming, sun-streaked California blond, and became Hollywood's most sizzling "in" gossip columnist, with her own radio and television show and a syndicated column that was carried by over two hundred newspapers across the country.

Erin's initial motivation in starting Lynn Powers on her career had been simply a matter of getting back at Randy Allen, for his unforgivable snub in not attending the party for her first picture. But she soon found herself becoming genuinely fond of the gutsy little Jewish girl from Brooklyn who fought so hard to achieve her dreams.

In many ways, Lynn reminded her of herself. More important, Lynn was as loving and loyal as she was smart and ambitious. She never forgot for a moment that Erin had been responsible for her success, and she repaid the favor in a hundred ways. If there was a hot new star about to appear on the horizon, Erin was the first to learn about it. If a studio was in financial trouble with a picture or about to lose an important screen option, Erin heard about it before anyone else. And if the vitally important trade unions were considering a strike, Erin got the word about that in advance too.

For the first time in her life Erin had a woman friend, and she thoroughly enjoyed the experience, looking forward to the daily phone chats with their deliciously spiced tidbits of gossip, and sympathizing with Lynn over her one continuing failure. Because despite Lynn's astounding success, there was a very important thing missing in her life . . . romance.

It wasn't that men didn't ask her out, because they did. As a matter of fact, she could have had three hundred and sixty-five dinner dates a year if she'd wanted to. The trouble was that all those eager, attentive men were only interested in Lynn Powers the columnist. No one was interested in Lynn Powers the woman.

At first, Lynn had eagerly accepted every invitation offered her in hopes that maybe this one would turn out to be different. But it never was. And she soon discovered that the loneliest feeling in the world was sitting across the table from a man who was ardently selling his client to you while at nearby tables couples touched and smiled, their ardor directed only at each other.

Soon Lynn began turning down almost as many invitations as she received, finding it infinitely more comforting to stay at home, curled up in the warm coziness of her small bed, watching old movies on television. And when lovers on the flickering screen came together in passionate embraces, causing tears of aching longing to stream down her checks, she could always get up and start writing her column.

Paradoxically, her sudden withdrawal from the social scene caused men to pursue her with frenzied desire. It became a real coup to get Lynn Powers to go out to dinner. Lynn was wryly amused by the accelerated courting she was receiving. It also made her accept fewer and fewer invitations. The only reason she agreed to have dinner with Garth Werner was because she was curious to find out what the man behind the talent was like.

Lynn had been genuinely impressed with the brilliant directorial work in the movie CountDown, which was based on the bestselling novel of the same name and had been handed over to a young unknown graduate of NYU's film school when budget problems and internecine battles within the giant studio that had optioned the book almost closed down production on the picture.

When the picture finally opened, Lynn devoted two columns to praising the director. She also discussed the film on both her radio and television shows. She didn't do this because any agents or public relations people had thrown themselves at her feet, abjectly begging for just a tiny bit of good press about the picture and promising to give her anything she wanted in return for the favor. No, she just did it because she liked the work. Which was one of the reasons Lynn Powers was so good. She couldn't be bought.

It also gave Lynn great pleasure to discover new talent. So when Garth Werner called her office in person to thank her for the reviews on his picture and ask her out to dinner, she hesitated only a few seconds before accepting. And it was the professionally interested syndicated columnist, not the wistfully lonely young woman, who opened the door of her apartment that night and smiled brightly at the tall, darkly handsome young director. But by the end of the evening Lynn Powers the columnist had been totally routed by Lynn Powers the woman, for she had fallen wildly, head over heels in love with Garth Werner. And, miracles of miracles, he seemed to really care about her too. Not her column, not her radio or television show, but her! She could hardly wait for Erin to meet him.

"Erin, you'll never guess what's happened!" Lynn cried ecstatically over the phone the next morning. "It's the most incredible, exciting thing you could possibly imagine!"

"You've met a man."

"Gee, how did you guess so easily?" she asked, crestfallen.

Erin burst into laughter. "Darling, what else could it be when you call at eight-thirty in the morning and tell me the most incredible, exciting thing in the world has just happened. Anyway, 1 think it's marvelous, and I told you it would happen one of these days. Now, who is he and how did it come about?"

Lynn happily launched into a detailed description of exactly how she'd met Garth Werner, where they went to dinner, what he said, what she said. Then she broke off in confusion when she came to the part about his coming back to her apartment.

"It was . . . well, it was everything I've ever dreamed about," she confided shyly. "If you know what I mean."

"Yes," Erin chuckled, "1 know what you mean. So when are you seeing him again?"

"Tonight. I'm cooking for him. He says he hasn't had a good home-cooked meal since he came out to Hollywood. I hope I remember how," she added worriedly. "I haven't fixed a real dinner since I went on my diet."

"You'll remember," Erin assured her. "And you'll probably hook him for life."

"I'd like to. He's really something special. You know who he is, don't you?"

"Well." Erin paused for a moment. The truth was that the name Garth Werner meant nothing to her, but she didn't want to hurt her friend's feelings. Then she suddenly recalled the column Lynn had done on the movie CountDown.

"Of course!" she said enthusiastically. "He's the bright young director Continental Studios hired out of nowhere to take over that picture they were having such budget problems with. He not only brought it in on time, he brought it in under budget, didn't he?"

"He did more than that, Erin. He turned the whole thing around. They've already made their money back, and the picture's been in general release for less than a month. But he's got more going for him than that. He happens to be a personal friend of the guy who wrote Street Scene. Every studio in town is bidding for the screen rights to that book."

"Are you saying what I think you're saying?" Erin asked cautiously.

"You bet I am!" Lynn exclaimed. "He's got a lock on that book. And what he's looking for is a producer who will give him a piece of the action. I kind of think you just might be that producer."

"I kind of think you just might be right. So why don't we set up a little intimate dinner party, just you and Garth and Anthony and myself, to discuss it?"

"You've got it!" Lynn said jubilantly. "Just name the night!"

****

The last thought on Erin's mind when she set up that intimate dinner party for Lynn and Garth was taking away her friend's lover. Erin's only interest was in making a deal with the young director who could get her the screen rights to a picture she, along with most of Hollywood, had been hungering after.

Perhaps the chain of events that was set in motion when Garth and Erin met was inevitable. But it is equally possible that they could have been avoided if Erin herself had not been so terribly vulnerable at that time.

Over the past two years Con-Well Productions had become an established commercial success. This was due in large part to Anthony's money, which allowed the young company to expand in a manner that was beyond the means of most independent producers, who had to wait, hope, and pray for the financial success of their first picture before they could even begin to think of going into production on a second. With Anthony's virtually unlimited funds, Con-Well had been able to acquire properties and start filming them immediately after work had been completed on the previous picture. This kept Con-Well continually in the public eye, and distributors were more than happy to book its pictures, knowing that every one came backed with a good-as-gold, seven-figure advertising and promotion budget.

However, the Connolly-Wellington marriage was not enjoying the same success. Erin had initially been charmed by Anthony's quiet, wry humor, gentle, courtly manner, and wholehearted worship of her. It had made her carefully planned seduction of him more pleasurable than she'd dreamed possible. But after two years, she found no charm in him at all.

His wry humor had become a bore, his gentle, courtly manner a drag, and his worship of her an almost intolerable irritant. He was, after all, almost twenty years older than she, and he had the body of an old man.

Erin was, by nature, a passionate, sensual woman. Curiously, it was the one thing she didn't understand about herself. All her life had been spent in fierce competition to win recognition and power, and in her headstrong battle to achieve those things she had sublimated her basic drives.

Erin had never become involved with a strong, dominant male, never known a man who could challenge and excite her mentally as well as fulfill the powerful emotional needs and desires inside her that were clamoring with increasing urgency to be satisfied. She was about to meet that man, with devastating results.

"Well, here we are!" a glowing Lynn Powers announced the following Friday evening as Erin opened the door.

She threw her arms around Erin and hugged her, then stepped back and gazed up proudly at Garth. "And this is Garth Werner, the brilliant young director all Hollywood will soon be talking about. Garth, honey, my very best friends, Erin and Anthony Wellington."

Erin smiled, extending a welcoming hand, and then her breath caught in her throat as he took it. Her whole body tingled as though she'd suddenly touched a live electric current. Their eyes met and she stood there frozen, unable to look away.

Anthony gave a gentle cough. "I'm afraid he isn't going to think we're such good friends, dear, if we keep them standing out here on the porch."

Embarrassed. Erin flushed as she retrieved her hand from his warm grip. "Good heavens, forgive me," she said breathlessly. "Please come in. We're so glad to see you."

Lynn and Garth made themselves comfortable on the long, low circular couch while Anthony went over to the bar to mix drinks. Erin fussed with the tray of hors d'oeuvres, keeping up a steady and slightly feverish stream of conversation while trying unsuccessfully to keep her eyes off Garth.

Garth Werner was an extraordinarily good-looking man in his late twenties. There was nothing pretty about him: his features were strong, bold, and totally male. He had an unruly mop of thick black curly hair, a dark slash of eyebrows over deep blue eyes that blazed with intensity, a square, stubborn-looking chin, and a low, husky voice with a rough, growling edge to it that gave it a distinctly sexual overtone. He was tall, two inches over six feet, and he had a lean, muscular body that always seemed on the edge of bursting free from some invisible bonds. He rarely sat still, prowling around the living room like a big cat as he talked.

Erin found herself fascinated with his hands. They were large and powerful looking with heavy-boned wrists, but the fingers were surprisingly long and sensitive. They were in constant motion as he talked, gesturing with such graphic precision that she could almost see them drawing pictures of the words he spoke. She shivered involuntarily as she thought about those hands moving on her body.

"Dear, I hate to mention it," Anthony whispered, "but I think Maria is getting a little anxious."

"Oh my God!" Erin leaped to her feet, and then smiled apologetically at her guests. "Maria is not just a cook, she's the last great cook in Hollywood. Everybody is always trying to steal her from us. So, if you don't mind, I think we'd better go on in to dinner before we ruin her creation and she quits on us. They say no one's irreplaceable," Erin remarked as she led them into the dining room, "but then they haven't met Maria."

"This is marvelous!" Garth announced with a smile of pleasure as his fork cut effortlessly into the exquisitely tender beef with its rich wine-and-mushroom sauce.

"Absolutely superb," Lynn said. She leaned over and whispered desperately in Erin's ear, "Will Maria give me this recipe? Because my dinner didn't really turn out all that well."

"I'll get it for you," Erin whispered back. "But don't ever tell anybody I gave it to you."

"I won't. Cross my heart. Oh, Erin, you're a real lifesaver," Lynn said fervently. "Because this guy is nuts about good food."

"To Maria," Garth smiled as he raised his glass of wine.

"Indeed," Anthony agreed. "Say, Garth, maybe you'd like to tell her yourself how much you're enjoying this. She'd really like that."

Maria was brought into the dining room and blushed with pleasure as the two men stood up and complimented her on the meal.

"You got a real nice guest tonight, Mr. Anthony," she beamed. "I'll cook for him anytime."

"To Garth Werner." Anthony laughed as Maria retired to the kitchen. "You may have just guaranteed me one of life's greatest joys, the delight of eating Maria's meals."

"I'd like to think so." Garth smiled. "Especially since I want the privilege of enjoying one of them again."

He finished his wine and set the glass back on the table. "So why don't we see if that's going to be possible. You want Street Scene and I want twenty-five percent of it. Can we do business?"

There was a stunned silence interrupted by Lynn's nervous whisper. "Honey, you can't just lay it on them like that. You have to lead up to it gradually, allow room for negotiation."

"That's a pretty big percentage you're asking for, young man," Anthony said. "Unless you're going to invest your own money in the production?" He gave Garth a quizzical look. "We hadn't been led to understand you were planning on that."

"I would if I could. Unfortunately, I'm not in a position at the moment to offer that. But what I do have to offer are the screen rights to a very powerful bestselling novel, and the very real possibility of an Oscar-winning picture for Con-Well Productions. I think that's worth twenty-five percent."

"Twenty-five percent is completely out of the question," Erin announced crisply. "That is not to say we are opposed to giving you some interest in the picture in exchange for your obtaining the screen rights. Lynn made it quite clear that's what you're looking for, and we agreed that would be part of the deal. What we had in mind was offering you five percent, which we feel is more than fair. And naturally you would defer your director's fee in exchange for it."

"Naturally I would defer my director's fee," he agreed. Then he started to laugh as a smug little smile crept over Erin's face, "But I won't take five percent. Or seven percent. Or even the ten percent you were probably willing to compromise on after haggling back and forth."

Garth leaned back in his chair and spread his large hands on the table. "Look, maybe Lynn didn't explain what a strange maverick I am. I don't believe in haggling. I believe in stating what I want, based on what I think is fair for what I have to deliver. People can take it or leave it. That, of course, is up to them."

"In that case there is absolutely nothing to discuss!" Erin snapped.

"The other thing Lynn may have forgotten to tell you is that I hate making unpleasant scenes," Garth said lazily, his eyes gleaming with amusement. "So, since we can't agree on the picture, why don't we just relax and enjoy Maria's dinner as good friends."

"I'll drink to that," Anthony said quickly, distinctly alarmed by the furious look on his wife's face.

"Me too," Lynn echoed faintly. She was almost in tears over the unexpected confrontation between Erin and Garth that was changing her beautiful evening into a nightmare.

To everyone's surprise, Garth managed to switch the strained situation into the relaxed, enjoyable dinner he'd suggested. He began talking about his early days in New York, and he had some very funny stories about how he'd gotten into directing, including an incredible saga about his apprenticeship at a small New York ad agency that specialized in retail accounts for underwear manufacturers.

Everyone was still chuckling about his account of the inflatable bra that suddenly deflated right on live camera when Maria came in to clear the table, and they moved to the living room for coffee and cognac.

Anthony lit the fragrant pine logs in the fireplace and switched on the five-thousand-dollar stereo set that gently flooded the room with warm sound as he made his way to the bar.

"Wow, this is living." Lynn sighed as she curled up in a chair next to the fireplace.

"The best," Garth agreed as he sprawled out on the sofa, his long legs stretched out in front of him.

"And this is the best cognac in the world." Anthony beamed as he handed each of them a giant balloon-shaped glass of Tiffany's finest crystal, and settled into the chair opposite Lynn.

Erin crouched at the far end of the sofa, her emotions in turmoil. She now hated Garth with as much passion as she'd desired him earlier. He was a totally impossible, arrogant bastard who not only had the incredible effrontery to turn down the best offer he'd ever get, but to insult her in the process.

She gulped down the potent cognac in fury. Then she thought about what he'd said. An Oscar-winning picture for Con-Well Productions. Erin's first three pictures had all been solid commercial successes, but no one had ever considered them for an Oscar. And Erin wanted to win an Oscar more than anything in the world.

"All right, you get your twenty-five percent," she announced, and braced herself for the cocky, triumphant grin she knew was coming.

But Erin was wrong. There was nothing cocky or triumphant about Garth when he turned and looked at her. The expression on his face was totally serious.

"I'm glad," he said simply. "Because I want to do this picture very much. And I promise you it will be a fine picture." He reached out and took hold of her hand.

Once again, his touch sent a tingling current of electricity surging through her body, and Erin's angry hostility dissolved, swept away by a rush of bewildering emotions.

"Well, this certainly calls for another drink!" Anthony exclaimed.

"Oh, Erin, I'm so happy you made this decision!" Lynn's face lit up like a Christmas tree. "You won't regret it, I promise you. He's going to give you your first Oscar. I just know it!"

For a while the four of them joined together to discuss the picture, all with their own eager suggestions for casting and locations. But gradually Lynn and Anthony became excluded from the conversation as Erin and Garth concentrated more and more on each other's ideas. And by the end of the evening, Lynn and Anthony found themselves sitting in silence as they stared at the vibrantly beautiful couple now sitting so close together on the soft, velvet sofa in front of the roaring fireplace that their heads almost touched as they continued to talk, totally engrossed in each other.

One week after Erin's intimate dinner party for Lynn and Garth, Hollywood's major trade papers reported that Con-Well Productions had scored a major coup by obtaining the screen rights to Street Scene. A small paragraph at the bottom of the story announced that the director on the picture would be Garth Werner, a young director who'd made his debut with Continental Studios' trouble-ridden production of CountDown.

One week after that, the major trade papers, along with every sensational tabloid, gleefully reported that a sizzling romance between Erin and the young director was about to break up the Connolly-Wellington marriage. It was the most delectably exciting news since Erin Connolly had broken up Marcia and Anthony's marriage and formed Con-Well Productions. Because without Anthony's money, how could Con-Well Productions survive? They waited with breathless anticipation to see what would happen.

Lynn Powers went back to spending her evenings alone in her small apartment. But she no longer wasted her time watching old movies on television. She was much too busy planning a way to destroy Erin Connolly.

TWELVE

The rain beat down steadily on the roof, sounding a counterpoint to the massive roar of the surf as the big waves crashed against the shore. There was a sudden sharp hiss as a gust of wind sent a shower of raindrops down the chimney where they sputtered furiously as they hit the red glowing logs in the fireplace.

Erin sat up, buttoned her blouse, and ran her hands through her hair, "We never even made it to the bedroom, did we?" she said shakily.

"No, we didn't." Garth smiled at her. "But then I always did want to make love on a fur rug in front of a roaring fire while a storm raged outside."

"Don't ever try to be a writer," she laughed. "They'd murder you for lines like that. Besides, this is hardly a fur rug." She grimaced as she brushed ineffectively at the lint on her custom-designed silk blouse.

"Complaints already?" he grinned.

"I wouldn't say that."

Suddenly uncomfortable with the memory of her total and ecstatic capitulation to his erotic demands, she got to her feet and walked over to the sliding-glass doors that opened on to the deck overlooking the pounding surf.

"This isn't bad for a tacky little beach house, Garth," she said lightly. "But you'll be able to afford a much more impressive place after Street Scene comes out."

"Maybe I like my little tacky beach house." He stood up and stalked over to where she was standing, grabbing her arm. "Did that ever occur to you?"

"Garth, stop it! You're hurting me."

He let go of her so abruptly she fell against the glass door. "I'm sorry. I didn't mean to do that. Are you all right?"

"I'm fine," she said stiffly. "But it's getting late. I have to leave."

"No. I'm not going to let you leave like this," he murmured huskily as he reached out for her.

Helplessly, Erin allowed him to pull her forward. It was an incredibly exquisite sensation, feeling him grow like that inside her, as though she'd been empty and hungry all her life and was finally discovering the miracle of being filled.

"Honey? Hey, honey, are you okay?" Garth asked with concern as he leaned forward and kissed the tears off her face.

"I don't know," she said tremulously. "I've never felt this way before."

"It's all right," he told her gently. "I won't ever hurt you, Erin. All I want to do is give you pleasure and make you happy."

And for the next few weeks Garth more than kept his promise. Erin drifted through them in a state of delirious bliss, totally caught up in the rapture of their relationship. They saw each other every day, meeting for lunch in small, out-of-the-way restaurants and then driving back with feverish impatience to his beach house to make love, clinging to each other until the last possible moment, when she reluctantly pulled herself away from him to get dressed and head back to the big Beverly Hills mansion where Anthony innocently awaited her.

It was a magical time, a world filled with lovely dreams and desires that grew more beautiful with each meeting, because the incredible chemistry between them became stronger each time they came together. And it was made possible by a set of unusual circumstances.

Anthony's lawyers were busy negotiating contracts with the tough agent who represented the author of Street Scene. Anthony was busy supervising his real estate empire, making sure there would be enough liquid capital to launch a major production effort for what he fondly thought of as his and Erin's first Oscar winner. Con-Well Productions, having completed its current picture, was in a holding action; waiting for the new film. Garth Werner had fulfilled his contractual agreements with

Continental Studios and had not signed up for anything else, awaiting production to start on Street Scene. And Erin, for the first time in her life, had no demanding schedules to meet, no challenges to face, nothing, in fact, that would force her to make a choice between her fierce, driving ambitions and deep emotional needs. But all this was about to change.

"But why can't you tell me over the phone?" Erin insisted.

"Because it's too important to discuss over the phone. I have to talk to you face to face."

"It's nothing bad, is it?" she asked, suddenly apprehensive.

"No, my love," he said in that husky growl that still sent shivers through her every time she heard it. "I would say it's something very good."

"Oh, Garth, suspense drives me crazy! I don't know how I'm going to wait!"

"Well, you won't have to wait very long. It shouldn't take you more than thirty minutes to get here from your place. You know how to get to Donkin's, don't you?"

"I think so," she said uncertainly. "Although it's been ages since I've been there."

"Just take the freeway to Marina Del Rey and turn off on Marquesas Way. You'll run right into it."

"All right, darling. I'll see you in a bit."

It actually took her just a little over twenty minutes to reach the attractive restaurant located on a choice piece of land overlooking the huge marina and Pacific Ocean beyond. Traffic had been relatively light on the busy San Diego freeway system and Erin, eager and impatient to hear Garth's news, had raced the powerful cream-colored Mercedes at a steady eighty miles per hour down the outside fast lane.

She pulled into the restaurant's parking lot with a muted squeal of brakes and leaped out of the car before the parking attendant had a chance to open the door for her.

"Hey, take it easy. He'll wait for you." The attendant grinned. Then his eyes widened as he got a good look at her, and he stared in open admiration. "Hell, anybody would wait for you," he said fervently. "Probably forever."

"You're sweet." She gave him an absentminded smile and patted him on the check. "Now take good care of the car, okay?"

"I will. You can count on it! How long . . ."

Erin whipped by him without waiting to hear the rest of his question, and he gazed after her as she disappeared inside the restaurant.

There was no sign of Garth in the lobby or at the bar. Erin glanced around anxiously, and then she looked through the wide glass doors leading to the deck and saw the solitary figure standing at the far end.

Garth was leaning over the railing, watching the sailboats tacking back and forth in the channel on their way out to the ocean. It was one of those rare perfect Los Angeles days where a hot, bright sun illuminated a pure blue cloudless sky and the air sparkled like champagne, miraculously free of even a taint of smog. A fresh breeze stirred off the ocean, causing the sails of the sleek long boats to dip gracefully as they heeled over. Garth's head rotated slowly, following their fluid motion. Then he sensed Erin's presence and turned around to face her.

He looked so handsome, her breath caught in her throat. The sun had burned color into his face, making his eyes a startlingly vivid blue. His eyebrows slanted black above them, and one lock of crisp dark hair fell over his forehead. His sports coat, a casual but elegant dark blue cashmere, hung easily from his broad shoulders, revealing a glimpse of the blue-and-white striped shirt under it; and his custom-tailored white slacks showed the lines of his long, lean body to perfection.

He smiled with pleasure as he saw her and walked over quickly to meet her, his arms outstretched.

"You look beautiful," he said as he took hold of both her hands and leaned down to give her a light kiss.

"'You're looking pretty great yourself," she replied a little breathlessly.

She linked her arm through his and started walking back toward the restaurant, then glanced up in surprise as he firmly guided her away from the door and led her over to one of the tables set up on the outdoor dining deck under a gaily striped umbrella.

"We're going to eat out here?" she exclaimed.

"Yes, why not?" he smiled. "It's such a beautiful day."

"Well." She wet her lips and looked around nervously at the crowd of people now filling the dining area, to see if there was anyone she recognized. "It's . . . it's not very intimate."

"No, but it's very bright and clean and open. Which is what I'm in the mood for today."

Erin was gripped by a sudden feeling of uneasiness. "Does this have something to do with what you want to talk to me about?"

"In a way." He pulled out a chair and seated her, then beckoned to a waiter. "What would you like to drink?"

"Just white wine, I think."

"Okay, now tell me what this is all about."

"First, I got a call from Derek Marston's agent. Derek wants the lead role in Street Scene. In fact, he wants it so much, he's willing to negotiate on price. You know he usually won't even talk about doing a part unless he's been guaranteed a million dollars up front."

"My God!" Erin was so excited she almost leaped out of her chair. "Oh, Garth, that's incredible! That is absolutely, totally marvelous! The hottest young star in Hollywood, and he wants to do our picture!"

Her triumph faded when he said nothing. "Is there a problem?" she asked uncertainly. "I mean, I know he has a reputation for being difficult on a set. And there are rumors about his being heavily into drugs."

"You're not going to turn him down, are you?" she said in sudden horror. "Garth, please don't tell me that!"

"No, I'm not going to tell you that. It's true he's difficult, if not impossible, on a set. And he is into drugs. He's also an animal. But he's a wildly talented animal," he said quietly. "He has more raw force and power than I've ever seen in an actor. And I know how to harness that force and power and turn it into what will be the greatest performance of his life. I think he knows I can do it, too. So I don't foresee any insurmountable problems in working with him."

He smiled at her then. "Besides, I said this was just the first thing I had to tell you."

"And what's the second?" she asked faintly.

"The author of Street Scene, Joel Greenberg, is my friend. His agent refused to let him do the screenplay because he's involved in a new book. And we've been bogged down for weeks trying to find a top Hollywood screenwriter who's free now."

Garth took a sip of his wine and grinned. "Well, we don't have to worry anymore. Joel wrote the screenplay on his own with nobody but the two of us even knowing he was doing it. He just finished it, and it's dynamite! It's the best script I've ever seen!"

"That's wonderful, Garth," she said slowly. "Both pieces of news are wonderful. But now let's get to the third act." She looked at him quizzically. "I assume there is a third act?"

"Of course. There's always a third act."

He propped his elbows on the table and tented his fingers, staring at her across them. "You realize that what I've just told you means we're ready to go into production. Which also means we'll be working like dogs every day from early morning until night, till the picture's finished. There'll be no more time for lunches like this. No more time for lazy afternoons on the beach. No more time for us to be together like we've been."

"W-what are you trying to say?" Erin's voice shook so badly she had to stop for a moment and fight for control. "Are you telling me that we're through?"

"Jesus Christ, no!" He leaned across the table and grabbed her hands. "How could you possibly think that? Don't you know how much I care about you?"

"But then what are you saying?"

"That I want you to leave Anthony. That I want you to come and live with me,"

"Oh, Garth," she whispered. "I want that too. And I will, after Street Scene is completed."

"After Street Scene?' he shouted. "Erin, didn't you hear a thing I said? It's now that you have to do it. That's the whole point."

"I understand, darling," she said quickly. "Of course I understand. But there are some things you don't understand."

"Like what?"

"Like this very important picture we both want so much to do. We can't do it if I leave Anthony."

"You're right," he said flatly. "I don't understand. Maybe you'd be kind enough to explain?"

"Darling, please don't look at me that way," she begged. "Believe me, I know what I'm talking about. We need Anthony for this picture. It won't be as terrible as you predict. I know how busy you'll be, but we'll always find a way to get together."

"Really? A quickie in wardrobe between shoots?"

"I don't think that comment was necessary," she replied stiffly.

"Well, what about us?" he demanded. "Are we necessary? Or have I just imagined this whole thing?"

"You know better than that," she said quietly. "You know how I feel about you. I also know how important this picture is to you. So why are you trying to destroy it?"

"I guess because I really don't understand. Why would it be destroyed if you left Anthony?"

Erin gave an unhappy sigh. "The only thing that's made Con-Well Productions possible is Anthony's real estate money. Money I have no access to. Anthony's attorneys took care of that," she added bitterly. "I'm not saying that Con-Well Productions isn't a success. We've done very well. All of our pictures have shown a profit. But there simply isn't enough money in the company to launch a major production like Street Scene."

She looked at him gravely. "Now do you understand?"

"That's the big problem?" He started to laugh. "Honey, you've been worrying your head about nothing. We don't need Anthony's money. Any one of the major studios would jump at a chance to back this picture."

"I don't think so, Garth." She smiled wryly. "I'm not exactly the most popular producer in Hollywood."

"What the hell difference does that make? Studio heads don't invest money on the basis of popularity contests. They invest on the basis of getting winning properties, and who's got a more winning property than us? A bestselling novel. A screenplay by the author of that bestselling novel. And Derek Marston, the hottest star in Hollywood. To say nothing of a brilliant director," he added with a mischievous twinkle. "So how can we lose?"

"It's not that easy, Garth. My first picture was based on a bestselling novel with the author doing the screenplay and I had Anthony's money backing me as well. I thought I had it made, but the major studios almost killed me."

Her eyes clouded as she remembered that struggle. "This can be a very nasty town, darling, and the people here have long memories."

"Hey, lighten up, love. That's ancient history. Who cares now that Martin Weinguard's daughter lost her husband to you? You're exaggerating the whole thing."

"You can say that because you weren't here when it happened. But I was, and I know what it was like."

She frowned. "Besides, let's not forget that Con-Well Productions is as much Anthony's as it is mine. He could make things very difficult. He could tie up the whole company in litigation, and no investor would touch us with a ten-foot pole."

"I don't think Anthony would do that," Garth said softly, "And I don't think you believe it either. He's a very decent person, and he knows Con-Well Productions is your creation. I think he'll sign the whole thing over to you."

"Probably," she admitted reluctantly.

"Well then, why are you creating these barriers?" he demanded. "Anthony will give you control of the production company. We'll take the property to a major studio and get financial backing. Then we'll make our Oscar-winning picture."

He reached over to touch her. "And we'll be together," he said huskily. "All the way. You and me. We'll make it, babe. You can count on that. So what do you say?"

"I'm afraid to take the chance," she said miserably. "Oh, Garth, I want this picture so much! You have no idea how much I want it!"

"I'm beginning to get the idea," he answered grimly. "It's the picture that's really important to you, isn't it? Not me."

"No, that's not true!" she cried. "You're both important. The two most important things in my life. Why can't I have both? Why do I have to make a choice? It's all there for us if you'll just be a little patient."

"I'm not a patient man. But I warned you about that when we first met. Remember, I told you I didn't believe in compromises, negotiations, or haggling over deals."

"Are you saying our relationship is a deal?" she exclaimed.

"No. You are."

"I don't believe this conversation. I really don't believe it!"

"Believe it," he told her quietly. "Because I mean it."

"You're crazy! You're not making any sense at all. You'll change your mind when you have a chance to think it over."

"I won't change my mind." He stood up. "Goodbye, Erin."

She stared in shock as he threw two twenty-dollar bills on the table and walked away.

THIRTEEN

"Hello? Hello?" Erin said feverishly.

"Hi there, Mrs. Wellington," a cheerful young voice announced. "This is Tina Andrews from The Hollywood Reporter, and we'd like your comment on the story that Derek Marston has just signed with Con-Well Productions for considerably less than his usual million dollar deal, just so he can get the juicy role of Wyeth in Street Scene. Is it really true he agreed to cut his price in half?"

"How did you get my private number?" Erin demanded furiously.

"Oh well, that's a trade secret. We couldn't reach you at the office, so we go where we have to in order to get the news. Is it true?" she insisted.

"Of course it's not true," Erin said coldly. "And if you want to find out what he signed for, I suggest you ask his agent."

She banged down the phone, then leaned over the desk and started to cry. "Goddamn you, Garth," she wept. "Why do you have to be so stubborn? Why won't you call me?"

It had been a week since that luncheon at Donkin's restaurant, the most miserably unhappy week of her life. The ache of missing him was so intense she felt it as a physical pain, like a cancer clawing at her insides. She couldn't eat or sleep. She'd lost five pounds. There were dark smudges under her eyes, and her face looked gaunt.

An anxious Anthony had begged her to go to the doctor.

"There's nothing wrong with me," she'd snapped, and then burst into tears in front of his astonished eyes.

"Erin, my dearest Erin, what is it?" His face filled with alarm as he put his arms around her and patted her ineffectually. "Please tell me. Let me help you."

"You can't help," she'd sobbed. "You're the very last person in the world who could help."

Erin filled with sudden remorse as she saw the look of naked pain in his eyes at her unthinkingly cruel words.

"Forgive me, Anthony," she'd said contritely. "I didn't mean that."

Forcing a smile, she'd leaned over and given him a quick kiss. "Put it down to preproduction nerves. You know how much I want an Oscar for this picture, and we both know how tough that's going to be with the way this town feels about me."

His face had brightened perceptibly. "Well, don't you worry about that!" he'd assured her. "We're going to produce such an outstanding film, they won't have any choice but to vote you that Oscar."

Beaming fondly, he'd hugged her to him. "And we're going out this Friday night to that ridiculously overpriced Beverly Hills restaurant where all the so-called Hollywood powers congregate to show our faces and celebrate the production start of Street Scene. And I bet you'll start feeling better immediately!"

As she went upstairs to dress, she looked into the mirror at her strained, unhappy face. "Have you missed me at all, Garth?" she whispered forlornly. "It's five o'clock now. Are you remembering how special that time was for us? We'd stand out on the deck of that little beach house of yours and look out over the ocean. It was always so beautiful at that hour. The sky all aglow as the sun hung in it like a big ball of fire. Then the wind would come up, we'd turn and see the faint shadow of the moon rising, and you'd turn and grab me. "Give me tomorrow," you'd always say. "Give me another tomorrow with you.'"

Erin suddenly slammed down the hairbrush that she had been listlessly pulling through her hair. "Goddamnn you, I know you haven't forgotten!" she said fiercely.

"You're suffering just like I am. It's only that stupid male pride of yours that's keeping you from me."

All right then, Mr. Macho." Erin began carefully applying her make-up. Two can play at that game. And I can wait as long as you. You'll be coming to me before long.

"You look absolutely beautiful!" Anthony said reverently as he: escorted her into the jam-packed restaurant.

"Thank you, sweetheart." Erin gave him a glowing smile for the benefit of the crowd as they were led to their table. "Now, who's here?" she hissed as they sat down and she pretended to study the menu.

"Well, let's see." Anthony glanced around the room and then broke into a big grin. "Erin, look!" he exclaimed delightedly. "Well, now we really will have a celebration!"

Erin looked, and felt her heart stop. Walking through the door was Garth, and by his side was an exquisitely beautiful young girl with an angelic, heart-shaped face, wide cornflower-blue eyes, and a mass of silky blond hair. Her arm was tucked through his, and she was gazing up adoringly at him.

Anthony leaped to his feet as they approached the table. "Garth, what a pleasant surprise!" he cried happily. "Erin and I are here to toast the beginning of production on our picture this coming Monday. You must join us!"

Garth's eyes rested briefly on Erin, then moved away as he introduced the girl at his side. "Thank you, Anthony," he said pleasantly. "But I hope you'll excuse me if I ask for a rain check. Melissa and I have some private things we need to talk over."

"I can certainly understand that," Anthony chuckled. "If I were with a gorgeous young lady like Melissa, I'd want to keep her to myself too, instead of spending the evening with an old married couple like us. But I do hope that sometime soon you'll give us the pleasure of getting to know her."

"That's a promise," Garth said with an easy smile. "Because if things work out the way I expect them to, Melissa and I will be seeing a lot of each other."

He nodded politely then before walking away, and Erin felt a sharp pain as her fingernails dug into the palms of her tightly clenched hands.

"They certainly make a lovely couple, don't they?" Anthony said admiringly as he sat down and gazed after them.

It took every ounce of will power Erin possessed to keep from screaming. "Yes, 1 suppose they do," she said through gritted teeth. "Although I must say I never envisioned our director as a cradle-robber. The girl can't be more than nineteen."

"Oh my, do I detect a little feminine cattiness here?" he asked with an amused twinkle in his eye. "After all, you're not much over nineteen yourself. And that makes me a considerably more serious cradle-robber."

"I'll he twenty-five this September." she snapped. "And that's a lot over nineteen."

"You'll also be the most beautiful twenty-five-year-old woman in the world, or for that matter the most beautiful woman of any age, twenty-three, twenty-one, or even nineteen."

"Do you really mean that?" she asked with a desperate eagerness. "Do you really think I'm still beautiful?"

"Of course I do!" He leaned over and took hold of her hand. "My dear Erin, how could you doubt it? Don't you ever look in the mirror? You're not just beautiful, you're the most exciting woman I've ever met!"

"Thank you, Anthony."

"Well, you hardly have to thank me for it," he smiled. "It's something mother nature blessed you with."

He picked up his menu and then peered at her over it. "I must say it pleased me to see Garth and the young lady here tonight. Not that I ever believed the rumors, but still it was nice to see them together."

Erin's head snapped up. "Rumors? What rumors?" she asked sharply.

"Oh well." He shrugged apologetically. "You know how this town is. When they don't have any real news, they start making it up. Things about you and Garth having ..."

He coughed suddenly and looked down at the menu. "Something between you. That sort of thing."

"You must be joking! I would sooner become a nun than become involved with that impossibly arrogant and obviously emotionally retarded excuse for a man!"

"Good Lord, Erin," he exclaimed in obvious alarm. "1 didn't know you felt that strongly. I mean, I know the two of you didn't hit it off too well at first, but I somehow assumed you'd patched up your differences. You're not thinking of bringing in another director on the picture at this stage, are you?"

"No, I'm not thinking of doing that." She gave him a wintry smile. "After all, how could I? He owns twenty-five percent of the picture."

"Well that's true, isn't it?" He fingered the menu nervously. "But if you really don't want him to direct it, aren't we going to run into major problems?"

"No," she replied curtly. "As long as he does his job and we do ours, there will be no problems. Now let's order, Anthony, and then get the hell out of this place!"

Anthony hastily summoned the waiter, who urged them to try the house specialty, veal with prosciutto ham in a white wine sauce.

"Will it take long?" Anthony asked anxiously.

"Oh no, sir. It's ready right now."

"Order it!" Erin commanded him in a savage whisper.

Anthony gave a nervous little cough. "Well then, I guess we'll both try it."

"You'll enjoy it very much," the waiter promised.

Erin doubted that seriously as she gazed bleakly after the waiter, who was now busily making his way through the crowded room toward the kitchen. She followed his progress, then found her eyes drawn like a magnet toward the small table at the far end of the room where Garth and Melissa were talking animatedly, their heads close together. A sick helpless rage filled her at the sight.

Anthony tried valiantly to carry on a conversation as the waiter returned with the steaming hot plates and placed them on the table, then discreetly withdrew, but he soon trailed off disconsolately when Erin continued to reply in curt monosyllables.

They finished the meal in silence, a silence which continued as Anthony paid the check, led his wife out of the restaurant, and drove home.

"I understand there's an excellent drama on PBS television tonight," he offered tentatively as they walked inside. "One of those splendid BBC productions. Would you like to watch?"

Erin stared unseeingly at her husband, her eyes still filled with the vision of Garth and Melissa. She suddenly focused on him.

"No, Anthony." Her hand reached out to caress him. "No, I don't think we'll watch a splendid production. 1 think we'll stage one. I want you to make love to me, Anthony."

"Oh, Erin!" he said worshipfully as she moved close to him.

"Well then, what are you waiting for?" she laughed. "Come on, race me to the bedroom."

Anthony charged up the stairs after her. When he arrived, breathless, at the door of their bedroom, she was already naked and waiting for him.

"My dearest love," he moaned as he flung himself on her. "My dearest, sweetest love."

"Is that good? Do you like that?" she whispered as her hands and mouth roved over him.

"Oh God, yes. Yes, yes, yes!"

It was over in less than a minute. Anthony sat up, his hands trembling as he tried to stroke her hair. "I'm so sorry," he whispered. "It's just that it's been so long. I tried to wait, but I couldn't."

He leaned over to kiss her, then flinched as she pushed him away. "A little time," he begged. "Give me a little time and I'll make it right for you."

"It's not your fault, Anthony," she said dully as she got out of the bed. "Go to sleep."

Erin barely made it to the bathroom in time. When the last retching spasm had passed, she stood up unsteadily and washed out her mouth.

Anthony was lying quietly in the bed when she returned. He'd gone to sleep just like she'd told him to do and he slept as he always did, stretched out on his back with his arms folded peacefully across his chest and his feet crossed neatly at the ankles.

It occurred to her, with sudden revulsion, that he looked like a corpse laid out in an undertaker's parlor, and she knew she couldn't possibly get back into that bed with him.

Turning around and running soundlessly across the thick carpet to her closet, she grabbed a pair of chocolate colored suede slacks and a bulky white turtleneck sweater, pulled| them on, then fled from the bedroom, down the stairs, and out of the house to her car.

Erin had no conscious plan of what she was going to do or where she was going to go. All she knew was that she had to get away. After an hour of mindless driving, pushing the accelerator of the powerful car harder and harder toward the floorboard, feeling the scream of the wind as she tore down the freeway at seventy, eighty, ninety miles an hour, she was aghast to discover herself in front of Garth's small beach house.

Oh no. I must be losing my mind. What in the name of God possessed me to come here?

She looked up and saw lights in the window. "He's still awake," she murmured to herself. Then her hands tightened on the steering wheel. "Of course he's still awake. He's in there with that bitch Melissa, and they're doing all the things we used to do. Except we never did them at night," she sobbed. We never had a night together."

She started to shake. "Get out of here, Erin," she told herself fiercely. "Get out while you still have a shred of pride left."

But her hands refused to release their tight grip on the steering wheel and put the car into gear and she knew that subconsciously she'd planned all along to drive up here and confront him.

With what, though, she asked herself in anguish. It was all my doing. Am I going to go up to that door and make a complete fool out of myself?

"Well, apparently that's exactly what I'm going to do,'" she admitted out loud. She turned off the engine, got out of the car, walked slowly up the steps to his place, and knocked on the door.

"Who the hell is it?" Garth yelled.

Erin swallowed hard and knocked again.   :

"Listen, if you've got a flat tire, why don't you try hiking down the road half a mile to that gas station instead of bothering people in their homes." He flung open the door.

"My problem isn't a flat tire," Erin said unsteadily.

"Jesus Christ!" Garth stared at her. "Jesus Christ, Erin, what are you doing here?"

"I'm not sure," she said miserably. "I think maybe . . ."

She never had a chance to finish her statement. He opened his arms and reached out for her. Not that he had to reach very far. She rushed toward him, trying to fit her body into every turn and curve of his, feeling him, touching him, stroking him.

Erin had no clear memory of what happened next. One minute she was standing in the doorway. The next minute she was in the living room in front of the fireplace feeling him surge inside her. They were so hungry for each other, they came in jolting spasms, like a wild horse bucking.

"That was hello, Erin," Garth said huskily. "That was just hello. Now come here and let me get to know you again."

Vaguely, Erin heard the same chord playing over and over again on the stereo. "Garth. Garth, the record's stuck."

"Let it stick," he growled. He stared deep into her eyes, holding her now so that she lay on her side, one leg resting high on his.

"Look, Erin!" he commanded. "Look at us."

She looked, and gasped. She could actually see him as he filled her.

He leaned over and kissed her, making the room seem filled with brightly colored lights that kept changing into different patterns.

"It's a kaleidoscope, Erin," Garth whispered in her ear.

He knows what I'm feeling, she thought in wonderment. He knows exactly what I'm feeling. And then the patterns went round and round and round.

They were both lying on their backs, and Erin felt like she was floating a foot above the floor. She reached out to find him. He was right there, and she took hold of his hand.

"You know now, don't you?" he said quietly. "You know you can't ever leave me."

"Yes, I know," she replied with a soft, contented sigh. Then her eyes suddenly narrowed and she struggled to sit up.

"But what about that bitch? What about her?" she demanded furiously.

He stared at her. "What bitch? What are you talking about?"

"Little Miss Puberty," she hissed. "Melissa, whom you so happily informed us tonight would be spending a lot of time with you."

Garth threw back his head and burst into laughter. "Oh, that bitch. Well, honey, actually she's not a bitch at all. She's a very sweet girl."

"I don't care if she's Joan of Arc reincarnated." Erin pounded on his chest with her fists. "You're not spending a lot of time with her. In fact, you're not spending any time with her. She's out of your life permanently as of this moment. Do you hear me?"

"How could I help hearing you?" he grinned. "They can probably hear you all the way to San Diego."

"It's not funny!" she stormed. "I don't know what your relationship with her was, and I don't want to know. I just want you to tell me it's over. What was your relationship?"

"That's what brought you up here tonight, isn't it? You saw us together, and you couldn't stand it. You had to find out what was going on."

"What would you have done if you'd found us here together?" he asked. "Pulled out a gun and shot us?" He picked up her purse and started rummaging through it. "Let's see, is the murder weapon in here somewhere?"

"Don't, Garth," she said tensely. "Don't tease me like this, please. 1 really can't take it."

"I have a feeling you can take anything," he said slowly as he gazed at her.

"That's not true." Erin's eyes filled with tears. Then she suddenly sat up straight and wiped them away.

"I need you, Garth," she said bravely. "I think I need you more than you need me. It's a difficult thing for me to admit, but I guess it has to be said. And if it's too late, well then I have to accept the blame for that." There was a certain quiet dignity about her as she looked squarely and unflinchingly into his eyes.

"Oh, babe, do you have any idea how long I've been waiting to hear you say that?" Garth reached out and gathered her into his arms. "I love you, Erin. I love you with all my heart. There's never been anybody else since the second I met you."

"But what about . . ."

"Hush," he said softly, rocking her in his arms. "Hush, love. Melissa is an actress. A young, talented actress a friend of mine saw playing in a little theater on Santa Monica Boulevard. I want her for the part of Janine in Street Scene. That's all our relationship amounts to."

"That's really all?" she said incredulously.

"That's really all," he smiled. "Now why don't we go to bed?"

"Bed," she repeated uncertainly. "But it's so late. I should be going ..."

"No," he said firmly. "You're not going anywhere except into my bedroom. To sleep with me. To be with me. Always."

He gripped her by the arms and stared at her. "You do understand that, don't you?"

"Yes, master," she laughed.

"Good. Come on, then."

****

The bedroom drapes in Garth's rented beach house were made of a cheap, flimsy fabric that offered no protection against the strong moming sun as it rose up over the horizon and bounced rays off the glittering blue ocean below. Erin sat up with a start as the demanding light streamed through the windows and illuminated the small room.

"Garth. Garth, wake up." She poked him in the ribs. "It's morning, and I've got to leave."

"Nuh," he mumbled indistinctly, burrowing deeper into their covers. "'It's night. Go back to sleep."

"It's not night," she insisted, poking him harder. "Look!"

"Jesus, babe," he grumbled as he turned around and squinted at her. "It can't be more than five o'clock. You call that morning?"

"It's not five. It's almost six-thirty."

"I don't believe this," he moaned. "I fell in love with am early morning freak."

He dug his knuckles into his eyes, shaking his head at the same time. "Honey, I'm crazy about you, but this is too much. If you're one of those up-at-dawn beach joggers, you're just going to have to go out and do it by yourself."

"What I have to do has nothing to do with jogging, Garth," she said softly. "I have to go home and talk to Anthony."

"Oh Christ!" He bolted upright and stared at her in dismay. "Erin, you must think I'm the most insensitive clod of all time. I don't know what to say except I just forgot all about Anthony for the moment."

He reached out and put his arms around her. "Honey, you want me to go with you? It'll only take me a couple of seconds to get dressed."

Erin gazed at him affectionately. "You're a darling to offer, and I appreciate it. But this is something I really have to do alone."

"You'll call me?" he said anxiously. "You'll call me right away after you've told him?"

"Of course." She leaned forward and kissed him, then slipped out of the bed and pulled on her slacks and sweater.

"Remember, I love you," he told her earnestly.

"I'll remember." She smiled and started to walk out of the room, then stopped by the doorway and turned around. "And I love you too," she said softly. Then she was gone.

****

It was a few minutes past seven-thirty when Erin pulled into the driveway of the handsome Beverly Hills mansion, parked the cream-colored Mercedes in the garage next to Anthony's long, black, gleaming Lincoln Continental, and walked through the breezeway into the spacious French country-style designer kitchen.

Anthony was waiting for her. He was perched on a stool at the breakfast bar, his eyes fixed on the door.

"Where have you been?" he asked tonelessly.

"Well." She swallowed nervously. "As a matter of fact, that's exactly what I want to talk to you about."

"I'm listening," he said in the same monotone.

"Is there . . ." She looked around distractedly. "Is there any hot coffee?"

"No."

"Oh." She forced a smile. "Then maybe you'd like me to make some?"

"I don't want you to do anything except tell me where you've been."

"This isn't easy for me to say, Anthony." Erin set her purse down on the counter and stared at it.

For a long moment there was no sound in the room except for the faint ticking of the kitchen clock that was mounted on the brick wall over the open-hearth fireplace.

"I guess the only way is to come right out with it," she finally announced shakily.

Erin looked up at him. "I've been with Garth, Anthony. And I want to be with him. All the time."

"Arc you telling me you went to him last night after making love to me?" Angry red splotches stained Anthony's normally pale cheeks.

Erin stared at him in alarm and briefly considered lying to him, telling him she'd just left the house that morning. But as he glared at her, she realized it would be futile. He knew what time she'd left the house. Oh shit, she moaned silently. This is going to be much worse than I imagined.

"I'm waiting for your answer," he told her coldly. "Is that what you did?"

"I love him, Anthony," she whispered. "I didn't want to. I made love to you last night to try and forget him, to make everything work with us. I never expected anything like this to happen. I swear to you, I never expected it. But I can't help it. I can't help how I feel. Can you understand at all?" she pleaded.

"Just what is it that you're saying?"

"I want to live with him."

"You mean you want to leave me."

"Well." She looked at him helplessly. "I would have to leave you under those circumstances, wouldn't I?"

"Yes," he said dryly. "You certainly would. And since you've figured out everything else, have you figured out how you're going to do that?"

"That's what I wanted to talk to you about."

"Of course. It must have been very much on your mind." He offered her a glacial smile. "Then let me resolve your unanswered questions. You may walk out of this house at this very moment. You are free to go to your lover. You may even take your clothes, your jewelry, and the car I bought for you."

He rocked back on the stool, crossed his long, stork like legs, and hooked his fingers around one knee. "However, that's all you'll take," he said evenly. "If you want any more, you'll have to go to court and fight me for it."

"But, Anthony, what about Con-Well Productions?" she cried in horror. "You know that's my company!"

"Ah, yes. Con-Well Productions. I wondered when that subject would come up."

He rocked back and forth on the stool, seemingly oblivious of the fact that it was in immediate danger of toppling over, a faraway look in his eyes.

"Most women would be concerned about getting the house," he mused. "Or alimony." He grabbed hold of the counter seconds before the stool lost its precarious hold on gravity and crashed to the floor. "Not you, though," he said thoughtfully as he gazed at her. "No, the only thing you're concerned about is Con-Well Productions. I'm finally realizing that's the only thing you've ever been concerned with, from the very beginning."

"Anthony, it's hard for me to believe this is you talking," Erin said shakily. "You've always been the kindest and gentlest of men. I really thought you'd understand. I never imagined you'd turn out to be so hard and cruel."

"There are apparently a number of things you've never imagined." He stood up and leaned over the counter, his long, bony fingers closing on her wrist like surgical pincers. "For example, that I have feelings."

His fingers tightened, and the flesh around her wrist turned white. "If you'd been honest with me from the start, if you'd told me about this when it began, I would have understood. I might even have been able to forgive you. But you lied to me!"

The red splotches on his cheeks spread, and his breathing became labored. "You sat in that restaurant last night and said there was nothing between you and Garth. Then . . ." His chest heaved, and he had to stop for a moment to get his breath.

"Then," he said between clenched teeth, "you deliberately seduced me when we came home. You used me and you made a mockery out of my feelings for you. And after you'd used me and discarded me, you walked out of my house and drove to your lover's house. Where you made love to him.

"You did make love to him, didn't you?" he shouted.

"Yes," she whispered.

"One truth." He let go of her wrist and sat back down on the stool. "Finally one truth out of you," he said heavily.

"Anthony, what are you going to do?"

"I'm not going to help you pack, if that's what you mean."

"You know that's not what I mean."

"Of course I know that." He looked at her, his eyes now cold and forbidding. "We're back to Con-Well Productions again, aren't we? Well, I'll tell you what I'm not going to do. I'm not going to give it to you. However . . ." He paused.

"What?" she said desperately. "What, Anthony?"

"However, I am willing to sell it to you. For six million dollars."

"Six million dollars! What kind of a sick joke is that?"

"I assure you, my dear, it is not a joke. Even I don't joke about six million dollars. That's my offer. Take it or leave it."

"But where would I get six million dollars?"

"Oh that won't be a problem." He regarded her with a thoughtful little smile. "I may no longer be the kindest and gentlest of men, as you so perceptively observed a few minutes ago, but I'm still a very generous man."

He plucked a small note pad from the shelf over the counter: and began jotting down figures on it. "According to my accountants, the current net worth of Con-Well Productions is six million dollars. The studio complex I built for you in the San Fernando Valley represents three million of that. One million for the land, two million for the buildings and equipment. The other three million dollars are in cash receivables, profits realized from our pictures."

Anthony looked up at her. "I'll take the three million in cash; receivables as a down payment, and you'll sign a note for the remaining three million, using the studio property as collateral. The interest on the note will be at ten percent a year, payments to be made quarterly. At the end of three years, the entire note will become due and payable.

"That seems a reasonable amount of time to me," he said reflectively. "Because if you haven't made enough money in the next three years to pay off a three million dollar loan, then you really don't belong in the movie industry, do you?"

"It's too bad you waited so long to become a bastard," Erin observed quietly. "Because if you'd started earlier, you might have become a genuinely interesting man."

"Unfortunately, my timing has never been very good." He stood up and peered at her. "Well, what's your answer?"

"I don't have much choice, do I?"

"Not if you want the screen rights to Street Scene."

"All right, Anthony, you've got your deal."

"Good. I'll have my attorneys draw up the papers."

He started to walk away, then turned around and stared hard at her. "There's one more thing. When the divorce is final, I want you to take back your own name. Wellington no longer belongs to you."

FOURTEEN

"Would you please quiet down?" Bobby Franken begged. "Just come up one at a time, give me your name and assignment, and we'll get back to you as soon as possible."

The young unit manager was standing at the entrance to Con-Well studios' Sound Stage 3, gripping his clipboard desperately to his chest as the angry crowd of film technicians and extras swarmed around him.

"They said shooting was starting today!" A burly extra in faded blue jeans and a tight white T-shirt strode up to Bobby and shook his fist threateningly in front of his face. "I turned down a chance to work in a television series, got up at four o'clock this morning, and drove fifty miles to get here. And now you're telling me you don't know when they're going to start shooting? What the fuck is going on, anyway?"

"Listen, just take it easy, will you?" Bobby wiped his arm across his forehead and it came away damp with perspiration. "There's a temporary problem with the script," he lied, improvising wildly. "The director isn't satisfied with the way the riot scene reads, and he wants it rewritten. They're working on it now."

"Bullshit!" a furious voice shouted. "You don't need a script for a hot scene. All you need are actors, a camera crew, and a director who knows what the hell he's doing. So maybe," the voice sneered, "what you're telling us is that we're stuck with a director who doesn't know his ass from a key light and is afraid to start shooting!"

"What's your name?" an authoritative voice barked out.

The crowd, which had started to catcall, abruptly fell silent as Garth came through the door of the sound stage and glared down at them.

"I'm waiting," he said softly into the sudden quiet. "I'm waiting to meet that unrecognized genius who knows all about directing. Would that gentleman like to step up here and be recognized?"

There was the muted sound of shuffling feet and a few nervous coughs.

"No? He prefers to remain unrecognized?" Garth smiled coldly. "Well, I think that's a wise decision. Because he doesn't know what the shit he's talking about!"

Garth's voice cracked out like a whip over the crowd. "The only one who knows is me! I'm your director. I will tell you what to do. And I will tell you when and where you'll do it. Now if that's too tough for you to take, then go back to your unions and ask for another assignment where things will be safe and easy. Where you won't have to put out all the way. Because I don't want you on my set. I only want winners."

He turned to Bobby. "Take their names. Anyone who still has complaints, pay them off immediately. And tell the unions to make a note of those names. We don't want them sent out to us ever again." Then he stalked away.

Garth's bluff worked. The men, now grinning sheepishly, formed an orderly line and gave their names to Bobby, who checked them off against the list on his clipboard. Then they got into their cars and trucks and drove away.

But Garth's proud, arrogant pose disappeared as soon as he stalked out of their sight and walked into the sound stage. Shoulders slumping and a worried frown on his face, he made his way down the corridor to Erin's office.

She was sitting behind the large mahogany desk, a tight unhappy smile on her face as she talked into the phone.

"No, Sol, I'm afraid I don't understand. What high risk? There's no more bankable star in Hollywood than Derek Marston. And there's no hotter property than Street Scene. May I also remind you that Con-Well Productions has never lost money on a picture? Which is more than any other studio in this town can claim," she added bitingly.

She paused for a moment to smile up at Garth, then bent down once more to the phone. "I'm sorry, Sol, I didn't catch that. You said what? Oh," she said heavily. "Of course I can see how it would make a difference. Yes, Sol, it was nice talking to you, too. Goodbye."

"Not going too well, I take it." Garth sighed.

"That, my love, is the understatement of the century," she said grimly. "Would you like to try for total failure?"

"But how can they turn it down?" He smashed his fist on the desk in frustrated fury. "They've got to know this is a potential Oscar winner, which is every investor's dream. They're not denying that, are they?"

"No, they're not denying that." Erin took a drag on her cigarette and stared moodily at the swirling smoke. "They're denying me."

"That's crazy!" he said furiously. "How do they do that?"

"Very politely." She gave him a wintry smile. "By an extremely odd coincidence, every important motion picture investor has just recently committed his money to a picture being produced by someone else. Which obviously ties up all his available funds, don't you see?"

"What about the major studios?"

"They don't even bother to be polite," she said distantly. "I have yet to get past a secretary to a production chief."

"Well hell, it's only Monday, isn't it?" He forced a cheerful smile and leaned over to kiss her. "Come on, babe, we haven't even begun to fight. We'll beat them yet."

"How?" she asked dismally. "Anthony really stripped this place. I don't think we even have enough money to pay the electric bills."

"We'll find a way," he said fiercely. "We have each other, and we have a great picture. We'll make it together."

"Will we?" She looked up at him miserably. "Will we really?"

"Yes, we will." Garth took a deep breath, then stared intently into her eyes. "But you're going to have to go to New York."

"What?" she said confusedly.

"New York," he repeated. "There's more money on one single street in Manhattan than there is in this whole fuckin' cow town. You go to New York, babe," he told her softly, "and you'll get our money for us."

Erin flew to New York the next day and spent two exhausting weeks talking to bankers, investors, promoters, anyone and everyone who had money. But it was all in vain. No one had any faith in the stability of Con-Well Productions now that Anthony Wellington and his money had withdrawn, and no one wanted to risk money on a picture that every major studio in Hollywood had refused to back. The ultimate humiliation for Erin was facing their thinly veiled, although always politely expressed, contempt for her. Because the contempt was based solely on the fact that she was a woman, and their comments made it clear they thought she was not only out of her depth but out of her place in trying to negotiate what was obviously a man's business.

An oil-rich Texas entrepreneur brought the matter home to her in a particularly painful fashion after a dinner at New York's famous Four Seasons restaurant where she had first argued, then explained, and finally almost begged him to back the picture before giving up and reaching for her purse as the check arrived.

"Now just stop right there, little lady," he'd smiled, whisking the check away from her. "The day that Jeb Stanton can't buy a pretty girl a dinner is the day that Jeb Stanton is in deep trouble."

"Mr. Stanton, you are not buying a pretty girl a dinner," she'd said through clenched teeth. "You are having a business discussion at a dinner where you are the invited guest. I will take care of the check."

"Honey, you're real cute when you get mad," he'd chuckled. "Always did like a spirited woman." He'd winked at the waiter then, who'd smiled back, taken Jeb's money as he totally ignored Erin's efforts to pay him, and walked away. "But can I give you a little advice? Don't push your luck, honey," he'd said earnestly, leaning toward her. Find a good strong man to handle these things for you. You'll be a lot happier and a lot more successful that way. Believe me, old Jeb knows."

Erin had barely restrained herself from picking up her wine glass and throwing it right into the smug, fatuous face. She'd taken a cab back to her hotel after icily refusing Jeb's offer of his chauffeur-driven limousine, thrown herself on the bed where she'd pounded the pillows in rage before picking up the phone to book a seat on the first morning flight back to Los Angeles.

****

Glittering rays from the sun burned through the airplane's window as TWA's Flight 502 passed through its fourth time zone on its journey from New York to Los Angeles. Erin turned away from the painfully bright light, pulling down the shade as she took off her watch and set the hands back three hours.

"We arc now approaching Los Angeles International Airport," the impersonal, antiseptic voice of a stewardess announced. "Please extinguish all cigarettes and make sure your seat belts are fastened. It has been a pleasure to serve you, and we hope to see you again soon on TWA."

There were two sharp bumps as the plane landed and then taxied up to the terminal. Erin stood up and collected her belongings, and then was almost knocked off her feet by the impatient crowd surging toward the door as she stepped out into the aisle. When she finally reached the exit and walked down the ramp leading to the airport lobby, she saw Garth waiting for her and ran toward him.

"Hey!" He grinned as she rushed into his arms and hugged him fiercely. "If this is what happens when you're away from me for a couple of weeks, maybe I should send you on more trips." |

"Oh, Garth, I missed you so much. I'm so glad to be home. I hate New York!"

"It was that bad, huh?"

"Worse," she said tersely. "It was so awful I don't even know how to describe it. The filth. The noise. And those people you call New Yorkers are even worse than their rotten, filthy city! I can't imagine how you could have lived there all those years."

"Okay, okay now," he said soothingly. "Take it easy, honey. You're back where you belong."

"That's for damn sure! And I'm never going back to that place. Ever!"

"I'm sorry, Erin," he said as he picked up her overnight case and led her out of the airport. "I'm really sorry. 1 truly thought it would work out."

"I know you did," she said contritely, squeezing his arm. "And probably what's really bothering me is that I failed to make it work, because I didn't know how to handle stupid bastards like Jeb Stanton."

"Who?"

"Never mind. That's a story for later. Right now all I want to do is go home and sleep for two days. I am so tired I can't believe it."

She offered him an apologetic smile. "After that, I'll start getting things together again, I promise."

"Do you think you could settle for five hours instead of two days?"

"Five hours? What do you mean, five hours?"

"Well." He hesitated for a moment. "The thing is that in a little over six hours we're due at a party Derek Marston's throwing."

"Oh, no, Garth!" she moaned. "Not a party tonight. Especially not the kind of party Derek Marston throws. I just couldn't face it."

"I'm afraid you're going to have to."

An expression of alarm crossed her face. "He's not giving us any problems about the picture, is he?"

"Not nearly as many problems as Barney Lipsky, his agent, is," Garth said grimly. "Lipsky's threatening to pull Derek out of his Street Scene commitment on the grounds that Con-Well Productions has failed to live up to its part of the contract by canceling the originally scheduled production start without sufficient prior notice, and being further delinquent in not providing a new production start date."

"Jesus Christ!"

"I don't think we can count on him to help us."

"And going to this party will?"

"I hope so, babe. I sure hope so."

"How?" she demanded wildly. "What do I tell him after this fiasco in New York?"

"First of all, he doesn't know that New York was a fiasco. Second, I don't think it would be all that important to him."

"Not important?" she said incredulously. "Garth, what are you talking about? We don't have any money. And without money we can't start production. You're telling me that won't be important to him?"

"Look, honey, you don't know this kid. You've never met him, so you don't understand where he's coming from. He's a New York street kid. He grew up being hassled by his parents, his teachers and the cops. Now he's being hassled by his manager, his agent, and his accountants, and he resents the hell out of it. He'd like nothing better than to stick it to all of them. He's got sympathy for the hassle we're going through. Besides, he really wants to do this picture."

"But he's not a total idiot, is he?" She stared at him. "I mean, it's nice to know he'd like to stick it to the establishment, but he's not about to throw away his career to do it. Is he?"

"No," Garth admitted. "No, he isn't about to do that."

"Then what in God's name do you expect me to do at this party tonight?" she asked despairingly.

"Buy time for us. Just buy time for us, Erin, and pray."

Derek Marston's house, set on a gently sloping bluff overlooking the ocean, was located in the Trancas area of Malibu, several miles north of Zuma Beach. As Garth and Erin approached it, they could see red-jacketed valet-parking attendants running frantically up and down Pacific Coast Highway, dodging traffic as they crossed the busy lanes.

Both sides of the highway were lined with parked cars stretching out for almost a mile in either direction, and the variety of the vehicles attested to Derek's eclectic taste in friends. Rolls Royces nudged bumpers with dusty Chevy pick-up trucks. Volkswagens crouched nervously in front of massive Harley Davidson motorcycles. Cadillacs sniffed at the tails of campers.

Erin gazed at the endless line of vehicles in stunned disbelief. "My God, do you think there's anyone he didn't invite?"

"Just his Malibu neighbors, who are undoubtedly busy once again filing complaints with the sheriff's department."

They pulled up to the gate and handed their car over to one of the attendants, then walked onto the spacious grounds. The house was set back a good five hundred feet from the entrance gate, surrounded by flower beds and a velvet green lawn. Off to the right was a regulation tennis court where a heated doubles match was in progress, cheered on by a crowd of spectators. To the left of the house was an Olympic-size pool and Jacuzzi, encircled by a huge free-form deck. A volleyball net stretched across the shallow end of the pool, and a noisy crowd leaped up and down in the water, screaming and laughing as they batted at the ball.

At the far end of the deck a rock group blasted away while a frenzied crowd of dancers performed in front of them. Occasionally an unwary dancer would get too close to the edge of the pool, whereupon a hand would reach up out of the water, grab the hapless dancer by the ankle, and flip him into the pool.

People of every size, shape, age, color, sex, and costume clustered around the chaises set up on the deck and the lawn, their voices loud and shrill as they drank and talked. Three nude couples paddled dreamily in the Jacuzzi, the glazed expressions on their faces making it clear they were stoned out of their minds.

"Apparently they're holding the party out here," Erin observed. "Do you see our host?"

Garth shook his head. "No, all you're seeing is the fringe element. The real party, as always, will be going on inside."

"If this is just the fringe element, I don't think I want to meet the real party," she said faintly.

"Don't worry. I'll look out for you."

Derek answered the door in response to Garth's knock. He was dressed in white shorts and a white silk shirt that was open to his navel. A gold chain hung from his neck, gleaming dully against the golden tan of his powerful chest. The short sleeves of his shirt were tight around his swelling biceps. His strong muscular legs were covered with golden sun-bleached hairs, but they were darker than the thick shock of white-blond hair that fell in careless disarray over his forehead. His eyes, the same tawny gold as a lion's, blazed out of his sensually handsome face. Those golden cat eyes now opened wide in admiration as he saw Erin.

"Well ol' buddy, so this is what you've been hiding away at that little pad of yours. Can't say I blame you. If I had her, I'd hide her away too."

He reached out to Erin, the tips of his fingers lightly caressing her cheek. "You ever get tired of this old grouch, you let me know. Because I'd be mighty happy to take care of you."

"Down, boy." Garth was smiling as he spoke, but there was a definite edge of warning in his voice.

"Hey, man, take it easy." Derek threw up his hands in mock fright. "Would I invade a friend's turf?"

"Of course you would."

"Of course I would," Derek agreed with an amused grin.; "But not without the lady's permission." He looked speculatively at Erin. "I guess I don't have that, huh?"

"I'm afraid not. But it was nice being asked." The warm smile she gave him took any sting out of the rejection.

"Well, maybe I'll ask you again sometime. People have been known to change their minds."

He started to laugh as Garth made a low growling sound. "But not tonight. Tonight is just for friends. So stop hanging around the door. Come on in and enjoy yourself."

"He really is a magnificent animal," Erin murmured as they followed their host inside.

"Just don't forget the animal part."

"Darling, you're not upset about what he said, are you?.'" She looked at him in genuine surprise.

"You mean, am I jealous?" He smiled. "No, honey, I'm not jealous. I don't have any reason to be, do I?"

"No. No, you certainly don't."

"I didn't think so." He kissed her absently, then frowned. "It's just that I have to warn you about something. I should have guessed that Derek would come on to you like that. The problem is that I'm not kidding when I say he's an animal. He sees something he wants, and if he gets any encouragement at all he'll go after it and forget everything else. So don't tease him. He doesn't understand that. Forget the flirting you might carry on with a normal human being and concentrate instead on appealing to the rational part of his brain that wants to do this picture."

"You're serious, aren't you?" she said in amazement.

"Very serious."

"Okay. Message received and understood." They walked into the living room behind Derek.

"Hey, listen up!" Derek yelled to the crowd sprawled around the large sunken living room. "These are my friends Garth and Erin, so treat 'em nice. You hear?"

"Yeah, man. We hear." The crowd clapped enthusiastically, then two exceptionally pretty young girls and a short black man with a beard sprung up and raced over. The two girls embraced Garth, and the black man took Erin's hand and bowed low over it.

"What's your pleasure, ma'am? You name it, we got it. Just tell this humble servant, and he will bring it to you."

"Well." Embarrassed and confused, Erin tried to pull her hand away. "I ... I don't know."

"You gotta know," he said urgently. "You gotta tell me, so I can bring it to you." His eyes, preternaturally bright, burned into hers.

"Scotch. Scotch and water would be fine."

"Brand?"

"I beg your pardon?"

"The brand. What brand of Scotch?"

"Oh, the brand." She cast a desperate look at Garth, who was trying to fend off the amorous advances of the two girls. "Well, how about the house brand?"

"Very good, lady. Very good." Chuckling gleefully, the black man danced off.

"What's the matter, baby?" Derek's eyes were gleaming with amusement as he looked at her. "Don't you like my catering service?"

"Well, they're certainly different."

Derek threw back his head and roared with laughter. "You can say that again, baby. As a matter of fact ..."

The rest of his sentence was drowned out as someone turned up the stereo and the raw, elemental sound of Mick Jagger screamed through the house. He grinned and shrugged, mouthing the words "Later, baby" as he plucked the two girls off Garth, holding one in each arm, then wandered off with the girls clinging to his neck and giggling.

"Garth, I want to go home," Erin announced. "Right now."

"We can't, honey. We haven't accomplished what we came to do yet."

"You're out of your mind if you think we're going to accomplish anything in this madman's zoo," she snapped. "Unless you count getting out alive as an accomplishment. And I think our odds on that are getting slimmer with every second we stay here."

He started to laugh. "Honey, it's not all that bad. You'll get used to it. Just try to relax."

Erin jumped in fright as the short black man with the beard suddenly appeared in front of her and pressed an ice-cold double old-fashioned glass against her lips.

"House brand, ma'am," he chanted happily. "House brand." He abruptly let go of the glass, and Erin caught it bare seconds before it crashed to the floor.

"Good," he said approvingly, then disappeared as quickly as he'd appeared.

"Relax? I'll get used to it? Is that what you said?"

Garth tried valiantly to keep a straight face, but Erin's outraged expression as she held the dripping glass was finally too much for him and he broke into helpless laughter.

"I'm delighted you find me so entertaining," she said frigidly. "Especially considering the competition I have all around me. And if you run out of chuckles here, come on home and we'll see what else we can do for you." With those words she turned on her heel and started marching toward the door.

"Wait!" He grabbed her by the arm.

"For what?"

"Hey, honey, I'm sorry," he said apologetically. "I didn't mean to laugh at you." His face was completely serious now as he looked at her. "Erin, I know how unpleasant this is for you, but you have to believe me when I say it's important."

"Then explain it to me!" she snapped, still furious.

"Derek wants to talk to us. He wants some assurance that we'll be producing this picture."

"Talk to us? You can't even hear yourself think in this place, much less talk. If he wants to talk, why doesn't he come to our offices?"

"Because it's not his way." Garth frowned unhappily. "I know it sounds weird to you, Erin, but you have to trust me. We had to show up here tonight, show him we were willing to meet him on his own turf, as he puts it. We have to do this if we want to save the picture."

"But what are we supposed to tell him?"

"That we believe in him."

"For God's sake, Garth, we'll probably never even see him again tonight. Look at this crazy party!"

"We'll see him," Garth said confidently. "He'll be coming over to us in a bit. In the meantime, let's go and sit down." With a gentle but firm hand, Garth led her over to the long curving sectional couch that filled almost half the living room and faced both the fireplace and the huge glass windows that looked out over the ocean.

An exquisitely fashioned antique coffee table, its rich, hand-rubbed surface brutally scarred with cigarette burns, sat in front of the couch. Silver cigarette boxes lined with cedar were open on it, offering a colorful variety of marijuana cigarettes. Some were wrapped in bright red, white, and blue Uncle Sam stripes. Some had smart Mondrian designs. A few were in dark chocolate-brown paper with sharply twisted ends. In the center of the table was an expensive crystal bowl filled with a fine white powder. Half a dozen small gold spoons surrounded it.

"Want to do a little coke?" A slim young boy who couldn't have been more than sixteen sat down next to Erin and politely offered her the bowl.

"No!" Garth said harshly, pushing it away.

"Hey, man, what's the matter with you?" the boy protested. "I was just trying to be nice."

He shrank back against the couch as Garth glared at him. "Jesus, the weirdos you get at these parties," he muttered, dipping his spoon into the bowl and inhaling. Then a sudden smile illuminated his face. "Peace, man," he sighed happily.

"Chow time!" A heavy-set man in his middle thirties with a swarthy complexion and the physique of a professional body builder stood in the middle of the living room, bellowing through a megaphone. "Everybody to the dining area! These are orders!"

Erin stared in astonishment as everyone stood up obediently; and filed out. In less than two minutes the entire room had been cleared, and a soft gentle silence fell as someone turned down the stereo and changed the tape. Then the voice of Sinatra quietly crept into the silence. It was vintage Sinatra, from an album recorded decades ago, and the sound was mellow, rich, and confident as the wistful lyrics of "My Funny Valentine" wafted through the room. The only other sounds were the distant roar of the surf outside and the hiss and sputter of logs burning in the fireplace.

"So what's happening?" Derek appeared abruptly from a side door and sat down on the couch, crossing his legs yoga-style as he dipped a gold spoon into the crystal bowl and inhaled.

"Well, it's really a fascinating party," Erin began.

"Fuck the party," he interrupted impatiently. "I mean, what's happening with the picture."

"Oh." Erin wet her lips nervously and glanced at Garth.

"Hey, don't look at him!" Derek grabbed her arm, forcing her to turn and face him. "Look at me! I'm the one asking the question."

Erin stared into the demanding eyes and tried desperately to think of something to say. Nothing came to her, and suddenly she felt too tired to even try making up any lies.

"Nothing," she said simply. "We still haven't found any backers."

"Okay, that's straight," he announced grudgingly. "I would have been pissed if you'd tried to waltz me around."

He leaned over and picked up one of the chocolate-brown joints from the silver box in front of him, inhaling sharply as he lit it and holding the smoke for several seconds. "These are the best," he told Erin as he passed the joint to her. "The fancy wraps are just low-grade shit."

Erin took a slow drag, waiting until the lighted tip glowed red before passing it on to Garth. Then her eyes widened in shock as it hit her.

"What's the matter, baby?" Derek laughed. "Not used to this grade?"

"No," she said dazedly. "It's certainly different from what we used to smoke in college."

"College? You telling me that's the last time you lit up?"

"Yes, I guess it is," she admitted.

"Weird!" He shook his head. "I never figured you for such a square."

Erin flushed with anger at the casual contempt in his voice. "Not square," she snapped. "Just too busy with important things to waste time getting strung out."

"Really?" He smiled tauntingly. "Don't look to me like all that important busy work of yours has gotten you too far. Or we wouldn't be sitting here with a dead picture."

"It's not dead!" she said furiously. Then she bowed her head to hide the unexpected tears that filled her eyes at the thought he might be right, and her picture really was dead.

"Hey," Derek said awkwardly. "Hey, I didn't mean to upset you like that. Come on, now," he urged. "Garth tells me you're a really good fighter. You're not going to give up now are you?"

"No." She looked up and managed a smile. "No, I'm not going to give up. But what about you?"

He shrugged uncomfortably. "I'm getting a lot of heat. From a lot of people. You know what they're telling me?"

"What?" Erin asked quietly.

"That I can't handle this part. They say I'm too young. That I don't have enough experience yet."

He scowled at Garth. "Is that true, man? I mean, shit, I'm twenty-four years old!"

"It doesn't have anything to do with age," Garth told him. "It has to do with discipline and dedication."

"Hell, then there's no problem," he grinned cockily. "When I want something, I'm the most disciplined, dedicated son-of-a-bitch in the whole world."

The grin faded as Garth regarded him thoughtfully. "You wouldn't fuck me around, would you? I mean, you really don't think I'm too young?"

"Of course not," Erin interjected crisply. "Do you know how old Marlon Brando was when he appeared on Broadway in A Streetcar Named Desire? Twenty-three."

"No shit!" Derek gazed at her, obviously impressed. "Brando was only twenty-three when he played Stanley Kowalski?"

"That's right."

"Well, whaddya know!" The grin flashed across his face. "Wait til I tell those cocksuckers that! Twenty-three!"

He turned suddenly and stared at Garth. "You think I could be as good as Brando?"

"Yes, I think so. And Street Scene could do for you what Streetcar did for Brando."

"Then we gotta make it!" he announced. "So where do we go from here?" he asked, turning back to Erin.

"I'm not sure."

"You tried everybody you know, right? Hollywood and New York. Well, maybe I know somebody you don't," he said slowly. "Somebody who'd be willing to come up with the bread. If you're willing to deal with him, that is."

"Willing?" Erin exclaimed. "Derek, I'd deal with the devil if he had the money."

"Yeah? In this case you probably would be."

"Are you serious? You really know someone who would back the picture?"

"Sure I'm serious. But it'll have to be on his terms. You gotta understand that from the beginning."

"What exactly does that mean? If he insists on owning rights to the film, we can negotiate that."

"Oh, fuck the rights, baby. That's not what he's interested in. Personal favors is what he's interested in.

"Not yours," he assured her laughingly as she looked at him in alarm. "He couldn't care less about sex. Power is his turn-on. Political power. Not that he'll back the picture without financial return. You'll pay through the nose for his money. Probably thirty or forty percent. And if you don't come up with the money when it's due, you'd better be prepared to leave town in a hurry. Unless you want to pick out your cemetery plot in advance."

"I don't understand. What personal favors could I possibly do for him?"

"Just one I know about. But I think it's pretty important to him." Derek dipped the gold spoon into the crystal bowl once again and inhaled deeply. "Beautiful," he said dreamily. "Cleanest high in the world."

"But what about this investor?" Erin asked desperately.

"Still interested, huh?" Derek smiled lazily at her. "Well just 'cause you're so pretty, I'll tell you about him."

****

No one in Hollywood was quite sure when Arnold Scorsi arrived in their midst. It seemed as though one minute he didn't even exist, and then they turned around and found him everywhere. Tall, lean, tanned, gracious, and smiling, with his lovely wife on his arm, he turned up at the most select parties. And he was always in the company of the most important personages.

But people quickly learned not to try and pry into his background. There was an aura about Arnold Scorsi that made even the most nosy, impertinent questioner stammer nervously and decide suddenly to retreat to another part of the room.

Ostensibly, Arnold Scorsi was an eminently respectable corporation lawyer who had left New York to settle in Beverly Hills because, as he explained smilingly, "My wife fell in love with California on our first trip out here, and I've never been able to deny her anything."

However, Arnold Scorsi's real job was much more important than any ever held by a corporation lawyer; for Arnold Scorsi was consiglieri to the most powerful man in organized crime in the country. He had been carefully groomed for his present assignment over the past ten years and was now entrusted with over fifty million dollars to invest in the right places in Hollywood.

His immediate responsibility was to control the vital pipeline that led from Hollywood to Washington. His ultimate responsibility was to make sure the "right" man was elected as the next President of the United States.

Now he looked up from the folder lying on his desk that contained the contracts for Street Scene and various legal documents detailing the corporate structure of Con-Well Productions, a faint frown on his face.

"I sympathize with your problems, Miss Connolly," he said carefully. "But I'm afraid I don't see any way in which I can help you."

Erin swallowed twice before she spoke. Arnold Scorsi was the first person she'd ever met who made her feel afraid. "Mr. Scorsi, I want to produce this picture more than I've ever wanted anything in my life."

She leaned across the desk, her luminous green eyes fixed on him. "And I would do anything to make it possible," she said in a low, husky voice.

"I'm sure you would," he remarked dryly. "But as I said; before, I'm afraid you've come to the wrong person for help."

"Someone told me you represent a number of clients who look to you for advice on investing their money. I was hoping that one of them might be interested in backing a major film with the potential of winning an Academy Award."

"My dear lady, all the people I know invest in stuffy things like municipal bonds. They would be terrified at the very thought of putting their money into something as flamboyant as movies," he said with a laugh. But his eyes were cold as stone as he looked at her.

"I understand Senator Ryan is quite enamored of the young girl who starred in my last picture." Erin wet her lips. "Unfortunately, she is as shy as she is beautiful. It's almost impossible for anyone to get to meet her. However, she will be coming to a little informal get-together I'm having this weekend."

Arnold gazed thoughtfully at her for several minutes. "Were you planning on inviting the senator?" he asked finally.

"I've never been formally introduced to him," Erin replied quietly. "So I fear it would be presumptuous of me."

A small smile lifted the corners of Arnold's thin lips. "Well, that is a problem, isn't it? Perhaps I could be of help to you in this particular matter."

Senator Johnny Ryan thoroughly enjoyed himself at Erin's intimate gathering at Garth's beach house that following weekend, even though he did leave early. Of course he didn't leave alone. The stunningly beautiful eighteen-year-old girl who had starred in Erin's and Anthony's last picture left with him. An hour later the phone rang.

"We start production on Monday!" Erin shouted ecstatically as she hung up the phone and raced into the living room.

Wild cheers went up from five of the six people who were comfortably sprawled around the big oak coffee table sipping wine and nibbling on cheese and crackers. The sixth, Garth, was conspicuous by his silence.

"Hey, man, what's the matter with you?" Derek punched him on the arm, an exasperated expression on his face. "Didn't you hear Erin? We've got our picture!"

"I just wish we could have gotten it some other way," he said moodily. Garth had been strongly opposed to soliciting Arnold Scorsi's help after discovering what was involved in making a deal with him, and it had taken Erin and Derek a full week to talk him into it. From the look on his face now, it was clear he regretted giving into them.

"Listen, my friend, I do not think there is anything wrong here." Paul Marriott, the brilliant French cinematographer Garth had signed up for the picture, smiled gently at his host. "It appeared to me that the young lady left most willingly with your handsome senator."

"You think so too?" Garth turned abruptly toward Melissa, the girl with the angelic face and mass of silky blond hair he'd introduced to Erin and Anthony that fateful evening many weeks earlier. "The two of you are good friends. She came here today mostly because of you. Are you happy about her going off with him?" he demanded.

Melissa flushed, nervously twisting the strands of her hair. "It was her choice, Garth, just as you insisted it would have to be. Besides," she added with a shy smile, "I don't think it was all that difficult. Johnny Ryan is as charming as he is good looking. It's not like you turned her over to some dirty old man."

"Absolutely right." Tom Sanders, a veteran character actor, gave an amused chuckle. "What you did was turn her over to a dirty young man, and that makes all the difference in the world. Believe me, I know."

"Okay." Garth grinned in spite of himself. "It's obvious I'm outnumbered and outvoted. So let's get on with the picture."

"Right, man!" Derek exclaimed exultantly. He stood up and filled everyone's wine glass, then extracted a bottle of pills and several glassine envelopes from his shirt pocket, throwing them down on the coffee table. "Now let's get this party rolling in style," he laughed delightedly. "Because we got a lot to celebrate!"

Garth's hand smashed down on the table, crushing the drugs. "We celebrate when we get the Oscar," he announced coldly. "In the meantime, we work our butts off. And the only high you're allowed is what you get from doing a good scene. Now, are there any questions?"

"No suh. No way, massa." Tom Sanders cringed in mock fright, then turned and grinned at the others. "I think we just heard the voice of God."

"Damn right you did!" Garth glared at them for several seconds, then allowed a small smile to creep across his face. "I don't have to tell you how good you are, because you all know it. And I don't have to tell you what I'm expecting from you, because you know that as well. Together, we're going to sweep the Academy Awards. You know that too, don't you?" he shouted.

"Yes!" they shouted back.

"Good." He leaned back against the couch and laced his fingers together behind his head. "Now get the hell out of here and enjoy your last free day before shooting starts," he ordered.

****

There was tremendous tension and pressure on the set from the very first day, and it increased steadily every week. The primary reason was the time problem. Because of Erin's difficulties in obtaining financial backing for the picture, their originally scheduled production start date had been delayed a full month.

Under normal circumstances, a one-month delay would not have made any particular difference. But these were most definitely not normal circumstances. For Street Scene was being produced as an Oscar contender, and that meant the picture had to be completed by the end of the year in order to qualify for the Academy Awards that would be presented the following spring. Which gave the cast and crew only five months to put together a highly complex and demanding film that would ordinarily have taken over a year to produce.

Two months into shooting, the time problem was compounded by a money problem. It was not that Arnold Scorsi had been stingy. He hadn't been particularly generous, but the financial backing he'd provided had been well within the accepted budget range for a major release.

Erin had been forced to siphon off some of the funds in order to meet the quarterly interest payments to Anthony for his sale of Con-Well Productions to her. But that wasn't what caused the problem. It was the demands of the distribution company who'd handled all of Con-Well's previous pictures.

"You can't be serious, Harry!" Erin had exclaimed in shock when the short burly owner of the distribution company had shoved her contract back across his desk without signing it and then stated his terms.

"Con-Well Productions has been dealing with you for over two years, and you've never asked for anything like this before. You've made a goddamn fortune on us!"

"Yeah, well, that was the old Con-Well. This is the new Con-Well." He chewed stolidly on the soggy end of his cigar, his small pig eyes regarding her coldly. "You get my drift, or do I have to spell it out for you?"

"No, you don't need to spell it out," she snapped. "You've made your meaning very clear. But has it occurred to you that you could be making a very important mistake?" she said furiously. "This picture is going to win the Oscar, and then Con-Well Productions will never need you again. Or forget this blackmail!"

"So?" He shrugged indifferently. "You win some, you lose some. You wanna take your business elsewhere, be my guest."

At that moment, what Erin wanted was to kill Harry, preferably by strangling him with her bare hands. The possibilities of accomplishing that were very slight, she had to admit. Harry's thick bull-like neck was probably twice the circumference of both her hands joined together. Even less possible was taking Harry's bored suggestion to place her business elsewhere. Because Harry owned the biggest independent distribution company in Hollywood, and without him she would never be able to get a successful release for Street Scene.

"All right, Harry. We'll go with your terms."

"Two million up front for advertising and promotion, right?"

"Right."

"And I see it logged on your books," he demanded. "Not a cent goes out from that account for production. It stays right there!"

"Yes, Harry. It stays right there." Erin pushed the contract back across his desk. "Just sign on the dotted line," she said dully.

Garth was stunned when she came home and told him. "My God. Erin, how could you have done that to us? We're already over budget by half a million. I was counting on that money," he told her, an anguished look on his face. "I need it, babe. I've got to have it!"

"Don't tell me you need it," she yelled at him. "Because we don't have it anymore."

"Okay, okay now. Just take it easy," he murmured as he put his arms around her. "We'll manage. Somehow we'll manage."

They managed, but barely, in the months that followed. A cameraman quit on the spot when he dropped a lens and was faced with the accusing eyes of both the cast and his fellow crew members. Two young supporting actresses walked off the set in tears after Garth screamed at them, "The reason this is take twenty-two is due entirely to your unbelievable stupidity. Didn't anyone ever tell you how to hit your marks?"

Paul Marriott found another cameraman, and Derek came up with replacements for the two supporting actresses, who were now filing a suit with the Screen Actors Guild, charging undue harassment. The shooting went on, with the pressure mounting visibly every day.

By this time only three people were holding the production together: Garth, Paul Marriott and, amazingly enough, Derek. No one had expected him to survive the intense pressure without blowing up, but he not only kept his cool, he helped everyone else keep theirs.

He showed up promptly at five every morning and stayed late into the night, even when his scenes weren't being shot, cajoling and encouraging the rest of the cast. Then everything blew sky high when Erin got the second piece of devastating news from Harry.

"Will everybody please hold it down? I have an important announcement to make." Garth's face was white as chalk, and it was only with the greatest effort he managed to keep his voice steady as he stood up and addressed the cast and crew, after Erin had run onto the set and whispered frantically in his ear.

"First of all, I want to tell you what a fantastic job each and everyone of you has been doing. 1 know what it's taken out of you just trying to keep up with this ball-breaking production schedule. But you've not only kept up with it, you've turned in consistently superior performances. At the rate we're going, we'll not only meet our December twenty-fourth deadline but bring in a picture we can all be very proud of."

There were a few scattered cheers. However, most of the people remained silent, looking up apprehensively at Garth. A strange chemistry comes into being between a strong director and those he's directing. It's almost as though their nerve ends become linked, and whatever happens to one is instinctively felt by all. Now, although none of them had the slightest idea of what Erin had just told Garth, they sensed there was a serious problem with the picture.

Garth knew they sensed it, and he took a deep breath before continuing. "Unfortunately, I'm going to have to ask even more from you," he said heavily. "We're going to have to complete filming earlier than we'd planned. Our new release date is November twenty-second."

"What?" Derek screamed in rage. "Have you lost your total fuckin' mind? We can't do that, man. We just can't do it!"

"We can do it. It won't be easy, but we can do it."

"No!" The outraged cry from Paul Marriott, the brilliant cinematographer, seemed even louder than Derek's because he had never been known to even raise his voice. "You are asking the impossible," he said hoarsely. "You are asking us to destroy our film."

"Goddammit, shut up and listen to me for a minute!" Garth yelled as a sullen swell of anger began to grow in the crowd. "There isn't going to be any film unless we meet this deadline. The distributor has just informed us that every major theater chain across the country is booked solid with Christmas releases from the big studios. Our only chance to get a decent showing and qualify for the Academy Awards is to break the picture before Thanksgiving."

"Jesus Christ, Garth, that's less than two months away! How can you stand there and tell us we can make a November twenty-second deadline when we need at least five more weeks of shooting? Or were you planning to forget editing and printing, and just send out the daily rushes?" Derek asked with an angry laugh.

"I can stand here and tell you that because we don't have any other choice."

"Well that's where you're wrong, ol' buddy," Derek snarled. "Because we do have a choice. And I for one do not choose to ruin my career and kill myself in the process by volunteering for a suicide mission that will only result in a hopelessly botched-up picture. The Academy Awards come around every year. I can wait for the next one." He turned around and stalked off the set.

"He'll be back," Erin reassured Garth with a nervous smile.

"I hope so," Garth said bleakly. "But I wouldn't count on it. I've already pushed him harder than I ever thought I'd have to, and I'm afraid he's reached his limit."

Garth's gloomy prediction proved to be right. Derek didn't show up the next morning or the one after that, and he refused to answer any phone calls. After a full week had gone by, the morale on the set hit rock-bottom. In desperation Garth tried shooting around the missing star, but it became harder and harder to do. For one thing, the upcoming scenes demanded his presence. For another, everyone on the set had stopped believing in the picture after he left, and their performances were leaden and uninspired.

"Maybe he's right," Garth said wearily the following Sunday night as he and Erin picked dispiritedly at their TV dinners in front of the fireplace in his beach house. "The Academy Awards do come around every year. So maybe the smartest thing for us is to follow his advice and wait for next year."

"Garth, we can't!" Erin's face filled with panic, and she clutched at his arm. "My God, darling, you said it yourself when you told them this was our only chance. And you know it is," she said feverishly. "We can't wait a year. Con-Well Productions will be dead in a year. The only way we can survive is if we make the picture now!"

"Do you mean we? Or just Con-Well Productions?"

"I didn't think there was a difference." Erin retreated from him, a stiff, hurt look on her face.

"Oh, babe," he sighed. "I guess you don't deserve that. We wouldn't be in this mess today if I hadn't insisted on your leaving Anthony."

"Are you sorry?"

"No." He smiled at her. "Of course I'm not. But are you?"

"You don't have to ask that. I think you know you don't have to ask that." Her hands reached out to him again, her fingers gently tracing the sharp planes of his face before moving down to caress his body.

He moved away abruptly. "I'm sorry, honey," he said miserably. "This goddamn picture is really taking it out of me. I hope you can understand."

"I'm trying, but it's not easy. It's been almost a month since you made love to me."

"Well, give me one more month and then I'll make it all up to you." He grinned at her. "In fact, I'll not only make it up to you, I'll have you begging for mercy."

"Is that a promise?" she asked huskily.

"You can count on it! After we wrap this picture, we'll go away somewhere. Maybe Mexico. I've got a friend who has a place in Mazatlan. We'll lie in the sun, drink Tequila, and—"

He broke off abruptly and gave a short, harsh laugh. "What the hell am I talking about? We don't have a picture to wrap. One more week like this past one and I'm going to have to shut down production."

"Oh. Garth, please don't do that!" Erin knelt in front of him her eyes begging.

"Babe, you know I don't want to, but what choice do I have?"

"You have a choice," she told him fiercely. "Get Derek back on the set."

"I'm afraid that's something I don't know how to do."

"Then I'll do it," Erin announced grimly.

FIFTEEN

The voluptuous young girl who opened the door of Derek's beach house in response to Erin's knock gazed at her uncertainly.

"Gee, you sure look different from the other ones Sylvia's been sending over. Did she clue you in on the action?"

"Not exactly." Erin felt herself flushing under the girl's scrutiny and had to fight a desperate urge to turn and run away.

"Well she should have, because it's really a weird scene. I don't mean to put you down, honey, but maybe you should split while you have the chance." Her hand went up and absently fingered a large bruise on the side of her mouth. "After all, we're sisters, aren't we? And who'll look after us if we don't look after each other?"

"Nobody," Erin agreed.

"Hey, where the fuck is that new bimbo? I heard the door! Now get her in here!" The furious voice of Derek echoed through the house.

"Listen, honey, you can split right now," the girl whispered nervously. "And I'll tell Sylvia you showed up too late. That he was busy with somebody else and didn't have time for you. It'll be okay, I promise."

"No, that's all right. But thanks anyway." Erin gave the girl a tentative wave as she stepped past her into the house and walked down the hallway toward the sound of the steady, pounding rock music.

Derek was lying stark naked on top of the rumpled sheets in a huge circular bed that sat in the middle of the bedroom under a mirrored ceiling. His eyes were closed and he was puffing on a water pipe, his head nodding in slow rhythm to the beat of the music. The air in the room was rank from the pungent reek of sex mixed with the stifling odors of stale booze and hashish.

As he heard the click of Erin's high heels on the parquet floor, he raised one arm and beckoned indolently. "You can start by going down on me, chickie,' he said in a bored voice without opening his eyes. "Then if you do good, we'll have a present for you later on."

"That's terribly generous of you, but I think I'll pass," Erin announced dryly.

Derek's eyes snapped open and he bolted upright in the bed, staring at her in disbelief. "Jesus Christ, Erin, what are you doing here?"

"Well, I'm not on assignment from Sylvia, if that's what you mean."

His face reddened with embarrassment as he groped ineffectively at the tangled sheets and tried to cover himself. Erin started to laugh at his desperate attempts to extricate the top sheet, which was trapped under his leg, and his eyes suddenly darkened with rage.

"Shut up, cunt!" he said tightly. "Nobody invited you here, and nobody wants you here. Now get out before I have you thrown out!"

"I didn't mean to upset you, Derek." She instinctively backed away as he got out of the bed and advanced threateningly toward her.

"What the fuck is that supposed to mean?" he demanded furiously. "You come in to my home, insult me, and expect me not to get upset? Where the hell do you think you're coming from?

"I said I was sorry. And I know it was probably wrong of me to come here like this, but it was the only way I knew to reach you. Now would you please calm down and put on some clothes, so we can talk?" she asked quietly.

"It just so happens I like being naked."

"All right," she said equably. "You stay naked and we'll talk." Erin walked past him and sat down in one of the boudoir chairs, then looked up at him with a pleasant smile.

Derek gave an unwilling laugh. "You got more balls than most men I've met." He went back to the bed and arranged himself cross-legged on it, staring down at her. "But this time it won't work, baby. I'm not going back to the set, and that's final."

"Why?"

"Oh, come off it! You know exactly why."

"Preserving your artistic integrity was the way I heard it." Erin's eyes coolly surveyed the filthy, disheveled bedroom. "This is what you meant by artistic integrity?"

"Listen, don't you talk down to me, bitch! I know what I'm worth, and I'm not about to compromise it."

"It's apparent to me you've already compromised it," she said curtly. "If I'd had any idea how fast you could slide downhill, I would never have come to you with this offer. Because it's painfully obvious you could never handle it."

She stood up. "Good luck on your B-pictures, Derek. And I hope you can keep them going. At least they're a little better than straight porn."

"Hey, you don't walk out like that!" Derek leaped out of the bed and grabbed her. "I know you're conning me," he whispered viciously as he fastened his hands around her neck and began to shake her. "But you don't get out of here until you admit it. You understand that?"

"What I understand is that you're through as a major star."

"Shit, I don't need this crap." He pushed her away. "Just get the hell out of here."

"With pleasure. And when they draw up the list of once talented actors who blew it, they'll mention the name of Derek Marston, who had a chance to do the final cut on an Academy Award picture. If they can remember you, that is."

"What?" He stared at her, completely dumbfounded. "Repeat that!"

"Why bother? It would just be a waste of time." She headed for the door.

He jumped in front of her, barring her way. "Well, you're going to repeat it whether you want to or not, if you expect to leave here," he announced grimly. "Now let's hear it again loud and clear."

"Final cut." She smiled at him coldly. "Now do I have permission to go?"

"Jesus Christ, you really did say that." He shook his head. "Erin, that's just not possible."

"I don't see why. It's happened before."

"Are you kidding?" he exclaimed incredulously. "Maybe three actors in the whole history of filmmaking have been granted that honor, and they were all superpowers. You know damn well that the final cut belongs to the director. It's his personal stamp on the picture, the signature that marks the film as his creation. I can't believe Garth would ever give that up."

"Perhaps that's because you're not thinking very clearly." Erin quickly reached out and put her hand on his arm, patting him soothingly. "I don't mean because of this, uh, party you're having today," she said hastily. "I was referring to your very legitimate concern about jeopardizing your career by being denied the proper time to build and develop the character you're playing."

Confusion replaced the belligerent look in his eyes. "What's that got to do with Garth giving me the final cut?" he asked in honest bewilderment.

"For heaven's sake, Derek, it has everything to do with it." She gazed at him earnestly. "Don't you see? If you have final cut, then the picture can't be released without your approval. And that means there's no way in the world your career can be jeopardized. Because only you will have the power to judge your performance. If it's not up to the standards you insist upon, then you'll have the right to demand more time. So you can't lose. You can only win. Right?"

"I guess so," he said uncertainly.

"Oh, Derek, what do you mean you guess so? You know perfectly well this will make you the power on the set. I can't believe you're suddenly getting modest at this stage of the game."

"Yeah, well, it still seems strange to me," he muttered dubiously. 'That picture really belongs to Garth. I just can't see him giving it up like this."

"The picture belongs to both of you," Erin said softly. "And Garth knows that. I thought you knew it too. Don't you remember him telling you this would make you the next Marlon Brando? And don't you also know that is the dream of every director? To find an incredibly talented young actor and bring him to the peak of his career? To create a major motion picture star? What's a little ego thing like the final cut compared to that kind of achievement?"

"He still thinks I can be as good as Brando?"

"He doesn't think it. He knows it!"

"Jesus, I don't know what to say." Derek ran his hands through his hair. "I promised Barney I'd start that new picture next week."

"Barney?" Erin stared at him in alarm. "You mean your agent?"

"That's the only Barney I know. You know some other Barneys?"

"But you can't do that!" she exclaimed in horror. "You're still under contract to us."

"You want to bet on that? Barney's broken more contracts than I've ever had."

Erin took a deep breath. "Well, we won't fight your agent," she said in a voice that remained steady only through tremendous effort. "If you recall, he never had any faith in you from the beginning of this picture. He was the one who said you wouldn't be able to handle the part. We know you can handle it. So we'll just have to leave the decision up to you."

"Okay, let's say I take your offer." His eyes drilled into hers. "There are less than seven weeks left before the November twenty-second release date. That means shooting will have to be finished in two weeks maximum, to allow time for editing and printing. Do you agree to release me from my contract in two weeks, whether we complete shooting or not, and also agree that I can refuse to let the picture out if I'm not satisfied with it?"

"I guess I have to, don't I?"

"Damn right you do," he announced, grimly triumphant. "All right. You've got it."

"Then we've got a deal."

"You won't regret it," she said fervently. "This is going to be your Academy Award picture."

"I don't know about that. There's so much work still to be done, and so little time." Then he smiled at her. "But I promise you this. I'll give it my damnedest."

"And you'll be on the set first thing tomorrow morning?"

He shook his head wonderingly. "You are some tough broad. You never lose sight of what you want for a minute, do you?"

"I never lose sight of what all of us want," she answered crisply. "And isn't that what you want in a producer?"

"Depends." His eyes regarded her cynically. "For example, I would hate to be that poor son-of-a-bitch Garth. But I feel just fine being me."

"You don't know what you're talking about, so I'll just ignore that last comment of yours," she said frigidly. "All I ask is that you continue to feel fine, so you'll be able to do your best."

"Oh, I'll do that all right," he agreed laughingly. "Now I'd offer to be a gentleman and walk you out of here, but I think you already know your way and would prefer to do it on your own. Did I figure that correctly?" he asked mockingly.

"Absolutely," she snapped. "See you first thing tomorrow morning."

"And have a good night," he called out cheerily as the staccato click of her heels echoed down the hallway.

****

Erin found her hands trembling so badly on the steering wheel of the powerful Mercedes as she drove it out of the circular driveway of Derek's beach house toward the access road leading to Pacific Coast Highway, she was forced to pull off to the side and stop.

The pervasive decadence of the orgiastic scene inside the beach house had affected her more than she realized.

Erin jumped as a car pulled up beside her, the horn beeping as the voluptuous young girl who'd greeted her earlier leaned out of the open window and called, "Hey, are you okay?"

"Oh, yes. I'm fine."

"Well, listen, you can't just park here," the girl announced with a worried frown. "The guard will be coming around soon."

"No problem," Erin assured her. "I'm leaving right now."

"And everything's okay?" the girl repeated anxiously.

"Couldn't be better." Erin forced a smile and waved as she started the engine and pulled out of the access road. But the smile faded quickly as she headed down Pacific Coast Highway and thought of the task that lay ahead of her.

When she'd first conceived the idea of offering Derek the final cut on Street Scene, she'd felt confident she could bring Garth around to accepting it without too much trouble. However, Derek's reaction had severely shaken that confidence.

She recalled the incredulous look on Derek's face as he'd exclaimed, "You know damn well that the final cut belongs to the director. It's his personal stamp on the picture, the signature that marks the film as his creation. I can't believe Garth would ever give that up."

Was Derek right? Would it really mean that much to Garth? Or would he be able to see, as she did, that it was only a symbolic gesture, a necessary concession to Derek's overweening ego?

Surely he would be able to see that and put the whole thing in perspective, she told herself desperately. After all, it wasn't as though she was letting Derek direct the film. The little bastard probably didn't even know how to do a final cut. He'd undoubtedly end up standing around helplessly while Garth did the real work.

Erin found herself cheering up at that thought. It would be a shock to Garth, of course, when she told him what she'd offered Derek. But after they'd talked it over, he was bound to admit she'd done the only thing possible to save the picture. Why, he'd probably end up chuckling over the clever way they'd manipulated their cocky star.

The smile was back on her face as she drove into the narrow garage underneath Garth's place and parked behind his battered MG roadster, then ran up the steep steps at the side of the garage that led to the small beach house perched on stilts above.

"Hello?" she shouted excitedly as she burst through the door. "Is anybody home?"

Garth poked his head around the bathroom door. He was naked except for a brief pair of bikini shorts that hugged his hips, and his face was covered with shaving cream. He looked like an improbably lean, muscular Santa Claus.

"Hello yourself," he grinned, his lips very red within the lathery white beard. "Come in and tell me what happened."

"Oh, Garth, I'm so glad to see you!" she exclaimed, putting her arms around him, slipping to her knees and kissing the small of his back.

"Hey, watch that!" he warned her laughingly. "I could cut my throat if you keep that up."

"Then put the razor down," she said huskily. "Because I plan to keep it up."

Unexpectedly he started to laugh, and she drew back in confusion. "What's so funny?" she asked defensively.

"You! Look at you!" He pulled her up and turned her towards the mirror.

"Oh my God!" Her face was covered with gobs of Garth's shaving cream, her eyes peering comically from the fuzzy froth of beard. "Oh, I don't believe this!" she cried, breaking into hysterical laughter. "How could you make love to someone who looked like this?"

"I must have been concentrating on some other area," he grinned, "Now let's see what you look like down here."

"Stop!" she pleaded, laughing helplessly at the same time. "I can't take any more."

"Not even a little?"

"No! No! I give up."

"Finally she admits it. The lady has met her master."

"I knew that from the first moment I met you," Erin said softly. "You knew it too."

"To tell you the truth, I wasn't all that sure." He gazed at her quizzically. "And you still haven't told me what happened today when you went to see Derek."

"Oh. Well . . ." Flustered, Erin grabbed a handful of Kleenex and started wiping the gobs of shaving cream off her face.

"I guess I didn't have to ask," he said ruefully. "If it had been good news, you would have told me the minute you walked in."

He patted her comfortingly. "Don't feel too badly, honey. I never really thought there was any chance of getting him to change his mind."

"Then I've got a surprise for you." She gave him a nervous smile. "Because he did."

"It's a tough break," he continued. "But it's not the end of the world. We'll—" He broke off abruptly as her words registered. "What did you say?"

"He changed his mind."

"He's coming back to the set?" Garth exclaimed incredulously.

"First thing tomorrow morning."

"My God, I can't believe it! That's fantastic!" he shouted gleefully as he swept her up in his arms, dancing her around the bathroom. "You're a goddamn miracle worker, Erin. You're a bloody genius! How did you do it? And why didn't you tell me right away?"

"I guess I got carried away with another priority."

"That you did, lady. That you most certainly did!" He shook his head wonderingly. "Jesus, babe, this is such marvelous news I hardly know what to say. We've got to celebrate!

"Come on," he announced as he set her down and took hold of her hand. "First we are going to open that bottle of champagne in the refrigerator, and then we're going out for the most lavish dinner you've ever had!"

Erin had to run to keep up with his long, excited strides as he pulled her out to the kitchen. The cork came out of the champagne bottle with a big, satisfying pop and the wine shot up to the ceiling in a golden spray. Beaming delightedly, he filled two glasses and handed her one. "To us, first. And then to success and the Oscar."

He gulped down the effervescent bubbles, laughing as they tickled his nose. "Okay, now tell me how you accomplished this miracle, you beautiful little thing."

"I just did what you told me to do," she said with a tentative smile. "I appealed to his ego."

"Oh sure," he replied mockingly. "Simple as that, huh?" He leaned over and refilled her glass. "Now cut out the false modesty and tell me what you really did."

The renewed confidence Erin had felt when she'd arrived back at the beach house some thirty minutes earlier now deserted her totally as she looked at Garth.

"Well, darling, actually there was only one major problem to overcome," she began nervously. "And once that was taken care of, the rest was easy."

"Hey, enough with the suspense! Out with it, now. Bottom line!"

"I promised him . . ." She stopped and swallowed. "I promised him he wouldn't have to worry about the stepped-up release date forcing him into a bad performance. You do know that was the only thing he was really concerned about, don't you?" she said feverishly.

"Of course I know that." He looked at her strangely. "But what could you possibly promise him that would allay his fears on that score?"

"Nothing that's of the least importance to you and me," she said quickly. "But you know his impossible ego. So I told him he could be in on the final cut of the picture and decide for himself if his performance was up to par."

She reached out and put her hand on Garth's arm. "Oh, darling, you would have laughed if you could have seen the expression on his face when I offered him that. He was so thrilled! He respects you so much, it was like I'd given him the keys to the kingdom."

"Erin, stop right there!" Garth stared at her, his eyes suddenly cold. "Just how many keys to the kingdom did you give away?"

"I don't know what you mean," she stammered. "I just told you. He gets . . ."

"Final cut. That's what you gave him, isn't it?" he shouted. "You bitch! How could you do that to me?"

"Darling, please let me explain," she begged. "It doesn't mean anything at all. You know that."

"It means nothing to you. I understand that all too well. Anything for the picture, right?"

"Garth, I can't believe you're reacting this way before you've even given me a chance to explain," she said frantically.

"Explain?" he yelled. "You think a man needs an explanation of what happened when his balls are cut off?"

He smashed the bottle of champagne down on the counter so hard that it broke into pieces, sharp splinters of glass flying everywhere, and he stalked out.

Erin ran after him as he disappeared into the bedroom and started dressing. "Garth, you're exaggerating this whole thing. Won't you at least listen to me?" she pleaded.

"Listen to what?"

"The reason. The reason,darling. Surely you can see why I did it."

"Of course I can see that." His eyes raked her with icy contempt. "Any fool could see that." He turned away and continued dressing, then headed out of the bedroom toward the front door.

"What are you going to do?" she asked as she followed him.

He stopped and uttered a short, harsh laugh. "What I'm going to do is get the hell out of here and try to get my head straight. But obviously that's not your real question, is it? You want to know what I'm going to do about the picture."

"That's not true. I love you, Garth."

"Sure you do." He laughed again but it was a cold sound, and there was no smile on his face. "Well I can tell you this much. I'm not going to walk out on the picture and let you hand it over to some other director. I've invested too much of myself in it to allow that to happen. I'll be on the set tomorrow morning and every morning after that until it's completed. And when I say completed, I mean completed the way I want it to be. Not the way you want it or Derek wants it or anybody wants it except me," he added fiercely. "Because this is my picture, and I'm not going to let anybody forget it."

He paused for a moment, a sudden bleak look on his face. "After that, I don't know what I'm going to do. I just don't know."

"Oh, darling, everything's going to be all right," Erin cried desperately. "Please just give it a chance, and you'll see we're going to be all right."

"Erin, we'll never be all right again." He turned and walked out the door.

SIXTEEN

"No!" Derek shouted angrily. "What the shit is your problem, anyway? I mean, didn't you even read the fuckin' script? Janine is trying to seduce me, for Christ's sake. And you're acting like a constipated virgin."

"Janine is trying to seduce a human being!" Melissa screamed. "Not some hairy animal. And, besides, who ever gave you the right to be a director?" She burst into hysterical sobs and ran off the set.

"Jesus! That's all we need. A stupid broad in a supporting role who suddenly becomes a prima donna."

"She'll be back," Garth said quietly from his chair behind the set. "But she's right. You're pushing her too fast. You have to let her come to you.'"

Derek flushed as he stepped out of the circle of bright lights and made his way over the complicated lines of cables snaking around the floor to Garth's chair.

"Yeah, I know," he grunted as he flopped down in the chair next to Garth. "And she was right about that last crack she made, too. I'm not the director, and I should have kept my damn mouth shut."

"It's okay." Garth smiled and gave him an affectionate punch on the shoulder. "The way you're going, you just might turn into a respectable director one of these days. In the meantime, you doing one hell of a job with the character you're portraying."

"You mean that?"

"I mean it."

"Jesus, man, that's great to hear." Derek hunched over, absently cracking his knuckles. "Because I'm giving it everything I've got. I just hope to God it's enough."

"Keep on going the way you have been and it will be."

"You know something, man?" Derek exclaimed suddenly. "You are something special. I mean, really special. Because I know damn well, no matter what Erin said, that giving me the final cut wasn't your idea. It was something that little conniver dreamed up herself. And you could have been shitty as hell about it, riding me on the set, slicing me up every time I goofed. But you've been just the opposite. You've gone out of your way to help me, to teach me stuff. So . . . well, I just wanted to tell you how much I appreciate it, and thank you for it," he finished awkwardly.

For a brief second, Garth's expression turned cold and forbidding. Then he shook his head and smiled at the young actor. "I'm the one who should be thanking you. You're not only giving a magnificent performance, you're sparking every one on the set to do the same. If we get an Oscar for this picture, it will be because of you."

Derek ducked his head, suddenly embarrassed. "Yeah, well, we won't get it with me parking my ass here," he mumbled. "I'd better get back to work."

He stood up and walked back to his marks. "Okay, you guys," he yelled. "Let's hit it! We're going after a perfect take this time."

To everybody's delighted surprise, it was a perfect take. Melissa returned to the set, still seething with rage over Derek's crude hut absolutely accurate assessment of her last scene, and turned in a bravura performance as the shy, lovestruck young girl whose terror at losing the boy she's adored since childhood goads her into a desperate competition with the woman he's turning to.

Derek and Melissa received a standing ovation from the cast and crew when they finished the scene. Erin, who'd quietly slipped into the sound stage a few minutes earlier, joined in the applause. And, as she'd done every day for the past ten days, once again crossed her fingers and gave thanks for the miracle occurring before her eyes.

After Garth had walked out of the beach house the previous Sunday, she'd been numbly prepared for total disaster. It had seemed impossible then to believe the picture could ever be saved. But it was not only being saved, it was achieving a brilliance she could hardly believe. The scenes shot before Derek had stalked off the set had been so good she'd despaired of ever matching them. The most she had been able to hope for was that the remaining scenes would go smoothly enough to allow a clever editor to cut and segue them into the earlier footage. But there was no chance of doing that, because Garth scrapped all the film shot the week before Derek left the set and started every scene over again to build the proper momentum. She'd been horrified when she saw what he was doing.

"My God, Garth, have you lost your mind?" she'd cried. "You're throwing away our only insurance on this picture."

"If you want another director, tell me now," he'd snarled. "Otherwise, shut up!"

She'd shut up after she saw the rushes. They were superb. She also stopped coming around to see the dailies three days later. She'd appeared as usual that evening, peering intently through the viewer at the tiny frames of film, and then announced in shock, "This shadow is terrible! Why hasn't someone cut it?"

There was a sudden grim silence in the room, and she had turned around to find three pairs of eyes staring at her hostilely. Sarah Lawton, the film editor, dropped her eyes when Erin looked at her but Garth and Derek had continued to glare at her.

"I-I'm sorry," she'd stuttered nervously. "Obviously everyone here has noticed it also. I should have realized there hasn't been time to fix it yet."

The oppressive silence continued and she stood up and fled from the room, knowing that she was not only not needed but not wanted. And she stayed away. But she couldn't make herself stay from the set, even though Garth pointedly ignored her presence.

He turned around now as he heard the door open and she waved eagerly, a bright smile on her face as she made a circle with her index finger and thumb indicating how pleased she was with the scene. He regarded her unsmilingly for a moment, then curtly turned back to the set, and her arm dropped awkwardly to her side.

"It's my picture too," she whispered. But no one was paying any attention to her. With an unhappy sigh, she slipped out of the room as quietly as she had come in and made her way to her car, which the guard had waiting for her immediately outside of the sound stage.

It was three o'clock, and she was due at the advertising agency in Beverly Hills for a three-thirty meeting. She'd be late, but at least she didn't have to fear any disapproving looks from them, Erin thought with a bitter smile. They'd wait for her until midnight, if necessary, and still greet her with enthusiastic cries of pleasure.

"No love so true as that bought with money," she murmured to herself as she drove out of the lot and onto the Ventura Freeway that led through convoluted ribbons of asphalt into the cold heart of Hollywood's show business capital. "As long as you don't lose the money."

The steel radial tires on the Mercedes hummed confidently along the sharp curves of the freeway as Erin stepped hard on the accelerator, racing along at eighty mile per hour. A check in the rear-view mirror showed a distant speck of black moving up fast. It was a highway patrol car. Erin quickly released the pressure on the accelerator, letting the car glide around the turn approaching the San Diego Freeway, and breathed a sigh of relief as the patrol car whipped by her. For Christ's sake, Erin, take it easy," she admonished herself. The last thing in the world you need now is a speeding ticket.

She looked up to check the rear-view mirror again. Sometimes the highway patrol cars traveled in packs. But the only image in the mirror was her own white, strained face. As it looked back, it seemed to mock her. And what's the first thing in the world you need, it asked.

"Oh shut up!" she said furiously. "I'm going to get my picture. That ad agency is going to produce the most exciting campaign that's ever been seen. I've given them the money to produce it and the product to back it, and I'm going to get that Oscar!"

And what about Garth, the image asked implacably. Are you going to get him too?

"I don't know. You know I'm trying. God knows I'm trying!"

It was true. Erin had been doing everything within her power to show Garth how much she loved him, believed in him, and wanted him. No matter how late he got home from the studio, she was always up and waiting for him; and as soon as she heard him drive into the garage she hurried into the kitchen to fix him something hot to eat.

At first she had tried to discuss the day's shooting with him, offering herself as a sounding board for his ideas and thoughts, but she quickly realized that was the last thing in the world he wanted. Gray-faced with exhaustion, he could hardly keep his head up while he ate. All he wanted was sleep. So she would serve him quietly, clear the table when he was finished, pick up the dirty clothes he flung off as he fell wearily into bed and lay out fresh clothes for the morning, then go out and clean up the kitchen.

Her own days were frantically busy as she rushed from one meeting to another, coordinating the massive advertising and promotion campaign that would launch the picture. In between conferences with copy and art directors, recording sessions for the radio and television commercials, and luncheons with syndicated columnists and film critics, she managed to make time for meetings with Con-Well's accounting staff, which assured Garth a steady flow of money to keep his production going smoothly. It was an almost impossible task, trying to keep everything going successfully at the same time, but somehow she did it. And she never bothered Garth about it. If there was good news, she told him. If there was bad news, she kept it to herself. And every free moment she was on the set, cheering him on.

But he doesn't seem to notice at all, she thought glumly as she walked into the office of the Beverly Hills ad agency, smiled absently at the eager young account executive who bounded out to meet her, and then frowned as he led her into the conference room and presented her with the layout.

"I don't know," she said hesitantly. "It seems exploitative somehow."

"Exploitative? My dear, I can't believe you said that!" Josh Engels, the silver-haired president of the ad agency sprang forward and seized her hands. "Look again," he urged her. "Sensual, yes. But never exploitative. And the power of the concept! It will turn on everyone who sees it. They'll stand in lines eight blocks long at the movie theaters for a chance to find out what's behind this ad!"

Erin shook her head. "I'm sorry, Josh, but you're going to have to change it. Get that hungry look off her face, and put some more clothes on her. I'll be back at ten tomorrow morning to okay the revision."

The art director groaned involuntarily and Erin turned around, giving him a sympathetic smile. "I know. It means you'll be working through the night to get it ready, and I am truly sorry. But this is a very important ad, and it has to be exactly right. I hope you can understand."

"Don't worry," Josh said gamely. "We'll do it, and it will be right. You can count on us."

"I'm sure I can." She made a point of shaking hands with everyone in the room and thanking them personally for their cooperation.

It was an effort to come up with a warm, personal comment for each individual, but she decided it was well worth it as she walked out of the agency to her car and recalled the appreciative smiles on their faces. It wasn't that she was worried about getting them to work all night. Josh was the original slave driver. If the money was right, he'd work his people to the bone and then bring in his mother, wife, and children to finish the job when they dropped in their tracks.

But although you could force people to work to death, you couldn't force them to be creative at the same time. She desperately needed that creativity, and she knew the only way to get it was to impress them with a sense of their own importance. Hopefully, she had now accomplished that.

But the brief surge of energy she'd felt faded as she climbed into the car and put the key into the ignition. Her head ached almost unbearably from the pressures of the past two weeks, her stomach was a tense knot of pain, and she found herself constantly rubbing her eyes, which felt like they were full of sand.

She leaned her head back against the seat of the car, trying to relax for a few minutes before she headed into the bedlam of homeward-bound traffic as thousands of irritable commuters poured onto the congested freeway, then started the engine and drove down Wilshire Boulevard to the freeway entrance, telling herself that all she needed to do was hang on for another sixty minutes and then she'd be home. At which time I'll pour the world's largest drink, empty a whole bottle of bubble bath into the tub, and collapse in style until Garth gets back tonight, she promised herself. It was such a pleasurable image, she found herself smiling in anticipation.

The smile changed into an expression of terror as she drove into the garage underneath the beach house and saw Garth's car. Heart pounding, she raced up the steps and burst into the living room.

"What's wrong, Garth?" she cried in panic.

He was sitting on the couch, his long legs stretched out in front of him, staring unseeingly at the cold ashes in the fireplace. He lifted his head at her cry and regarded her blankly.

"Wrong?" he repeated vaguely.

"My God, darling, what happened?" She rushed over to him. "Is there a problem on the set?"

"No, there's no problem."

"But you're home! It's only six o'clock."

"Oh, that." He gave her a tired grin. "That's not a problem. It's a plus. You see, I think we can finish the shooting tonight. So I gave everybody five hours off to rest and prepare themselves. We go back to the studio at ten and film straight through tomorrow morning. I think we'll have a wrap then."

"Garth, that's incredible!" Erin's face lit up with joy. "Oh, darling, I can't tell you how proud I am. To think you've brought it in a day early! It's a miracle."

"Yeah, well, save your praise until next week. We still have to cut and edit. That will be the real test. When we see just what we've got."

"It's going to be superb." she announced confidently. "I just know it."

"Maybe. Maybe not. We'll have to wait for that." He started to stretch and then winced.

"What is it, darling?" she asked anxiously.

"Getting old, I guess," he said ruefully. "At this moment I feel like a geriatric case. Every bone in my body aches."

"Let me help." She moved quickly over to the couch and started massaging his neck.

"Hey, you don't have to do that."

"I know," she said softly. "But I want to. Now lie down. Come on, Garth, lie down," she insisted as he looked at her quizzically. "It's going to feel good, I promise."

He shrugged, then did as she ordered. A minute later he gave a low groan of pleasure.

"I told you you'd like it," she smiled. Her hands patiently kneaded the tight muscles at the base of his neck. His skin was warm and smooth, and she could smell the clean, fragrant odor of his thick black hair. With an effort she restrained herself from burying her face in it.

"You want more there, or should I do your back now?" she asked. There was no answer, and she realized he was fast asleep. "My poor tired baby," she whispered, leaning over and kissing him gently. "Sleep well, and have pleasant dreams."

Erin let him sleep for a little over two hours before waking him. He sat up with a start when she shook him by the shoulders. "Jesus, what time is it?" he demanded.

"It's still early," she reassured him. "Just a little after eight. Dinner will be ready in twenty minutes, so you have plenty of time to shower and dress."

He rubbed his eyes wearily, then blinked as he looked around. While he had been sleeping, Erin had cleaned up the small living room, lit a fire in the fireplace, and set two places for dinner on the oak coffee table. There was a basket of crisp French rolls in the center of the table, along with an uncorked bottle of red wine. Candles glowed softly at each end.

"Hey, this is really nice!" He smiled at her then. "You've been pretty nice too. And I appreciate it."

It was all the reward she needed. "My pleasure, darling," she said happily.

She was humming contentedly under her breath as she went back to the kitchen and started fixing the salad, after checking the casserole which was bubbling nicely in the oven. It's going to be all right after all, she told herself confidently. Everything's going to work. The picture and us.

Garth finished the filming that night just as he'd hoped. Then came the backbreaking work of editing and cutting. The release date was now less than a month away. Hesitantly, remembering her earlier rejection in the cutting room. Erin offered her services.

"I don't know," Garth had said dubiously. "God knows we need all the help we can get, but what can you do?"

"Whatever you order me to." She'd smiled at him diffidently. "I don't claim to be an expert, but there's lots of scut work I can do. After all, there was a time when I got job offers as an assistant film editor."

"You did?" He looked at her in surprise. "I never heard about that."

"Well, it wasn't one of my starring roles," she'd admitted with a small grin. "But they thought I was good enough to give me a try. And I don't think I've forgotten how to do it. So what do you say?"

"Are you kidding?" He grinned back at her and grabbed her arm. "Come on, lady! We've got ten cans of film waiting just for you."

It was a mind-numbing process, and there were times Erin thought she wouldn't be able to stand one more hour of viewing the endless reels, marking off the next section of cuts. But somehow she managed. More important, she also managed to keep her mouth shut when Garth, the film editor, and Derek announced their decisions about the editing. Her role was as a lackey and she kept it that way, rushing off with each completed can of film to the lab that was now working twenty-four hours a day to print it.

Con-Well Productions delivered the finished prints to the distributor one hour before the deadline, and Erin threw a party to end all parties to celebrate the event. The main sound stage at the company's San Fernando studio was thrown open to welcome the cast and crew along with their families and friends. Dom Perignon champagne flowed freely. Two rock groups played continuously. Enough food to feed a small country filled the wide-planked redwood tables set up around the area. But despite the lavish and almost frenetic display, most people left early. The simple fact was that they were exhausted. Completing the picture had taken almost every ounce of energy they possessed, and after eating and drinking they just drifted off.

"Do you think they liked it?" Erin asked anxiously as she and Garth drove away.

"Sure," he said absently, concentrating on the traffic in front of him.

"Well, but maybe I should have waited a week or so," she persisted. "When everybody had a chance to rest up first."

"Erin, would you please stop harping on it?" he said irritably. "You gave the party when it should have been given, it was a fine party, and everybody appreciated it. Now can't you just let it go at that?"

Hurt, she subsided and leaned back against the seat, staring out the window at the cars roaring by. They drove the rest of the way home in silence. But once they reached the beach house, Erin's spirits revived.

"I don't know about you, but I'm not through celebrating yet," she announced gaily as they walked inside. "Why don't you light a fire and put on some music while I fix us a couple of drinks?"

She dropped her evening wrap and purse on an end table and walked briskly into the kitchen, where she arranged a variety of bottles and glasses on a tray.

"How's this for a dazzling array?" she laughed as she walked back into the living room. "Not that I expect us to drink all of it, but you never know what the night might . . ."

She trailed off uncertainly as she looked around the empty room. There was no fire, no music, and no sign of Garth. "Darling?" she called nervously. "Where are you?"

"In here," he called back, his voice sounding slightly muffled.

"Garth, what are you doing?" she exclaimed in shock as she appeared at the doorway of the bedroom and saw him backing out of the closet with a load of clothes in his arms.

"I thought I told you." He pulled a suitcase out from under the bed and started packing the clothes in it. "Don't you remember I said that as soon as the picture was completed I was going to take a vacation in Mexico? At my friend's place in Mazatlan?"

"Of course I remember!" She clapped her hands in delight. "But I thought you'd forgotten. You've never mentioned it even once since you first told me about it."

She ran over and hugged him. "What a marvelous surprise, darling! But you really shouldn't have sprung it on me like this. I know you men only need some slacks and shirts and a change of underwear to be off and running but us women folk like to do a little shopping first. I don't have even one decent outfit I can wear down there. Or did you think I could buy the clothes once we got there?"

"Erin, I thought you understood," Garth said slowly. "We're not going there together. I'm going by myself."

"We're not going there together?" she repeated numbly. "But you told me...

"Things were very different when I told you that. And you know it."

"No, I don't know it. We've been together practically every minute in the past two weeks. We've been as close as two human beings can get. How can you say things are different?"

"Please, Erin, don't make things more difficult than they have to be," he sighed. "It's true we've been close these past two weeks. But that was a professional relationship. We were working together to save the picture. That's not the same as a personal relationship."

"I don't understand what you're saying!"

"No, you probably don't." He smiled sadly. "To you, there's no separation between your feelings for your business and your feelings for people. But to me there's a big separation. And that's why I'm leaving you."

"I don't believe you! We mean too much to each other. Is this some last minute macho move on your part to try and prove something to me?"

"If it makes you happy to think that, then go ahead," he said indifferently as he snapped the clasps on his suitcase.

"Garth, don't do this to us," she pleaded. "You know you love me."

"Past tense, babe. I did love you."

"Then how could you stop?"

"I didn't stop, Erin," he said evenly. "You killed it."

"That's bullshit, Garth!" She glared at him. "All right, I admit we've had some rough times, I've done some things you didn't like, and you've done some things I didn't like. But I never stopped loving you because of it. I love you just as much today as I did when we first met."

"Then I feel sorry for you," Garth said quietly.

Her face went white at the cutting words. "How dare you tell me that?" she spat furiously. "No one ever has to feel sorry for Erin Connolly, because she doesn't need anyone!"

"I'm sure that's true. Which is probably the problem."

"What the hell is that supposed to mean?"

"Nothing you'd understand in a million years." He carried his suitcase over to the door. "I'll be gone for at least six weeks. You're welcome to stay here while I'm away, but I'd appreciate it if you'd find another place to live before I return.

"You needn't worry about that!" she snapped. "I'll be packed and out of here before you get to the airport tonight."

"Suit yourself." He picked up his suitcase and walked past her through the doorway.

She stared after him in numb disbelief. It couldn't end like this. It just couldn't! She willed him to turn around, come back and put his arms around her and tell her he couldn't leave her. He continued walking steadily through the living room to the front door. She heard it open and then slam shut. It was a very final sound. She began to shake uncontrollably.

It's just that it's cold in here, she told herself. I'll light a fire, and then I'll be fine.

She moved stiffly into the living room and crouched down in front of the fireplace. The gas jet came on with a hiss, and flames leaped up as she held a match under it, causing long ominous shadows to fill the silent room. She quickly adjusted the flow of the gas, and the old charred logs sputtered feebly before collapsing through the grate in a smoldering pile of ashes. They gave off no warmth at all.

"What am I going to do?" she sobbed. "Where am I going to go?" The thought of a lonely, impersonal hotel room was more than she could bear.

Unexpectedly, the phone rang. For a wild hopeful moment she thought maybe Garth had changed his mind, that he realized their love was too strong to kill. But the voice on the other end was the last person she ever expected to hear from.

"Derek, I'm sorry if you wanted to talk to Garth but he's already left for Mexico."

"I know that, Erin. And I know he left you because you gave me final cut. The reason I'm calling is because I think we might be able to help each other.

SEVENTEEN

Erin's first reaction to Derek's offer of moving into his place was an immediate "No." The very thought of living in that madhouse filled with drug addicts and prostitutes made her nauseous. But when Derek explained why he wanted her to, and showed her a beautiful, quiet suite hidden away on the top floor, far away from all the chaotic madness, she decided to give it a try.

As he explained, he was constantly deluged with books and screenplays and led her to a large room packed with them. "I never read them," he told her. "There are so many, and they just keep coming. I get a headache at the very thought of trying to read them. But you have the best eye for quality I've ever met. So I want to hire you to go through them, and if you find a winner, then we'll do another film together."

"But why doesn't your agent read them?"

Derek laughed. "The first time I opened the door and showed him the stacks inside, he said there wasn't enough money in the world to persuade him to touch even one of them. He added he already had more scripts in his office than he could handle."

"But why have you saved them, Derek?"

"Because I believe somewhere in there is the screenplay that will bring me an Oscar."

"I assume you've hired other people to go through them."

"Yeah, I tried for a while, but nobody has your gift for not only knowing what's great but what's right for me."

Going through the mass of manuscripts and screenplays in Derek's office reminded her of the ghastly mess she'd faced with her first job at Film-Star, working for Andi Steiner. It was especially hard to concentrate on them when all she could think about was their film Street Scene.

Erin had diligently collected every press notice on Street Scene from the moment it had been released on November twenty-second. It had opened to extremely favorable reviews, and the box office had responded with enthusiasm. In its first few weeks the film had audiences waiting in theater lines all across the country to see it.

Derek looked at her in amazement when he walked into the room and saw the huge scrapbook in her lap. "When did you put all this together?"

She blushed. "Oh, a couple of weeks ago when I had a little free time." Actually Erin worked on the book every single day, hungrily combing newspapers and magazines for every scrap of news about the picture.

He sat down beside her and began flipping through the pages, quickly becoming absorbed in the clippings. There were reviews from every major film critic and columnist in the country. He paused at a full-page newspaper ad featuring his photo. STREET SCENE IS A WINNER! it proclaimed in bold type. AND DEREK MARSTON MAKES IT A WINNER. GOLDEN GOLD AWARD FOR BEST ACTOR!

"How about that?" he exclaimed gleefully. "Derek Marston makes it a winner! That's me they're talking about."

"It certainly is. And you are a winner. Just like the picture. But we still haven't gotten any Academy Award nominations."

"You're jumping the gun, baby. The academy hasn't even announced them yet."

"But when they do, we will be nominated, won't we?" she asked anxiously. "You do believe that?"

"Sure I do."

She relaxed and smiled at him. "That's good. Because you have to have faith in order to make things work."

****

Two weeks later, on a cold, rainy February morning, Erin sat behind her desk in the executive suite of Con-Well Productions' business office, located in Century City, and stared tensely at the phone. There were three other people in the suite with her. Paul Marriott crouched on the edge of his chair and chain-smoked steadily as he gazed unseeingly at the carpet; Melissa was curled up in a tight ball in the corner of the couch and Derek was restlessly pacing up and down from one end of the room to the other.

It was the third Monday in February, and in less than fifteen minutes the doors of the Motion Picture Academy on Wilshire Boulevard in Beverly Hills would open to admit the hundreds of domestic and foreign journalists who were crowded around the entrance.

Inside the building, academy staffers had worked through most of the night preparing the announcements on this year's Oscar nominations. The noise from the crowd began to build as the time came closer.

"Derek, you're driving me crazy!" Erin snapped. "Can't you sit down?"

"No!" he snapped back.

"Can't say I blame you. Jesus, when will they call?"

"When they know," Paul muttered somberly as he lit another cigarette. "You have good people there?"

"The best. They'll be right in front, and get the news first. Oh God, I'm not religious, but do you think it would help if we prayed?"

"It's too late," Melissa sighed. "Either we got it or we didn't. They've already made their decisions."

The phone rang then, and everybody in the room jumped. It rang again and Erin reached out for it, but her hand was shaking so badly she dropped it before she could bring it to her ear. When she finally managed to pick it up, there was only a dial tone.

"There's no one there."

"Jesus Christ, Erin, you disconnected them!" Derek: shouted. "Let me handle this." He leaped over and reached for the phone, but she shoved him away sharply.

"They'll call back, and I'm the only one who's going to answer," she announced, her face white. "It's my picture."

As though she'd ordered it, the shrill ring sounded once again in the room, and she grabbed the phone. "Yes, Andy, I'm here," she said hoarsely. "Yes, I can hear you. What? What? Oh, Andy, I can't believe it. Say it again. Yes. Yes, I've got it. And thank you, Andy. Thank you!" She hung up and leaned back in the chair, an expression of pure bliss on her face.

"For Christ's sake, Erin, tell us!" Derek shouted.

"Six," she said ecstatically. "We got six nominations. Best Picture. Best Director. Best Screenplay."

She turned and beamed at Paul. "Best Cinematographer."

He was so overcome that tears sprang to his eyes, and he went into a coughing fit to try and hide them.

She turned back to Derek and Melissa, and grinned mischievously. "I said six, didn't I? Now let me think . . ."

"Erin, please!" Derek groaned.

"Best Actor and Best Supporting Actress!" she finished triumphantly.

The room exploded with noise as they screamed with joy and began dancing around, hugging and kissing each other first and then running over to embrace Erin and Paul.

"Any chance I could get in on this party?" a warm, deep voice inquired.

They whirled around to face the door, and Melissa's eyes lit up with delight. "Garth!" She raced over and threw her arms; around him "Oh, isn't it the most incredible news? Isn't it just fantastic?"

She stepped back and shook her finger accusingly at him. "But where have you been all this time?" she demanded. "We haven't heard one word from you in months!"

"Well, Mexico turned out to have more charm than I expected," he said with an easy smile. "But it looks like I came back at the right time."

"Hey, man, you can say that again!" Derek bounded over and pounded him enthusiastically on the shoulder. "Any better timing and we could make you an actor."

"No, no!" Paul protested laughingly as he came forward. "We need him too much as a director." He took hold of Garth's hands. "Congratulations, my friend," he said softly. "We pulled it off after all, didn't we?"

"Yes, we did. Thanks to all of you."

"Enough of this sentimental slop!" Derek yelled. "We are going to celebrate!"

"Right!" they all shouted, grinning like idiots at each other.

Erin watched them from a distance, a painful lump in her throat as she gazed at Garth. He was deeply tanned from his two and half months in Mexico, and he had never looked more handsome. All the strain lines in his face, the exhausted slump of his body, had disappeared. He stood tall and proud, the crisp black hair curling over his forehead and the intense blue eyes glowing out of his smiling face.

"I still love you," she whispered. "And I'll do anything you want if you'll just give me another chance."

He looked up and met her eyes, then walked over to her. "Well we really did make it. didn't we?"

"Yes," she replied unsteadily. "Yes, we did. And I'm very glad you're back. It wouldn't have been the same without you."

"It's not something I would have missed." He smiled. "Looks like we're both on our way now."

"And there's so much we have to talk about," she said eagerly. "Have lunch with me, Garth."

"Thanks, Erin, but I'm afraid I'm tied up. I have a lady waiting for me."

"Oh." The sudden pain that pierced her chest was so sharp she was unable to breathe for a moment. She closed her eyes, feeling beads of perspiration break out on her forehead as she tried to swallow.

"Erin? Are you all right?"

She opened her eyes and forced a smile. "Of course. I think it's just all the excitement. It made me a little dizzy there for a second."

"You're entitled. It's a very exciting day."

"Yes it is, isn't it? Well, I'd better let you run along," she said brightly. "You should never keep a lady waiting. See you at the awards, Garth."

"Right. See you then."

Erin kept the smile on her face as she watched him walk away, telling herself it would be absolutely ridiculous of her to cry. How could she possibly cry when everything she'd dreamed of and worked so hard for was finally coming true?

This is the happiest day of my life, she told herself fiercely. The very happiest day of my entire life.

EIGHTEEN

Street Scene swept the Academy Awards, winning Oscars in every single category for which it had been nominated, and Erin became famous overnight. Not only was she the only woman producer to ever achieve such honors, she was young, beautiful, and a highly controversial figure in the Hollywood film industry.

The press fell on her with cries of delight, and she was courted, catered to, and eulogized. Her photograph made the cover of both Time and Newsweek, and her phone rang constantly. Literary agents, including some of the biggest and most powerful in the business, called to offer books and scripts. Theatrical agents, who controlled an impressive stable of stars, begged for a moment of her time to discuss future projects. And, the sweetest triumph of all, major executives from three of Hollywood's top studios made overtures to discuss a possible deal on her next picture.

She basked happily in the glory for a full month. Then on a warm, sunny May day while she was sipping a glass of wine on the patio of an exclusive Beverly Hills restaurant and smiling across the table at the eager reporter leaning toward her, she felt the first grip of pressure.

"So, Miss Connolly, the big question for all of us is what you're going to do now. Rumors are flying all over the place about the next picture you're going to produce, but you still haven't given us any definite word."

He smiled engagingly. "And I don't have to tell you how important that word is. You've got options on some of the biggest properties around, and everyone is waiting breathlessly to see which one you choose. Because you made a commitment when you won those Oscars; a commitment to excellence, and another Academy

Award for Con-Well Productions next year. No producer in the history of this industry has ever had the courage to make that kind of commitment, and I don't need to tell you what kind of excitement that's generating in this town. Everyone, and I do mean everyone, is watching and waiting."

"Well, I can't believe I ever put it in such egotistical terms as that," she said with a nervous laugh. "Every producer is committed to excellence, and I think I was talking about all of us if I did say anything like that. So we'll just have to wait and see what next year brings."

"Come on, Miss Connolly, surely you don't expect me to believe that. You know as well as I do that this next film is crucial, because now that you've been proclaimed the best, you can't get away with just producing good pictures. You've got to top your own performance, and everybody in this town will be gunning for you."

****

"That miserable little creep!" Erin stormed later that night as she and Derek sat on the couch in the living room of his beach house, having their usual evening cocktails while they waited for dinner to be prepared. "First he comes out with this preposterous statement that I've challenged the entire film industry to a new standard of excellence, and actually has the nerve to claim he's quoting me, and then he finishes up by telling me if I don't have another Oscar next year, I'll be washed up in this town."

"Welcome to fame, baby," Derek grinned. "Ain't it fun?"

"No. It isn't fun at all. I've won my Oscar, I've established myself, and now all I want is to be left alone to make more pictures."

"What? Is this the same Erin Connolly who's been spreading herself around like a smorgasbord for the press that I hear talking now?" he inquired with a mocking gleam in his eyes.

"That's a pretty lousy remark, Derek, especially considering that you've been spreading yourself around as a smorgasbord for considerably more than the press." Her eyes surveyed the living room. "But perhaps I should thank you for cleaning up before I get home. Or is there a surprise waiting for me in a bedroom or bath somewhere?"

"Hey, take it easy." He took the glass out of her hand, got up and walked over to the bar to refill it, then leaned against the counter and gazed at her curiously. "I didn't know that bothered you. You've never mentioned it before."

"You mean the girls you run in and out of here every day? No, that doesn't bother me, Derek," she said coldly. "True love was hardly one of the conditions we had when I moved in with you."

"Then what is bugging you?" he asked, genuinely puzzled.

"That the little prick might be right," she muttered. "I've read so many books and scripts, I'm going blind. I don't know what to choose for the next picture. I don't know what's the right one. Do you?"

"Jesus, Erin, don't ask me. I can't make that kind of decision."

"But you've read the material I've given you, haven't you?"

"Uh, sort of " He shrugged uncomfortably. "Actually, I let my agent do it. I mean, he's more into that scene."

"Oh my God, I don't believe this! You took all those scripts I gave you and handed them over to Barney Lipsky?"

"Well what the hell did you expect me to do?" he said defensively. "After all, he's the one who knows what works best for me."

"Really? What about the fact that he wanted you to turn down Street Scene? What about the fact that he could have lost you the Oscar?"

"That was different. I had Garth's guarantee on the picture."

"Garth's guarantee?" she said furiously. "What about mine? I was the one who bought that property, in case you've forgotten."

He turned away, refusing to meet her eyes, and she sighed.

"All right, Derek, maybe you have a point. I know how important the director is to an actor. So what if I go to Garth with these properties? Let him read them and make the decision?"

"You can't."

"Of course I can. We may not be lovers anymore, but we're still professionals. We can work together. As a matter of fact," she said with sudden enthusiasm, "I don't know why I didn't think of doing this sooner. We'll get hold of Paul Marriott and all the rest of the crew that worked on Street Scene. We'll bring the whole winning team back together again, and we'll produce our second Academy Award picture. How does that sound to you?" she asked him, her eyes sparkling with excitement.

He shook his head. "You're too late, Erin. Garth is going into production on his own picture at the end of this month."

"What?" She stared at him in shock. "But. . .but he never even mentioned it to me. He never said a word! How could he do a thing like that?"

"Well, Erin, I hardly think he felt he needed your permission," Derek said dryly. "And as far as the Academy Awards go, I think he's planning to win them on his own next year, without your help."

"With you? He signed you?"

"No. Not that I wouldn't have signed if he'd asked me. He's the greatest director I've ever worked with. But the part just isn't right for me. I could see that when he explained it to me."

"You went to him without telling me? Knowing what I'm going through?"

"Jesus Christ, Erin, what is all this shit?" he said irritably. "We live together, but that doesn't mean you own my career! And if you think it does, then maybe you'd better move out right now."

There was no question but that he meant it, Erin realized as she looked at him. And with the realization came panic. He was her ace in the hole for her next picture. She had to have him and his incredible box-office magic. And up until this moment it had never occurred to her that she'd have any problems getting him. Because despite the constant parade of young girls he brought into the house, she knew how dependent he was on her, how important she was to him.

He saw her as someone superior to himself, and he desperately needed the reassurance that a superior being could want him. But now she saw by the way he was looking at her that she'd lost that superior status, which meant she could lose him. And that couldn't be allowed to happen.

"I think you missed my point," she said lightly, taking a sip of her drink. "Of course I don't think I own your career. What I was saying was just the opposite. No one but you owns your career, and no one else should try to. Not Garth, and certainly not Barney Lipsky! You're much too major a talent for that.

"By the way," she added idly, "what was the role Garth turned you down for?"

"He didn't turn me down," Derek scowled. "He just said it wasn't right for me."

"But what was it?"

"Andrews. In The Olympic Connection."

"He turned you down for that? Good God, Derek, you would have been magnificent!"

"He said I was too young. And I think he was right," Derek said defiantly. "After all, the guy's over forty."

"Forty is too old for you to play? Derek, did you ever see James Dean in Giant! He was only twenty-four years old when he appeared in that, and the character he played aged over fifty years during the course of the picture."

"Yeah, well, I'm not gonna be any new James Dean in Garth's picture," he said morosely. "Because I'm not gonna be in it."

"Frankly, I think that's Garth's loss," she told him crisply. "Don't feel badly about it. I've learned these things work out for the best. It simply wasn't meant for you to play that part because somewhere there's another picture, a much more exciting picture, that's going to be offered to you."

"You really think so?"

"I don't think so, I know so. And that's something you can count on. Because I'm Irish, and we have special gifts for seeing into the future."

"I sure hope you're right," he sighed, hunching over and staring into his drink. "Because I get a little crazy between pictures. Like, I don't know what to do with myself."

"It won't be much longer now."

"But what if a picture comes along that I feel is right and it isn't your picture?" he challenged. "Say it comes to my agent from some other producer and I want to sign. Are you going to hassle me about it?"

"Derek, I am never going to hassle you. All I want is the best for you, and I'll back you in any decision you make." She smiled warmly at him. "I'm never going to let you down, either. Somehow, I just know that when I get home tonight I'm going to have that perfect picture for you. It's going to be waiting on my desk when I go in this morning."

"Jesus, I almost believe you."

****

It wasn't waiting on the desk, it came in on a telephone call from Joel Wiseman. "Are you ready for this?" he shouted ecstatically into the receiver. "The only novel that won both the Pulitzer Prize and the National Book Awards, and I'm giving you first chance at the screen rights to it."

It was like an answer to her prayers, and she barely restrained herself from letting out a cry of delight. "I don't know, Joel," she said slowly. "It sounds interesting, but I've practically committed myself to another project, and I don't think I want to take on a second one at the same time."

"Sweetheart, you owe it to yourself to look at this before you make any commitment. Because I am talking quality here. I am talking prestige here. I am talking Oscar potential! Now have lunch with me today. And I won't take no for an answer."

"Joel, you literary agents are bigger hucksters than all of Hollywood put together," she laughed.

"So where do you want to eat?"

"The Bistro? At one?"

"You've got it, sweetheart. Ciao."

She was still laughing as she hung up, then a slight frown crossed her face as she realized he hadn't told her what the book was. She punched down the intercom button on her phone and buzzed her secretary.

"Nancy, what novel won both the Pulitzer Prize and the: National Book Award this year?"

"I haven't the foggiest," Nancy admitted cheerfully. "But give me a few minutes and I'll find out."

Fifteen minutes later Nancy walked into her office. "The book is called Body Count and boy is it controversial!" she exclaimed. "Eight publishers turned it down flat before the author found someone who was willing to go with it. And even then they only printed a minimum number of copies. The critics had to ferret it out on their own.

"By the way, in case you're interested, it took him decades before he found himself able to write it. He was a Marine lieutenant in Vietnam, and he had to take over a squad or platoon or whatever the hell they call them when the captain in charge of the outfit was killed. By his own men."

"Are you serious?" Erin said incredulously.

Nancy shrugged and gave her an apologetic smile. "Hey, don't blame me. I just do research here."

"But why haven't I ever heard about it? I mean, something that explosive should have been on all the bestseller lists."

"It never made the bestseller lists, Erin. The L. A. Times book editor I talked to said that people in this country just want to forget about all the bad things our soldiers did in Vietnam.

Nancy looked at her uncertainly. "Are you considering this as a property?"

"I don't know right now. I really don't know."

****

"This book was a loser right from the moment the author started it," Erin stated coldly as she looked across the table at Joel Wiseman. "So what the hell are you trying to pull by peddling this thing to me?"

"Nothing that wins the Pulitzer and the National Book Award is ever a loser," he replied with equal coldness. "My mistake was in not realizing that you're a coward just like most of the other Hollywood producers."

He signaled briskly to a waiter as he drained his drink. "So order, and we'll call it quits. You get a nice lunch, and I learn a lesson."

"That's the first intelligent recommendation you've made all day. I'll have the filet of sole, and please ask them to bring it as quickly as possible, because I have a great deal of important matters awaiting me back at the office."

"Two filets of sole," he said glumly to the waiter who came up to their table at that moment. "And we'd like them served right away. The lady's in a hurry."

The waiter nodded understandingly and was back with their orders in less than ten minutes. They ate silently, then Joel gave an unhappy sigh.

"It's really a goddamn shame." He absently pushed the uneaten portion of his fish around on the plate. "Derek Marston is absolutely perfect for the part of the lieutenant. With that raw, primal energy of his, he'd make the picture. The author wants him for the part in the worst way. That's why he asked me to come to you."

Joel sighed again before looking up at her. "I suppose you have him under contract?"

She glanced at him sharply, the unwelcome feeling of panic stabbing at her once again. But it was obvious from the expression on his face that he wasn't testing her. He clearly believed she had Derek locked up.

"Joel, is that a serious question?"

"No, not really," he admitted ruefully. "There's no way you'd let him out of your clutches after the performance he gave in Street Scene. Everybody knows that."

"Well I don't think having him in my clutches is quite the way I'd put it. But if you mean has he signed with Con-Well Productions for his next picture, the answer, naturally, is yes. Joel, would you forgive me if I leave you to settle the check? I really do have the most frantic schedule ahead of me this afternoon."

"If you'll do me one favor."

Halfway out of the chair, she paused for a moment and looked at him in surprise. "Favor?"

"Read the book." He reached into his briefcase and pulled out a copy of the novel, holding it out to her. "Erin, just do this one thing for me."

"But, Joel, I don't see any point to it. I've already explained to you why Con-Well Productions isn't going to option it. The material is simply too controversial. My reading it isn't going to change my mind at all. In fact, if the book is anything like what I've heard, it will just confirm my decision."

"I'll take my chances." He leaned forward quickly, laying the book on the table and taking hold of her hands. "'Please, Erin," he said imploringly, "Just read it. That's all I'm asking,"

He released her hands then and gazed at her. "Surely that isn't too much to ask, is it? A few hours of your time? They could be the most important hours you've ever spent."

Uncomfortable with the naked intensity in his eyes, she nodded. "All right, Joel. I'll read it."

"Thank you. And I promise you, you won't regret it."

Erin was quite sure she wouldn't regret it, because she hadn't the slightest intention of reading the book. She took it from the agent dutifully and then tossed it on the front seat of her car. As she drove away from the restaurant and back to her office, she felt a headache developing as she thought of the pile of scripts not only waiting for her there but at Derek's place. God, let there be one winner among them.

There weren't any at her office and she'd pretty much given up on the ones at Derek's. Sending Nancy out for coffee, she burrowed back into the pile and it seemed to her that every script she picked up got progressively worse.

"Oh, hell!" she finally exclaimed in disgust. "You don't even know what you're reading anymore. Give it up for the day."

"I've had it, Nancy," she announced as she walked into the reception area. "If anything important comes up, you can reach me at home."

"Bad day, huh?" Nancy said sympathetically.

"There may have been worse, but I can't remember them at the moment."

"Tomorrow will be better," Nancy smiled. "It's in our horoscope."

"Well, let's hope the horoscope is right." She managed a weary smile in return, then gave Nancy a brief wave and left the office.

It was still fairly early when Erin drove through the tunnel at the end of the Santa Monica Freeway and headed north up Pacific Coast Highway to the beach house. The sun sparkled off the ocean, the air was warm and balmy, and she felt her spirits reviving. Maybe Nancy's right, she thought, and tomorrow will be better. In the meantime, I think I'll treat myself to a nice lazy afternoon by the pool.

As she pulled into the long circular driveway, turned off the motor, and started to get out of the car, her eyes fell on the book lying on the seat beside her. She hesitated for a moment, then shrugged philosophically and picked it up. Since she had the rest of the afternoon free, she might as well give it a look. It wouldn't take her very long to skim through it, and then she could report back to Joel tomorrow and get him off her back.

But to Erin's surprise, she found she couldn't just skim through it. The writing was intense, compelling, forcing her to read it in depth. It was also haunting and deeply disturbing. She shook her head as she came to the part where the Marine captain is executed by his own men. Her initial reaction had been right. The subject matter was simply too controversial. A shame, though. God, what a powerful film it would make. And Joel was right. Derek would be outstanding as the young lieutenant. Sighing, she laid it down on the chaise, stretched out, and let the last warm rays of the sun caress her as she drifted off to sleep.

"Hey! Hey, Irish!"

She sat up with a shock of surprise as the exuberant voice boomed in her ear, and stared in confusion at Derek who was leaning over her, grinning from ear to ear.

"What?" she said bewilderedly. "What did you say?"

"Irish." He picked her up and hugged her so hard, she had trouble breathing. "Don't you remember? You told me this would be my day! The day I found my picture. Because you're Irish, and you can see into the future. Well, you were right, baby, because I did find it. I went into Barney's office today and he handed it to me. And it's perfect! Just like you told me it would be. Isn't that great?" he crowed as he set her back down on her feet.

"You signed a picture contract today?" The color drained from her face as she looked at him. "No, you couldn't have!"

The delighted joy on his face abruptly faded. "Goddamnit, Erin! I came home to celebrate, not to get hassled. You told me you wouldn't hassle me."

"I'm not hassling you," she said faintly. "It...it's just a little unexpected, that's all."

"What do you mean, unexpected?" He glared at her. "Didn't you tell me it would happen today?"

"Yes, I certainly did." She walked back to the chaise and picked up the book. "The only thing I didn't expect was that you'd get two pictures in one day." She held out the book to him. "This is your next Oscar, Derek. Did Barney guarantee you an Oscar too?"

"Listen, Erin, I'm in no mood to be conned. So what the fuck is this thing you're handing me?"

"To tell you the truth, I'm not sure," she said quietly. "I just think you should read it."

"You're not sure? Then why the hell should I bother?"

"Because I'm Irish," she told him with an oblique smile. She laid the book down on the table next to the chaise, picked up her beach towel, and walked off the patio.

He stared after her as she disappeared into the house; then, with a grudging curiosity, he reached out for the book and flipped it open to the first page.

When Erin reappeared on the patio an hour later after bathing and dressing, she found Derek stretched out on the chaise, a frown of concentration on his face as he slowly turned the pages of the book.

"Do you want a drink?" she asked.

"Yeah," he muttered without looking up. "Bring it out here."

She mixed the drinks herself and carried them out, setting the two glasses down on the table next to him as she curled up in the lounge chair opposite. "Gin and tonic okay?" she asked.

"Sure," he said absently. He reached out for the glass, took a brief gulp, and returned to his reading.

He was still reading when Rosa came out to the patio forty minutes later to announce dinner, and he carried the book with him into the dining room. The plump Mexican maid gazed uncertainly at Erin.

"It's all right, Rosa," Erin assured her. "Just serve the meal."

Derek read steadily through dinner, grunted irritably when Rosa tried to clear his plate away, then pushed back his chair; and stood up, still holding the book.

"Bring my coffee to the study," he ordered.

At midnight Erin gave up her vigil, as Derek continued reading, and wearily made her way into the bedroom. She fell asleep almost immediately. Then she groaned in protest as a bright light blazed in her face and she found Derek leaning over her, shaking her.

"For God's sake, Derek, what are you doing?"

"You were right, Erin!" he announced feverishly. "This is my picture. It's absolutely dynamite! I want it. I want it more than I wanted Street Scene. I want it more than I ever wanted anything in my whole life!"

She was fully awake now as she looked at his flushed excited face.

"I thought you'd feel that way. But what about the contract you signed today?"

"Oh that's no problem," he shrugged. "I just finished talking to Barney and told him to get me out of it."

"You woke Barney Lipsky in the middle of the night to tell him you're breaking the picture deal he just finished making for you?" Erin let out a peal of laughter. "My, how I would have loved hearing his reaction to that."

"He wasn't exactly delighted."

"I'll just bet he wasn't. Well, darling, you've made my day with that little tidbit of news."

But Erin's feeling of glee about Barney was replaced by a sudden cold shiver of apprehension and she found herself wondering if she had paid too high a price to keep her box-office star.

Erin's apprehension turned into grim reality as work began on Body Count, for the production was plagued by major problems from the outset.

Joel Wiseman explained that one of the conditions the author insisted on, in selling the property to Con-Well Productions, was that he would get to write the screenplay.

Erin agreed readily because she naively assumed that good novelists would make good screenwriters. When she saw the first draft of the script for Body Count, she found out how wrong that assumption was.

""It's a disaster, Joel!" she'd moaned over the phone. "It's so bad, I can't believe it came from the same man who wrote the book. We can't possibly go with this!"

"Now calm down, Erin. I'm sure you're exaggerating. Besides, remember our deal."

"Have you read this?'

"Yes."

"And you have the nerve to remind me about our deal after seeing this piece of crap? Have you gone completely bananas?"

"Look, Erin, the man is a novelist. A highly talented novelist. There's no one writing today who can equal his power in rich narrative interior scenes, evocative descriptions, and character delineation."

"Then let him go write another novel," she'd said furiously. "And let me get somebody who knows a few simple things like dialogue and camera action!"

"Sweetheart, I think you're blowing this whole thing out of proportion," he'd said soothingly. "Of course you can go out and get someone who knows those technical things. I would expect you to. After all, this is just a first draft. So please feel free to turn it over to one of your professional craftsmen for polishing."

"Professional craftsmen? And what about the screen credits for this particular professional craftsman you're referring to so casually? What exactly does he get out of this?"

"Well." A nervous cough had followed. "Equal credits?"

"He does all the work and then has to share the credits? You're crazy, Joel. No first-class screenwriter would touch it on that basis."

"He'll have to," Joel had replied unhappily. "Because my man wants those screen credits. Without them, there's no deal."

It took Erin two months to find a screenwriter who would agree to those terms. The top writers turned her down flat, as she'd expected, and it was unthinkable to hire a second-rate hack for such an important and complex film. Finally she found a competent professional who was having severe financial difficulties at the moment and agreed to do it if she would pay him double the going rate.

Another three months passed before he completed the revisions, because the author of the book had become totally paranoid at the thought of having another writer work on his script and insisted on going over every word the exhausted screenwriter wrote with a fine-tooth comb. By this time, production on Body Count was five months behind schedule and not a single foot of film had been shot. Then the real problems started.

Erin had hoped that with this picture she would be freed at last from the onerous responsibilities of financing and distribution and could concentrate solely on producing. But the major studios who had made overtures to her earlier were frankly appalled by the property and backed away from it in horror, warning her with much head shaking that she was crazy to even consider making such a film.

"There are much easier ways to commit suicide," one told her dryly. Their reactions, although they depressed her somewhat, didn't surprise her; and she glumly prepared to take on the whole burden once again. What did surprise her, and seriously depress her, was the reaction of Con-Well Productions' comptroller.

"That's ridiculous, Max!" she'd snapped. "We grossed over thirty million on Street Scene. So how can you possibly tell me I'm in trouble if I finance this picture?"

"Look at the figures," he'd said gloomily. "You had to pay Garth Werner twenty-five percent of the profits for his share in Street Scene. You had to pay off the loan to the backers, and you know the interest rate Arnold Scorsi wrote into that contract. Then you had the payment to Anthony Wellington on his note. After subtracting all that, plus expenses and taxes, you've got less than five million left."

"Well, come on, Max," she'd smiled. "Five million is hardly peanuts."

"The way you're going, it'll be peanuts any day now," he'd said sadly. "You're over budget on script. You're over budget on casting. And you still have location shooting ahead of you. That's going to cost a fortune."

"Then we'll just tighten our belts."

"You'd better, Miss Connolly." He'd frowned, absently pushing up the glasses which had slid down his nose. "Or you're going to run out of money before this picture is finished."

She hadn't counted on being so much over budget on casting. Derek had wanted the picture badly enough to waive his usual million dollar fee, just as he'd done on Street Scene. Unfortunately, the other actors hadn't waived their fees at all. In fact, they'd increased them. Con-Well Productions had just turned out an Academy Award winner, and all the actors' agents had demanded top dollar for their stars on that basis.

It wasn't something that Erin could negotiate. She desperately needed the draw of top actors for this highly controversial film, and so she had to pay what they demanded. But as their contracts rose in price, Derek's had to rise also. Because his ego demanded that he make a minimum of fifty percent more than anyone else. He was, after all, the consummate star. So casting costs, which had originally been figured at two million, rose to three million. Erin just swallowed hard and paid them. Then came the problem with the director.

Anson Konrad was a dark, saturnine man who never smiled. In fact, his usual expression was a ferocious glower. But he was generally acknowledged as one of the few directors in Hollywood who deserved the title of genius. Erin paid a small fortune to get him, and then her investment went up in smoke the second week of filming.

"If he does not do as 1 say this time, I leave!" Anson hissed as she came on the set.

"If you keep this cocksucker on the set one more minute, I leave!" Derek yelled.

"Please, can't we just sit down and talk about this?" Erin: begged.

"No!" they shouted in unison.

She looked at the director first, then at Derek. There was no doubt about the rage in his eyes. It wasn't at all like his occasional fury with Garth. He clearly hated and distrusted this director.

"I'm really sorry, Mr. Konrad," she sighed. "But Derek stays."

"Your problem, Miss Connolly," he said icily as he stalked off the set.

"Oh shit, Derek, what do we do now?"

"You got nothin' to worry about, baby," he said confidently. "I know a really first-class director. A guy who can bring this whole thing together. I'll have him come over tonight and talk with us."

He smiled then and gave her a hug. "You're first class too, baby. You stood up for me when it was important. I won't forget that."

Erin was less than enthusiastic about the director who showed up at the beach house that night. "All he did was agree with everything you said," she frowned as they got into bed. Goddamnit, Derek, you need direction, and I can't see that man offering any!"

"Did it ever occur to you he agreed with me because I was right?" Derek retorted angrily. "Or have you forgotten how closely I worked with Garth on Street Scene? I learned a hell of a lot on that picture, and Garth himself told me I had the makings of a fine director."

"Oh, I'm not questioning your ability for a moment. You're not only enormously talented, you have a sixth sense about what makes a scene work that's really extraordinary. And no one is more aware of that than I. It's just that the role you're playing in this picture is so demanding, I worry about you taking on any additional responsibilities. You should be free to concentrate totally on it."

Mollified by her words, he smiled and patted her hair. "Your problem is you worry too much. Believe me, I can handle it. And you'll see that everything is going to work out just fine."

But Erin saw with increasing despair that everything was not working out fine. In fact, it wasn't working at all. Derek assumed more control over the set every day, to the detriment not only of his role but the picture as a whole. He was blowing up his part to ridiculous proportions, invalidating the integrity of the character he played and reducing the rest of the cast to one-dimensional figures.

The director meekly went along with him. She tried on numerous occasions to point out what was happening, but he became instantly hostile at the mere suggestion of criticism. Finally she was forced to admit the unhappy truth that she couldn't control him. He would either do it his way or quit.

Garth would have been able to whip him into line in one day, but there was no Garth on the set. It was extremely painful to her to realize how little real power she had. Of course she could hire and fire, but that was meaningless compared to the power of creating a successful picture. Only a strong director could do that, and although she was strong in many ways, she wasn't a director.

As the weeks and months went on, she worried more and more. Costs went up and the money supply from Con-Well productions shrank, with Max nagging at her constantly.

The trades were filled with stories about problems on the set. Two major actors had quit when Derek slashed their parts. The distributor was making ominous noises about theater chains that didn't want to show the film after hearing what it was about.

She found herself drinking too much and jumping at sudden noises. It was a problem trying to sleep. When she finally dozed off, terrible nightmares would bring her awake with a start, trembling and drenched in perspiration.

They were shooting the final scenes of the picture on the Yucatan peninsula in the southern part of Mexico, where the tropical jungles and marshes offered a close approximation of the Vietnam geography. At the end of the first week on location, over half the cast and crew had come down with dysentery. Erin was far and away the hardest hit. The local doctors, seriously concerned about her extreme dehydration and generally weakened condition, insisted she return to California for treatment. She spent three days in Cedars-Sinai Hospital and was released only on condition that she stay in the Los Angeles area for a ten-day convalescence period.

She went crazy pacing around the empty beach house, worrying about what was happening to her picture. It was almost impossible to get phone calls through to the location site, and when she did, the news was invariably bad. More cast and crew members had come down sick. Equipment broke down and replacements had to be flown in from California, causing crucial delays in shooting. Worst of all, neither Derek nor the director ever returned her frantic calls, and she found herself reduced to screaming over the phone to some minor assistant.

She announced to the doctors at Cedars-Sinai that she was cured and was going back to her picture. They tested her and reluctantly agreed. The virulent bug was gone. But they warned her it could attack her again with even more serious consequences if she went back. She laughed them off. "This time I'll be tougher."

There was nothing but disaster on the set, though. An unexpected rain of monsoon proportions closed down shooting for four weeks. When it finally let up, the sick and despondent crew members and cast who'd remained on the set had no energy for anything. Neither the director's pleading nor Derek's raging could force them into giving viable performances. Foot after foot of film was scrapped as scenes had to be reshot.

The picture was now more than a year behind schedule, and it had long ago missed the deadline for the next Academy Awards nominations. Erin found some small comfort in knowing that Garth's picture was suffering similar problems. He'd been on location for six months, and it was reported that he had at least one more month of shooting ahead before filming would be complete. So at least he wouldn't be one up on her. They'd be competing at the same time—both a year late—for the Oscar.

But as it turned out, Erin was denied even that small comfort. Her picture, which had opened to mixed reviews and bombed at the box office, didn't get a single Academy Award nomination. Garth's got eight. She hung up the phone in her Century City office after the call came through and stared at the people who were sitting in front of her, gazing tensely up at her.

"We didn't make it," she said bleakly. "We got nothing."

Derek let out an anguished scream and ran out of the office. The rest of the people continued to sit there and look at her.

"Go home," she said harshly. "There's nothing here for you."

Derek didn't come back to the beach house that night or any of the following nights that week, but Erin was barely aware of his absence. Numb with grief and despair, she spent hours huddled on the couch in the living room, staring unseeingly out at the ocean, refusing Rosa's frightened pleas to eat something, rousing herself only when the room grew completely dark, to make her weary way to bed.

On the fourth day of her self-imposed exile, she accepted the mail from Rosa and listlessly picked up Daily Variety. There was a feature story on the Cannes Film Festival. A picture she'd never heard of had swept the awards. She shrugged, started to glance away, then blinked in surprise as the familiar name registered.

"Cyclorama, written and directed by James Lee Norton and produced by James Lee Studios Ltd.," the article read, "has proved to be not only this year's biggest sleeper but one of Hollywood's most unsettling surprises. The brilliant but decidedly controversial James Lee has not been heard of in this town since he walked off an International Pictures set two years ago and instigated a lawsuit against that studio for infringement of civil rights, claiming that minorities were not only discriminated against but were threatened with blacklisting if they filed any complaints.

The suit never reached the courts, and most Hollywood insiders agreed that James Lee had committed professional suicide. Several months later he moved to France, confirming that opinion. But he's certainly turned the tables now! He's kept his American citizenship, entered Cyclorama as a U.S. (read Hollywood) entry, won all the awards in sight, and is now being courted by every major film producer in Europe. By the way, he never withdrew that suit against International Pictures. So watch out, Hollywood!"

"Well, you finally made it," Erin murmured. She knew she should feel happy for him. She tried for a moment, but it was too much of an effort. It seemed like everyone but herself was now successful. Even Anthony Wellington was doing well. He'd moved back to New York and for once in his life had done something right. The first play he'd backed had turned out to be a smash box-office hit, he was now producing a new play, and there were rumors of romance between himself and the leading lady.

Forget it, she told herself tiredly. It doesn't matter. Nothing really matters anymore. She turned the cover page of the green and white tabloid, then froze in shock as the headline on the second page leaped up at her.

DIRECTOR AND STAR OF THE OLYMPIC CONNECTION NOMINATED FOR EIGHT ACADEMY AWARDS PLAN JULY WEDDING."

The print blurred as she began reading about Garth's upcoming marriage.

"Miss Connolly, there's a phone call for you." Rosa stopped; abruptly in her tracks as she saw Erin's shoulders shaking, tears streaming down her cheeks. "I-I'm sorry, ma'am," she stammered. "I'll tell them you're busy."

"No." Erin looked up at her, wiping away the tears and forcing a smile. "No, Rosa. You don't have to tell them that. I've had my final piece of bad news, and nothing can be any worse. It's time to pull myself together and make a new start. I'll take the call."

It turned out to be the greatest mistake of Erin's life.

NINETEEN

"I don't care if she did it with three midgets while she was standing on her head!" Lynn Powers snapped with considerable irritation into the phone. "I'm not running a sleazy gossip column here. What movie stars do in the privacy of their homes is their private business. All I report on is their public business. Now if you can't understand that important distinction, I have a number of suggestions as to what you and your hot little tips can do. And my favorite is drop dead!"

She slammed down the phone without giving the stunned caller a chance to answer, then sighed as she saw every extension line on the panel light up.

"Hey, Sally, which one should I pick up now?" she asked as she walked into the adjoining office.

"What?"

"The next call," Lynn said patiently. "What's the most important?"

"Well, Andi Steiner's on three and she says she has something vitally important to talk to you about."

Lynn raised a skeptical eyebrow. "Andi Stciner? The woman at International Pictures? Sally, I think you're losing your touch. The day that a studio publicist has anything vitally important to say is the day I'll go into another business, because the flacks will have taken over this one. Now let's try again."

Sally, who'd been with Lynn ever since she left Randy Allen and started her own column, and who probably knew more about her famous and powerful employer than anyone else in the world, hesitated a moment before speaking.

"Andi's not calling to push studio product," she said finally.: "Andi wants to talk to you about Erin Connolly."

"Oh." The sound of the word as Lynn uttered it was not unlike the surprised gasp of someone who has unexpectedly been hit in the stomach. She recovered quickly, her eyes narrowing in speculative interest. "In that case, Sally," she said softly, "I think you got your priorities right."

She turned around, walking quickly back into her office, and settled into the swivel chair before punching down line three and picking up the phone.

"Andi, how are you?" she exclaimed warmly. "I swear, I don't know where the time goes. It's been ages since we've talked. What are you people up to these days?"

"Did Sally tell you why I'm calling?" the tense voice asked.

"Why, no, I don't believe she did," Lynn replied innocently. "She just said you had something very important to relate. A new picture, darling? Is that it? Or are you about to confirm the rumors that you've stolen Frederick Landsman from Columbia, she chuckled. "You do know I had that story first, don't you?"

"Actually, it's none of the above, as they say," Andi laughed nervously. "It's Erin Connolly I want to talk to you about."

"Erin Connolly?" Lynn said vaguely. "But whatever for, darling? She's washed up. Her last picture bombed terribly! Surely you people aren't considering bringing her into the studio as an independent producer? I mean, I wouldn't consider that a news story. More like a requiem mass, I'd say."

"Please, Miss Powers, don't play games with me," Andi implored her. "I want to destroy Erin Connolly, and I think you do too. Just let me come to your office and I'll tell you how we can do it."

"That's a very strange statement," Lynn announced coldly. "I assure you I have no interest in destroying anyone, much less Erin Connolly. She's accomplishing that quite well on her own. I think this phone call of yours was a big mistake. For your sake. I'll try to forget it."

"You owe it to your public to give them the facts," Andi pleaded. "Won't you at least let me come to you with those facts?"

"You're very determined, aren't you?" Lynn said curiously.

"Very determined," Andi answered grimly.

"Well, that in itself is rather interesting," Lynn said slowly. "All right, Andi Steiner, I'll see you in my office at two o'clock, tomorrow. But please don't be late. It will be enough of a problem just finding time to fit you in."

"I won't be late, Miss Powers," Andi promised fervently.; "And you won't be sorry you took the time, when you see what I have for you."

****

"This is your big story on Erin Connolly?" Lynn said incredulously. "That she takes drugs?"

"It's been enough to ruin a lot of people in this industry," Andi replied defensively.

"But you have no proof! You expect me to go with a column based on nothing but gossip? Hell, if I published blind items about suspected drug users in the movie industry, I'd be out of business in two weeks from libel suits alone."

Lynn leaned back in her swivel chair and stared thoughtfully at Andi. "What is it with you, anyway? Why do you want to bring her down?"

"It's a long story, and it happened a long time ago," Andi said bleakly. "Suffice it to say that 1 trusted her, I thought she was my best friend. Then she betrayed me and stole the one thing I wanted more than anything else in the world."

"I see," Lynn remarked quietly. She closed her eyes for a brief moment, remembering with pain how Erin Connolly had done exactly the same thing to her.

When she opened her eyes and looked at the unhappy woman sitting in front of her, Lynn's expression was kind and gently pitying. "I'm very sorry, Andi. I know how much something like that can hurt. But I don't see any way I can help you. I just don't print unsubstantiated rumors."

"But what if they aren't unsubstantiated?" Andi's hands twisted nervously in her lap. "What if you got a sworn statement from the doctor who supplies her with cocaine?"

"Doctor?" Lynn asked sharply.

"Warren Felber. Surely you've heard the stories about him? That he supplies half of Hollywood with its drugs?"

"Yes, I've heard that," she frowned. "I've never wanted to believe it, though. Warren is an excellent doctor and a very nice human being. I went to him to have my nose done, as a matter of fact. Did you know that?"

"No, I didn't." Andi dropped her eyes.

"Well, that's neither here nor there," Lynn said with sudden briskness. "Anyway, what you're suggesting is totally preposterous. Even if Warren is involved in the drug trade, he's hardly about to jeopardize his position by admitting to it, no matter what guarantees I give him about confidentiality. And I have no interest in doing an expose on the man. I'll leave that up to those so-called investigative reporters."

"He'll sign that statement for you," Andi said. "Just as soon as you show him this." She reached into her large handbag, drew out a manila file folder and laid it on Lynn's desk. "Once you read that, Miss Powers, you'll never doubt for a minute that he'll sign it."

Andi stood up, a twisted smile on her face. "And all I can ask from you is to do what's right." She walked out of the office.

Lynn stared after her in confusion. The phones began to ring again. She looked down at the brightly lit buttons, started to punch one of them and pick up a call, then shook her head.

Damned if the woman hasn't gotten to me, she muttered as she opened the file folder. Her eyes immediately widened in|shock as she saw the headline in the first article.

"Jesus Christ!" she exclaimed. "Jesus Christ, Warren, how did you|get away with this for so long?"

Warren Felber, a small, dapper man with warm, friendly eyes and quick, deft hands, was Hollywood's most prestigious plastic surgeon. Stars who were outraged at the thought of having to wait for anything—a salesperson at Gucci's, a table at the Bistro, or even a traffic light—meekly signed up six months in advance to get an appointment with him.

Part of the reason for Warren's fame and popularity was that he did truly marvelous work on sagging faces and bodies. But mostly it was due to the way he took care of his patients. As a plastic surgeon, he had legal and almost unlimited access to the very best cocaine. He was also a very considerate man. The street price for an ounce went as high as $3000. Warren charged only $1000. And no one begrudged him his considerable profit, even though they knew the pharmaceutical companies gave him the standard professional rate of $27 an ounce. After all, he was a doctor and could be counted on to warn an overenthusiastic sniffer when his or her septum was in danger of being destroyed. It gave his patients a comfortable feeling of being cared for.

Most of the time Warren was a very happy man. He made $250,000 a year legally, and $600,000 a year illegally. And he didn't have to pay one penny of tax on the $600,000.

But there were nights when suppressed fears broke through his guard, emerging in the form of nightmares which brought him awake, sweating and trembling, to find his wife bending over him anxiously.

He and his wife never spoke at these times, for there was nothing comforting to say. She would simply hold him against her breast, stroking him gently until he fell back to sleep. And the next day he would try to forget that even the $250,000 he earned was basically illegal.

Warren Felber, once a brilliantly promising young surgeon, had lost his license to practice medicine when he was thirty years old and the nurse at his hospital tearfully admitted to her superior that he had performed an abortion on her. The matter was quickly hushed up by the hospital's governing board, and he'd gone three thousand miles away to try and forget the whole terrible experience.

During the next five years, he surreptitiously practiced medicine in a small New Mexico town. No one ever challenged his credentials. Emboldened by his luck, he moved to Arizona and worked openly for a government-sponsored clinic. A full year passed, and there wasn't even the slightest ripple of suspicion about him. Excited and hopeful, he took his family to Los Angeles and opened an office in Beverly Hills.

Business was very slow at first. Then one day an aging and almost forgotten actress came to him. When he'd asked her curiously who had recommended him, she had smiled wryly and replied, "The Yellow Pages." Later, she admitted that she'd called fifteen plastic surgeons before him, but he was the only one she could afford.

It had been a number of years since she'd worked, and she'd been existing on her Social Security checks and a small savings account. Then her agent called with a job offer for a TV commercial.

"It's absolutely perfect for you!" he enthused. "The only thing is," he added apologetically, "you'll have to get rid of those bags under your eyes."

The operation was a success and she not only got the part in that commercial but was soon signed up for three other commercials.

There was only one problem. Under the fierce lights of the camera, the sensitive new skin around her eyes dried and tightened, causing her excruciating pain.

Warren, who had become genuinely fond of the spunky little woman, compassionately gave her a prescription for the anesthetic cocaine to ease her suffering. She was tearfully grateful and promised she'd find some way to show her gratitude.

A few months later, Warren was astounded to find new patients pouring through his doors, all recommended directly or indirectly by the aging actress.

"Who would ever have imagined she knew all these people?" he said wonderingly to his wife. But it didn't take him long to realize that most of them were more interested in his prescriptions than his surgery. He agonized briefly about how to handle the situation, then decided since he was living on borrowed time anyway he might as well make the most of it.

It had worked out very well. The world he operated in was a very protective one. His patients needed him more than he needed them, and so everything was kept very quiet. There had never been a hint of scandal or trouble.

Warren comforted himself with the thought that he had never been responsible for anyone's addiction. He had never "turned on" anyone in his life. They only came to him after their drug habits had been well established. Actually, he told himself, he was performing a humanitarian service. For God knows what might happen to those people if he sent them out into the streets to buy the dangerously polluted drugs that sold there.

But Warren's rosy-eyed view of himself was about to be brutally shattered as he walked into his examining room, where Lynn Powers waited for him.

"Well, Lynn, what brings you here today?" he asked cheerfully. "Nothing serious, I trust." He reached out a gentle hand to touch her face. "Nose bleeds? Trouble breathing?"

"Don't!" Her voice held a peculiar mixture of command and entreaty as she pulled away from him.

Baffled, he dropped his hand and gazed at her with concern. "Good heavens, my dear, what's wrong?"

"Warren." She stopped and swallowed. "Warren, there's nothing wrong with my health. I'm here on business. I want to talk to you about Erin Connolly. And the fact she regularly picks up drugs from you."

His face went as white as the immaculately starched surgical smock he wore. "I . . .1 don't think I understand."

"Yes you do, Warren. You understand perfectly."

"What is it you want?"

He looked so stricken, so bewildered, she had to turn away for a moment. When she finally managed to speak, her voice was unsteady. "I'm really sorry to involve you in this, Warren. Please believe me when I tell you I mean you no harm. All I want is to see justice done. Erin Connolly is a vicious, unprincipled creature who deserves to be punished. And with your help she'll get that punishment. All you have to do is acknowledge she's a heavy drug user. I won't use your name, I promise! And her attorneys won't be pressing any charges after they see the statement you sign," she added with a wintry smile.

"But she isn't," Warren said hoarsely. "She only picks up the drugs for Derek Marston. She doesn't even know they're illegal drugs. She thinks they're just medications. I would be committing professional suicide if I signed a statement like that. You don't know what you're talking about when you say you'd protect me. I wouldn't have any protection at all! I'd be indicted on so many counts, I can't even add them up."

He collapsed on the small stool in front of the examining table and buried his head in his hands. Then after several long moments, while he forced himself to take slow, shallow breaths to reduce his frantic hyperventilation, he raised his head and looked at her.

"But I can't imagine why we're even having this conversation." he said evenly "You've come to me with a completely unfounded charge. One that you most certainly can't prove and one that I will deny categorically, " he added with sudden grimness. "Now I think you should leave."

"No, Warren. You're not going to kick me out. Not after you read this." She handed him the manila folder which revealed in excruciating detail the truth about how he lost his license as a doctor, had been practicing illegally for years and become the major supplier of illegal drugs for celebrities.

He took one look at it and uttered a groan like a mortally wounded animal. "Oh God. Oh dear God!" He gazed at her with haunted eyes. "Where did you get this?"

"Does it matter?"

"No," he said dully. "No, I guess it doesn't." He sighed and passed a trembling hand over his brow. "You can give me the statement now."

She took it out of her purse and started to hand it to him, then paused.

"Wait a minute, Warren. I think I have a better idea." She nodded thoughtfully to herself, a small smile beginning to play around her mouth. "Yes indeed, Warren. A much better idea." The smile grew into a broad grin as she looked at him. "And this time I really can guarantee you'll be safe. Your name will never come into it. Now listen to me very carefully."

****

"Arc you sure, Rosa?" Erin asked with a puzzled frown.

"Yes, Miss Connolly. A Dr. Felber. He says it's important."

"Well, I think I geared myself up needlessly to take this call." she laughed ruefully. "I was all prepared to bravely confront Harry who's announcing my picture is being withdrawn from distribution or, at the very least, to hear Max inform me I'm on the brink of bankruptcy."

The maid stared at her uncomprehendingly, and Erin gave an apologetic shrug.

"Never mind, Rosa. It's all right. I'll take the call in the study. And maybe I'll have a little lunch afterwards. One of those special enchiladas of yours with salad."

"Oh yes, Miss Connolly!" Rosa beamed, the gold tooth in the front of her mouth gleaming. "I go start that immediately!"

"Hello? Warren? Are you there?"

"Yes. Yes, I'm here. I hope I didn't catch you in the middle of something."

"No, nothing important. Just looking over some scripts." She hesitated. "How are you, Warren?"

"Me? Oh, I'm just fine." He coughed. "Well actually, not perfectly fine."

"Good Lord, Warren, what's wrong?"

"Well, certainly nothing serious." He gave an uneasy laugh. "Mostly my wife's nagging. She thinks I'm overworking. But then, I guess all wives feel that way."

"Yes, I suppose they do," Erin said uncertainly.

" I don't want to bore you with all this," he announced with sudden vigor, "The point is. . . the point is that I'll be leaving at the end of this week for a medical conference in Switzerland, and my wife insists we stay there for a long holiday. Maybe two months. Or more."

"Two months or more? Wow, that could be a real problem for Derek. Do you have anyone who'll fill in for you?"

"I know," he interrupted quickly. "It was the first thing I said to my wife. How could I possibly leave my patients alone without treatment for all that time? Well, obviously I'm not going to do that. Which is why I'm calling you."

"Well, Derek will really appreciate that. He depends on your prescriptions. What do you suggest?"

"A visit as soon as possible. Do you think you could make it into my office tomorrow morning?"

"Of course. What time?"

"Would ten o'clock be convenient?"

"Yes. Ten would be fine."

****

Erin leaned back against the car seat as she patted her purse, which bulged slightly from the large package inside it, before starting the engine and driving out of the underground garage that served the exclusive Beverly Hills medical building where Warren Felber's office was located.

Maybe it would be a good idea to continue this stockpiling even after Warren came back, she thought. It would save her all those weekly trips to his office, because Derek was practically a one man pharmacy, supplying all his friends when they came down with anything.

The traffic light at Topanga Canyon and Pacific Coast Highway flickered a warning yellow before changing into red. Erin was only a few feet away from the intersection and going very fast. She took a chance and sped through it. Seconds later she heard the siren and saw the Highway Patrol car zooming up behind her.

"Oh shit!" she exclaimed in disgust. As the car approached her, she slowed down and pulled off on the shoulder of the highway.

"Could I see your driver's license, ma'am?" the officer asked politely as he peered through the open window at her.

"The light was yellow, officer," she said earnestly. "If you were behind me, you could see that. The only safe thing to do was go through it."

"Yes, ma'am. Now, your driver's license?"

She heard footsteps crunching on gravel, looked around in surprise, and saw a second uniformed cop circling her car.

"What's he doing?" she asked in confusion.

"Please, ma'am, just give me your driver's license," he said stolidly.

She opened her purse and reached for her wallet. The cop's eyes narrowed sharply as he saw the package inside.

"Step outside the car," he barked suddenly. "Don't make any sudden moves. Open the door, and come out as I direct you."

Erin stared in terror at the gun pointed at her.

****

"Isn't this one of your patients?" Warren's wife asked.

She had unfolded the newspaper left by the room service waiter who'd just brought the breakfast tray into their elegant suite in New York's Plaza Hotel, where they were resting up before catching their flight to Europe.

Warren stared at the headlines which screamed, "FAMOUS HOLLYWOOD PRODUCER IMPLICATED IN DRUG RING"

With a sick feeling, his eyes dropped to the story below.

"The Los Angeles police received an anonymous tip at ten-thirty yesterday morning that Erin Connolly, the brilliant and beautiful twenty-eight-year-old Hollywood producer whose film Street Scene swept the Academy Awards two years ago, had just picked up a large shipment of cocaine that would later be sold and distributed by Miss Connolly to various members of the film industry whom she has been supplying for several years. When California Highway Patrol officers stopped and searched her car on Pacific Coast Highway shortly after receiving the anonymous phone call, they discovered . . ."

The newspaper print blurred in front of Warren's eyes and he bolted from the table, reaching the bathroom barely in time.

TWENTY

The oversized metal key jangled harshly in the lock as the guard opened the door of the large, crowded holding cell. Erin was numb and sat with her head bowed, not even bothering to look up. During the first few hours of her confinement, she'd leaped to her feet and run forward eagerly each time the door had opened, sure that this would be the time someone had come to release her. But as the slow, agonizing hours of the afternoon passed into night with no sign of reprieve for her, she gradually began sinking into a state of hopeless depression.

"Why, oh why," she moaned for at least the fiftieth time, "was I so incredibly stupid as to call the beach house instead of my attorney?" In her first frightened panic, all she'd been able to think of was getting hold of Derek. But of course he wasn't there when she called, and Rosa came completely unhinged at learning Erin was in jail, breaking into tears and lapsing into rapid Spanish so that Erin was unable to make any sense at all out of talking to her. Nor was her desperate pleading with the police to allow her another phone call of any avail. The law allowed her one call. She'd made it, and that was all she'd get.

"Connolly. Erin Connolly," the guard shouted.

Absorbed in the miserable litany of self-castigation, her mind screened out the words. She rocked back and forth, continuing to moan softly to herself. The guard, an impatient edge to his voice now, yelled her name again.

"Hey. Hey, honey, ain't that you?" the woman next to her whispered, nudging her.

"What?" she said blankly. Then as the guard yelled her name once more, the words suddenly penetrated.

"Here!" she cried frantically. "Here!" She stood up and ran toward the door.

"You're Connolly?" he asked suspiciously.

"Yes."

"Well, it sure took you long enough to answer," he grunted, examining her carefully. "Still strung out, huh?"

"Is that a legal question, officer?" she asked with a sudden cold bite to her voice.

He shrugged. "None of my business, lady. Come on, there's someone waiting for you."

Erin gazed unbelievingly at the trim, dapper figure who came forward to meet her, his hands outstretched in a welcoming gesture.

"Well, my dear, this is hardly the occasion I would have chosen to renew our acquaintance," Arnold Scorsi smiled. "It certainly doesn't compare with that delightful party you gave after your picture won the Academy Award, where you so graciously entertained my wife and myself."

"Arnold, what are you doing here?" she asked in a stunned voice.

"Surely that's obvious, isn't it? To get you out of this dreadful place. Come on, now," he said soothingly, "we have a few papers to sign, then you'll be free and we'll go somewhere to talk."

"But I still don't understand," Erin said as Arnold led her out to his car and considerately held the door open for her. "How did you hear about this? And why did you come down to help me? We haven't talked to each other since that party."

"My dear Erin, there's no time limit on friendship," he chided her gently. "As to your first question, I happen to know several police reporters quite well."

"Are you going to defend me, Arnold?" Erin asked hesitantly as she got into his car and he drove them to a quiet restaurant where there'd be no Hollywood people in it and sat down in a booth at the back of the room. "I know everyone probably says this, but I'm really not guilty. I was just picking up what I thought were legal medications for Derek Marston."

"But Mr. Marston is not about to admit that, is he?

"Apparently not. Oh, God, I can't believe how stupid I was! I knew Derek took drugs. And everyone who passed through his place used drugs. But I'd become a hired hand. First, it was reading manuscripts and screenplays for him. Then it was shopping for Rosa, his cook, because she didn't drive. I even took his clothes to the cleaners. So picking up his medications just seemed like part of the job."

"The thing is . . ." Erin paused as the waiter set the large seafood salad in front of her. "The thing is," she continued in a small, unhappy voice, "I'm not sure I can afford your fees. I know you're very expensive, and I've had some financial setbacks lately. Actually, I don't really know what my financial status is at the moment."

"Don't worry about it, Erin. Just consider this a favor between friends. I'm confident you'll find a way to repay that favor one of these days."

Erin felt a cold shiver go through her at his words. The thought of being in Arnold Scorsi's debt was the most awful thing she could imagine. No it wasn't, she realized suddenly with a choking feeling of terror. Being sent to prison was much worse. Anything, anything at all, was preferable to that. And there was no doubt in her mind that she could be sent to prison. The police had made that all too clear. Would her attorneys be able to save her from that? They were careful corporation lawyers. They wouldn't even know where to start on a case like this. They probably wouldn't even care, she admitted miserably to herself. Con-Well Productions was their only genuine concern. So that left Arnold Scorsi as her one hope.

"Thank you, Arnold," she said huskily. "I accept your favor with gratitude, and I promise to repay you whenever and however I can."

"It never occurred to me that you wouldn't. But you must do exactly as I tell you."

"Well. . . well, that goes without saying," she stammered, unnerved by his swift and unexpected change from warm comforting friend to cold, demanding accuser. "What is it that you want me to do?"

"First, you move out of that beach house. I don't want any continuing connection between you and Derek Marston. It will only hurt our case. Everyone knows Derek is into drugs. It's an angle I may be able to play up."

He paused for a moment and gazed at her quizzically. "Unless you feel a need to protect him?"

"No." Her throat was very dry, and it took her a few seconds to swallow. "No, I don't need to protect him."

"Good," he said approvingly. "That's one problem out of the way. Now, the next thing you're going to do is move into this apartment in Westwood. A friend of mine owns the building, and the penthouse apartment is currently available. You'll love it."

"But how can I afford it?" she asked in shock.

"Erin, I already told you not to worry about these things," he said a little impatiently. "I'm taking care of everything." He handed her a card. "Here's the address of the building and the name of the manager, who'll be expecting you. I want you to move in there today. Is that understood?"

"Yes."

"All right. Now, after you get settled in I want you to make an appointment with this doctor." He flicked through his wallet and pulled out another card. "He'll give you a complete physical, start you on vitamin shots, and get you back into shape. When we go into court, you have to look like a clean, healthy, all-American girl."

"Do I look that bad, Arnold?"

"You look exhausted. Things have not gone well for you recently and it shows. Just take a look in a mirror, Erin. You're only twenty-eight years old, but you'd never know it from that face."

"Do I really look that bad?" she asked pitifully.

"I'm afraid you do." Then his cold smile grew warm. "But it's hardly fatal, my dear. You're young and basically healthy. We'll have you looking the way you should in no time at all. And that, believe me, is very important." There was a sudden faraway look in his eyes. "Very important indeed."

The strict health regimen Arnold Scorsi's doctor put Erin on worked wonders with her appearance. The vitamin shots, plus a carefully planned diet and a special therapy and exercise program, had restored the luminous glow of health to her complexion. She had gained ten pounds, which did away with the gaunt, haggard look that had aged her and gave her back her natural youthful vitality. She was sleeping well, her brilliant green eyes once again sparkled with life, and she had never looked more beautiful. Arnold was visibly delighted.

"If I weren't a happily married man, I think I'd fall in love with you on the spot."

"In that case, let's hope the judge is an unhappily married man."

He threw back his head and laughed. "Well put, my dear. I shall endeavor to find such a judge." He gazed at her appreciatively. "You have spirit, Erin Connolly. I like that."

She smiled as she thanked him, then the smile faded as she thought of what was still ahead of her. "Have they set a date for the trial yet?" she asked a little tremulously.

"I've got us on the docket for next week. Now don't worry," he said quickly as he saw the sudden apprehension in her eyes. "Do exactly as I say, and everything will work out just fine."

Arnold Scorsi was as good as his word. He presented Erin as an innocent victim, an unknowing courier for Derek Marston. It was on his instructions, Arnold told the judge, that Erin had driven into the city that day to pick up the package. She had no idea what was in it.

His defense was skillful and extremely persuasive, with witnesses who swore that in all the times they had been at Derek's beach house Erin had never used drugs. That in fact she had tried to persuade Derek to stop using them, and believed she had succeeded in that endeavor. What finally convinced the judge was his quiet but impassioned plea to consider the facts of what had happened when Erin was stopped by the police and subsequently taken into custody.

"Now, your honor, you know as well as I that people who deal in drugs are all too well aware of the consequences if they get caught," Arnold said softly. "Which is why they always have attorneys on tap to rush to their rescue. An unfortunate situation," he added sadly, "because all too often those attorneys manage to free them and then they go on peddling their dangerous wares.

"But that didn't happen in this case!" he announced, his voice rising sharply. "Erin Connolly, like everyone else in these circumstances, was allowed only one phone call. And what did she do with that one phone call to freedom? Did she call an attorney, who could be counted on to race down and bail her out of jail? No! She did what any normal, bewildered, frightened, and innocent person would do. She called the man who had sent her after the package, in the trusting belief that he would come down and explain the whole nightmare away. Of course he didn't. He didn't even accept the phone call from her. And so this poor woman was forced into the incredible humiliation of spending a night in jail, not even understanding what had happened."

Arnold wearily let his arms drop to his side at this point. "Your honor, 1 will leave it up to you to decide where justice lies in this case."

The judge, who had become increasingly mesmerized by Erin's glowing green eyes, which had been fixed soulfully on him during Arnold's entire speech, almost lost his grip on the gavel as he pounded it down and announced with more than a trace of huskiness, "The court finds Erin Connolly not guilty. Case dismissed."

"You were wonderful, Arnold," Erin said gratefully as he escorted her out of the courthouse and drove her back to her apartment. "I can't thank you enough. But how in the world did you manage to keep Derek from contesting that charge you made against him?" she asked curiously.

"Oh it wasn't all that difficult," he said casually. "After all, he wasn't on trial. You were. And when his attorney pointed out to him how messy things could get if he came into court, he immediately saw how wise it would be to disappear for a while until things blew over. Besides, by the time the police showed up at his beach house with a search warrant, there wasn't a trace of drugs to be found anywhere in the place. So then it comes down to a case of his word against yours, and since you've been tried and acquitted I rather imagine the police will simply drop the whole matter.

"Of course," he added with a dry smile, "I must tell you that Derek does not harbor particularly warm feelings toward you at this juncture. I hope you were not planning to continue your relationship with him."

"No. It occurred to me during the trial that would not be a very feasible idea. Nor one that even interests me," she announced with sudden grimness. "It's a chapter of my life I would like to put behind me and forget as soon as possible."

"A highly intelligent decision." He pulled up in front of her apartment building. "Because all the good chapters are still ahead of you. Now take care, and we'll be in touch soon."

Erin felt a sudden cold chill go through her at his words. "In touch soon?"

"Well of course. You don't think I'm just going to desert you at this point, do you? I'll want to know how you're getting on. And if you have any problems, please feel free to call me."

"Yes, Arnold, I'll do that. When . . . when do you want me to call you?"

"Good heavens, my dear, only when and if you need to. What in the world did you think I meant?"

"I-I don't know. I thought maybe ..."

"Erin, I can see this trial has been a terrible strain on you. You need time to relax, to pull yourself together. Go on, now," he commanded, leaning over to open the car door. "Start building those nice chapters in your life. All I ask is that you remember I'm a true friend, ready whenever you need me."

As the next few months passed and Erin slowly began picking up the shattered pieces of her life and putting them back together again, she forgot all about Arnold Scorsi. He never called, wrote, or even made his presence known at the apartment building he had found for her. The manager of the building appeared during the second month of her occupancy and somewhat diffidently asked her if she wanted to sign a lease on the place.

"As you know, ma'am, the owner's original lease is up now," he said with a shy smile. "And apparently he's not going to renew it." He cleared his throat. "I know you've been subletting, something we don't ordinarily allow, but you've been such a fine tenant that we'd be happy to turn the lease over to you, if you're interested."

She signed the lease immediately, because she'd fallen in love with the beautiful, spacious penthouse apartment that offered spectacular views of both the city and the ocean. She also signed it because she was finally able to afford it. The recent sessions with Max, Con-Well Productions comptroller, had been as grim as they were exhausting; but she was forced to admit that everything he said made sense. She really had no choice except to follow his advice.

His gloomy predictions about Body Count had come true with a vengeance. The picture had come close to forcing her production company into bankruptcy. Only the money from the foreign-distribution sales of Street Scene had saved Con-Well Productions from going under. But that money had just about run out, and the upkeep on the Century City business offices and San Fernando studio was slowly but surely bleeding the corporation to death.

"Which is a ridiculous situation," Max said with considerable asperity. "You could be realizing a considerable profit by renting out the studio to independent producers. It's an excellent facility. Anthony did a first-rate job when he built it. I know at least ten companies who'd pay top dollar for the use of it."

He took off his glasses, polished them vigorously, then frowned as he put them back on. "The same is not true of these offices," he said as he looked around. "They are, to put it bluntly, a total waste of money. We have no business to transact in them. Ergo, we have no business being in them. Close them down. Lay off the staff. And the sooner the better!"

"I know you're right, Max," Erin sighed. "But where does that leave Con-Well Productions?"

"Alive, and isn't that what you really want? A year from now, when all this unpleasant publicity disappears, you'll be in shape to start producing again, if you're careful about the way you handle your money."

"You don't have to worry about that," she assured him with a grim smile. "This town hasn't seen the last of Erin Connolly. I'm going to be back bigger and better than ever. And if it takes a year of scrimping and saving to accomplish it, well then, I'll be the best scrimper and saver you've ever met."

It wasn't in Erin's nature to scrimp and save, and she loathed every moment of it. But she did it, knowing she had no other choice. Even if she had money, there was no way she could produce a successful picture at this time. Arnold Scorsi had saved her from a jail sentence, but there was no way he could save her from the harsh judgment of Hollywood. She was a pariah now in that close-knit society. She'd originally forced her way into it as an unwelcome outsider, which was a sin in itself, and then compounded that sin by becoming notorious in an ugly drug scandal. Half the town wouldn't even speak tot her. The other half licked its chops in eager anticipation of destroying her the moment she tried invading their ranks again,

Less than a week after Erin gave her reluctant approval, Max had rented out the sound stages at the San Fernando studio, and she realized wryly that he'd had the prospective tenants lined up all the time. But she could hardly complain. The combined revenues from the six-month leases would put Con-Well Productions solidly in the black for a full year, and Max assured her there would be no problem in either renewing the leases at the end of the six-month period or bringing in new tenants.

Erin then closed down the Century City offices, laying off all the staff except her secretary Nancy, and rented a tiny, cramped suite in an old run-down building whose only virtue was its Beverly Hills postal address.

"Well, Max, Con-Well Productions can't go completely out of business for a whole year," she said defensively when he found out what she'd done

"For all the business you'll be doing, you could work out of your apartment and be a lot more comfortable," he told her bluntly.

"But I wouldn't be. I just wouldn't be, Max."

"Oh all right," he grumbled. "If it's that important to you, go ahead. The amount of rent you're paying for the little rat trap isn't enough to make any difference anyway."

Erin had to admit Max's description of her new offices wasn't too far from the truth, as she looked around that first day after the movers left.

"You think you can hack this place, Nancy?" she asked doubtfully.

"I've seen worse." Nancy grinned at her. "Come on, boss, cheer up. It's only temporary. You'll put me back into the style I'm accustomed to in no time at all."

The phone rang, and they turned and stared at each other in shock. Then they both began to laugh.

"My God, Nancy, if that surprises us so much, we're in worse shape than I thought," Erin said ruefully, wiping the tears of laughter from her eyes.

"Are you expecting a call from anyone?"

"No, not even a bill collector."

"Well, in that case I guess it's safe to answer it." Nancy made her way around the packing boxes to the desk and picked up the phone.

Good afternoon, Con-Well Productions," she said brightly. "Yes, I believe she just came in. May I tell her who's calling? Thank you, sir. Just a moment, please." |

Nancy cupped her hand over the receiver and looked up at Erin. "Someone named Arnold Scorsi. You want to . . ."

She broke off abruptly as Erin's face turned a deathly white. "Erin? What's the matter?"

"Arnold Scorsi? Is that what you said?"

"Hey, take it easy," Nancy said in alarm. "I'll tell him you're not here. Now sit down before you fall down, and I'll get you a glass of water."

"No, it's all right." Erin took a deep breath. "I have to take the call." She walked stiffly over to the desk and held out her hand.

Reluctantly, Nancy handed over the phone, her eyes wide with concern as she watched Erin take another deep breath before speaking into it.

"Hello? Arnold?"

"Hello yourself. How's my favorite client doing?"

"Just fine," she said faintly. "How are you, Arnold?"

"Couldn't be better. Understand you signed a lease on that apartment. Glad to hear it. I knew you'd love it."

"Arnold, I know I still owe you for the first month's rent on it." She swallowed. "As a matter of fact, I was planning to call you about that this week. I'm really sorry it's taken me so long, but my financial situation is just beginning to get straightened out. However, I have some really good news." she continued feverishly. "It looks like I'll not only be able to pay you back for the apartment but take care of your legal fees as well. Just tell me what they are, and I'll get a check off to you immediately."

"Erin, Erin, what is all this ridiculous talk?" he protested. "Didn't I tell you all that was just a favor between friends? Surely you don't think I'm calling to ask you for money?"

"Well, you certainly have the right to." There was complete silence on the other end of the telephone, and Erin felt herself starting to perspire. She plucked at the blouse that was clinging damply to her. "Arnold? Are you still there, Arnold?"

"Sorry, my dear," he murmured. "One of those infernal transatlantic calls finally came through and my secretary inadvertently switched lines to take it. Please forgive me for keeping you on hold. Now, where were we?"

"Talking about the money I owe you," she replied tensely.

"No, no." His voice was a brisk reprimand. "How many times must I tell you that was a favor? Ah, now I remember! This time it is I who have a favor to ask of you. I do hope you're free this coming Wednesday evening."

"What?"

"Wednesday evening. You are free, aren't you?"

"I'm sure I can arrange it."

"Wonderful!" he exclaimed enthusiastically. "1 can't tell you how much I appreciate it. I know it's terribly short notice, but Senator Ryan made a special point of asking to have you there. He was most impressed with you when he met you, and this is quite an important party for him. He'll be announcing his official candidacy for the next Presidential race, and he's eager to have all his friends there."

Arnold chuckled. "I don't think you'll find going too much of a burden. It promises to be a most delightful party, and I can assure you that you won't be asked for any political contributions. This is simply a fun occasion."

"A party?" Erin was so giddy with relief to learn that all Arnold Scorsi wanted from her was to attend a party with him that she started to laugh. "Arnold, you've got a date!" she told him happily. "I'm long overdue for a good party."

It wasn't until the next day that she realized how strange the invitation was. Why would Johnny Ryan, a Presidential candidate, request the presence of a Hollywood producer who had been involved in a drug scandal, been on the verge of bankruptcy, and was being avoided like the plague by everyone in town? It made no sense at all. It was crazy!

There was only one answer. They wanted something from her. But that's just as crazy, she thought. Because she had absolutely nothing that could be of any possible use to them.

TWENTY ONE

There were over three hundred guests at the party, including some of the biggest names in Hollywood, but the man who commanded the most attention, after Johnny Ryan, was an advertising executive named David Bernstein who was rapidly becoming known as one of the prime movers and shakers in the world of politics.

All the experts agreed that his stunningly creative campaign had been responsible for putting the current President of the United States into office, and David had been besieged by offers from both parties when the incumbent President decided not to run again. To date, David had not announced that he'd accepted any of the offers, but his presence at the party caused reporters to buzz around him.

Erin had always been fascinated by men with power. She made her way quietly but determinedly through the crowd that surrounded David until she found an opening left by a harried waiter fighting his way back to refill his drink tray. She slipped into the vacant spot and stood there looking up at David, her green eyes glowing with interest. She had no idea that Arnold Scorsi was watching her from the far side of the room, a quiet contented smile on his face, as David turned away from a particularly obnoxious reporter, met her eyes, blinked, and then took her by the arm and moved her out of the crowd.

They left the party together and David took her to a restaurant named Melisse, which she'd never heard of before.

"It's my hideaway," he told her. "I never bring anyone from the business here. So I'm trusting you to keep it a secret."

It was a small, elegant, formal place, and the food was superb. The other patrons were quiet, expensively dressed couples who murmured to each other in soft voices and seemed several light-years away from the frenetic world she knew. She couldn't imagine that they had ever had to fight for anything in their whole lives, and that impressed her. She was also very impressed with David Bernstein. He was nothing like she'd imagined advertising executives to be. Everything about him suggested quiet, confident authority. He also possessed an immense charm and warmth that relaxed her and drew her out. For the first time she could remember, she actually talked about herself instead of manipulating the conversation into areas designed to make the other person open up and reveal himself. And by the time the cappucino was served, Erin thought she'd discovered the man she'd been looking for all her life.

During the next few weeks Erin existed in a state of delirious happiness, oblivious of everything but David. He was all she thought about, all she cared about. When she wasn't with him, she daydreamed about him, lovingly recalling the way his dark intense eyes lit up when he was excited about something, seeing the delicious curve of his lips as he grinned in amusement, hearing the rich sensual quality of his resonant voice, feeling his hands as he cradled her head between them and leaned down to kiss her, his mouth so warm as it fastened on hers.

Nancy sighed as she watched Erin staring dreamily into space, the contract on her desk lying just as she'd placed it over an hour ago, still unread.

"Hey, I'm all for love, but don't you think you're carrying it a bit far?" she announced from the doorway.

"What?" Erin blinked and gazed at her vaguely.

"That thing on your desk. You're the one who asked for it, remember? The television deal for your pictures."

"Oh that." Erin smiled. "Well, it's not really such a good deal, is it? I mean, they're insisting on the rights to Street Scene before they'll agree to pick up the other pictures. But Street Scene won't be available for another three months. So I think I'll just wait out those three months and auction off the rights to the highest bidder. And double my money in the process."

"I guess I should give thanks you haven't forgotten everything."

"Nancy, I never forget anything."

"Are you sure?" Nancy hesitated for a moment, then took a deep breath and resolutely plunged in. "Listen, Erin, I know it's none of my business, but you do know the guy's married, don't you? And he's got kids. I mean, I just don't see any future for you."

"You're really concerned, aren't you?" Erin said wonderingly.

"Are you kidding?" Flushed and embarrassed, Nancy tried a cocky smile. "It's my future we're talking about here, too."

"Of course it is. And I'm not going to let you down, Nancy. This thing between David and me is the best thing that's ever happened to me. It's making me stronger, more sure. Everything is going to work out for the best. Not just for me, but for the business and you as well. I promise you that."

"But what if he lets you down? What happens then?"

"David will never let me down."

****

The call from Arnold Scorsi came two days later. "Well, I think you enjoyed that party even more than I promised you would," he announced genially. "David Bernstein is a most enchanting fellow, isn't he?"

Erin felt an instant flash of apprehension, her instinct telling her that Arnold Scorsi was finally calling in his debt.

"Yes," she said cautiously. "He seemed quite pleasant. Actually, everyone did. It was a delightful party."

"Come now, my dear. Pleasant is such an anemic word. According to my sources, you're finding David a great deal more than pleasant."

Erin hesitated, unsure of how to answer. She and David had been very discreet. Did Arnold really know anything or was he just making an educated guess based on the fact that they'd left the party together? No, she thought dismally. He knew. He always seemed to know everything. Well the hell with it, she decided, suddenly angry. I'm sick and tired of his cat-and-mouse games.

"You're absolutely right, Arnold," she said evenly. "I find David Bernstein considerably more than just pleasant. Now, what's it to you?"

"Well, that's certainly direct." He sounded slightly taken aback. There was a pause, but when he spoke again his voice was once more smooth and assured. "I forget sometimes how forthright you can be, Erin. It's an interesting quality. It also has the virtue of saving time."

He coughed and paused for another brief moment before continuing. "I am correct, am I not, in assuming David's interest in you is as strong as yours in him?"

"You're correct, Arnold."

"Yes, I rather thought I was. Well, then, we shouldn't have any difficulties here. It's a very simple thing I'm asking. Get David Bernstein to handle Johnny Ryan's Presidential campaign."

"What?"

"Erin, you did hear me, didn't you?"

She stared baffledly into the phone. "Yes, Arnold, I heard you. But I don't understand you. At all! What has Johnny Ryan's campaign got to do with me and David? I mean, David was practically the main attraction at that party. I thought he'd already agreed to handle it. Besides, I don't know anything about these things. What could I do?"

"Please, Erin, no games," he said wearily.

"Arnold, I swear I don't know what you're talking about," she told him bewilderedly.

There was a long pause now on the other end of the phone. When Arnold finally came back on the line, his voice was thoughtful.

"I believe you, Erin," he said quietly. "Politics has never been your game, has it? Pictures. Film. That's what turns you on. It never occurred to you that David showed up at that party as a spy, did it? That he was checking out the competition because he'd already secretly pledged himself to another candidate and wanted to find out what they'd be up against."

"Are you serious?" Erin started to laugh. "David a spy? I've never heard anything more ridiculous in my life. He's the most honest, open person I've ever met. If I didn't know better, Arnold, I'd think you were smoking something. Believe me, you're completely wrong about this."

"I certainly hope so," Arnold said calmly. "It would make everything a great deal easier. In the meantime, I can look forward to your call tomorrow morning assuring me that David will be handling Senator Ryan's campaign, can't I?"

The happy, confident laugh suddenly died in her throat. "Arnold, I already told you I don't know anything about these matters. I thought you understood that. If you have any questions, you really should talk to David."

"If I could talk to David, I wouldn't be wasting my time with you," he remarked coldly. "That's apparently something you don't understand. Now, can I expect that call from you tomorrow morning?"

"Arnold, I can't do this!" she exclaimed frantically. "I can't make David's career decisions for him! How can you expect me to do such a thing?"

"How you manage it is of no concern to me," he said, sounding bored. "All that counts is that you do manage it. Because if you don't, you'll never make another motion picture in this town. And that, I assure you, is something I can manage." He hung up before she had a chance to say another word.

****

"You know, if it hadn't been for Johnny Ryan, we would never have met," Erin announced as she carried a tray of hot hors d'oeuvres out of the kitchen and set it down on the coffee table.

"Without question one of his finest achievements." David gave her an amused grin. "Does that mean he's won your vote?"

"Well, first he has to get the nomination. But of course that won't be any problem if you handle his advertising campaign," she remarked as she snuggled up next to him on the couch. "Everybody says that the candidate who has David Bernstein behind him is a shoo-in."

"I didn't know you were so cynical about politics."

"Cynical? I don't know what you mean, darling. I was complimenting you."

"But hardly the system," he said dryly. "Apparently you buy Joe McGinnis's thesis."

"Who?"

He shook his head. "Sorry, love, I guess that was way before your time. Joe wrote a book called The Selling of the President 1968. He was one of the first to contend that getting a man elected President of this country isn't too much different from selling a new detergent. Both go after the same national market and both, he claimed, succeed or fail based on their advertising efforts, irrespective of their merits. Remember Hubert Humphrey?"

"Hubert Humphrey?" She stared at him blankly. "What does Hubert Humphrey have to do with anything?"

David picked up his glass and absently swirled its contents. "Wait a minute. Let me see if I can remember how he put it. 'I'm fighting packaged politics. It's an abomination for a man to place himself completely in the hands of the technicians, the ghost writers, the experts, the pollsters, and come out only as an attractive package.' Now doesn't that sound just like selling soap?" David asked her with a wry smile.

"But that's your business you're talking about," she exclaimed in shock. "How can you do it if you feel that way about it?"

"Because I don't feel that way about it." He took a swallow of his drink, suddenly looking quite serious. "Erin, politics today is a mare's nest, and media holds a prime responsibility for putting it into that condition. All I try to do is even the score. Give the right people a chance to make it in this crazy arena. Because our country deserves it.

He shrugged and gave her a slightly embarrassed grin. "Forgive the soap box speech. And no pun intended. Now enough of all this. Where would you like to go to dinner?"

"David." She reached out tentatively and touched him. "David, are you going to handle Johnny Ryan's campaign?"

He looked at her in surprise. "No, of course I'm not. Where did you ever get that idea?"

"But you were at that party! Why did you go to the party if you weren't planning to run his advertising campaign?" she asked desperately.

"Hey, what is all this?"

"The thing is . . ." She paused. "The thing is I was thinking about giving a fund-raising affair for Johnny after you officially announced you'd be handling his campaign. You see, I've known Johnny for several years and am quite fond of him. So 1 thought it would be a nice thing to do."

She wet her lips nervously. "I was really looking forward to it. It never occurred to me that you wouldn't be handling his campaign. I mean, you were at that party."

"Honey, I don't understand why you keep harping on that," he said with an exasperated laugh. "If a movie producer gives a party to announce a new picture and a well-known director happens to show up at that party, does that mean he's going to direct the picture?"

"Yes," she said flatly. "It usually does."

"Oh." He looked faintly startled. "Well, that proves politics and show biz aren't as much alike as I feared."

"David." Erin leaned forward, her eyes fixed intently on him. "David, I want you to handle the advertising campaign for Johnny Ryan. He's a fine man, and I really want you to do it."

"You don't know what you're talking about," he said impatiently. "Johnny Ryan is a lightweight. Just another pretty face. He'd make a lousy president. Now why don't we make a bargain? I'll let you take care of the movie business and you let me take care of the political business. That way we'll both be fine."

"Aren't you being awfully unfair?" she asked tensely. "Why should Johnny Ryan be penalized just because he's good looking? After all, he's also a senator with an established record. Does being ugly mean you're automatically a better person? I mean, look at the other candidates! That dreadful Thurgood Ralston, for example. I wince every time I see him. Is it someone like that you're going to support?"

"No." David set his drink down on the coffee table and regarded her strangely. "As a matter of fact, the man I'm supporting is Richard Longworth. It's not for publication yet, though."

"Richard Longworth? I never even heard of him!"

"Well, that's a problem I'll be correcting soon," he smiled. "Longworth's one of those unsung heroes, an honest man who gives an honest day's work and has no time to play around and get media hype. He's a congressman from Wisconsin and one of the finest legislators around today. His voting record is outstanding, and his integrity is without question. He'll make a superior President."

"Were you already committed to handling his campaign before you came to Johnny Ryan's party?"

"Yes." David frowned as she continued to stare at him. "Why? What's the problem?"

"Oh God, Arnold was right! You were there as a spy."

"What?" He broke into laughter. "Erin, I don't know who Arnold is, but I think you should send him back to one of the studios. Maybe he could become the next Hitchcock."

"It's true, though, isn't it? You did come to that party, knowing you were going to support another candidate, just to check out the competition."

"Of course. That's standard operating procedure." His amused grin started to fade as she kept on staring at him.

"What the hell is the matter, Erin?"

"Everything," she said miserably. "Absolutely everything!"

"You want to tell me about it?" he asked, his eyes dark with concern.

"Do you love me, David?"

"You know I do." he said huskily. "I love you more than anything in the whole world."

"Even more than your principles?"

"Jesus Christ, Erin, what is this?" he asked in alarm. His face whitened as she turned away, refusing to speak. "That stupid little speech you made about wanting to hold a fundraiser for Johnny Ryan was all crap, wasn't it?" She nodded, unable to answer.

"Then lay it on me," he said heavily. "Tell me what it's really all about."

****

There was a long, painful silence in the room when Erin finished telling him about Arnold Scorsi.

"Please, David," she begged. "Please help me."

"Erin." He shook his head, not trusting his voice, then reached for his drink and gulped at it. "Jesus, Erin, how could you have let yourself get involved with someone like that? You must have known what kind of a person he is. You've lived in this town long enough to know that!"

"But what else could I have done? I was in jail. I was all alone. There was no one else to turn to. Besides, how was I to know this would happen? I didn't even know you then, David. I thought . . ."

She started to cry. "I thought the worst thing that could happen was that he'd want something from my production company. And I was willing to give him whatever he wanted. Because nothing could be as bad as going to prison. Nothing, David! Can't you understand that?"

"Christ!" He rose and started to pace the room. He stopped and turned to face her, his expression bleak.

"Don't you see what this means, Erin? If Arnold Scorsi wants me to handle Ryan's campaign, it means that your pretty little friend is something more than just a lightweight. Something very frightening. It means Ryan's a pawn for the people behind Arnold Scorsi."

"Do you want me to be responsible for electing a President who has to answer to those kind of people?" he shouted with sudden fury.

"David, I'm not asking you to get him elected. All I'm asking is that you handle his advertising campaign."

"Goddamnit, Erin, don't play the hypocrite to me now!" He turned on her savagely. "Or have my talents abruptly diminished during this past hour? After all, it was just a scant sixty minutes ago you assured me that any candidate who had David Bernstein backing him would be a shoo-in."

"'I'm sorry, David," she said quietly. "I don't have any of the answers you'd like to hear. I'm not an idealist. I know very little about politics, and I have to admit I don't really care very much. I've never known any politician that really changed this country for the better. Maybe your man Richard Longworth could accomplish that. But if he destroys me in the process, I would not find it a worthwhile accomplishment."

She gazed at him, her eyes steady now. "What we're really talking about is me. Which is the only thing I do know. And I don't want to be destroyed. You can save me, David, if you want to. It's all up to you."

He looked at her helplessly, this beautiful, bewitching, green-eyed woman who'd brought him to heights of ecstasy he'd never dreamed existed and so obsessed him that he could hardly eat or sleep for thinking about her. The thought of losing her was literally unbearable.

"All right," he said in a voice he had trouble recognizing as his own. "I'll take on Johnny Ryan's campaign."

"Oh, darling!" She flew over to him, covering him with kisses. "You've made me so happy, darling. You'll never know how much this means to me. And you mustn't worry. It's all going to work out just fine. Why, in no time at all we'll have forgotten the whole thing."

He knew she was wrong. It would not work out fine, and he would never forget it. But he could live with it, he told himself, as long as he had her. He could live with anything as long as he had her.

TWENTY TWO

Two months after David took on Johnny Ryan's campaign, Ardis Kendall's first book was published. It was titled Liberation and the advance publicity on it created such excitement that bookstores across the country were deluged with requests for it weeks before it came out. It was number one on all the bestseller lists within its first week of publication, and every studio in Hollywood was bidding for the screen rights.

Much of the excitement was generated by the notoriety of the author herself. Thirty five years ago, at the age of twenty, Ardis Kendall had made the front page of every major newspaper in the country when she publicly accused twenty of the top U.S. corporations of using women as slave labor, and backed it up with documented wage and salary figures she had managed to obtain, by what means no one ever learned, from the personnel files of those prominent corporations.

She continued to make news as she joined forces with the National Women's Political Caucus and Women's Active Alliance, and quickly became one of the most famous and, to many, most feared leaders of the feminist movement in America due to her startling exposes of the power elite in the country. Now, with her first book, she promised to deliver the most sensational revelations of her entire sensational career, for Liberation was reputed to rip the lid off some very explosive secrets in the lives of some very well-known public figures.

Erin had never felt such a fierce hunger for a property. David listened with patient indulgence as she paced like a restless tiger back and forth across the living room of her penthouse apartment, telling him in short, staccato sentences what a dynamic opportunity this was, how it could turn her whole career, her whole life, around and bring her back to the top for good. Of course he didn't believe for a moment that she had the faintest chance of getting the screen rights. It was obviously impossible. But then David still had a lot to learn about Erin.

Ardis Kendall's agent was horrified when his prize property announced that she was going to talk to Erin Connolly before she signed any studio contract.

"Have you lost your mind?" he shrieked. "She's poison, Ardis! Everything she touches dies. Please, please listen to me. You know I only want what's best for you."

"Nonsense, Leonard," she replied crisply. "You only want what's best for you. And you exaggerate ridiculously. Poison indeed," she sniffed scornfully. "The lady may have had some problems, but she's hardly poisonous. Besides, her lawyer did get her acquitted of that drug charge on the basis that she was deliberately framed. Which she probably was, considering that Derek Marston, that stupid stud, was involved. His manager undoubtedly set up the whole thing. Pigs, all of them."

Ardis munched pensively on the dry piece of whole wheat toast that, along with a cup of black coffee, comprised her entire breakfast as she sat in her expensive bungalow at the Beverly Hills Hotel watching her agent wolf down scrambled eggs, ham, and bagels thickly slathered with butter, jelly, and cream cheese. And once again she cursed her peasant ancestors who had given her a body and an appetite that would have been perfect for a truck driver but was a disaster for a bestselling female author. Sighing, she forced down the last, tasteless crumb and looked across the table.

"Anyway, Leonard, you're missing the point. Erin Connolly is the only major woman producer in this male-dominated town, and I think it would be a great mistake for me to ignore her totally. It would be a little hard to explain to the sisters."

"Well, if that's all there is to it." Leonard relaxed visibly, leaning back in his chair and giving her a relieved grin. "Okay then, go ahead and do your good deed, and I'll make sure we get some nice publicity out of it. But don't take too long about it," he warned her. "This town isn't like New York. It cools off as fast as it heats up. Today your book is the hottest property around. Tomorrow it could be forgotten."

"Don't worry, Leonard. I'm just as well aware of that fact as you. Which is why I scheduled a luncheon meeting with the woman today."

She pushed back her chair and stood up. "Now run along and do your publicity thing and let me get dressed."

"My pleasure, sweetheart," he beamed. "And tomorrow we'll get down to serious business." He blew her a kiss as he left the room.

She waved absently in return, then looked down longingly at the two bagels left in the basket next to his plate. "No, Ardis," she said firmly. "Be a good girl, and maybe we can give you a little treat for dinner."

But as she walked into the bedroom and gazed at her reflection in the full-length mirror, she decided glumly that there wouldn't be any treat for dinner either. "I wonder if Erin Connolly is as slim and beautiful as her pictures," she mused. She smiled and gave the finger to her mirror image. "So what if she is?" she announced. "Look where it got her. Nowhere! I'm the one with the power. Dumpy fifty five year old body and all."

Considerably cheered by that realization, she bypassed the expensive but dreary black dress designed to slim down her beefy contours and chose instead a bright, colorful pantsuit. While the pantsuit made her look like a balloon, it also made her feel relaxed and comfortable. And as she dressed, she found herself looking forward with interest to the upcoming lunch.

Ardis had been both amused and admiring about Erin Connolly's approach to her. Less than an hour after she'd checked into the Beverly Hills Hotel, the hand-delivered telegram had arrived at her bungalow. Its message was challenging, and its delivery more than a little arrogant. For Erin had blithely ignored all the sacred rules of procedure, going over the heads of publishers, managers, and agents to zero in directly on her quarry, the author of the book. Such things were rarely if ever done, especially when the producer not only had no ties to a major studio but was, in fact, practically ostracized by the entire movie industry.

Ardis had chuckled when she read the telegram and was still chuckling when the phone in her bungalow rang precisely fifteen minutes after the telegram had been delivered.

"All right, Erin Connolly, you've made your point." she'd announced into the receiver. "Let's have lunch tomorrow, and we'll discuss the matter."

"Ms. Kendall?" The voice on the other end of the line sounded slightly stunned. "You knew it was me calling?"

"Of course, child," she'd laughed. "Whatever your faults might be, I doubt that subtlety is one of them. So when my phone rings fifteen minutes after I get this telegram, who else could it be? You see, I've got you all figured out. So you'd better watch your step with me. You're dealing with a pro here, you know."

"Yes, I know. Which is why I'm making this effort. And if you'll allow me, may I thank you for being exactly that? A pro?"

"Oh, I think so." Ardis smiled, amused again. "Now I hope you don't mind having lunch here at the hotel, because I never go out in this crazy town. I wouldn't even know how to pilot a car down your insane freeways."

"Good Lord, Ms. Kendall, I wouldn't dream of asking you to do that," Erin had exclaimed. "I'd planned on our having lunch in the Polo Lounge. If that's all right with you."

"Sounds just fine, my dear. I'll see you there tomorrow at noon."

Ardis turned slowly now back and forth in front of the mirror as she recalled her conversation with Erin Connolly, then frowned unhappily as she saw the way the top of her pantsuit bulged out around her waist. Oh what the hell!" she told herself in disgust. Who cares? Certainly that woman won't. The last thing in the world she'll notice is how I look.

Ardis couldn't have been more mistaken.

"Ms. Kendall!" Erin raced forward as Ardis came through the doorway to the Polo Lounge and walked inside, holding out her hands in welcome. "What a pleasure to finally have the opportunity of meeting you."

"And what a pleasure to find you here waiting for me. Ardis cocked her head, a faint smile on her face. "I thought it was against the law in Hollywood to be on time."

Erin laughed. "I'm afraid it must seem that way some times, but it is not a practice I subscribe to. And I most certainly would not have been late for this meeting! I know how very valuable your time is, Ms. Kendall. May I thank you again for your courtesy in seeing me?"

"If you'll drop that Ms. Kendall crap and call me Ardis." The small, shrewd eyes roved over Erin in frank appraisal. "You really are as pretty as your pictures. Maybe even prettier."

Erin's own eyes narrowed slightly in sudden speculative interest as she observed the way the famous feminist author was looking at her. She returned the searching gaze with one equally searching, carefully noting every detail about Ardis as she took in the short cropped hair that was turning gray, the square face with its blunt features and pugnacious jaw, the thick shapeless body in its garish pantsuit.

"Being pretty in Hollywood is more a liability than an asset," she said lightly. "For every girl who's pretty, there are a thousand girls who are beautiful. It's the cheapest and least respected commodity in this town. I don't know a single woman who wouldn't gladly trade it all for what you have."

"Really?" Ardis said dryly.

"Really." Erin gave her a warm, glowing smile. "But of course you know that. It's what makes women everywhere care so much about what you write, and care so much about you as well. I hardly need to belabor the point to you, of all people.

Please forgive me, it just happens to be something that's quite important to me. Now let's go on in and get comfortable."

She took hold of Ardis's arm and started to lead her into the restaurant, then stopped abruptly. "Ms. Kendall? I mean, Ardis. I booked a booth for us inside, so we'd have a chance to chat in quiet. But maybe I'm being selfish. It's a beautiful day today. Perhaps you'd rather eat out on the patio?"

"No, you did just fine. To tell you the truth, I hate your California sunshine. It makes me squint, and puts lines on my face. And those rotten little patio chairs put creases on my bottom."

Erin gave a delighted laugh. "Ardis, you're wonderful! Because, you know, that's exactly how every woman in Hollywood feels. We've just never had the courage to come out and admit it. I think you should do a piece about it, and liberate us poor souls."

Ardis found herself laughing along with Erin as the maitre d' led them to a large, comfortable booth. "Maybe I will," she chuckled as she settled back in the booth, spreading her thighs to let air circulate between them. "Now, what do you recommend?" she asked as she opened the menu.

"For openers, the seafood salad."

Ardis blinked, feeling a sudden rush of heat as the luminous green eyes gazed into hers. "And then what?" she demanded hoarsely.

Erin smiled, a slow, teasing smile. "Well, why don't we wait and see how the seafood salad works out first?" she suggested mischievously.

****

"I don't believe it!" Leonard screamed in anguish the next day when Ardis brought him the contract from Erin. "Have you completely flipped out?"

"Stop foaming at the mouth, and just read the contract," Ardis instructed him calmly. "I think you'll find it an excellent deal. Erin has offered a higher percentage of the gross than any of the major studios. And, as you well know, that's where the real money is for a writer."

"Oh it's Erin, is it?" Leonard snarled. "A week ago you didn't even know the bitch. Now you're on a cozy first-name basis."

He tore at his thinning hair in frustrated rage. "Christ, if I didn't know better, Ardis, I'd think she got to you in some way. I mean, it's common knowledge she'll do anything to get a picture she wants—lie, cheat, steal, and God knows what else."

"She's a woman trying to make it in a man's world, and her options are limited," Ardis said gently.

She flushed and straightened in her chair as she saw her agent staring at her peculiarly. "And in case you've forgotten, that happens to be what my book is all about," she added with her usual crispness. "Besides, Erin Connolly is a first-class producer. I don't think you can argue with the quality of her work."

What Ardis refrained from mentioning was that Erin Connolly was also the most breathtakingly exciting woman she'd ever met. Her pulse began to race just at the memory of the way Erin had looked at her as she talked in that low, husky voice about how moved she had been by Ardis's book, and how deeply she felt that women owed each other a special commitment.

Ardis could hardly wait to see her again. Because she believed the promise she imagined in those beautiful, tantalizing eyes would turn into fulfillment. And oh what a fulfillment it would be! Ardis had never felt such desire in her whole life, as she signed the contract for film rights to her book.

She showed up unannounced at Erin's place the following evening, carrying two large bags of groceries. "I thought we'd eat in," she announced cheerfully as she barged inside without waiting for an invitation, setting the bags down on the counter in the kitchen, and opening the refrigerator door.

"My God, child!" she exclaimed in horror as she peered inside. "You don't have a single thing in here! I think I got here just in time."

" Ardis, I can't have dinner with you tonight," a stunned Erin exclaimed. " I already have a dinner date."

"Well, then, you'll have to cancel it." Ardis turned around, placing her hands on her hips and giving Erin a long, hard look. "Because you and me, baby, have some unfinished business to take care of. Business that can't wait any longer. You understand?"

Anger flared in Erin's eyes. "I'm afraid you're the one who doesn't understand. I don't take orders from anybody, and frankly I'm appalled that you should try giving them. It goes against everything I thought you stood for, everything that made me believe in you. I am equally appalled," she continued tightly, "by your storming into my home without even the bare courtesy of calling first to find out if it's convenient for me to see you. Now I think you'd better leave."

"What the hell are you trying to pull?" Ardis grabbed hold of Erin's arm.

"It's obvious we have a very basic misunderstanding here," Erin replied icily, freeing her arm with a curt gesture. "One we should clear up as soon as possible."

"Oh no you don't!" Ardis said, suddenly grim. "If you think for one moment I'm going to let you get away with making a fool out of me, you've got a lot to learn. Nobody, but nobody, makes a fool out of Ardis Kendall! My agent will have that contract nullified before you're through your first course with your dinner date tonight."

"I don't think so. Not when he finds out what's involved. After all, my dear Ardis, I'm not the one who has a reputation to protect. They could hardly say anything worse about me than they already have. But you? Well, that's an entirely different matter, isn't it? Imagine the shock and horror when your devoted public finds out that their esteemed leader is not only a lesbian, but a lesbian who used her position of power and influence to try and bully the only real woman producer in Hollywood into bed in exchange for the screen rights to her book."

Ardis withdrew but she didn't retreat. The story broke simultaneously in the Hollywood trade papers and the national newspapers shortly after production started on Liberation. "ARDIS KENDALL SAYS STAY AWAY FROM MY MOVIE!'" the headlines announced.

In the story that followed, Ardis stated that Erin Connolly had totally compromised the integrity of her book. "I don't know what she's afraid of, since she refused to tell me," Ardis was quoted as saying. "All I know is that I was proud of my book, but I can't be proud of the movie she's making out of it. She's killed all the truth in it, and left it without heart or guts."

The three leading actors cast in the movie broke their contracts the day after Ardis's story came out, and the director walked off the set two days later. A week later International Pictures triumphantly announced that they had just acquired the screen rights to Ardis Kendall's new book and would be starting on the picture immediately. Production on Liberation was quietly canceled.

Erin's career hit rock bottom after that, and her relationship with David deteriorated right along with it. There was no way she could tell him what had really happened, and his innocent questions and misguided sympathy drove her mad.

"Would you please do me a favor and just shut up about it?" she screamed. "How do I know why the woman planted that insane story? Because she's insane. What else can I tell you?"

Making matters worse was the fact that David was now thoroughly caught up in the campaign for Johnny Ryan, traveling around the country almost three weeks out of every month; and when he came back to Los Angeles he had the demands of his family to meet.

Erin, on the other hand, had nothing to do. The forced cancelation of Liberation brought her production company close to the edge of bankruptcy again. The New York investor who had put up the money for the picture angrily demanded the full amount of his investment back, plus interest, leaving Erin to absorb all the expenses that had been incurred. As a result, Con-Well Productions found itself completely stripped of its liquid assets.

Max sighed and muttered as he tried to find some financial solution out of the chaos, and Erin cursed and often cried as one long, lonely hour followed another while she paced back and forth in her apartment, staring out the window and waiting for David to come back to her.

Inevitably, she turned on him. "It's obvious you don't have time for me," she shouted one afternoon when he came over. "You have lunch with your business people, you have dinner with your family, and you fit me in between when it's convenient for you. Well, I'm not going to put up with it any longer! I'm going to find someone who has time for me all the time." She burst into tears.

"Erin, please," he begged.

"No," she sobbed. "This is it. Get out of my life. Give me a chance to find someone I can count on."

He left, but he couldn't stay away. Three weeks later he showed up at her apartment, pale and exhausted looking. "I can't live without you, Erin. I'm getting a divorce."

"Oh, David!" She threw herself into his arms, hugging and kissing him. "Oh, darling, I love you so much."

For the next few months they were very happy. David started taking her on his business trips with him, and since he had an extremely generous expense account they were able to enjoy the best that places like San Francisco, New York, Miami, and New Orleans had to offer. But it didn't last. Because all the exciting, glamorous, romantic trips in the world couldn't make up for the fact that she wasn't making pictures. So Erin went back to Hollywood to try again.

This time, however, she was stopped cold before she could even start. In the past, she'd been able to overcome all the incredible obstacles in her path because she'd always possessed the one big trump card, a bestselling property. But now, after Ardis Kendall's scathing denunciation of her, she found the world of literary agents and writers had implacably closed ranks against her. There wasn't one decent property in the entire town that she could get her hands on, because the major agents and writers flatly refused to sell to Con-Well Productions.

She fought it like she'd fought everything in her life, but nothing worked. The final humiliation was that all the third-rate agents and hack writers in Hollywood descended on her like vultures. There are no secrets in Hollywood. Everyone knew about the boycott being imposed on her, and they assumed she'd been brought to the point where she was desperate for any material. So they deluged her with their wares: books that had died after a minimal first printing; unsold and unwanted screenplays; shoddy, hastily improvised treatments; even pornography.

At first she haughtily rejected them. But as the months passed, and she became as desperate as they'd originally assumed she was, she swallowed hard and agreed to look at their material. She and Nancy spent hours at their desks in the small, cramped offices of Con-Well Productions in Beverly Hills, reading through the huge stacks of submissions in the forlorn hope that one, just one, might have some value.

Sometimes she and Nancy broke up at what they were reading, striking dramatic poses and declaiming various passionate purple passages to each other before collapsing into helpless laughter. That was on the good days. But there weren't many of those. Most of the days Erin just buried her head in her hands and tried to keep from crying.

And as the bad days steadily increased in number, Erin found her fighting rage turning into depression. Nothing was working, and she began to believe that nothing would ever work for her again. She came home one Friday afternoon, crawled into bed, and just stayed there.

When Nancy called anxiously the following Monday to find out why she hadn't shown up at the office and discovered the state Erin was in, her concern and alarm were so great it managed to penetrate through Erin's lethargic fog. Frightened now by the seriousness of the depression that held her in its grip, she realized she had to do something to break out of it before it destroyed her. But what?

The only real cure would be getting Con-Well Productions back into the business of producing pictures. However, the way things stood now, she reflected dismally, there was no chance of that.

Making things worse, David became increasingly unhappy about his campaign for Johnny Ryan after he'd learned the truth about the situation that had forced him into it. And his depression grew as he found out what was happening to Richard Longworth, the only candidate he'd truly believed in and committed himself to; for Longworth was desperately strapped for campaign funds and fighting a hopelessly uphill battle with minimal support from an advertising agency and public relations firm that was, to put the best possible face on it, second-rate.

Compounding David's depression at abandoning his political principles was the terrible guilt he felt at leaving his family. His wife had taken the divorce very badly, and his youngest son had run away. It took two private detectives almost a month to find him.

Consequently, he was moody and morose a great deal of the time. And this weighed heavily on Erin. She had finally managed to break out of her own depression, and she was damned if she'd let David drag her back into it. So they quarreled about that as well, with Erin frequently threatening to leave him.

After one particularly bitter fight, David showed up at the apartment with an armful of flowers and announced with forced gaiety that he was taking her to a party.

"It's just what we need to get us out of the doldrums."

"I don't want to go to a party," she said sullenly.

"Come on, honey," he coaxed. "It will do us good to go out and be with people for a change. You'll enjoy it, I promise."

"No I won't. I'll be bored to death. You know how I feel about politics."

"Of course I know how you feel about politics. I also know how you feel about the movie industry."

"What?"

"Surprise!" He grinned at her. "This is a very lavish party, in the best Hollywood tradition. No politics, all entertainment, and a cast of thousands. So what do you say?"

She looked at him uncertainly. "Whose party? And what's the occasion?"

"Harry Kingston, the man who invented the Hollywood party, will be our gracious host. And the occasion, I suspect, is some high level wooing of Sheldon Avery."

"Sheldon Avery?" Her head snapped up. "You mean the author of Secret Rites?

"The one and only," he agreed smilingly.

"But that doesn't make any sense." She shook her head, frowning. "Why would Kingston bother holding a party for Sheldon at this late date? Everybody knows that

Columbia offered a million dollars for his book, and frankly I thought his agent had sewed up the deal."

David shrugged. "I guess hope springs eternal in the hearts of movie producers when an Academy Award winning property is up for grabs. Especially when there's still no official announcement of the sale. On the other hand, maybe Harry Kingston knows what I do. Although I can't think it would be very useful to him."

Erin straightened suddenly and stared at him. "What do you mean, David? What do you know about Sheldon Avery?"

He looked at her, puzzled. "Well, I didn't realize it was all that big a secret. Avery is practically queer for the actor Keith Ramsey. He's worshiped the man all his life, even though he never met him, and his dream has always been to get Ramsey in one of his pictures. There's no doubt in my mind that Avery would happily give up a million dollars if some producer could guarantee delivering Keith Ramsey for the lead role in Secret Rites. Of course it's impossible. Ramsey is a very stubborn maverick."

David chuckled. "I must say I admire the hell out of that man Ramsey. He told the industry to fuck off after his last picture. He was retiring for at least a year, and he wouldn't be back until he felt like it. He meant it too. He's completely disappeared. No one knows how to reach him."

"Well in that case, I imagine you're right," Erin said softly. "It certainly doesn't sound like Harry Kingston has much of a chance."

She stood up, walked over to him, and gave him a kiss. "But I guess we don't have to worry about Harry Kingston's problems, do we?" she murmured as the tips of her fingers caressed the back of his neck. "We can still enjoy his party, can't we?"

"You'll go, then?"

"I wouldn't miss it for the world."

Erin closed in on Sheldon Avery forty minutes after she and David arrived at the gala party. "There's something extremely important I have to talk to you about," she whispered in his ear. "Something nobody else can hear. Meet me out on the patio in five minutes."

"Are you sure?" he gasped, hope and disbelief mingling in his wrinkled pixy face. "I mean, everybody told me . . ." -»

"Everybody told you wrong," she assured him quietly. "Because Keith Ramsey is available for the right property. Don't you remember what he said before he took off? That he would come back when the right picture appeared? Well, he told me that Secret Rites is that picture."

"He really said that?" Joy blazed out of Sheldon's face.

"He said more than that." Erin smiled warmly "He said it was the only picture that could bring him back."

Suspicion suddenly shadowed the happy face. "Then why doesn't anybody else know about this?" he demanded accusingly. "Why didn't Harry Kingston tell me about it? Why didn't my agent? Why didn't Columbia Pictures?" he screeched, his voice rising dramatically.

"Why ask me?" Erin spread her hands in a helpless gesture. "Maybe because they don't have any way of getting in touch with Keith."

"That's true," he muttered to himself. "They don't. They told me that." He looked up at her. "And you do? You can guarantee that?"

"Why else would I be talking to you?"

"Okay. Okay." He started pacing around the patio, then turned back to give her a hard stare. "Can you deliver Keith Ramsey, signed contract and all, one week from tonight?"

"It could take two weeks. Because he really is out of touch." She gave him a light smile. "I might have to take a canoe up river to deliver the contract."

"So start paddling. Because two weeks is all you've got."

"Hey, I was right, wasn't I?" David beamed as they drove away from the party. "You really did enjoy yourself."

"Yes, David, you were right," she said dreamily. "It was indeed a marvelous party."

Erin curled up in the seat, resting her head against the window as she gazed absently at the flashing lights of the passing cars and began to figure out a way to get hold of Keith Ramsey.

"So let's go celebrate tomorrow night. A private party for David and Erin, who've just made it through the doldrums and are coming out just fine!"

"Tomorrow night?" she said vaguely. "No, David, I don't think I can make it tomorrow night. I've got a lot of things to think about."

"What the hell are you talking about?" He braked abruptly and turned around and stared at her. Horns screamed in protest as the line of motorists behind him pushed desperately on their own brakes to avoid hitting him, swerving wildly around him and hurling curses as they passed.

"Jesus Christ, David, what's the matter with you?" Erin shouted. "Are you trying to kill us?"

"It's a thought." His smile appeared strangely twisted in the glare of headlights from approaching traffic.

"That's not funny, David," she said furiously. "And, for that matter, you're not much fun these days either. I think I was right when I suggested last month that we take a rest from each other. And I think now is the time to do it!"

"You can't do that to me, Erin." His voice was low and calm as he pressed down on the accelerator and began moving the big car down the highway once again. "I've given up too much for you. My career, my family, everything I believed in. You're all I have left. So you can't leave me. Ever. Do you understand that?"

"No, I don't understand that," she snapped. "If want to leave you, I'll leave you. And that's all there is to it."

Then she swallowed in fright as his hands tightened so hard on the steering wheel that his knuckles gleamed white, and the car leaped forward in a surge of uncontrolled power.

TWENTY THREE

"Will you please stop telling me you're just his answering service?!"

"But I am just his answering service," the girl said, her voice trembling.

Erin took a deep breath and tried to control herself. "Now look," she continued, dropping her voice to the warm, low contralto that had successfully charmed a number of people into doing things they didn't want to. "I, of all people, understand Keith Ramsey's need for privacy. As the most exciting and sought-after actor in the industry today, I know he's constantly besieged by people who want to grab a piece of his glory. But I am not one of those people and I assure you that Keith will be not merely upset but infuriated if he learns that you have refused to put me in touch with him."

"Erin Connolly?" the girl from the service repeated uncertainly. "Are you a personal friend? I don't see your name on this list he gave me."

So he had left a number where he could be reached! Erin slumped back in her chair and breathed a sigh of relief. You never knew about that independent bastard. He'd been known to disappear for months at a time with no one knowing his whereabouts.

"My dear," Erin said softly, "I am a little more than a personal friend. He has been waiting for word on a major script that I've been negotiating for. Well, I've got it for him, and I need to talk to him immediately!"

"Oh!" The girl sounded slightly awed. "In that case, I'll certainly pass your message on to him right away. Could you give me your number?"

"There's no need for that," Erin said quickly. "Just tell me how to contact him, and I'll call him myself."

"I can't do that," the girl said firmly. "Mr. Ramsey specifically instructed me to do nothing but pass on messages."

"I think you're making a major mistake, young lady," Erin said threateningly. "Mr. Ramsey could lose the most important role of his career due to your obstruction. Would you give me your name and the name of your supervisor?"

"My ... my name is Susan Laskey, and my supervisor is Mrs. Morganstern, but you won't be able to reach her until tomorrow." The girl started to cry. "I'm sorry. Miss Connolly but I have to do what I'm told."

Jesus Christ, Erin muttered to herself. Have I sunk so low I'm now down to intimidating innocent kids from an answering service?

"It's all right, Susan," she said. "You're doing the right thing. Just make sure that Keith calls me as soon as possible. I'll give you two numbers."

The minute Erin hung up the receiver, her intercom button flashed red. She punched it down and picked up the phone. "Yes, Nancy, what is it now?"

"Sheldon Avery is on line two. He's been waiting almost five minutes, and he's really steamed."

"Oh God." Erin groaned. "That's the last thing I need. All right, I'll take him."

"Hi, Shel. Really sorry to keep you waiting, but the damn phones have been screwed up all afternoon. Would you believe that I placed a call to Marty Jessup at CBS in New York and ended up talking with a housewife in Crestline, Ohio? I mean, honestly . . ."

"Just cut out the shit, will you?" Sheldon said furiously. "I want to know now if Keith Ramsey has signed a contract for the part."

"Shel, luv, what in the world has got you so upset?"

"You know damn well what! I've been stalling my agent for two weeks now because I was nuts enough to believe you when you said you could deliver Ramsey. You got any idea what it's like to stall Irving?"

Erin laughed. "Darling, I most certainly do. It's like trying to stall a bulldozer that's headed straight at you with its throttle open full."

"It's not funny, Erin. Irving told me today that Columbia's dropping the option on my book unless they get a definite commitment in the next forty-eight hours. That's a million dollars we're talking about, darling," he added viciously. "So it's put-up or shut-up time for you."

"I don't much care for your tone of voice," Erin said evenly. Now I do understand the kind of pressures you've been under, so I think I can excuse that last remark. But I would appreciate it if you'd remember that you're not talking to some cheap, one-shot producer or money-hungry agent. You're talking to Erin Connolly who, among other things, won both the Oscar and the Cannes Film Festival award for Street Scene "

"That Oscar was four years ago," Sheldon snapped. "What have you won lately?"

For one terrifying second Erin went completely blind as the rage generated by Sheldon's remarks blazed inside her. A few seconds later the room came back into focus and she looked up gratefully at the late afternoon sun streaming through the sheer curtains and reflecting off the brilliant paintings hung on her walls.

"Hello? Hello? For Christ's sake, is anyone there?"

"Sorry, Shel," Erin said calmly. "Must be those damn phone lines acting up again. Anyway, to get back to what we were talking about, I'd like you to answer one question for me. And I want you to think about it very carefully before you answer." She paused for a beat and when she did speak again there was an almost solemn tone to her voice.

"Do you really believe wholeheartedly and without reservations, as I do, that Keith Ramsey is the only actor alive today who can be totally trusted to portray the most important character you've ever created without compromising the artistic integrity you wrote your guts out to give him?"

"Well yes, of course I do," Sheldon said, momentarily distracted by the thought of his artistic integrity being compromised. "But . . ."

"No buts." Erin said firmly. "That's the answer I was looking for, and you gave it to me. Now, can Columbia guarantee you Keith Ramsey?"

"You know damn well they can't. There isn't a studio in town who can, because nobody knows how to reach him." Sheldon's suspicions flared up again. "And I think that includes you."

"Really?" she replied coolly. "Then it must have been my overactive imagination that I spent a full sixty minutes earlier today talking to that very same Keith Ramsey. He absolutely loved your script, by the way."

There was a stunned silence on the other end of the line. When Sheldon finally managed to speak, he was so excited his voice cracked.

"He did? I mean, he really said that?"

"Among other things. Like it was one of the few scripts he'd ever read that was worthy of the book that inspired it. He told me something else I think you might be interested in hearing. 'Erin,' he said in that marvelous, deep resonant voice of his. 'When I finished this, I knew I was holding an Academy Award picture in my hands.'

"My God. Oh my God, I can't tell you what that means to me," Sheldon babbled. "I am so thrilled. Did you know Keith Ramsey has always been an idol of mine? My whole life I've dreamed of having him play one of my characters."

"Of course."

"Well, this is such wonderful news I hardly know what to say. Listen, Erin, please accept my apologies for the way I talked earlier. I was just so uptight with this deadline hanging over my head that I didn't know what I was saying."

He gave a small, embarrassed laugh. "I know this probably sounds a little crazy, but do you think there's any chance you could set up a luncheon or something where I could meet him in person now that he's signed the contract?" Sheldon paused. "He did sign the contract, didn't he?"

"'Luv, can you imagine that he wouldn't after the way he fell in love with the script?"

"Erin, that's not an answer." There was a sudden ominous note in Sheldon's voice. "Now, either he did or he didn't. Which is it?"

"Honestly, Shel, sometimes I wonder why 1 put up with you." Erin sighed. "I give you everything you've ever asked for and in return I get hit with your paranoid fears. "No!" she said sharply as he started to protest. "You listen to me! Now I told you I just finished talking with Keith. The operative words are talking. As your own wonderful agent along with all those super powerful studios reported to you," she said sarcastically, "no one could get Ramsey for your picture because no one could reach him. Well, I reached Keith Ramsey and sent him your script. And he called me to say he wanted to do it. But he's two thousand miles away in one of his hideouts. So we're just going to have to wait till he gets back for the actual signing."

"I can't wait, Erin."

"Then you want to lose the whole thing?"

"Look," Sheldon said desperately. "You know I don't want to lose him, and I'd never ask him to come back here just to sign a contract. But I have to have that contract. Now you know where he is, so why can't you fly up to wherever that is and have him sign it there?"

"You really ask a lot. Shel."

"I'll pay you for it," Sheldon said frantically. "The plane tickets, your time, whatever you want to charge. I don't have any other choice. Do you understand that? Forty-eight hours. That's all I've got."

"I understand," Erin said slowly. "Okay, Shel, I'll get back to you."

There was a hesitant tap at the door. "Excuse me, Erin." Nancy peeked in. "I just wanted to check and see if there was anything else you wanted me to do before I left for the night."

Erin gazed at her blankly for a moment then blinked. "Is it five already?"

"Five-thirty, actually."

Erin looked at her watch, a faintly startled expression on her face "The day seems to have gotten away from me," she said vaguely. "I'm sorry to have kept you overtime."

"Oh for heaven's sake, you didn't keep me overtime!" Nancy burst out impulsively. "Why, I remember when we worked straight through till ten o'clock every night and... " She stopped abruptly.

"It's all right," Erin said gently as she watched Nancy flush crimson. "I remember too. But don't worry," she announced with sudden grim determination. "We're going to get those days back!"

"You betcha," Nancy grinned. "We'll show 'em all! Right?"

"Right," Erin smiled. The smile faded as she thought of the forty-eight-hour deadline facing her. Sheldon Avery's script was her last, her only chance to make a comeback. But she was going to lose it unless she got Keith Ramsey. And at the moment she couldn't think of a single way to do that.

"Are you okay?" Nancy asked anxiously.

"Of course I'm okay," she said, forcing the smile back on her face. "Now run along, Nancy, and enjoy your evening."

"You're sure?"

"I'm sure. Now scat!" she said firmly.

"Well, all right then." Nancy started for the door, stopped abruptly, and whirled around.

"Oh wow, I almost forgot! David called and asked me to remind you that he was picking you up for dinner at seven." She grinned and gave a cheerful wave as she headed back for the door.

"Have a nice evening," she called over her shoulder. "You deserve it."

****

The traffic was unusually heavy as Erin headed west on Wilshire Boulevard toward the elegant high-rise apartment; building that dominated the skyline of the expensive Westwood Village area.

She whipped her white Porsche around the big Cadillacs and Lincoln Continentals that moved with maddening slowness in front of her, switching from one lane to another, accelerating rapidly as she came up to each intersection, trying to beat the light.

Pulling up to the iron gates that guarded the entrance to the underground garage of her apartment building and inserting her plastic card into the electronic lock, she cursed as she looked at her watch. Despite all her frenetic maneuverings to get home quickly, it was already six-twenty. Erin had been counting on at least an hour to relax and pull herself together before David arrived. Now she'd barely have time to bathe and dress. And if David was in one of his sullen, depressed moods, which was about the only mood he'd been in for the past month, she thought irritably, then she was going to have to deal with that along with everything else that had gone wrong on this rotten, miserable day.

Well, the hell with it. There's no law that says I have to meet his damn seven o'clock timetable. He made the date, not me. So he can wait till I'm ready!

Erin stepped off the elevator on the lobby floor to check her mailbox. It was stuffed with envelopes: bills from Saks, Bonwit Teller's, Gucci's, Giorgio's,

Jorgensens, and Vendome Liquors. There was also a small white envelope,
unstamped, from the manager of her building reminding her the rent on her apartment
was now five days overdue.

"Welcome home," she announced with a grim smile. "It sure is good to get all
these loving letters from family and friends."

Shoving the envelopes into her purse, she walked to the elevator and pressed
the button for the penthouse apartment.

The six-foot grandfather clock bonged one slow, solemn note as she entered
her apartment, which was freezing. Goddamnit, why couldn't she remember to turn
the air conditioner off when she left in the morning? That's going to be another
hundred and fifty dollar electric bill, she thought unhappily

Walking quickly into the bathroom, she filled the tub, slipped into the soothing
water and closed her eyes. Then faintly she heard chimes. They stopped for a
moment and then sounded again.

It was the doorbell. It was David! She scrambled out of the tub, grabbing a
robe and wrapping it around her as she ran to the door, her bare feet leaving damp
imprints on the thick pile carpet.

"Am I too early?" he asked.

"No, I'm late. It's been a hell of a day. Let me fix you a drink."

`"Why don't I fix my own and let you get dressed?"

"You're a dear." She blew him a kiss and pattered down the hall to her
bedroom, standing in front of the closet that took up one whole wall, trying to decide
what to wear. She finally settled on the red velvet pantsuit that had set her back
fifteen hundred dollars. But it was worth every penny, she thought as she admired her
image in the mirror.

The pants, which she wore without any underwear, clearly outlined her small
waist, flat tummy, slim hips, and firm, tight ass. The short velvet jacket was cut to

reveal the low-necked white silk blouse with its crisp ruffled front. The contrast of the sheer white blouse against the rich red velvet jacket set off to perfection her small triangular face with its flawless ivory complexion, brilliant jade green eyes and lustrous short cap of dark hair.

Not bad for a thirty-year-old broad," she announced thoughtfully to the mirror. Then she laughed. "Hell, it's damn good for a twenty-year old broad."

"Well, I'm ready," Erin announced brightly as she appeared in the entrance way of the living room. "Now that didn't take too long, did it?" Then her eyes widened in shock as she saw the oversized double old-fashioned glass in David's hand which was filled to the brim with a dark amber liquid.

"My God, David, is that all Scotch in there?"

"You don't mind, do you?" He raised the glass and gulped down a third of its contents.

"No, of course not," she said uncertainly. "It's just that I . . . well, I've never seen you drink like that."

He gave her a twisted grin. "I'm celebrating," he announced. "An anniversary."

"'Anniversary?" She looked at him blankly. "What anniversary?"

He took another large swallow. "I guess it was foolish of me to think you'd remember. You see, it was exactly a year ago tonight that I left my wife and family for you."

Erin's eyes narrowed in anger. "Is this going to be one of those blame-Erin-for-everything-that's-gone-wrong evenings? Because if it is, I'm going to cancel it right now before it starts."

"Oh no, my love, you're not going to cancel this evening," he said softly. "This is very definitely a non cancellable evening."

He stood up and walked over to her, his hand cupping her chin and tilting it up to him as he kissed her lightly on the lips. "You're looking unusually beautiful and desirable tonight," he murmured in the deep, warm voice that had turned her on so totally when she first met him.

Unexpectedly, tears stung her eyes as she looked at the husky, broad-shouldered man with the dark, intense eyes and remembered how things had been then. They'd been so much in love, so ecstatically, wondrously in love that the whole world had glowed. And he'd been everything to her. Friend, lover, the father she'd always longed for. Why had it gone wrong? Why had she lost it?

"I still love you, David," she said tremulously.

"Do you?" He looked at her intently. "But you're not in love with me anymore, are you?"

"I don't know." She gave a helpless shrug. "If only . .."

"If only you still wanted to go to bed with me," he interjected harshly. "That happens to be one hell of an if, doesn't it?"

"I can't help it," she said unhappily. "It's not something I can force."

"But you're not the kind of woman who can go too long without a man," he said broodingly. His eyes clouded. "Soon, very soon, you'll find someone who turns you on," he murmured half to himself. "And that's the one thing I cannot stand to see."

"David, you promised it wasn't going to be one of those evenings. I told you, I just can't take it tonight."

"That's right. You did, didn't you?" He smiled suddenly, an engaging smile that lit up his face. "Well, as a man who keeps his promises, I now declare a moratorium on the subject. It shall never be mentioned again."

He offered her his arm. "Shall we leave for dinner, my lady?"

"Oh Christ, I almost forgot!" she groaned. "David, I've got to call my answering service and tell them where I'll be this evening. Where are we having dinner?"

He frowned. "You're not planning to meet anyone later tonight, are you?"

"Don't be silly. Of course I'm not." She patted his cheek. "It's just a business thing."

"What kind of a business thing?" he asked suspiciously.

"It's a long story." She smiled. "No, that's not true. It's a very short story. About forty-six hours short, now. I'll tell you about it at dinner. Which is going to be? "

He hesitated. "I made reservations at Melisse." he said finally.

Erin lifted her eyebrow, wondering just what was going on in that complex head of David's. That five star, fantastically romantic Santa Monica restaurant had been "their place" for every special occasion in their lives. It was where they'd first admitted they were in love with each other. It was the place where David told her he was getting a divorce and wanted to marry her. It was where they first talked about having a child. Her eyes closed in sudden pain at the last memory.

"I hope you don't mind," David said quickly. "I was just hungry for their food, that's all."

"No, I don't mind." She forced a smile. "Now that I think about it, I'm a little hungry for their food myself."

He looked relieved. "Good. You go ahead and call your answering service, then, while I finish my drink."

****

The maitre d' broke into a delighted smile as Erin and David walked into the restaurant, and rushed toward them. "Miss Connolly, Mr. Bernstein, what a pleasure to see you again. It has been so long!" He looked at them reproachfully. "Why do you stay away for such a time? It is not right for friends to behave so."

"You're absolutely right," David agreed solemnly. "But you see Miss Connolly's business has been most demanding lately. And how could I come here without her?"

"Ah. In that case, you are forgiven." Then he shook a reproving finger at Erin. "But you must not let business deprive you of the joys of life. Work less and enjoy more," he commanded her as he led them briskly to their table where a waiter stood at attention."

"Would you like to see a menu now, sir?" the waiter asked.

"No. We want to relax for a few minutes first. A double Scotch on the rocks for me and a martini for the lady."

The waiter was back with the drinks in minutes and David lifted his glass toward Erin as though he were about to propose a toast. Then his eyes, which had been fixed on her, suddenly grew distant as he brought the glass to his lips and drank deeply, staring into space.

Erin shifted uncomfortably as the brief pause in their conversation grew into a lengthy silence. "How are things in politics these days?" she asked with determined brightness.

"So so," David replied briefly. "How are things in the silver-screen business?"

"Worse than so so." she said with a grimace, "Christ, I don't know what I'm going to do if I lose this picture!"

She began telling him in detail about the conversation with Sheldon Avery, then trailed off as she saw the amused glint in his eyes.

"And just what the hell do you find so funny about all this?"

"Your attitude." He smiled. "To hear you tell it, you're the innocent victim of a cruel and malicious fate. While the truth is it's your own sweet, charming, lying, cheating, conniving, manipulating self that put you in this box."

"Why, you supercilious son of a bitch!" she spat, white with rage. "Who the hell do you think you are to talk to me that way?"

"The person who knows you better than anyone else in the world," he said, the faint smile still on his face.

"Don't flatter yourself," she said contemptuously. "After all, you're just one in a long line of men who felt the same way."

David's fists clenched involuntarily as rage blazed out of his eyes. With a visible effort, he regained his composure.

"Well, that tender loving moment in your apartment didn't last long, did it?"

"None of them do." Erin was furious. "Because you spoil them all. We should have ended this whole relationship two months ago like I wanted to. It's become destructive for both of us, and I have enough problems without having you drag me down too."

"Poor Erin. You do suffer terribly, don't you?" he mocked.

"There was a time you cared about my problems. Now all you care about is your own sick self!"

"That's certainly sick," he agreed coldly. "After all, what could be more important than the meteoric rise and fall of Hollywood's most important producer? Especially when her fall is almost as meteoric as her rise."

"You have two choices. We can order, or you can take me home now. And frankly I don't much care which you choose as long as I don't have to talk to you. Because I am really, finally, finished with you."

David signaled the waiter. "The lobster Fra Diavolo for two and a bottle of Pouilly Fuisse. He glanced at Erin. "Unless the lady wants another drink?"

"No, just the wine." She looked up at the waiter. "And could you bring it now?"

"Of course, madame." He bowed politely before leaving.

"Miss Connolly?" The maitre d' appeared suddenly in front of them, a frown on his face. "There's a telephone call for you. Do you wish to take it?"

Erin's face lit up. "Indeed I do!" She looked triumphantly at David. "I told you I'd get through to Ramsey," she gloated as the phone was brought to their table.

"Hello, this is Erin Connolly," she announced with a vibrant warmth.

"It's Susan Laskey," the worried young voice answered. "I'm terribly sorry to disturb you at dinner, but you did say how important it was to call you. The thing is, well, I haven't been able to reach Mr. Ramsey. His housekeeper at their lodge told me he's backpacking in the mountains and isn't expected for at least another day."

"For Christ's sake, don't they have forest rangers or something that can reach him in an emergency?"

"I ... I really don't know anything about that. Is it really an emergency?"

"His whole career is hanging in the balance and you ask me if it's an emergency?" Erin took a deep breath and lowered her voice. "Susan, maybe I didn't explain it fully. If Keith doesn't get back to me in the next twenty-four hours, he's going to lose it all. The script, the picture, the Academy Award. Now do you understand?"

"I didn't realize all that, Miss Connolly. Let me try to reach him again."

"Mr. Ramsey and I would both appreciate that, Susan. Just make sure you succeed this time." She hung up the phone with a crash.

"Bravo!" David smiled sardonically. "A virtuoso performance."

"Oh just shut up." She took a swallow of the wine, wondering if this kid from the answering service did reach Ramsey, would he call her?

Yes, she decided, he would. Not because her dramatic messages would arouse his curiosity. He was too smart and savvy to fall for that. No, the reason he'd call her would be to give her hell for scaring little Susan Laskey half to death. Which was just fine with her. All she needed was that vital personal contact with him.

Once she got that, somehow she'd figure out a way to persuade him to read the script, even if she did have to end up doing what Sheldon had begged her and fly up to that godforsaken wilderness where Ramsey was camped out. But the timing is so goddamn fuckin' tight, she thought desperately. What if he doesn't come back to his crappy rustic lodge before the forty-eight-hour deadline is up? Well he's going to, she told herself. I am willing him to come back, and it's going to happen.

"Pardon me, madame."

Erin looked up, startled, as the waiter stood patiently beside her, holding the steaming plate of lobster Fra Diavolo. "Sorry," she murmured automatically, leaning back to allow him to set it down in front of her. Her eyes focused on David, who was staring at her with a peculiarly intent expression.

"Are you all right?" she asked apprehensively.

"Couldn't be better." He continued to stare at her with the strange glitter in his eyes. "And how are you?"

"Tired." She eyed him carefully. "I'm really very tired, David. I'd appreciate your taking me home as soon as we finish dinner."

"Don't get upset," he said softly. "I'll take you home. But I have to make a phone call first." He stood up abruptly and walked away, leaving Erin to gaze after him bewilderedly.

****

An elderly man carrying a miniature poodle under his arm was coming out of Erin's building as she and David walked up to the entrance. He smiled and held the door open for them, bidding them a pleasant good evening as he set the dog down and headed off down the block.

"Some swell maximum-security building," Erin grumbled as they crossed the lobby to the elevator. "Might as well send out engraved invitations to every burglar in Los Angeles and be done with it."

"Um," David murmured noncommittally.

Erin shrugged irritably and gave up all attempts at polite conversation as they rode in silence to her floor. The headache which had started in the restaurant was now pounding steadily at her temples.

One of the hall lights had burned out, and Erin stumbled as she stepped out of the elevator, cursing under her breath as she fumbled in her purse for the key to her apartment.

"It's all right, I've got it," David said as he opened the door.

She glared at him in outrage as he reached inside and switched on the light in the foyer. "Goddamnit, David, what are you doing with a key to my place?"

"Don't get so excited. It's an extra one I just discovered after I gave you back the others."

"Just discovered? Don't give me that shit! I know damn well you've kept it all this time. What the fuck were you planning to do with it? Catch me with someone else? Well, maybe that's what you deserve. But it's not going to happen that way. So give it back to me right now," she demanded.

"I was planning to," he smiled. "We'll have a nightcap, and I'll turn over all the keys of your kingdom to you."

"No nightcap," she said grimly. "Just the key."

"Well, then, just the key." He looked down at her, his body blocking the doorway. "But I do have to bring you your gift."

"Oh Christ, David, no more gifts!" she exclaimed. "You're always bringing me gifts, like you think they're going to solve all our problems. Just give me the key."

"No, this time you're wrong. You want this," he insisted. "It will only take me a minute to bring it up from the car."

"David, please. Just leave me in peace tonight. I am totally wiped, and I need to be alone. Can't you understand that?"

"Of course I understand that," he said gravely, "That's why you need this."

"All right," she said resignedly. "Bring me the gift. But do me a favor, okay? Bring it into the bedroom where I am going immediately to collapse. You can leave it there along with the key."

Erin headed down the hallway to her bedroom without waiting for David's response, kicking off her shoes and unbuttoning the white silk blouse.

"What a waste," she muttered as she walked into the bedroom and stared into the mirror. "Five hundred dollars worth of clothes for a two-bit evening." Angrily, she ripped off her pants and jacket, threw off the blouse, then crawled into bed, pulling the covers up to her chin and closing her eyes.

She didn't hear the soft opening and closing of the door when David returned, and the thick-pile carpet muffled the sound of his footsteps as he walked down the hall and into the bedroom. The first intimation she had of his presence was when the bed moved under his weight as he sat down at the foot of it.

Her eyes opened lazily and she turned her head to the pillow next to her, David's favorite place for putting the beautiful expensive presents he loved to get her. But there was nothing there. Puzzled, she turned away and looked down the length of the bed, then gave a short, choked gasp as she saw the gun in David's hand. He held it loosely, its long black barrel pointed at her.

"What kind of filthy, sick joke is this?" she demanded hoarsely.

"It's not a joke, Erin."

"Stop it, David! Stop it this minute!" She sat up in the bed, clutching the covers to her. "This cheap melodramatic trick is beneath you. Now take that ugly thing out of here right now!"

His fingers played with the gun, turning it over so that it lay flat in his palm for a moment. He gazed at it idly, then brought it upright again, the snout directed at Erin.

"I am warning you, David, I will not put up with this! You take that thing out of here or I'm calling the police."

"Are you afraid?" He smiled at her, amused. "That would certainly be something to see. I thought Erin Connolly was never afraid of anything."

"I am not afraid," she said evenly. "I am disgusted. Now, do you take it away or do I call the police? You may not care about yourself or me anymore, but I don't think you'll want your kids reading about something like this."

"Oh, they'll understand," he said quietly. "They know what it's been like for me lately." He looked at her quizzically. "I thought you realized that. Didn't you know I was calling them when I left you for a moment in the restaurant?"

And then for the first time Erin was afraid. It was impossible, of course. This whole scene was impossible. David couldn't do a thing like that, she told herself. She swallowed hard as she looked at the man who'd given her so much love. The man she'd loved at one time almost as much as she needed him. No, this couldn't be real. It was just another Hollywood scenario. He would beg her forgiveness when it was over, and she'd make him pay long and hard before she gave it to him. But eventually she'd forgive him. Despite everything, they were still too close to stay away from each other for very long.

"I'm calling your bluff," she announced with narrowed eyes. "Right now!" As she reached for the phone, the shockingly loud report of the gun echoed throughout the room, making her ears ring.

David leaned forward on the bed, his arms outstretched as though he were reaching for her, and Erin dropped the phone as she flung aside the covers and held out her hands toward him. But she was too far away and he slid off the bed to the floor, dragging the bedspread with him. She scrambled frantically over the rumpled bed to where he had fallen.

"David? David, what did you do?" she whispered.

His eyes were open, looking at her, and tears of relief streamed down her cheeks. "Oh, David, you fool, you goddamn fool," she cried. "How could you do a stupid thing like this?"

He refused to answer her, and rage mixed with her tears of relief. She grabbed his shoulders, shaking him savagely. "Tell me," she commanded. "Tell me how you could try such a thing!"

His head fell against her breast. It was terribly, terribly heavy. And then she knew he wasn't going to answer her. Ever.

TWENTY FOUR

It was three o'clock in the morning, and thirteen days, seven hours, had passed since Harry Kingston's party. Twelve hours had passed since a furious Sheldon Avery had called Erin at her office and delivered his final ultimatum: deliver the signed contract from Keith Ramsey within forty-eight hours or lose the picture. Six hours had passed since she and David had sat in a booth at Melissse's restaurant and the maitre d' brought the phone to their table, whereupon she learned from Keith Ramsey's answering service that the actor was backpacking somewhere in the Sierra Mountains and there was absolutely no way of reaching him. Three hours had passed since David had walked into her bedroom and sat down at the foot of her bed, a faint, mocking smile on his face as he idly played with the gun in his hands, pointing it at her for a few heart-stopping moments before turning it around, pulling the trigger, and killing himself instantly.

The police were gone now, and the apartment was very still. Erin huddled on the couch in the living room, unable to face the thought of going back into the bedroom. Convulsive sobs continued to rack her body, although her eyes were dry, for by this time there were no tears left. She rocked back and forth in silent agony, pausing occasionally to drink from the large crystal brandy snifter in her hand.

Finally the potent liqueur, combined with the two sleeping pills she'd taken earlier, did its work. Her rocking became slower and slower, then stopped altogether as her head fell wearily against the arm of the couch, and she slept.

The phone rang, shrilly and persistently. Erin struggled out of her narcotic fog and groped for it. "Hello?" she mumbled thickly.

"Erin Connolly? Is this Erin Connolly?" The voice was crisp, sharp, and obviously angry.

She blinked, then grimaced at the terrible taste in her mouth, running her tongue around her teeth and trying to swallow, "Yes," she said with an effort. "Who's this?"

"Keith Ramsey," the voice barked. "And I have some questions for you, Miss Connolly. Like what the hell did you think you were doing harassing my answering service that way?"

Still numb with grief and shock, Erin was for once without a cleverly contrived story. She simply blurted out the truth about her outrageous promise to Sheldon Avery and the desperate reason behind it, then began to cry as she told the actor about David's death.

It was, although she didn't realize it at the time, the only way in the whole world she could have gotten Keith Ramsey to consider taking the part in Avery's picture. Because Ramsey was, in addition to being one of the most powerful stars in Hollywood, a genuinely sensitive, compassionate man, and his instinctive reaction to the terrible thing that had just happened to her was to offer whatever comfort and help he could.

An hour after the phone call, a copy of Sheldon's screenplay was on its way by chartered plane to Keith Ramsey's lodge in the Sierra Mountains. The following day, a special messenger brought Erin the signed contract from the actor.

****

Hollywood was rocked by the news of David's suicide and even more stunned to learn that Con-Well Productions had not only obtained the screen rights to Sheldon Avery's smash bestseller but signed Keith Ramsey for the lead. Executives at the giant studio that had originally optioned the book fumed in impotent rage. They had a legitimate suit against both Sheldon Avery and Con-Well Productions, but what the hell would it look like if they sued and took the picture away from Erin Connolly, who was now being portrayed as a tragic figure gallantly striving, in the best show business tradition, to rise above her personal afflictions, past and present, and make a comeback. They knew exactly what it would look like. Ruthless big business heartlessly crushing one lone, brave human being who was not only a small, independent producer but a woman. Cursing and gritting their teeth, they let the picture go.

Keith Ramsey's agent was equally furious, as was Twentieth Century-Fox. Just three weeks ago the agent had flown up to Ramsey's mountain lodge with a major new property, and the actor had agreed to take the part, subject to certain conditions. Jubilant executives at Twentieth Century-Fox had agreed to every condition and moved immediately to start production, not bothering to wait for the signed contract since it was just a formality.

Now they found it was a great deal more than just a formality. They'd lost their star, and without him the picture would never get off the ground.

But there was probably no one, in the long list of stunned and furious people, who was more upset than Arnold Scorsi. A man who prided himself on his ability to remain cool, calm, and totally in control no matter what happened, he found himself suddenly shaking like a terrified child, perspiration soaking through his elegantly hand-tailored silk shirt, as he picked up the private phone in his office and dialed an unlisted number that was known to only five people in the entire country.

"Yes, we heard," a flat voice replied. "Will the suicide seriously hurt Johnny Ryan?"

"No. Not per se. Voters never pay any attention to the ad agency or public relations firm that backs a candidate."

"Any incriminating evidence?"

"I'm sure there isn't."

"How sure?" the voice asked. It was still flat, emotionless, but now there was an undercurrent of threat in it.

"Positive," Arnold said quickly. "Our investigators have already, uh, surveyed David Bernstein's office."

"Good." The voice was approving. "No traces, I assume. "

"Oh no! None at all."

"Can you replace Bernstein with somebody as good?

"I'm working on it." Arnold cleared his throat. "But…

"What?" the voice snapped.

"It looks like we're going to be facing some unexpected opposition," he said unhappily. "A major power in Hollywood has recently come out for Richard Longworth. As long as we had David Bernstein handling Johnny's campaign, I didn't see any real problems from it. But now that David's gone …. He trailed off.

"We do not accept that as an explanation," the voice informed him coldly. "Your job is to neutralize the opposition. That's one of the things we pay you for. So you will manage it, won't you?"

"Of course." Arnold forced a smile into his voice. "Haven't I always?"

"So far you have," the voice said distantly. "But you're only as good as today's success." The voice laughed. "Isn't what they always say in that show biz world of yours?"

"Yes, that's what they always say," Arnold agreed shakily.

"Well, then, we understand each other. We'll expect another report from you within the month. In the meantime, be sure to give our best to your lovely wife."

"I'll certainly do that." Arnold hung up the phone, wiped his perspiration off the receiver, and started thinking very hard.

****

Erin was oblivious of the rumors, uncertainties, private rages and public speculations that swirled around Hollywood after the twin announcements of David's suicide and her acquisition of Secret Rites. The only thing she knew was that this was her last chance, and if she didn't make it with this picture, she was finished.

But this time around it looked like she was finally going to get support from the film industry that had so relentlessly shunned and ostracized her. Her phone rang constantly. People extended their sympathies for what had happened to David and wished her luck on the new picture; actors and agents were eager to discuss casting possibilities; directors, cinematographers, even set designers and film editors, offered their services.

Many of the calls came from some of the biggest and most respected names in the business, and Erin accepted them gratefully. But the most important call of all didn't come . . . the one from the money men. And without that call, all the support in the world couldn't help her. Because Con-Well Productions was, quite simply, incapable of producing Secret Rites on its own.

At the most conservative estimate, it would take ten million dollars to bring in the picture. Con-Well Productions' current financial statement showed the company had total liquid assets of $75,000.

In the first flush of excitement and pleasure generated by all the warm, friendly calls pouring into her office, Erin had failed to notice that no one was offering any financial support for her picture. But as a second week passed, the calls dwindled, and both Sheldon Avery and Keith Ramsey's agent began to press her about the start date for production, she realized with sudden shock that she was committed to a picture she couldn't afford to make.

She got on the phone quickly to those few major studio executives who had called her, remembering now that there had been very few of them indeed. Most of the calls had come from the private sector of Hollywood: actors and actresses, directors, film technicians, agents, and press people. Now she discovered that even those few studio executives who had called had suffered a sudden relapse of memory. They were in fact such victims of amnesia, they couldn't even come to the phone.

Erin found herself talking to an endless line of bright young executive assistants who all sounded faintly bewildered by her call but assured her cheerfully that they would pass on her message to their bosses. The message coming back from them to her was unmistakable. Erin Connolly might have finally won the sympathy of the film industry, but that's all she'd won. There wouldn't be a single penny of financial support.

In desperation she went to New York, where she found there wasn't even sympathy to be had. The money men there hadn't forgotten the disaster that had occurred the last time one of them had invested in an Erin Connolly production, when Ardis Kendall had forced a close-down of her picture Liberation. They turned her down flat.

That left Erin with only one place to go. She put it off as long as possible, filled with dread at the thought. But eventually she reached the point where she was forced to admit she had no other choice unless she gave up Secret Rites. And that she couldn't do, because doing that would be tantamount to giving up her life. So, pale and tense, she picked up the phone and dialed the number that once again would deliver her into the hands of the one person in the world who utterly terrified her.

"This is not an easy thing you're asking. Not easy at all." Arnold Scorsi peered at her over the top of his glasses as she sat in his office, nervously twisting her hands in her lap.

"Things are considerably different now than they were when you came to me with Street Scene. I'm sure you understand that."

"No, Arnold," she said with difficulty. "I'm afraid I don't understand. It seems to me this is an even better proposition for your investors. When I came to you with Street Scene, I was virtually an unknown producer. It's true I had a bestselling novel and a box-office star in Derek Marston. But this time I come to your people with a proven record as an Oscar-winning producer, to say nothing of having the hottest property in town and the most prestigious actor in Hollywood. Surely you'll agree that the combination of Sheldon Avery and Keith Ramsey is something very special. In terms of money alone, they have to be valued at ten times what Derek Marston and that now forgotten author of Street Scene were worth."

She swallowed and smiled nervously. "And there's also the fact that for the first time Hollywood is behind me. I get calls, Arnold. I get calls all the time from important people, wishing me luck. I think even the academy will be supporting me this time around. I really believe they'd like to be able to give me another Oscar. That's money in the bank for your investors."

"Somehow I doubt they'd look at it that way," he remarked dryly. He took off his glasses and tapped them reflectively on the desk for a moment, then unexpectedly smiled at her. "However, I suppose there's no harm in trying. After all, we've been friends for a long time, Erin, and I think one should make a special effort for friends. Give me a week or so to see what I can do. I'll be in touch."

"Thank you, Arnold," she said tremulously. "Thank you very much."

"Please, my dear, don't thank me yet," he protested as he stood up to escort her to the door. "I haven't promised you anything, you know. All I can do is try. So save your thanks for if and when I accomplish something. In the meantime, relax and take care of yourself."

There was no question in Erin's mind, as she left Arnold Scorsi's quietly expensive suite in the exclusive Century City high-rise building which only a few short golden years ago had housed the flourishing business offices of Con-Well Productions, that the cold, smiling man could accomplish anything he wanted to. The question was, did he want to? And if so, why?

She'd been prepared to give up virtually everything she owned in order to get the financing for her picture, but not once during their conversation had he asked for anything in return for that financing. There hadn't been even a hint of what terms he would require. The obvious conclusion was that he was giving her a polite brush-off. Except polite brush-offs were not Arnold Scorsi's style. He never bothered with such amenities.

Erin found herself incapable of following Arnold Scorsi's advice to relax and take care of herself while she waited to hear from him, pacing around her apartment and snapping at the few people who continued to call her, when she couldn't stand to think about the problems facing her for one more second.

Exactly one week after she had gone to see Arnold, he called her. "Well, I think we may have something possible here," he announced cheerfully. "Can you come down to the office today? At two?"

Erin arrived promptly just as the exquisitely fashioned miniature grandfather clock on the wall in the reception room chimed the hour. Then she sat on the edge of the couch, opening and closing her purse, before Arnold finally appeared and smilingly beckoned her inside.

"Sorry if I kept you waiting, my dear."

"That's all right, Arnold. I know how busy you are." She sat down in the chair he indicated, then waited tensely as he settled himself behind the desk and extracted a sheaf of papers from a folder.

"Are you familiar with the Marchison brothers, Erin?"

"The Marchison brothers?" she repeated nervously. "No, I can't say that I am."

"Hm. Well, I suppose that's understandable. They're not exactly a household name in Hollywood. But they're very smart men. Built a billion-dollar empire by taking over small quality retail clothing stores across the country. Continued to operate them under their own names, of course, but by putting them under the Marchison corporate umbrella they were able to achieve extraordinary discounts from the major fashion houses through volume buying.

"And they're interested in backing my picture?"

"Ah, as usual you come directly to the point." He beamed at her. "Most refreshing, I might add, for a lawyer who is forced to spend the majority of his time with clients who tiptoe around every issue, waiting for someone else to speak the first word "

"Will they put up fifteen million dollars? Arnold, I must have at least fifteen million dollars. I know the prospectus I gave showed ten million, but that was bare bones. To do it, I need that cushion."

"Erin, they're not cheap people," he chided her gently. If they decide to come in on the picture, they'll come in with style. After all, they want a winner just as much as you do."

"Well, they sound like the kind of backers every producer dreams of," she said with a shaky laugh. "Now what do I have to do to get these Marchison brothers?"

"Very little, actually. Outside of the usual, normal terms, they've made only one condition."

He paused, and Erin took a deep breath. Here it comes, she told herself.

"Okay, Arnold," she said, managing somehow to keep her voice steady. "What's the condition?"

"That you bring in a co-producer."

"A what?" It was absolutely the last thing in the world she'd expected, and the worst thing she could ever have imagined. A co-producer on her picture?

"Please, my dear, try to calm yourself," he said reprovingly. "If you'll just stop and think for a moment, I'm sure you'll be able to understand why they're requesting this. Investors need to feel a sense of security when they entrust their money to someone, and your profit-and-loss statement these past few years has been . . . well erratic, to say the least. Naturally this troubles them. However, they are still willing to take a chance on you. And all they're asking in return is a little simple insurance on their money, the security of having a responsible co-producer with a good solid track record. Frankly, I think they're being more than generous."

He squared the edges of the papers on his desk. "Their choice is Mike Sobel. He has a number of advantages to offer, including the fact that he can operate both as co-producer and director. I think it's an excellent choice. Do you agree?"

Erin wanted to stand up and shout that she not only didn't agree, she absolutely refused to even consider it. This picture was hers! She'd fought for it all alone, won it all alone, and nobody else had the right to come in and take over production on it. But as she looked at Arnold Scorsi's coldly appraising eyes, she knew she wouldn't say anything at all. Because if she didn't accept his terms, she'd lose the picture altogether. Numbly, she took the contract he handed her and signed where he indicated.

It wasn't until she'd left his office that Erin allowed the bitter tears of rage and misery to fill her eyes. Mike Sobel! Oh God, why of all people did they have to choose him? The thought of having any co-producer on her picture was practically unbearable, but with someone else she would have found a way to manage.

There were all kinds of ways to take care of co-producers. You flattered them, then worked around them so they never knew what was really happening; you gave them impossible assignments; you shunted them off into dreary administrative duties;

if nothing else worked, you bought them off. But you couldn't do that with Mike Sobel. He'd been around the track, there was nothing that ever escaped him, and he was the most demanding bastard in the whole world.

"He's going to take my picture away from me," she sobbed as she drove out of the Century City parking lot.

By this time the anguished tears were running down her cheeks in such a steady stream she could barely see. There was a sudden terrifying screech of brakes as she headed blindly onto Santa Monica Boulevard, and a car making a right turn smashed full force into her. Her radiator exploded, sending up a furious spout of steam, and she stared at it in horror as the driver of the other car shouted, "You crazy bitch! You could have killed both of us!"

Unexpectedly, she started to laugh. "Well, I'll be damned if I'm going to make it this easy for you, Mike Sobel. Nobody's going to hand you my picture on a silver platter. You'll have to fight for it. And I warn you right now it won't be an easy fight. When it's over, there'll only be one of us still alive in this business."

TWENTY FOUR

Mike Sobel was only eighteen when a Broadway producer spotted him in a summer-stock production of Oklahoma and promptly signed him for the juvenile lead in his upcoming play.

The play opened to lackadaisical reviews and closed after a short, disappointing ten-week run, but critics and audiences alike were wildly enthusiastic about the young, unknown actor who appeared in it. "An exciting new presence has arrived on Broadway," one critic raved. "A brilliant newcomer redeems mediocre play," another announced. "Mike Sobel is unquestionably the big find of this season," a third critic proclaimed.

The audiences, mostly female as the play drifted into matinee performances, couldn't have cared less what the critics said. They came to see the young actor who gave them back their youthful dreams, gazing raptly at him as he gently introduced the fragile-looking ingenue to the mysteries and delights of making love.

"Oh God, isn't he beautiful!" they sighed rapturously to each other as the curtain fell for the intermission.

He wasn't beautiful, of course. He wasn't even handsome. Only five feet nine inches tall, with sandy hair, a thin, angular face, and a tight, wiry body, he would have been completely undistinguished looking if it weren't for his eyes, which were an extraordinarily clear, penetrating blue.

But the way he looked was totally unimportant, because Mike Sobel possessed a magnetic vitality that drew people like a light draws moths, and he completely mesmerized audiences.

During the next five years he became one of the most sought-after young actors on Broadway, but he grew increasingly dissatisfied with the narrow, restricted world of acting. What he really wanted, he finally realized, was the freedom to create his own world through directing and producing.

He made it big on his first production, Ducktail, a wildly energetic musical parody of the fifties and after that he could pretty much call his own shots. Musical comedies, though, left him with a curiously empty feeling. He needed to create something that made people think and feel, and maybe even weep. But serious dramas just weren't making it on Broadway at that time. So, despite the pleading of his friends, he packed his bags, and took off for the West Coast to accept an almost impossible assignment offered him by a major studio.

Hollywood was not only skeptical but downright hostile when the twenty-nine-year-old Mike Sobel was brought out to replace the beloved veteran director who had lost his last battle with the bottle and had to be literally carried off the set of Amnesty. But less than two weeks after he'd taken over, word was out that a new genius had arrived. And when Amnesty walked off with eight Academy Awards, the entire audience stood up and cheered. Mike Sobel had proved himself a professional in every sense of the word.

But in spite of the unqualified success of his first picture, the next six months turned out to be the most frustrating and unhappy period of Mike Sobel's entire life. At first he was deluged with offers from studio executives eager to cash in on the reputation of Hollywood's new reigning genius. However, those executives quickly became dismayed and then infuriated by the attitude of the young director. For Mike Sobel was a perfectionist. And the only thing Hollywood dislikes more than a failure is a perfectionist. Because perfectionists are stubborn and argumentative. Perfectionists make impossible demands. Worst of all, perfectionists cost money.

They warned him, then they threatened him. When the warnings and threats failed to bring him around and make him accept their way of doing things, they used their ultimate weapon. They refused to let him make pictures.

He almost starved to death, but he never gave in. He was saved by a struggling young independent producer who took a chance on him. It was the smartest thing that producer ever did. Mike gave him an Oscar-winning picture that same year, and after that Mike Sobel never had any problems with Hollywood again.

Ten years later he'd established his own production company, and was one of the most respected director/producer in Hollywood. He was smart, he was knowledgeable and, above all, he possessed that most unusual attribute, integrity. It became a mark of honor for the money men in the business to claim they'd backed a Mike Sobel production. Which was unusual in itself.

Generally, money men only go where there are big profits to be realized, and Mike Sobel rarely produced big money makers. He waited for the right pictures to come along, the ones he really believed in, and he never went into television. Sometimes two years went by before he came out with a new film. But his films always won awards, and the industry revered him as someone who had set a new standard of excellence in their often tawdry world.

They were also more than a little afraid of him. He never socialized with them, living alone on his huge ranch in the San Fernando Valley after his wife was tragically killed in an automobile accident. Not that he became a recluse. Just the opposite, in fact. He was extremely active in civic affairs and worked closely with a number of important community leaders. But he never went to the parties Hollywood gave or showed up at the chic "in" restaurants. So they rarely saw him, and what little they knew about him came from occasional stories in the newspapers about his activities. Recently there'd been quite a number of those stories, for Mike Sobel had come out with the announcement that he was actively supporting the Presidential candidate Richard Longworth.

"We have a problem," Arnold Scorsi said abruptly as Erin picked up the phone. "Mike Sobel has refused our offer to act as director and co-producer on Secret Rites."

"Well." Erin leaned back in her chair. "To you, Arnold, it may be a problem. To me, it's the best piece of news I've had in days. I never wanted the stubborn bastard in the first place."

"I repeat, we have a problem. Because without Mike Sobel you don't have a picture. Now does that clarify the situation for you?" he asked coldly.

"Arnold, you can't be serious," she protested. "To tell you the truth, I never understood why you wanted him to begin with. He's hardly the biggest moneymaker in Hollywood. I can think of at least ten other people who would be a better risk."

"What you think is of no importance at all," he snapped "It's what the Marchison brothers think that counts."

"Are you saying they won't settle for anybody but Mike Sobel? But, Arnold, that doesn't make any sense at all. From what you tell me, they're just a couple of shrewd businessmen who want a maximum return on their investment. Can't I make them understand that they'd be much better off with someone else?"

"No," he said flatly. "This is their first venture into the movie business and, as I told you earlier, they like to go in style. To them, Mike Sobel is style."

"Oh for God's sakes, Arnold, that's a bunch of crap and you know it. Now explain the facts of life to them."

"For some reason, Erin, you seem particularly obtuse today. That's not like you. I certainly hope I'm mistaken, because that would be a most unfortunate development. It would force me to withdrawn all financial support from your picture."

"You are wrong, Arnold," she choked, her hand gripping the receiver so tightly that her wrist began to ache. "Believe me, you're wrong."

"I'm glad to hear that," he said, now sounding quite cheerful. "So we understand each other then, don't we? You'll get in touch with Mike Sobel and convince him to come in as co-producer, we'll make ourselves a fine Oscar-winning picture, and everybody will be happy. May I suggest you drive out to his ranch to discuss this with him, instead of calling him on the phone? It's so easy to turn someone down over the phone, but if you show up on his doorstep he'll have to talk to you. He's much too much of a gentleman to close the door in your face."

"What?" she gasped when she was finally able to find her voice. "Arnold, I don't even know the man. How in the world can you possibly expect me to talk him into doing the picture when your own investors couldn't manage it? I'm the last person in the world he'd listen to!"

"For your sake, I hope that isn't true," he remarked quietly. "Because you either get Mike Sobel or lose the picture." There was a click, then a faint, empty buzz.

"Oh shit! Oh shit, why does it always have to be this way? Why can't I be free to make pictures like everybody else?"

"Are you okay?" Nancy asked nervously when she walked into the office and saw Erin slumped over the desk, staring dismally into space.

"No, I'm not okay! I'm absolutely rotten! Any more questions?"

"Sorry I asked." Nancy started to back out of the office.

"Hey, forget it. It's not your fault."

Nancy paused, a frown on her face. "Is there anything I can do to help?"

"I guess so." Erin sighed. "I need the home address of Mike Sobel. That ranch. And you'd better get me a road map along with it, because I understand it's a million miles out in the boondocks."

"Are you serious?" Nancy asked incredulously.

"Unfortunately, I am."

"Well, why . . ."

"No, Nancy, don't ask me any questions. Just get me the information."

Erin swiveled around in her desk chair and stared at the blank wall behind her, leaving her secretary standing there.

When it became obvious that Erin wasn't going to say anything else, Nancy walked out of the office and began calling her contacts. It took an hour to find out Mike Sobel's home address. The road map was easier. It was a standard California Auto Club map, detailing little known access roads leading into the ranch spreads of the original San Fernando Valley settlers. Most of those original settlers and their families had long since disappeared, but the roads remained the same.

The huge brass door knocker that still bore the marks of the artisan who had hammered it into shape made echoes throughout the old Spanish ranch house as Erin lifted it by the handle and then let it fall against the massive oak door.

Mike Sobel opened the door and gazed in surprise at the slim young woman with the luminous green eyes who stood there smiling uncertainly at him.

"May I help you?" he inquired politely.

"Mr. Sobel, I'm Erin Connolly, and I'd very much like to talk to you."

The pleasant expression on his face vanished abruptly as he recognized her. "I'm afraid we have nothing to talk about, Miss Connolly," he announced with cold formality. "I have no interest in working as a co-producer on your picture, and I assure you there's nothing you could say that would change my mind. Now, if you'll excuse me, I'm rather busy."

"Please, would it be all right if I just came in for a moment?" Erin swayed, then reached out for the door jamb to steady herself. "It was a terribly hot, long drive up here, and I'm not feeling quite well."

"Good Lord, of course!" Concern momentarily darkening his clear blue eyes, he put his arm around her shoulders and quickly led her inside. "Here, sit down and let me get you something. Lemonade? I just made a fresh pitcher."

"No, a glass of water would be fine," she said faintly. "You're most kind."

As he hurried off to the kitchen, Erin curled up on the long, low, comfortable couch and let her head fall wearily back against the cushions.

"Now drink it slowly," he ordered as he came back into the living room and handed her the glass.

"Tastes marvelous," she murmured, sipping it as he'd instructed.

"Genuine well water." He grinned at her, an engaging grin that gave his thin, angular face a puckish charm. "Can't get that in Los Angeles."

"Seems like I can't get anything in Los Angeles," she said ruefully. "Maybe you had the right idea moving out here."

The friendly grin disappeared as his eyes thoughtfully surveyed her. "That's the way life works, Miss Connolly. You give up some things to get other things. For me, it was this ranch and a certain way of living. But somehow I don't get the feeling that you'd give up the Los Angeles life-style even if you were guaranteed all the fresh well water in the world."

"Somehow I have the feeling you're right," she admitted with a reluctant smile, realizing that it was going to be impossible to con this man.

She sat up, staring at him. "I want you on this picture very much, Mike Sobel, and I'd appreciate it if you'd tell me why you're refusing. It's your kind of picture, a fine quality film. Everyone agrees it could well be the next Academy Award winner. So is it just ego that's making you turn it down?" she challenged him. "Because you'd only be a co-producer and have to share the glory with someone else?"

He laughed with undisguised amusement. "That's quite a speech coming from you, Miss Connolly." His eyes narrowed and he gazed at her speculatively. "But since you've brought up the subject, I confess to a certain amount of curiosity. Why do you want me on this picture? It seems to me that if anyone would object to the thought of co-producing, it would be you. Especially since this was your project from the beginning."

"That's true," she said calmly. "Personally, I don't want a co-producer. Personally, I hate the very thought of it."

He blinked in surprise, clearly taken aback by the frank statement. "Then why in the world…"

"Because I don't have any choice. The investors insist on a co-producer before they'll put up any money. And it can't be just any co-producer. It has to be you. Those are their terms, and they won't budge."

She leaned forward, her eyes fixed entreatingly on him, "This picture is my last chance. If I lose it, I lose everything. So please, please won't you reconsider? Believe me, I wouldn't dream of asking you if I thought it would compromise your standards in any way. But surely you can see that isn't the case here. We're talking about a film anybody would be proud to produce. A film that would do credit even to your distinguished career. And I promise I'll give you a free hand in directing it. I'll never get in your way."

"Look, Miss Connolly, I wish I could help you." He stopped and shrugged uncomfortably. "But the fact is I have a number of commitments now, and I simply don't have the time available to get involved in a new film."

"Then forget about the directing. I'm sure the Marchison brothers will agree to getting another director. All they want is your name as co-producer. So this way you won't have to spend any time at all on the production. You can just come in on the set when you want and I'll handle everything else."

He looked at her quizzically. "Maybe the Marchison brothers would agree to that, but do you really believe I would?"

"No," she said miserably, bowing her head. "You're the kind of stubborn son-of-a-bitch who'd insist on supervising every single step of the picture."

He chuckled in spite of himself. "Well, apparently you know more about me than I realized. So you also must know that the whole thing is impossible."

"Would you do me one favor? Would you read the screenplay before you say no?"

"I'm sorry," he replied gently. "I'm afraid I can't do that."

"Then will you do me this favor?" She stood up, collected her purse, and walked toward him, her hand resting for a moment on his arm. "Will you please not say no today? Will you let me walk out of your house without having to hear that?"

"Why?" He regarded her with genuine puzzlement. "It's not going to change anything."

"If I told you it would make it easier for me to leave, would that be a good enough reason?"

Embarrassed by her intensity, he nodded. "All right, Miss Connolly. But the answer will still be the same tomorrow as it is today," he warned her as he walked her to the door.

"Well, I'll deal with that tomorrow."

There was no doubt in Erin's mind as she drove away from the big old Spanish ranch house that Mike Sobel meant what he'd said. He was not going to do the picture.

If only I could get him to read the screenplay, she thought despairingly. It was truly a superb script. She couldn't imagine any director turning it down once he'd seen it. But how was she to get him to see it? He'd been polite but absolutely firm in refusing to look at it, and she could hardly stand over him with a gun and force him to read it.

What if she sent it up to his house tonight by special messenger with a pleading note attached? Erin shook her head. No, that sort of trick wouldn't work with Mike

Sobel. He'd simply return it unopened. Then, just as she was about to give up hopelessly on the whole thing, the idea came to her.

****

It was shortly alter eight that evening when Mike Sobel opened the door of his house in response to the heavy knock, and gazed in disbelief at the tall, impressive figure standing there.

"Oh my God, not you too!" he groaned. "What is this? A conspiracy?"

Keith Ramsey gave him a faint, apologetic smile. "Sorry, old buddy. But you know how it goes. They always send in the marines when everything else has failed."

"Jesus Christ!" Mike muttered feelingly. "And I didn't even know I was in a war."

"It's a very friendly war," Keith assured him with a grin. "Even though you don't know it, we're both on the same side."

"Yeah? You couldn't prove it by me."

"So how about giving me a chance?"

"Okay. You can come in and do your number as long as you promise to leave me in peace once you're finished."

"Would I leave any other way?" he protested, laughing. "A peace-loving fella like myself?"

"Very funny," Mike replied sourly. "All right, let's go. What's your pitch?"

"This." Keith walked into the living room, laid the screenplay down on the coffee table, and opened it to a well-creased page. "Just read, my friend. Just read."

Reluctantly, Mike approached the script and looked down at it. The words leaped out at him, and he bent closer. Then, without conscious volition, he turned the page. An hour later he was still reading.

****

Mike Sobel and Erin Connolly circled warily around each other during the first few weeks of production on Secret Rites. It was at best an armed truce, their relationship limited to short, clipped, impersonal discussions about budgets and shooting schedules, set designs and location sites. But by the second month Erin's guarded hostility toward the man who had been forced on her as a co-producer began to relax. And by the third month it had disappeared completely. Because Mike Sobel was just as good as his reputation, and she found herself excited and stimulated by his genius. For his part, Mike was genuinely impressed with Erin's crisply competent professionalism and fierce, hard-working dedication to quality.

They soon got into the habit of going out for dinner together after the daily rushes, and one night Mike didn't leave Erin's apartment after he took her home.

They were both a little stunned by the incredible chemistry that leaped between them in that first lovemaking, and they both wore similarly dazed expressions when they showed up on the set the next day. Which didn't escape the sharp eyes of the cast and crew, who guessed immediately what had happened. There was a lot of sly kidding around the set that day, but it was basically good-natured. Everybody respected Erin and Mike as top-flight professionals, and they couldn't have been more pleased that the feud between them had been settled in such a rewarding way.

As it turned out, they had every right to be pleased, for the picture flourished right along with Erin's and Mike's love affair. Even the most difficult scenes went smoothly. Cameras and lights worked perfectly. Nobody forgot lines, stepped on the wrong marks, or tripped over cables. And everyone involved in the production looked forward each morning to coming to work. It was that rarity, a "happy set."

Secret Rites came in under budget, finished shooting a full two weeks ahead of schedule, and showed such brilliant clarity and power even in rough cut that the cast and crew were already congratulating each other on an Oscar winner.

"I think we deserve a little time off for a private celebration," Mike told Erin as they left the jubilant wrap party. "I've already postponed final editing until next week. Hope you don't mind."

"Well." She grinned at him mischievously. "That depends on whether or not you're going to make me an offer I can't refuse."

"How about coming with me to paradise? A beautiful place with fields of flowers and sparkling mountain streams, warm golden days, and star-filled nights. The ones from the sky, not Hollywood."

"I think I just got that offer I can't refuse," she said a little breathlessly. "Do you really know a place like that?"

"Just pack your bags, lady, and I'll show you."

They left Los Angeles early the next morning and arrived in the glorious wine country of California, located just north of San Francisco, shortly after dusk. Mike had booked a room for them in a charming, rustic inn situated in the center of the lush Napa Valley vineyards. Erin fell in love with it immediately. "Everything smells so clean and fresh!" she exclaimed.

"That's because it is. Now go out on the balcony, take a deep breath, and look around. It might even convert you permanently to the natural life."

By the third day of their stay, Erin was coming close to being converted. Everything was just the way Mike had promised it would be. Their mornings and afternoons were spent in explorations of the idyllic countryside, and their nights were filled with slow, sweet lovemaking. On their last evening they had a quiet dinner at the inn, eating by the glow of slender tapers and drinking an exquisite chardonnay produced by a fine local winery. They were so obviously in love that everyone in the room smiled on them.

After dinner they went into the lounge, where Erin curled up in a dark leather chair and slipped off her shoes. Mike moved his chair closer to her, reaching over and caressing one slender foot as they gazed into the cracking flames in the fireplace

They had Courvoisier in large crystal brandy snifters, and kissed between sips. When the flames finally died down and the logs had settled with a comfortable groan into embers, Mike gently pulled her to her feet and handed her the shoe she'd tucked under her chair. Then they walked outside and strolled along the path that led from the main building of the inn to their snug little cottage. The moon was very bright, and there was no sound at all except for the whisper of their feet on the fragrant pine needles.

Once inside their room Erin unzipped her dress and carelessly tossed it into the closet, then smiled as she climbed into bed and watched Mike undress. He was so neat and careful that she loved observing him. First he removed his jacket, making sure it was perfectly aligned as he hung it on the clothes hanger. Next came the shirt and tie, followed by the shoes and pants. Then he turned out the light, slipped into bed and pulled her close to him. They fell asleep in the middle of a kiss.

The phone woke them the next morning. The voice on the other end informed them they had only thirty minutes left to make breakfast before the dining room closed, and apologetically reminded them that check-out time was noon.

"Well, I guess it's time to pack up and leave," Mike told her with a regretful smile as he hung up.

"1 wish we didn't have to," Erin said sadly. "It's been so special here."

"Hey, honey, don't look so unhappy," he protested, leaning over to give her a hug. "Don't you know we have lots of special times ahead of us?"

****

The message from Arnold Scorsi was waiting for Erin when she walked into her office the following morning.

"Did he say what he wanted?" she asked Nancy, puzzled.

"Just that it was important, and you should call him the minute you came in."

"Strange." Erin shook her head, frowning, then shrugged. "Oh well, I guess there's only one way to find out." She picked up the phone and dialed his number.

"We have to talk," Arnold announced peremptorily as he came on the line. "Can you come over to my office now?"

"Now?" she repeated, stunned. "You mean right this very minute?"

"Yes, that's what I mean."

"But, but why? What's happened?"

"We'll discuss it when you get here." He hung up.

As Erin drove the short distance to Arnold Scorsi's office in Century City, she kept telling herself there was nothing to worry about. How could there be, when everything had gone so well? The Marchison brothers had received more than they could possibly have dreamed of in their first motion picture venture, and they should be among the happiest investors in the world at this moment.

But despite her efforts to reassure herself she had absolutely nothing to be concerned about, Erin found her throat dry and her hands clammy with fear as she stepped off the elevator and opened the door that led into Arnold's coldly elegant reception room.

Arnold came out from his inner office a bare three seconds after she'd shakily given her name to the plain, middle-aged, receptionist.

"You made excellent time," he said approvingly. "Come in, Erin."

She followed him, jumping nervously as he closed the door behind him with a resounding thunk.

"Good heavens, my dear, you seem a bit on edge," he observed with a faint smile. "That surprises me. I thought you'd just returned from a most relaxing vacation."

"Please, Arnold," she said tensely, clutching her purse to her. "Please tell me what this is all about."

"Right to the point as always," he nodded as he walked behind the desk and sat down, leaning back in his chair and regarding her thoughtfully. "Unfortunately, we're facing a rather unpleasant problem with our picture. It appears our esteemed co-producer, Mike Sobel, has embezzled a million dollars from the production company, which he has turned over to Richard Longworth's presidential campaign in return for certain favors to be granted once Longworth comes into power. As you know, the election is only two weeks away. The story will appear in next week's papers."

"Have you lost your mind, Arnold?" Erin exclaimed incredulously. "That's the most insane thing I've ever heard! Mike Sobel wouldn't steal a penny from anybody, and I can assure you he hasn't touched any of the production company's funds, because I've personally handled all the disbursements. Who is this idiot anyway that's planting this ridiculous story?" she demanded in sudden fury. "Just give me his name, and I'll take care of him!"

"It's not a him," Arnold said softly. "It's a her. And the name is Erin Connolly."

"Oh no," she whispered, sinking into the chair opposite him. "Oh no, Arnold. I beg you, don't do this to me."

"It's really a very simple matter," he smiled. "All the details have already been taken care of. You won't be involved in any way. Just follow my instructions and you'll have your Oscar-winning picture all to yourself."

"You don't understand," she said desperately. "I don't care any longer about having it to myself. I love Mike Sobel. I want to share it with him. I want to share my whole life with him!"

"Well that's too bad, because I'm afraid you'll find that a little difficult to accomplish after you break this story. However, you mustn't brood about it. I'm confident you'll get over it and go on to someone else. After all, you always have. That's one of the things I admire most about you, Erin. The way you put the past behind you and go on to new ventures unburdened by any regrets."

"You can't do this to me, Arnold," she said grimly. " Every penny of that fifteen million dollars the Marchison brothers invested in Secret Rites is fully accounted for, and I will be more than happy to allow a public auditing of our books. There's no way in the world you can prove Mike Sobel siphoned off a million dollars of it unless I agree to fix those books. And I am not going to fix those books. I flatly, totally refuse!"

She stood up. "Good bye, Arnold."

"You really disappoint me, my dear," he said quietly. "How could you possibly imagine I would leave such an important matter up to the vagaries of your emotions? I thought you knew me better than that."

She had already started to march out of his office. At his words she froze awkwardly in mid-step, then turned back and looked at him, swallowing hard to get rid of the lump of terror in her throat.

"Don't try to bluff me, Arnold. I won't buy it."

"I never bluff," he replied coldly. "That's something else I thought you knew."

He swiveled slowly in the big, leather chair, idly contemplating his templed fingers. "The fact of the matter is that the Marchison brothers didn't invest fifteen million dollars in your picture. They invested sixteen million dollars." He looked up at her. "So even you can see that leaves one million unaccounted for."

"That's impossible!" she cried. "My records clearly show fifteen million dollars is all they invested."

"Really?" he murmured. "Then I wonder why the Marchisons' corporate records clearly show that sixteen million dollars was paid to Con-Well Productions. To say nothing of a contract signed by you acknowledging a loan from them in that amount."

"I don't care what your phony documents say, Arnold," she declared, white-faced. "You'll never get away with this, because no one in this town will ever believe Mike Sobel embezzled that money. Especially when I swear he never had access to the company's funds."

"You have an interesting point there, Erin. I wouldn't be surprised if you were right."

He tilted forward in his chair, startling her with a sudden, cheerful smile. "So it looks like you're worrying needlessly about this whole thing, doesn't it? The odds are good that Mike Sobel will be acquitted by the jury when he comes to trial. At the very worst, he'll be sentenced to a few short years, and even that sentence will probably be suspended. In no time at all he'll be back in Hollywood, making bigger and better pictures than ever, and the whole unpleasant matter will have been buried and forgotten.

"Of course it wouldn't work quite that way in your case," he added softly, his eyes narrowing as he studied her.

"What?" she said bewilderedly.

"The embezzlement charge, my dear. You see, there is a deficit of a million dollars, and naturally it causes the Marchison brothers considerable anxiety. Now suppose you should be the one charged with that embezzlement?" he inquired politely. "After all, if it isn't Mike Sobel, it has to be you. Those are the only two choices available. And somehow I don't think this town would find it too difficult to believe you'd embezzle funds. Actually, I believe you'd be tried and found guilty. You might serve as long as ten years in prison. Even if you should get off with a lighter sentence, it seems highly unlikely that you'll ever be allowed to make another picture."

"Well, the choice is yours," he concluded quietly. "What's your answer?"

"I cannot give you an answer until I have a chance to look at the Marchison's books. You'll need to set up an appointment and I'll be bringing my accountant with me."

"That's not a problem. I'll check with the Marchisons and call you tomorrow. In the meantime, I suggest you think carefully about what I've said. Mike Sobel can survive this crime. You can't."

TWENTY FIVE

Erin called Mike on her cell phone the minute she got in her car. Please be there, she begged as the phone kept ringing. Finally he picked up, sounding a little breathless. She belatedly remembered he always did his running at this time and never took his cell phone with him.

"Thank heavens I got you. I have to see you immediately."

"What's the matter, honey?"

"I can't tell you over the phone."

"My God, what's going on?"

"I'll tell you everything as soon as I get there and then we have to figure out what to do."

Mike was standing outside, waiting for her when she drove up. He ran up to the car and grabbed the door before she even had a chance to open it. "Are you all right?" he asked, his face pale.

"Physically yes," she said. "Let's go inside. I have to tell you things I never wanted you to know and if you never want to see me again, I'll understand. But we need to work together now."

"It's no excuse," she began slowly, "that I was so ignorant about the significance. My whole life has been about producing films. I never knew anything about politics. You knew David Bernstein, didn't you?"

"Yes. His suicide was a terrible tragedy."

"I now know I was responsible for that suicide."

"What in the world are you talking about?"

"Have you ever heard of a man named Arnold Scorsi?

"No. Should I?"

" I wish with all my heart that you would never need to hear of him, but I must now tell you about him."

"Erin, you're driving me crazy with these cryptic comments. Would you please just come right out and tell me exactly what's going on."

"Arnold Scorsi wants me to say that I found out you embezzled a million dollars from our production company the Marchison Brothers, which you've turned over to Richard Longworth's presidential campaign in return for certain favors to be granted once Longworth comes into power. As you know, the election is only two weeks away. He plans to have the story appear in the papers next week."

"WHAT? That's insane! I don't even have access to those funds. What did you tell him?"

"Precisely that. He then said if I refused, I would be accused of embezzling the money and he was confident that with my very checkered career that he'd have no problem seeing that I ended up in jail."

"I can't believe what I'm hearing. What is this all about?

"It took me a long time to figure out Arnold Scorsi but I believe he works for some very powerful people who are trying to rig the election of our next president. When he rescued me from prison, after I was picked up for carrying drugs, he told me I had to make David back Johnny Ryan for president and drop his support for Richard Longworth. I managed that because David was so crazy about me but I now know it ate away at him and that, combined with leaving his family for me, drove him to suicide."

"And you've lived with that guilt all this time?"

"I've lived with a lot of guilt, Mike. I just managed to hide it most of the time. But if I never do anything else in the world, I want to put Arnold Scorsi out of business forever. Do you think you could contact the FBI and get them to move on him?"

"Let me talk to some people I know. I believe I could generate some interest on this bastard. But what do we do in the meantime?"

"I've saved us a little time by insisting on bringing my accountant to the Marchison Brothers tomorrow to examine their documents. Then I'll call Arnold tomorrow morning and tell him my accountant wants to bring along a forensic expert to see if someone at Marchison changed the figures on the contract but he won't be available until the end of the week. As you know, they loaned us fifteen million dollars but they've rigged things so their contract that we signed shows they actually loaned us sixteen million dollars, leaving one million dollars unaccounted for.

"Jesus bleeding Christ, I can't believe all this! But if they've rigged things, they're not about to let a forensic expert examine their contract, are they?"

"They're very clever, Mike. I'm quite sure their contract shows sixteen million but has not been rigged. It's almost certainly the contract we have that's been rigged so it looks like we laid fifteen thousand over their sixteen thousand."

"I hope you know that I can't allow them to lay that on you!"

"They don't want to send me to prison because that will do them no good. I've led Arnold to believe that I'm so terrified about going to prison that I'll betray you. You're a real problem to them and I'm scared to death that they might kill you. But as long as they think I'll cave and save my own ass, you'll be safe."

"I can't believe all this," Mike said in a dazed voice.

"It would make a great movie."

He started to laugh in spite of the horror. "God, Erin, do you ever stop thinking about producing a film?

"When I'm with you," she said softly.

TWENTY SIX

Giant searchlights stabbed at the sky as the long line of gleaming black limousines glided up to the entrance of the Pavilion and let off their distinguished passengers, who emerged with uniformly smiling faces that concealed the desperate hopes and even more desperate fears that raged inside them on this most important of all nights, the Academy Awards presentations.

Gary Morrison, a popular local TV talk show host, bounded forward eagerly each time another limousine pulled up, a camera crew hot on his heels as he thrust his microphone into the faces of the arriving celebrities with such force they barely refrained from cringing back in sheer self-defense.

"And here's Keith Ramsey!" he panted deliriously as the tall, commanding figure stepped out of a limousine, then turned around and gently held out his hand for the small, shy woman who had been his wife for twenty years.

"Well, what do you think, Mr. Ramsey?" Gary cried. "They're saying you've got it locked up for Best Actor. You feel that way too?"

"I feel I'm going to have to wait, just like everybody else, to find out," he smiled politely.

"But what about the scandal?" Gary's voice dropped to a conspiratorial whisper. "You think that could affect your chances?"

Keith Ramsey's expression turned suddenly cold. "Actually, what I think is that you exhibit extremely bad taste, Mr. Morrison. Now, if you'll excuse me," He took hold of his wife's hand and curtly walked away.

"Well," Gary babbled, embarrassed. "There we have a very loyal man. Now let's see who else . . . oh wait a minute!" he shouted happily. "Here's someone we really want to talk to. It's Erin Connolly herself, the controversial producer of Secret Rites."

With the camera crew racing after him, Gary rushed up to the next limousine as Erin stepped out. "Miss Connolly, I must say we've all been waiting rather breathlessly for your arrival," he announced, shoving the microphone at her. "Keith Ramsey has already told us that the scandal won't affect the picture's chances of winning. What do you say?"

"In my opinion, Gary, the only scandal will be if Keith Ramsey doesn't win," she informed him with a pleasant smile. Because he certainly deserves to, don't you think?" And with that she walked quickly away, leaving him with his mouth open and a slightly foolish expression on his face.

But Erin's smile faded as she entered the lobby, and her hands clenched involuntarily as she felt the sharp cramping pain in her stomach that occurred every time someone mentioned the embezzlement. The FBI were slower than molasses on indicting Arnold Scorsi and the Marchison Brothers. Mike explained that the Feds had quickly discovered this was way bigger than Erin had imagined and they wanted time to follow the trail all the way to the top. It was some comfort to her that they were also protecting Mike but in the meantime his reputation was being totally destroyed.

The immense theater was filled almost to capacity as Erin walked inside. Voices rose and fell in short, explosive bursts of nervous energy, occasionally punctuated by shouts of laughter. A myriad of lights cast a soft glow over the luxurious pelts of several thousand sacrificial minks, and then sparkled brilliantly as they caught the reflections from a million dollars worth of diamonds. Frantic television crews rushed up and down in response to the barked commands from their directors and the air was almost oppressively sweet with the mingled scents of several dozen expensive perfumes.

As Erin made her way down the long, red-carpeted aisle toward the front of the theater where her reserved seat was located, people stopped abruptly in the midst of their conversations to stare at her. No one called out a greeting, for everyone in Hollywood was convinced that Erin had set Mike Sobel up to save her own skin.

The ceremonies started with the presentations of relatively minor awards. First came Special Effects, followed by Best Sound Score, Best Feature-Length Documentary, Best Short Subjects in a Documentary Film, and Best Achievement in Sound. The presentations halted briefly before the awarding of the Irving Thalberg Lifetime Achievement Award to give the millions of television viewers at home a little entertainment.

Erin fought back tears as the names of the nominees for Outstanding Achievement in Directing were read off without mentioning Mike Sobel. Now Leon Aronson, a talented young director with a wild mop of black curly hair and a reputation for exuberant risk-taking, seemed curiously subdued as he stepped up to accept his award. The audience stirred expectantly as he fingered the Oscar placed in his hands and looked out at them. But the moment of potential drama passed as he simply muttered his thanks and walked away.

The next award was for Best Screenplay adapted from another work, and Sheldon Avery won it. His wrinkled pixy face beamed out at the audience as he gushed his thanks to Keith Ramsey for making this possible. No one missed the fact that he refrained from making any mention at all of the producer of the picture.

There was a hush in the audience when the nominees for Best Actor were announced, then a wild screaming as the envelope was opened and the presenter cried out, "Keith Ramsey"

Erin leaped up along with everyone else, clapping delightedly as she moved toward the distinguished actor who was just now getting to his feet. He turned around as she approached, his face a mask of icy contempt. The FBI had made it clear that absolutely no one, no matter how trustworthy they were, should learn that Mike was not guilty.

Unable not to feel humiliated, she stumbled back and allowed him to cross in front of her as he made his way up to the stage.

"And now it's time for that big one," the emcee said, "the one everyone here tonight has been waiting for—Best Picture. He glanced over at the two famous movie personalities who'd just appeared on the stage. "Are we ready?"

"We're ready," they smiled back.

Erin swallowed hard as they read off the names of the nominated pictures, and the TV monitors flashed scenes from each of the films. "And the winner is . . ." The presenter was overcome by a sudden coughing fit, and Erin stared at the palms of her hands where tiny flecks of blood had appeared as she'd dug her fingernails into them.

"And the winner is Secret Rites, he shouted. "A Con-Well Productions. Producer, Erin Connolly. Co-producer . . ." He broke off awkwardly. "Erin Connolly, producer," he finished lamely.

For one brief awful moment there was no sound at all in the huge theater. Then pandemonium broke out when Mike Sobel suddenly appeared, walking down towards the stage.

Erin ran towards him, almost tripping and falling in her haste to reach him. "You're all right? You're safe?"

"Would I be here otherwise?" he grinned.

"And they got Arnold Scorsi?"

"Arnold Scorsi will never bother you again, love. He's in prison for life, which makes him lucky because the people he worked for tried to kill him. But they're all headed for prison as well."

"Then why are we standing here?" She grabbed his hand and started running for the stage as people stared in disbelief.

"Sorry to be late," he said to the stunned audience. "You'll understand why when you read tomorrow's papers. In the meantime, I would like to say that Erin Connolly is not only the finest producer I've ever worked with but the bravest. She put her reputation on the line to save my life."

www.ingramcontent.com/pod-product-compliance
Lightning Source LLC
Chambersburg PA
CBHW070045030726
47506CB00002B/354